YA            6/05              $14.95
SLO                      0-689-87438-3

Sloan, Brian                          ✓
A really nice prom mess

# a really nice **prom mess**

## brian sloan

Simon & Schuster
*New York London Toronto Sydney*

*For Beau, the bestest*

SIMON & SCHUSTER
1230 Avenue of the Americas, New York, New York 10020
This book is a work of fiction. Any references to historical events, real people, or real
locales are used fictitiously. Other names, characters, places, and incidents are products
of the author's imagination, and any resemblance to actual events or locales or persons,
living or dead, is entirely coincidental.
Copyright © 2005 by Brian Sloan
All rights reserved, including the right of reproduction in whole or in part in any form.
Book design by Greg Stadnyk
The text for this book is set in Utopia.
Manufactured in the United States of America
10 9 8 7 6 5 4 3 2 1
Library of Congress Cataloging-in-Publication Data
Sloan, Brian.
A really nice prom mess / Brian Sloan.— 1st ed.
p. cm.
Summary: Gay high school senior Cameron Hayes endures a disastrous prom night when
forced to take a girl as his date, and after fleeing the dance in disguise, he finds himself
involved in a surprising on-stage performance, a high-speed police chase, and unexpected
revelations.
ISBN 0-689-87438-3
[1. Homosexuality—Fiction. 2. Gays—Fiction. 3. Coming out (Sexual orientation)—Fiction.
4. Interpersonal relations—Fiction. 5. Proms—Fiction.] I. Title.
PZ7.S6323Re 2005
[Fic]—dc22        2004011314

# ACKNOWLEDGMENTS

My deepest thanks and gratitude go to my editor, David Gale, who let me do things with this book that I didn't ever think I could do. Like *write* it! But seriously, his excitement and guidance through this somewhat foreign process was totally awesome, to borrow a Cameron-esque phrase. Thanks also to Will Lippincott, for being a great agent and laughing at my immature jokes. Also, thanks to the following folks for their inspiration, encouragement, and support in this endeavor: Tim Allis, C. Bard Cole, Kevin Donaldson, Kevin Dwyer, Katie Fleischer, Julian Fleisher, Ariel Foxman, Jade Gingerich, James Hoffman, David Levinson, Scott Mendelsohn, David Roccosalva, Mark Sam Rosenthal, Tor Seidler, Kevin Sloan, Tim Sloan, Mom and Dad Sloan, Vanessa Spevacek, Andy Volkoff, Jeff Wenger and David Zellnik. Finally, props to everyone at S&S who had a hand in taming this beast, namely Alexandra Cooper and Jordan Brown for keeping it real (as they say), and Katrina Groover for gently reminding me of all those grammatical things I forgot in Honors English. As for high school itself, major thanks to all the girls who tried to date me (not that there were *that* many), namely Laura and the Goose. And I guess I have to thank old St. John's, where my strict Catholic education served to repress and inspire me all at once. Shout outs to Mr. Donellan, Mrs. Opalack, Mr. Costa, Mr. Kramer, Mr. Dent, Mr. McCarthy, and that priest who called me a hedonist . . . *that rocked!* As for all the old school friends, you know who you are but isn't it fun to see your names in print? Thanks for all the crazy memories to Dave Brune, Ian Coburn, Russ Coller, Jeff Davidson, Tim Emerson, Gerry Hodgkins, Charlie McNamara, Charles Strachan, and Jay Talbott. Go Johnny Mops!

"Would you guys please hurry up! I'm breaking, like, thirty major laws here."

—The Geek
*Sixteen Candles*

# CHAPTER 1

*Virginia McKinley is a wild beauty.*

That's exactly what I was thinking as she emerged from her bedroom and stood behind an elegant white railing on the second-story landing of her swank Georgetown mini manse. Virginia had untamed, naturally beautiful features, unsullied by hair, skin, or facial care products; a large square face, like a vintage movie star, accented by the sharp jawline of a supermodel and eyes that were the most dangerous looking orbs since Bette Davis. Up top was an explosion of unruly hair that was not merely a fiery shade of orange but, from a distance, looked like it truly could have been ablaze. And finally, draped over her tall, robust, and generously voluptuous form was an Oscar-worthy prom dress in red velvet (see Catherine Zeta-Jones) with a neckline that risked an NC-17. I mean, whoa! Bathed in the smoky rays of an early summer sunset streaming through the foyer, her porcelain skin glowing with the radiance of an old-school goddess, Virginia McKinley truly took my breath away. Honest. Which is not too bad, considering I'm totally gay.

All right, well, I guess not *that* totally if I was taking Virginia to the senior prom. But you know what? Attending a conservative, all-boys school in Washington, D.C., it's not like there's a lot of other options for a guy like me when it comes to the prom. Sure, I've read stories online about radical formals in left-leaning hamlets such as Seattle or San Francisco where these bold guys take each other to the main event. But Washington is seriously conservative, and not just because President Bush is in charge. I mean, let's be real here. . . . It's not like there were dude couples macking to Mariah on the dance floor during the Clinton years. Please!

So that said, you must be wondering what the hell I was doing going on a fake date to the prom anyway. This is the new millennium and all, and you'd think people would be over that sorta fifties Rock Hudson, playing-it-straight crap. Well, you know what? I am *totally* with you on that one. This whole prom thing was *not* my idea. Honest. I mean, I have nothing against the prom per se as an institutional rite of passage. I'm not some Starbucks-smashing anarchist who wants to firebomb the Marriott ballroom or something in protest of the hypocrisy of male-female slow dancing in a world where love is a whole lot more complicated (and generally, like, faster) than that.

Actually, I have to admit that in theory I'm fond of the prom. In fact, I'm a bit of a sucker for a good tacky high school prom movie. You know the genre: *Down to You, Never Been Kissed, Pretty in Pink,* etc. But let's be real here; those movies are about as honest as your average member of Congress. It's a fantasy, people! The reality of the prom is not so pretty in pink or turquoise or lavender. . . . It's just pretty terrible. C'mon, you've heard the stories. (Hell, you've probably *lived* some of them.) Anyway, here's a few that pop to mind: the poor band geek who has to ask about ten girls before some tragic junior on the Potomac Forensics Team says yes; the insecure rich chick who buys her Stella McCartney gown at Nordstrom's, only to have her intended say it looks "kinda weird"; longtime steadies who plan their prom night like it's their friggin' wedding, only to have one of them drink too much and puke all over the back of the limo, causing a melodramatic breakup and ruining any chance of their getting hitched for real. Okay—do you want me to go on? I mean, seriously, do you really think anything approaching romance happens at the goddamn prom?!

Sorry—I'm getting a little hysterical. You see, I'm still a bit raw over the events that transpired on the evening of June 6, a.k.a. prom night. Though a couple weeks have passed, I'm still trying to piece it all together. It was absolutely insane. What—you think I'm being all exaggerated and über-dramatic? Oh, I wish it were the case.

If you think those previous anecdotes about the prom are scary, what happened to me is downright frightening. If you take those tales and multiply all of them by 10 and add about five other tangential incidents, that might begin to approach the manner in which my wonderful night at the senior prom devolved from the highest romance imaginable to the most utter chaos in just under five hours flat. And that's not even getting into the part where the police got involved. Or the strippers. But I'm really getting ahead of myself.

So let's get back to Virginia, where I left her, standing at the top of the stairs. Where, in major retrospect, I probably should have left her. You see, the first hint of trouble was when Virginia tried to come down those stairs. To put it nicely, she was a little wobbly. I know, I know—Virginia's a statuesque girl wearing vertiginous heels, and is relatively new to this adult balancing act that began with her debut at the Mayflower Hotel last November. I should have cut her some slack. Let the record show, I did. Until, that is, she tripped over her own left foot and went down.

"Virginia," I said, rushing up to her, sprawled out over five steps. "Are you okay?"

"Shit," she said, reaching for one of her Jimmy Choo's that had escaped the grip of her big, floppy foot. "What do you think, asshole?"

What did I think? Asshole? Let's see . . . uh, the first thing I thought was that her severe tone of voice and mildly abusive language were not really the nicest way to address her prom date, even if he was a big homo.

"Oh my god—Virginia!"

That was Virginia's mother. On hearing her daughter's collapse, Mrs. McKinley came racing in from the kitchen, a highball in one hand and a copy of *Town & Country* in the other. She was an equally tall woman with similarly reddish hair, except that hers, whipped into a curly meringue and radiating a color found only on Mars, was clearly a wig.

"What happened?"

Huffily, Virginia pushed herself up on her elbows.

"What does it look like, Mother?"

Given Mrs. McKinley's mortified look on Virginia's use of the same venomous tone of voice with her, I offered an answer.

"She, uh, she tripped."

"I told you those heels were too high for you, Virginia."

As she went up to help her daughter, bad morphed into worse when Mrs. McKinley tripped on the stairs as well. The magazine went flying but miraculously the drink barely sloshed as the lady of the house went down, losing one of her flats in the process. It was a pretty remarkable feat, this saving of the booze. I thought to myself, *Hmmm, maybe Virginia's mother is a woman who has had some experience falling down with a cocktail.*

"Jesus Christ, Mother!" said Virginia, standing up now and slipping her Choo back on while clinging tightly to the ornately carved handrail. "You're gonna spill all over my Armani. Gimme that."

Virginia reached for the tumbler, snatching it out of her mother's hand. Flustered, her mother tried to pretend that this hadn't happened, attempting to finesse the snatch with a question.

"Would you like a sip, darling?"

Ignoring this moot question, Virginia turned toward me with a wicked glance. I had seen this look before. I remembered it distinctly from the night I first met Virginia at an illegal parents-out-of-town party on Q Street, where she challenged some members of the football team to five consecutive shots of Jagermeister, one for all the games they'd lost so far that year. (With a grand total of only three hundred male students, my school is severely sports challenged.) Fixing me with this flashback look, she took a sip of her mother's drink, and she sipped and sipped and sipped until the drink was all gone. Then after her mother righted herself, Virginia handed her the empty glass, the marooned ice clinking sadly. Mrs. McKinley exchanged a brief, bitter look with her daughter and then turned her attention to me.

"Well, don't you look nice. . . . It's Cameron, right?"

"Yes, ma'am," I said, self-consciously pulling at the sleeves of my rental. It was the James Bond–style tux from Formal Friends in Wheaton. Being retro and all, it was a fashionable bargain at $99.90, consisting of standard-issue black pants with a thin, sporty strip of satin down each leg, a white dinner jacket with padded shoulders that was slim cut in the waist, and a .350 Magnum concealed in the pocket. (Okay—kidding!) Anyway, I thought Virginia might get a kick out of the spy theme.

"It's the James Bond tux."

"What?" said Virginia, interrupting a nanosecond of civility with a boozy bawl.

"That's, uh, that's what it's called. Or what the rental place called it. You know, like the old Bond wears, old what's his name . . . oh, Roger Moore."

Not particularly attuned or interested in what I was saying, Virginia approached me with a few unsure steps, and the problem with the state of Virginia was instantly clear. She was stinking drunk and it was not from her mother's highball. This was a drunk that had been in the works for a while, hours probably. I mean, her eyes were looking in opposite directions. Honest.

"A rental, huh?" she said casually but brutally. Then, reaching with her perfectly shellacked rose fingernails, she started molesting my lapels. It was as if she'd assumed the role of a Bond girl, you know, whose aim was the seduce me first only so that she could kill me later. Sensing her daughter's homicidal intent, Virginia's mother tried desperately to steer things back to the social niceties.

"So . . . Virginia tells me you're going to a dinner party first?"

"Yeah—at my friend Shane's house. But first we've gotta stop by my house. My folks want some pictures."

"Oh—that's nice," she said, beaming. "I meant to take some of you two here but the camera is . . . I don't know. . . . I can't keep track of where anything in this house is."

Then, done with leering at me and my lapels, Virginia barked out her next desire.

"I'm hungry," said Virginia, abruptly swinging the spotlight back on her. "I want to eat now!"

Noticing the panic in my eyes, Mrs. McKinley nodded secretly to me as if we were both dealing with an unruly child. Which I guess we were, though most unruly children don't down shots in the middle of the afternoon.

"You'll be at the dinner party soon enough, darling," said her mom. "But you'll want to get some pictures first, to remember your big night."

"You mean *you* will," she said, shooting her mother a more overt, menacing glance. Ouch. "I'm really starving *now*. Can't we just skip the formalities and get to the grub?"

Ohmigod. It's true. She actually said *grub*.

*What is wrong with this girl,* I wondered? My mind was now reeling in reverse, desperately searching for some horrible thing I had done in the recent past to deserve this sort of behavior not only from a date, but from my prom date. My senior prom. The first and last one I would ever be attending. I mean, I knew that this was not intended to be some grand night of romance between Virginia and me. But still, I didn't expect my date to be sloshed and spouting words like *grub*. It's like someone had replaced my Catherine Zeta-Jones with Anna Nicole Smith. A ravenous Anna. On a bad day.

"My parents are really expecting us," I said, trying to motion Virginia toward the door. "My dad is a bit of a shutterbug when it comes to these sort of things."

"Oh, isn't that sweet," said Mrs. McKinley as she leaned toward her daughter, attempting to will her to smile with the force of her own grin. It didn't work.

"I hate pictures."

Okay—to give Virginia some credit here, I probably would not have been too psyched to have a photographic record of myself if I was this trashed during daylight hours.

"Now remember, Virginia," her mom said, as we headed to the door. "Make sure you get home by two A.M. I don't want to be up all night, worrying about—"

Interrupting her mother, Virginia turned around and stated her intentions.

"I'll be home when I feel like it!"

Then just as quickly, she swerved back toward me, and grabbing me brusquely by the arm, yanked me out the door.

"Okay, Hayes, let's hit the road."

And as the weight of Virginia practically dragged me across the transom, I turned around to say good-bye to Mrs. McKinley. But it was too late. We were already halfway down the front walk, as Virginia had quite a stride with her long legs and determined pace. Despite this I managed to offer her mother a half-wave as she stood in the doorway, her brow furrowed with concern as she mouthed *Two A.M.*

I was like, *Wishful thinking, lady. Wishful thinking.*

# CHAPTER 2

It was beautiful out. Gorgeous even. Driving up Connecticut Avenue toward the 'burbs, the June air was ripe with trees and flowers and everything busting out all over. The sky was a clear pale blue, and through the thick canopy of leaves I could discern the outlines of a full moon coming up in the Eastern sky. Now, being a Libra, I'm technically not supposed to be a terribly superstitious type of guy. But when I see a full moon, I always get a little *uh-oh* going on in my gut. It's not like I have scientific evidence that a full-on lunar event is a setup for insane happenings. But on this night that moon was giving me a pretty decent hunch that bad things were rising. It seemed like an omen that things were only going to get worse as the night progressed, the moon rising higher, growing ever whiter, bolder, crazier.

As for Virginia, once she got in my car she was surprisingly docile in a way that was almost unnerving. Every now and then I'd glance over at her and she'd be staring straight ahead, her eyelids heavy and half-closed. I still couldn't figure out what had prompted the bender and her ensuing surly mood. I mean, sure, people have a tendency to imbibe a little too much on prom night. But usually it's on prom *night,* not prom midafternoon. The only reason I could imagine for her terrible 'tude was that maybe, somehow, she had found out I was gay. But how could she have? I mean, no one knew, not a soul. Honest. None of the girls at Potomac and none of the guys at Prep had a clue. I mean, it was the best-kept secret of the academic year, second only to Brittany Monroe's tummy tuck. Seriously . . . the gay thing was a total information blackout. Except for my boyfriend, not a single person knew.

Oh yeah—my boyfriend. I know, I know . . . I didn't really mention him right off the bat. Don't give me that look, okay? Believe me, I have my reasons. Anyway, even though my boyfriend knew I was gay (as he would have to, being my boyfriend and all), I can assure you that he was definitely not going to be telling anyone anytime soon. I mean, no one. Honest. You can trust me on that one.

So I remained utterly baffled as to what had gotten Virginia in a rotten enough mood to get totally sauced. Granted, I didn't know Virginia all that well, so maybe this was just an average afternoon for her. Actually, the one impression I *did* get from our first meeting was that she had a strong predilection for The Drinking. It was at that illegal house party in Georgetown where Virginia had impressed everyone with her limitless capacity for imbibing Jagermeister. I met her via Shane's ex-girlfriend, Jane, who was friends with Virginia from Potomac. But other than that night, the only time I'd hung out with her was Memorial Day weekend, when Shane invited all of us to his parent's country club for opening-day festivities at the pool. And it was there on the sundeck that this whole double-date plan got hatched.

After a round of general razzing about how the prom sucks, Jane posited that the event could actually be fun if you went with the right people. Then, commenting on what a blast we'd had hanging out at the pool that afternoon, Jane floated the idea that we should all go to the prom together; her and Shane as one couple, and me and Virginia as the other. Still, I thought it was crystal clear from the get-go that Virginia and I were not going to be dates, nor would Jane and Shane since they weren't even dating anymore. The whole thing would be more like a group of pals going in a loose yet friendly foursome. At the time, everyone seemed cool with this arrangement. As the planning for the big night progressed, everything went smoothly. I got the 411 on Virginia's outfit, discussed the color of the dress at length so I could order a matching corsage, and made arrangements for picking her up. In fact, I had even talked to Virginia the day before the prom and all systems seemed fine. She was chatty and funny and even somewhat flirty on the phone, which I guess is pretty normal with girls who like guys. Of course, there was one little lurking problem: She didn't know I wasn't her type of guy.

Crossing the District line, Virginia's sour mood continued. As we were now only about ten minutes from my parents in Silver Spring, I was getting anxious about this impending meet-and-greet, given Virginia's condition. I figured I had to at least try to make some peace before getting to my house or, at a minimum, beg her to put on a happy front for the parental photo op. So I opened my big mouth.

"Virginia, is something, uh, wrong?"

She turned and gave me that same wicked look as when she'd stolen her mom's cocktail. Uh-oh. Bracing myself, I sensed a highly dramatic, Oscar-worthy moment approaching.

"Is something *wrong*?" she said, her voice rising way up on *wrong*, like a preacher winding up for a killer sermon. *Oh, God,* I thought, *save me . . . save me now!* "Is something WRONG? Let's see . . . I think that's more a question for you, Hayes. Because there is nothing 'wrong' with me, but you . . . *you* . . . I think there are some serious things *wrong* with *you!*"

*All right,* I thought, *what is so wrong with me?* Sure, I rented a tux when she is definitely a buyer. But then again, girls don't rent dresses. She had something else in mind.

"What are you implying exactly—"

"Look, Hayes," she said. "Are you a fag or what?"

Shocked to hear her question, a question I'd never quite heard before, ever, I jerked my head to look at her and the steering wheel went with me. This caused my parents' practical little Neon to swerve off East-West Highway and onto the dusty shoulder. Virginia screamed as the car shook, vibrating wildly with the rough surface of the shoulder. Not one to be outdone by a female's scream, I shrieked as well. Quickly, though, my arms instinctually spasmed as I swung the car back onto the road, the tires letting out a discreet high-pitched scream of their own.

"Christ," she said, brushing her hair out of her eyes. "So I'll take that as a yes?"

Stunned by her accusation, I tried to dissuade her of the notion that I was gay, even though it was true and I had just proved it by screaming like a supersize sissy. Still, denial is my strong point, so I thought I'd play to it.

"I don't know what you're talking about."

Yeah, well, what can I say? Even though I knew I was gay and had known for quite some time, when she blurted it out in public like she had just done, even if it was in the privacy of my parents' car, it was so alarming that my knee-jerk reaction was to be all like . . . uh, what? But I couldn't play this with Virginia. She was no dummy when it came to gay men.

"And don't try to give me that denial bullshit."

I gave up on denial and went for the specifics on what exactly had tipped her off.

"Wait a minute. What made you even *think* that I was—"

"The corsage," she said, interrupting me.

"The . . . huh?"

"On the phone the other night," she said, to my continued blank look. "You asked me very specifically what color dress I was wearing so that you could order a matching corsage."

"But that's what a guy's supposed to do," I said protesting.

"Not a *straight* guy," she said, emphasis way on the *straight* in case I didn't get the point. "They don't care about the color of the dress or what fabric it is or who the hell made it. They just want to get the damn thing off. But *you* kept going on and on about my dress like you were a special guest host on E! or something."

Well, according to *Seventeen,* Rule number 3 of having a "dreamy prom" is to have a date who is constantly inquiring about and complimenting your outfit. Then again, I'm guessing that real straight guys probably don't read *Seventeen*, And perhaps therein lies my error. . . .

"Look, Hayes—you can be as closeted or uncloseted as you want at school or at home or in your own bedroom. I honestly don't give a shit. But right now, in this car, between you and me and East-West Highway, I need to know for real. . . . Are you a fag or what?"

Again with the fag! It was annoying and insulting, and what can I say? It got to me. On a deep level. I mean, by taking this tack she was asking for it, you know? Virginia had, unwittingly, unleashed my inner gay bitch.

"I don't know, Virginia," I said cockily. "Are you an alcoholic?"

This approach, however, was a huge mistake, as it merely incensed her even more.

"Only because I am going to the *prom* with a goddamn *faggot!*"

It was at this moment that I thought of maybe driving the car off the road again, this time on purpose; a minor accident maybe, something that would be just enough to get Virginia and I into the ER and out of our commitment to an evening together of prom hell. However, realizing that a car wreck would probably mean I would not be allowed to drive for, well, about the rest of my life, I opted for something else. I tried to get her to ease up on the harsh language.

"Can you please stop saying that?"

"What . . . *fag?*" she said, spitting it out. Again!

"Virginia, you just said it again."

"Oh yeah? Well, maybe I'll stop saying it if you answer the god-damn question."

All right—was she joking? There was, like, no *way* I was gonna answer that question, even though, sure, on a technicality I could have said that no, I was not a "fag" but was merely a guy who happened to dig guys. But I didn't sense that Virginia was in a mood for technicalities. She was equally not in a mood for me giving her the silent treatment on this issue. So undeterred by my unwillingness to speak, she launched another tirade.

"Look, Hayes—I've known a few in my time, and you seem pretty faggy to me. And I have no intention of going to the prom with a known fag and being labeled a fruit fly."

"A . . . a what?"

"A friggin' fruit fly . . . a girl who hangs out with fags."

*Hmmmm—fruit fly. Clever little slang,* I thought to myself, *and a lot sweeter than fag hag.* Still, I guessed that it was probably not so cute when you're the one getting tagged with it. But it definitely had a sweeter ring than *fag.* Especially when you factored in the harsh manner in which Virginia said it, which was truly getting on my nerves.

"Virginia, can you please stop using that word? It's totally offensive."

She shrugged, that wicked sideways grin reappearing.

"I'm just being real here . . . that's all, Hayes. Calling a fag a fag."

And that was it. Her double fag broke me. I slammed on the brakes and Virginia's hair lurched forward, her head following. Now that I had her full attention, I laid into her in a manner that surprised even me.

"Virginia, I swear to God, if you don't stop using that word I'm gonna run this car off the road and we'll both die terrible deaths together and thus be perpetually linked till eternity or something!"

Virginia regarded me like I was somewhat crazy, which at that point, I guess I was. Adjusting her disheveled hair, she brought her tone down a few octaves.

"Okay, I just need to know what the hell's going on here. When Jane set this whole thing up, I thought I was going on a legitimate prom date—"

"We said we were going as friends!" I said, my voice rising.

But she continued talking. "With a heterosexual male. But, after some consideration, it appears that I've been duped into being your show pony so that the rest of Prep won't figure out that you'd rather be slow dancing with some guy. Now, am I right or what?"

She poked my arm, fingernail first. Ow. But what hurt even more was that she had me. Sorta.

"Well," I said, concentrating on driving again. "You're not exactly wrong."

"So you *are* gay?"

I froze. I had never really admitted this to anyone. Ever. (Okay, well, other than my boyfriend.) So confessing this to some random prom date was not exactly the first person I imagined I'd be sharing this highly personal information with, especially a person who'd been drinking since 4:00 P.M.

Sensing my apprehension at copping to this admission, Virginia shifted gears.

"I don't have anything against gay guys, okay? My older brother's gay and I don't hate him. He can get on my nerves sometimes and the guy he used to date is a retard, but other than that, it's fine. No big deal. To each his own and all that shit. But this is my prom night we're talking about here. And if you really are gay, it basically means that I have a zero chance of getting any action whatsoever. Zee-ro. Probably in the negative numbers even. So how do you think that makes *me* feel, huh?"

All right, she had a point. It made me feel kinda bad, actually. At least I knew that no matter how terrible the prom was going to be for me, I would eventually get to make out with my boyfriend at some point towards the end of the evening. And maybe even get some action, too, as Virginia put it.

"Okay—you're right," I said, feeling vaguely guilty. "But taking you to the prom is not some lame attempt to make everyone at the dance think I'm not gay. That's not the point of this at all."

"Then what exactly *is* the point?" she demanded, crossing her arms across her ample chest.

Oh, man. Talk about the million-dollar question. The funny thing is that this was the exact same question that had been bothering me ever since this whole prom scheme was hatched. But I couldn't get into this with Virginia. I'd been sworn to supreme secrecy. Still, I began to wonder if by even having this conversation with her, I'd already compromised that top secret vow and the whole scheme itself by inadvertently coming out to my fake date.

"The reasons for going to the prom are . . . well . . . it's complicated."

"Hmmm," she said, her mind practically whirring, trying to figure this whole puzzle out. "Lemme guess. This have something to do with your parents?"

"What!"

"Do *they* know you're gay?"

"Uh . . . no. But that has nothing—"

Virginia cut me off, suddenly sure of what was behind this charade.

"Oh, I get it. . . . Playing straight for Mom and Dad. I totally know *this* whole tired routine. My brother did it all through high school, even into college, which was lame considering that at that point he wasn't even living at home. I had to out him to get everyone to deal with the whole thing."

"Wait—you outed your own brother?"

"His stupid boyfriend kept calling when he was living at home during the summer," she said, trying to downplay her role in this outing. "So one time when he called and my brother was up in his room, I yelled up the stairs 'Hey, your *boyfriend's* on the phone!'"

"Ohmigod," I said, my mouth agape. "That is evil."

"No, it's not," she shot back at me. "It was the truth, that's all. There is nothing evil about telling people the truth and waking everyone up to the goddamn elephant in the upstairs bedroom. I mean, the sheer volume of lying going on it that house . . . it was absurd and driving everyone crazy."

"Still, it was so not your right for you to out him like that."

"Believe me, it was for the best. Everyone freaked out for a month, but in the end it made life at home about ninety percent more bearable. Look, I'm sure your little secret is making things tense with you and the 'rents, right?"

Remarkably, she had a point. In the previous few months my conversations with my parents had gone from full sentences to the basic multiple-choice answers of yes, no, or maybe. Family meals were these increasingly awkward, silent affairs punctuated only by sad clinks of silver. I don't have any brothers or sisters so, in effect, I *was* the family, and suddenly I was not really there.

My dad tried to talk to me once, back in March, about the change in my behavior. In response, I covered up the real reason for my lack of communication, saying I was stressing because of the pressures of senior year, waiting to hear about colleges, and on top of all that, being in charge of editing the yearbook. But of course, I failed to mention the real reason: the guy who'd turned my world upside down with a stolen kiss at a Homecoming Weekend rager.

"That shut you up," said Virginia.

"Huh?"

I didn't realize it but I had gone totally mute, dropping my end of the conversation as I mused about my clueless parents.

"Sorry, I was just—"

"Thinking you should probably tell your folks?"

I turned toward her with my best sarcastic squint.

"Uh . . . no."

Virginia squinted back at me, her well-lubricated head bobbing with every bump the car encountered. We came to a stop at a traffic light and she lurched slightly forward again. She was still decidedly drunk. Not that I thought that she would have sobered up in the car. But I realized this was going to be a real problem in a few moments, as we were only a block away from meeting the parents.

"You know," she said, trying to be helpful and wicked all at once. "I could tell your parents for you."

"Are y—are you insane?"

"C'mon, Hayes, aren't you tired of the whole charade? You're what, eighteen, almost nineteen years old, and you're basically scared of your parents because of this? What kind of life is that?"

"Uh, it's my life. *Mine*. And you have no right to—"

And again I set her off.

"*I* have no right. What about *you* having no right to ask me as your date to the prom under totally false pretenses. How about *that*?"

When she was done letting me have it, all I heard was honking. Lots of cars honking. The light had turned green and I hadn't even noticed. I slammed my foot on the accelerator and Virginia slammed backward into her seat.

"We're almost at my parents' house," I said, on the verge of begging. "Please, Virginia, all I ask is that you just act like a normal date for ten minutes and don't mention anything about—"

"You being a fag?"

*Ohmigod,* I thought. This was bad. This was badder than bad. This was a family crisis about to be triggered by a sloshed girl in a very bad mood. If I can analogize here for a minute, she was a loaded gun and I had given her all the ammunition she needed to blow some severe holes in my entire life! Okay—maybe that was a little over the top. I can get a little dramatic sometimes. But I am a gay boy in training. Comes with the territory, you know?

"I'm serious, Virginia," I said, giving her my best pleading look, working my adorable droopy dawg eyes (that's what my boyfriend called them!) to full effect. "Please don't hint or allude or say one single word about this to my folks. Please . . ."

So for the record, these sort of big-eyed charms don't exactly work on a girl when she knows you like guys. In fact, in this situation they had the opposite effect.

"All right, Hayes," she said, her own eyes brimming with sheer craftiness. "What's it worth to you?"

# CHAPTER 3

As we pulled up to the curb of 2020 Crestwood Drive, I could see my parents sitting in the kitchen window, waving like lunatics. Let me say this: My parents are *very* excitable people. I guess it could be because they're relatively young for old people, both of them not even forty yet. You see, they had one of those too-cute-for-words meetings when they were freshman at the University of Maryland. The details are pretty nauseating, and I won't make you ill by relating all of them here. Let me just say that it happened in the library as they both were looking for a copy of *Romeo and Juliet*. Need I say more? Anyway, they got married right after graduation and had me a few months afterward. Yeah, it's true—I was a shotgun baby, but in a good way since they were already engaged when I was conceived. Apparently, they were so damn horny for each other, they couldn't wait for the marriage vows to consummate the whole deal.

Now, before you start thinking that it must be totally cool to have such young hipster parents, let me make something very clear. My parents are *not* cool. Honest. They are both geeks—I mean über-geeks. Get this: They are both research scientists—that's right, *scientists* at NIH in Bethesda. Some people might think this is cool, finding cures for cancer and making the world a healthier place and all that. But the people who think this do not have to live with my parents. I mean, c'mon, do you really want to listen to conversations regarding the periodic table at breakfast? Or how about, oh, let's see, the ionization of particle beams in binary lasers? Had enough?

On the cultural side of things, it's even worse. Just because someone's under forty does not mean they might have actually listened to cool bands like the Smiths or Black Flag during their formative years in the 1980s. Oh no—my parents listened to jazz. (Sorry, that's Jazz—I'm always getting corrected on this.) My folks are total Jazz music buffs, the radio dial in our kitchen permanently affixed to WAMU, the local NPR affiliate. And get this: They actually go to Jazz concerts. I know because I've been dragged along with them, less so in recent years, thank God. They also have countless numbers of old, arcane Jazz records that are "groundbreaking" and "monumental" and "historic." But to me, I don't know, Jazz sounds like a bunch of guys who don't know how to read music just sitting around and playing whatever the hell they want.

All this is to say that my parents get very excited about Jazz music and scientific breakthroughs and life in general. Thus they're kind of spazzy and prone to embarrassing things like waving out the kitchen window like a couple of freaks.

"Okay," I said to Virginia. "Here's the plan."

"Plan?"

"I'm going to get out and open the door for you—"

"Such a gentleman."

"And then you take my arm and I'll walk you up to the front door."

Virginia looked at me, not too happy about the plan.

"Take your arm?" she said, revolted. "Isn't that a little too cutesy couple-y?"

"Uh . . ." I said, trying to be polite about the real reason for arm holding. "Actually, I don't want you to trip on the way in."

Virginia glared at me. Uh-oh. I probably shouldn't have mentioned that.

"I am *not* taking your damn arm."

I glared back.

"I thought we had a deal," I said, forcefully reminding her of our negotiations regarding the home visit. Just before turning onto Crestwood, we'd reached an agreement to guarantee her silence on the fag issue.

"Fine."

With that I got out of the car and enacted my plan. Under the excitable gaze of my mom in the kitchen window (my dad had already excitedly gone to open the front door), Virginia and I made our way up the stone path that lead to the front door of our one-story, white brick sixties-style ranch house. Though I tried to keep us going at a stately, regal pace, Virginia's head bounced slightly with each high-heeled step, like one of those bobble heads that people stick to their dash. I gripped her arm tighter, somehow thinking that might stiffen up her neck muscles or something. Bad logic.

"My arm is falling asleep," she muttered under her breath.

I gave her some slack.

Just then the front door flew open and there was my dad, decked out in his scientist's finery: yellow plaid shirtsleeves, khaki pants with various stains of experiments gone awry, and a pair of Converse sneakers dating from the Reagan years. He did not have a pocket protector but, frankly, could have used one for the various pens, security badges, and Metro fare cards that sprouted from his pocket like a synthetic bouquet.

"Look, honey," he said, yelling to my mom. "The king and queen of the prom are here!"

Virginia gave me a morose but knowing look. At least she felt my pain.

My mom appeared in the doorway a moment later and practically squealed upon seeing us standing there on the front porch, looking like plastic figurines on a wedding cake. Uh, make that a rum cake.

"Oh—you two look *so* cute."

"Mom, Dad . . . this is Virginia," I said by way of introduction.

"Well, hello there, Virginia," my dad said, cheerily offering his hand for a shake. But instead of a handshake, his face swooped down and kissed Virginia's hand as if he were some seventeenth-century nobleman. Ohmigod—did he kinda curtsy, too? It is due to things like this that some nights I awake in a drenching sweat, convinced I am adopted.

"My, my, Virginia . . . what a beautiful state *you're* in," said my dad with a goofy grin. "Get it—Virginia . . . state?"

"Howard," said my mom, elbowing him at the bad joke. You see, my dad has this thing for puns that result in so much elbowing by my mom that, after nearly twenty years together, he must have a permanent indent on the left side of his abdomen.

"It's nice to meet you, Mr. and Mrs. Hayes," said Virginia in a surprisingly normal manner. "I've heard a lot about you two. Cameron was talking about what wonderful parents you were in the car ride here."

Though she was obviously baiting me with that last comment, she had my folks utterly charmed. They beamed at each other.

"It's wonderful to meet you, Virginia," said my dad. "Come on in and let's get some pictures."

My parents' excitability extends to their one discernible hobby: photography. No event, no matter how big or small, goes undocumented. I know, I know . . . everyone's parents take pictures. But seriously, I am not exaggerating when I say that my parents have a strange and unique obsession with recording every detail of my life. Example: There are two rolls of snapshots from the day I took the SAT's.

Virginia and I made our way into the living room, the traditional studio for the more formal events in the ongoing pictorial history of me. The centerpiece of the room is a large, earthy fireplace made out of various igneous rocks that my dad likes to identify for visiting company when things get really boring. Fortunately that evening he merely stood us in front of the fireplace, grabbed his Nikon 284x-SLR and started snapping away.

"Okay, ready?" he said so damn eagerly it hurt. Hurt me, that is.

I nodded and tried to muster a smile. Virginia looked distracted and stone-faced and pretty much like someone under a gag order. (Uh, which she was.) As we settled into our poses, standing side by side in front of the fireplace, I released her arm. Virginia then shook it out a bit, waking it from its slumber.

"Here we go," said my dad as he switched to his best *Fantasy Island* voice. "Smiles, everyone . . . smiles!"

The flash rigged atop his camera was so enormous and powerful that its first explosion of megawhite stunned Virginia. Literally. She teetered on her heels, blinking her eyes as she tried to regain her balance and her sight.

"Jesus Christ!" she muttered under her breath. Deftly, I reached out for her hand to give her some needed balance, keeping her from pitching into the mantle.

"Okay, ready?"

Not really, but my dad started shooting again anyway. FLASH-FLASH! Virginia was reeling from the shock of the flashes, her body swaying back and forth as if caught in an incongruous indoor lightning storm. My dad, fortunately, didn't seem to notice this, engrossed as he often was in the technical details of his camera, setting the exposure, checking the focus, etc. Looking closer, though, it seemed that when he framed us, my dad wasn't exactly looking at us in the viewfinder. It looked like he was aiming a little low. Wait a minute—was he taking pictures of Virginia's ample cleavage?

FL-FL-FLASH. FLASSSH. FLASHHHH!

"Dad, isn't that enough?"

He fiddled with the focus ring and forwarded the film, oblivious to my question. He was under the spell of Virginia's busting-out boobs.

"Couple more, Cam . . . okay, everyone say *Cheez Wiz!*"

FLASH-FFFFLASH-FLA-FLASH.

"Jesus Christ," said Virginia, her muttering more audible this time, so that my mom took notice. Or maybe she innately sensed that my dad was actually doing a photo essay on the teenage breast.

"Honey," my mom said sheepishly, tapping his shoulder. "Maybe that's enough."

"Just a few more . . ."

Then I remembered something, a diversionary tactic perhaps, that could end the pics.

"Dad, can you get Virginia's corsage?"

"Oh, my *matching* corsage!" exclaimed Virginia, solely for my benefit. Charming, huh?

"It's in the fridge," I said to my dad.

"I'll get it," my mom replied, racing off to the kitchen. Great. Unfortunately, I'd gotten rid of her, which was not my intention. Meanwhile, my dad kept snapping as Virginia's fake smile was wearing off.

"Such sad faces. This is the prom!" my dad said, getting excitable again. "The most exciting night of your life!"

Which makes me wonder—do parents have any sort of long-term memory? I remember getting this whole "most exciting" crap on my sixteenth birthday, which my parents turned into a megaevent rivaling the Super Bowl. But for me, all I recall of that birthday was being totally depressed about turning sixteen and still not having kissed anyone in my life that I had a romantic feeling for. It was probably the most depressing day of my life. But with a drunk date who wanted to out me and an endless semiperverted photo session, prom night was on track to trump even that low point.

My mom raced back into the living room with the now infamous corsage. Instead of stopping the photo op, it only inspired a whole new round of pictures as I placed the red roses with the matching velvety band on Virginia's wrist.

"Oh, wait," said my dad. "I was out of focus. Can you do it again?"

"Dad—"

My pleading did nothing to stop him as he kept on shooting, making spastic gestures with his left hand in an attempt to direct me for take two of Placement of the Corsage while clicking away on the shutter button with his right. FL-FLASH. FLASSSSH. FLASH-FLASH.

FFFFFLASH. FLASH. Virginia seemed to be getting dizzy as the clicking wore on, her balance woozy, her heels increasingly wobbly. After about a minute of corsage shots, a weary, bleary-eyed Virginia tilted toward my ear, her voice low and raspy.

"I think I'm gonna be sick."

Fortunately at that moment, the flashing stopped as my dad ran out of film.

"Whoops—gotta reload."

Trying to avert a puking disaster, I was about to lead Virginia to the bathroom when my mom started chattering away. Very excitably.

"We can get you some copies for your mom, Virginia. Would she like that?"

"Yeah," said Virginia, looking paler by the second. "Sure."

"Cam tells us your parents are separated. So maybe another set for your father."

"Whatever."

I regarded my dad to see if he noticed the true state of Virginia, as it were. However, he was still checking out her body. I guess it'd been a while since my dad had seen a live teen babe, and he was enjoying the scenery. You see, I hadn't exactly been bringing girls home every other weekend, you know what I mean? Still, you'd think he'd be able to restrain himself somewhat, given the fact that, technically, she was supposed to be my date. But I guess that's the other drawback to having parents under forty—they still actually have a sex drive. Gross, right?

"So . . . Cam tells us you live in Georgetown," my mom continued. "That must be *very* exciting."

"Yeah," responded Virginia, wholly unexcited.

"I would love to live down there. But on our salaries we were lucky we got this place when we did. But it must be so convenient for you, going to Potomac. Do you like it there?"

"Yep."

Uh-oh. Her responses were getting shorter. The countdown to calamity had commenced.

"It's such a beautiful school. And the history in those old buildings must—"

Virginia flashed me a discreet look of panic. *Puking in 4 . . . 3 . . . 2 . . .*

"Uh," I interjected. "I think Virginia wants to use the ladies' room."

"Oh, sure—to freshen up a bit," my mom said with a knowing look. Ah, but if she only knew. "Let me show you."

As my mom led Virginia away, I experienced some blessed relief, at least for a moment.

"Wow," said my dad, coming back with a newly loaded camera. "She's quite a girl, Cam."

"Gee," I said, not knowing how to respond to a pervy parent. "Thanks, Dad."

"Don't be modest about it. She's really cute. Where did you meet her again?"

"At that party in Georgetown . . . she's a friend of Jane Pierce."

"And hopefully she'll be friendly with you," he said, creeping me out. "Looks like you're going to have quite a memorable evening, that's for sure."

Evening? At this rate, the afternoon alone was going to be hard to forget, though not in the way he meant it. Clamping his hand onto my shoulder in typically fatherly fashion, my dad seemed to be implying that I was going to get laid. It was at this horrific point that all of Virginia's ranting about the truth hit home. Literally.

"Dad," I said as plainly as I could. "Virginia and I are just friends. Really."

"It's okay, Cam," he said with a wink and shoulder squeeze. "You don't have to be ashamed about these things with me."

"But really, Dad . . . it's not like we—"

"Hey, I understand. You should have a good time. Just be safe."

With that little gem, I thought that *I* was going to be sick.

"You know, I think I better hit the head too before we go."

Sprinting downstairs, I headed to the other bathroom. I wasn't really going to get sick. I just needed to get away before my dad said something truly disgusting about having sex with my date.

Locking the door behind me, I didn't really have to do anything in the bathroom except hide from everyone. So I turned on the water to make it sound like I was busy in there and checked out my pre-prom appearance in the mirror. I have to say, despite how I felt inside, I looked fairly good on the outside. I guess even a tux can make a stick figure like me look like I have shoulders and a chest and something resembling arms. It actually gave my wiry twig of a body some formal heft, which was nice for a change. As for the rest of me, my looks were about as hopeless as usual, though it didn't stop me from trying to improve on the situation.

I futzed with my thick, muddy brown hair, but there was not much to do with it. Though tamed by some of my mom's conditioner for the big night, it seemed as expansive and unruly as ever, its bangs covering up my massive forehead. That's probably the one thing I liked about my hair: it did a good job of hiding the high, flat expanse of prairie above my dark brows. Next I pursed my nonexistent lips a bit, trying to make them bigger and failing as usual. You see, way back in tenth grade, my former best friend, Franklin Taylor, was nice enough to point out to me one day during lunch that I had no lips. (Sweet, huh?) Ever since that day, I've been hyperaware of this fact, checking out other people's lips, taking comparison notes, contemplating that weird procedure female celebrities have that pumps them up like a bicycle tire. Strangely, my boyfriend thinks my lips are perfect and all that. But you know what? Considering what these lips have done for him, he's probably not the most objective person to ask about this.

Okay—so standing there in front of the mirror I continued the usual inventory of things about my face that bug me. My ears are huge, which is why I'd let my hair get so long and unruly in the first place. It did a decent job of hiding at least half of their satellite dish shape. My eyes are all right, if maybe a little too close together, with a pleasing green cast that my mother has doted on for years and that the boyfriend digs too. My nose, however, is definitely less than desirable; short and pointy, like an elf or something silly, which doesn't help matters when you already have an elfin build. I think Franklin once mentioned a resemblance I shared to that elf in *Rudolph,* the one who wants to be a dentist. (And he wonders why we're not friends anymore?) I read in *Jane* magazine about some makeup tricks one can deploy to camouflage a "sharp" nose, but I don't think that would work for me really. I mean, c'mon, it's not like I'm a drag queen or anything. Please!

Anyway, as I stood there critiquing my looks per usual, I was struck by the fact that I had much bigger problems at play that night that dulling the point of my nose. Looking at myself in the mirror, there was something less tangible than my physical features that was bothering me; namely, the fact that my formal, put-together look was itself a lie. It was like this nice and fancy outer shell covering a person that was really not so nice and fancy. In fact, after the unsettling car ride with Virginia, I was coming to the realization that I was basically a huge liar, having wholly falsified my life to my date, to my parents, maybe even to myself. I was beginning to feel like I needed a drink as much as Virginia. Then I remembered the deal. The one I had struck with Virginia.

Discreetly twisting the doorknob, I exited the bathroom so that no one would hear and slipped around the corner. Crouching down in my white dinner jacket, I imagined myself in a Bond movie as I gingerly made my way across the basement, hugging the wood-paneled wall. If you're ever trying to do something sneaky, let me tell you that trying to tiptoe in hard shoes is not easy, especially on a linoleum floor. Arriving at the liquor cabinet, I scanned the room quickly for dramatic effect that was appreciated only by me. Then putting one hand on the oaken door of the cabinet, I grabbed the stubby metal knob with the other, trying to quiet the *click* of the magnetic latch. It popped open with barely a sound, thank God. I reached in for the quart of Jack Daniels that I had promised Virginia in return for her silence. It was hush liquor, though I was unsure whether she would exactly need or want it, postpuking. Still, it was part of the deal and I was trying to be a man of my word.

FFFLASSSH!

The dark rec room went white as I spun around on my heel and saw my dad standing there, his camera aimed right at me. Bond was in a bind.

"Hey, Dad," I said nonchalantly, slipping the bottle behind my back and clasping both my hands there. Suave, huh? If only . . .

"What you got there?" he said, totally seeing through my attempts to hide the Jack.

"What . . . me . . . got . . . uh—"

Just so you know, I get very articulate in tense situations like this.

"Getting a little sauce for later?" he asked, approaching me for closer examination.

Sauce! So young but, really, so old, you know what I mean?

"It's okay, Cam," he said, tilting his head to indicate what I was concealing. "What you got there?"

"Nothing really," I said not so convincingly. "I was just—"

However, the nervous sweatiness of my palms conspired to show me up as—*CLINK!*—the bottle of Jack hit the floor and, fortunately, did not break.

"You've disappointed me, son," he said with a disturbing grin on his face.

"I'm sorry, Dad," I said, feeling beyond mortified. But he wasn't disappointed that way.

"I thought you'd go for the good stuff, at least."

Wait a minute—so he apparently *wanted* me to steal the Maker's Mark? I didn't get this line of reasoning, so I tried to explain. Well, maybe not everything, but at least something. All right, how 'bout one thing.

"You see, Virginia asked me to—"

"You don't have to explain, Cam. I understand."

Again he put his hand on my shoulder and clamped down tight. Okay—so what exactly is this shoulder-hold thing? The international sign for parental understanding or something?

"I get it," he said. "A little grease for the wheels, as it were."

Again I was sick to my stomach.

"No, Dad—really. It's just—"

"You know, Cam . . . I remember my prom. And my date. Wow. Melanie Johnson . . . we were both National Merit semifinalists and co-chairs of the Computer Club . . . and that was even before they had personal computers!"

He sighed, lost in hazy memories of geek love.

"She was a big girl, too, you know," he said, pantomiming her breasts.

Nausea alert. I was ready to be puking myself in 3 . . . 2 . . .

"But she was not easy. Actually Mellie was a bit of a prude. So I had to take 'extra measures.' I got my older brother to buy me a fifth of whiskey, and later, at this after-party, I got her a bit sauced. And . . . well, we had a *great* time. But don't tell your mother!"

All right, was he joking? Seriously. Like I would ever tell anyone this hideous story of parental lust run amuck. Ever.

"So it's okay, then?" I said, unsure whether or not my dad was really encouraging illegal underage drinking.

"Sure. But no driving if you're gonna have any, got it?"

"Uh . . . okay. It's really for Virginia anyway."

At least that was the truth. My dad nodded, pleased with my answer.

"And don't tell your mother," he added. "This is *our* little secret."

*Our* little secret, huh? I had to smile on hearing that. Though my dad thought this smile was a complicit grin, I was really thinking about my not-so-little secret and how being offered illegal booze paled in comparison to the fact that I'd had a boyfriend for the past six months.

Thinking I was off the hook, I started to head back upstairs, the bottle tucked away into my breast pocket. But stopping me on the landing, Dad reached into his pants pocket to offer me something else. Oh, no—was he actually going to give me a condom, too?

"Here—"

I practically closed my eyes, not wanting to see what sort of birth control he was offering. Was it going to be ribbed for extra pleasure? Maybe Magnum-sized with a reservoir tip? Or, God help me, not the prelubricated, treated with Nonoxynyl-9 deal? I was incredibly relieved to see it was not a Trojan but a Benjamin. Benjamin Franklin, that is.

"Whoa—a hundred?" I said. "What's this for?"

"It's an emergency fund."

I was dumbfounded. Emergency . . .

"You know . . . in case you can't get home."

Still in the dark here, folks . . .

"And have to stay . . . downtown."

Ohmigod! He doesn't mean—

"And need to get yourselves a room."

Okay—have you ever felt like reporting your parents to Social Services? Well, neither had I until the moment my dad decided to secretly fund my premarital sexual relations with a drunk Amazon. But as horrified as I was, I can see in retrospect what was going on. Basically, my dad had made the big mistake of thinking that I was him at eighteen, eager and horny to get it on with my bodacious babe of a date. I guess all parents assume that you are them until you start to tell them otherwise, especially if you look like them and I am pretty much a carbon copy of my dad at this age. (In fact, there is a whole compare-and-contrast album with photos of us, side by side at different ages, to prove this lovely theorem.) That's when I realized that Virginia really did have a point about the whole coming-out-to-your-folks thing. The point being that this lack of communication only leads to terrible misunderstandings, which end up being majorly embarrassing for all parties involved. You know, misunderstandings like thinking your gay son is really going to get it on with his female prom date in some skeevy motel room. Please!

"You look like you don't want it," he said as I stared at the bill like it was a condom.

"Uh . . . no . . . it's just—"

All right—how to break this to him? Sorry, Dad, but I'm actually a homo and was wondering if I could maybe use this to get a room for me and my *boyfriend*? But with Virginia waiting upstairs, Shane's dinner party already underway, and a long night ahead of me, I didn't really have the time or the energy to drop this sorta bomb in our basement. So I just smiled at my dad, smiling like my dad. We have the exact same smile, my mom likes to say. And seeing it always pleased him.

"Thanks, Dad."

"Hey, have a great time," he said with a wily look in his eyes. "And don't tell your mother!"

# CHAPTER 4

Safely back in the Neon, I hit the gas and practically peeled away from 2020 Crestwood, trying to put all the embarrassments and near disasters of the home visit behind us as quickly as possible. Virginia, however, didn't feel the same way, as she waved way too enthusiastically at my parents, who were back in the kitchen window taking pictures of our getaway. With my right arm, I batted Virginia's corsaged hand down.

"Don't encourage them," I said.

"God—you're no fun. You know that?"

"That's not what you said the night we met."

"Hmmm," she considered, "I must've been drunk."

"Hmmm . . . seems like a recurring theme in your life."

"Ha-ha-HA," she said in a mockery of laughter. Then, snapping her fingers twice, she thrust out her palm.

"So where's my hooch?"

"Hooch?"

"You did get it, right?"

"Yeah—when you were puking upstairs," I said, emphasis on the *puking*. "I hope you flushed real good."

"I didn't puke, smart-ass."

Virginia went on to explain, however, that she did nearly pass out while sitting on the toilet. Fortunately under the sink she found some Pepto to tame the beast that was her stomach.

"So let me get this straight," I said, no pun intended. "Already this afternoon you've had tequila in your bedroom, your mom's highball, Pepto, and *now* you wanna do shots of Jack?"

"Uh, sure. Why not?"

"Because, hmmm, I don't know," I said facetiously. "Maybe I don't want you to puke all over my parents' car?"

"I can handle my liquor, Hayes," she said, speaking like a boozy old movie star. "It's a genetic thing, tolerance and all. Runs in the family."

Despite having witnessed her mother's skill with a drink, Virginia's mixing seemed like it could turn into a potentially messy situation. But Virginia and I did have a deal; her silence for my dad's Jack. And as I said, I was trying to be a man of my word for once in my life, you know? So I handed her the bottle, and she took a healthy swig.

"Cheers," she said to herself. "You want some?"

"Uh, driving here."

"Oh, right. Well, at least you're a conscientious fag."

And again we were back to the *fag*.

"I thought we'd agreed to stop using that word."

"What word would you prefer? Homo, fairy, cake boy, Mary?"

I looked over at her, astounded she could be so damn offensive so effortlessly.

"If you don't like those terms, I could go on—gay blade, fudge packer, rump—"

Okay—that was enough. Now it was my turn to give her a reality check.

"That's cute, Virginia. Very cute. However, I'd like to remind you that the night we met, we made out for, oh, about forty-five minutes, and you seemed to enjoy it quite a bit, as I recall, so maybe I'm *not* so gay after all."

Oh yeah—I'd forgotten to mention this part. I have made out with girls, not a lot but more than once. What? These things happen. It's sort of an unavoidable hazard in a world that is majority hetero-sexual. In fact, when you're attending a raucous party at someone's parentless town house, it's downright inevitable. Not that I make a point of it to put myself in situations like this. Hardly.

You see, it was Shane's idea to go to that party in the first place. Ian Harrison, his best friend from the football team, had gotten him all jazzed about this illegal party on Q Street. Initially I said I didn't want to go, feeling it would not be a welcoming environment for someone like me, who wasn't exactly on the football team. Don't get me wrong, though. It's not like I'm a total geek. I mean, I'm not in marching band or anything. Please! But on the other hand, I would never be mistaken for a linebacker on the Prep varsity squad. So as a rule I tended to avoid those sort of jock-filled events as much as possible. But when Shane gets insistent about what to do on a given night, resistance is futile.

Anyway, by the time we got to Georgetown, the party was in full swing. After having decimated the contents of the wine cellar, the members of the team and their personal "cheerleaders" were scattered throughout the various living rooms, sitting rooms, and bedrooms, making out and getting it on. Shane and I arrived about the same time as Jane, Shane's ex who goes to Potomac. And it was Jane who had Virginia in tow with her. Virginia was already slightly buzzed when I met her, and despite this (maybe because of it?) took a liking to me. We hung out in the downstairs living room while Jane and Shane went upstairs to find Ian, who supposedly had some pot.

After Virginia plied me with a flask of hers containing Jagermeister, we started making out. Well, actually, she started making out with me. That's how these things happen with girls; they attack me and I just go along with it. Seriously—what's the big deal? I mean, really, when it comes down to it, lips are lips, right? And Virginia was not a bad kisser. So writhing around with her on an enormous leather couch, I kissed Virginia and thought about my boyfriend and no one was the wiser. Or so I thought.

"Frankly, Hayes," she said to me angrily, "you kissed like a gay guy!"

"Really? How many gay guys have you kissed?"

"Too many," she said with the weariness of a bitter divorcée.

"So how does a gay guy kiss?"

"Uh . . . let's see," she said, winding up her delivery. "Poorly?"

Okay—so as you may have surmised, I was clearly dealing with someone who had it out for gay men. With that kissing comment I instantly knew why. Virginia had been down this road before, probably with someone she actually liked, and it had not been a fun ride. On top of that, she definitely had some issues with her brother being gay too. Still, I wasn't going to sit there and take her bitchiness sitting down, even if I was driving. I was going to bitch right back.

"Poorly, huh? That's not what my boyfriend says."

"What boyfriend?"

"*My* boyfriend."

She looked me over, assessing the truth quotient of my statement. At that point she knew better than to take me, like most people had, at face value. Yet her lie detector was not infallible.

"You don't have a fucking boyfriend."

"Actually, if you want to be literal about it, I *do* have a fucking boyfriend."

That bit of graphicness silenced her. Points for me, huh?

"Look—if you really had a boyfriend, then why are you going to the prom with me?"

Oh, man—this question again. More like why am I going to the prom at all! Like I said, the whole prom thing was not my idea. Honest. I really didn't know why I was doing this and, with every passing minute I was questioning the whole thing more and more. But I couldn't get into this with Virginia. It was complicated. It was beyond complicated in a way that would probably only serve to make her even angrier and more embittered than she already was. Also, making a familiar turn, we were only about a minute away from the dinner party.

"Maybe we can talk about this later. We're almost there."

"It's about time," she said, dropping the subject easier than I'd expected she would. There were more pressing matters, namely her stomach. "I'm starving!"

Hooking a left off Foxhall Road, we drove past the walled compounds and gated entryways to some of the most exclusives homes in the city. Just as the road was about to come to a dead end, a hand-carved, wooden sign read RAVENSWOOD, the nickname of the Wilson estate. As a reverse sign of exclusivity, there were no imposing walls or tall hedges or electronic gates surrounding the Wilson's expansive property. In their naturally secluded ravine, they felt no need for these modern battlements. Also, as Shane had once remarked, his mother felt that those security devices just screamed "new money."

Shane Wilson was a rare bird, a true Washington native. Though I was born and raised in Maryland, my parents were not from the area, having grown up in rural parts of Massachusetts and Connecticut. Generally that is the case for the majority of people living in D.C. and its surrounding suburbs, due to the transitory nature of the government and military jobs in the area. But Shane was the real thing, a Washingtonian. Not only was he born and raised in the District, but so was his father. And his father's father. And so on and so on, back to sometime in the midnineteenth century.

The reason for this is that Shane's family had little to do with the governments that came and went on a four- to eight-year basis. The Wilsons were bankers and businessmen, the behind-the-scenes players on the D.C. stage whose names do not garner headlines but whose holdings make them some of the wealthiest people this side of the Rockefellers. Not that you would know it, really. Wealth in D.C. is not as auspicious as it is in other cities. Befitting a city where diplomacy and Southern charm rule, being loaded is much more discreet and secretive. The one sure way that wealth *can* be ascertained, though, is location. And the Wilson house was smack in the middle of the Beverly Hills of Washington.

"Jesus," said Virginia, staring out the car window like a child, her face nearly pressed to the glass. "Shane is loaded!"

"You've got pretty nice digs, too," I said recalling her Georgetown address.

"But he's got a yard. Hell—they've got a wildlife preserve."

There were about ten limos idling on the expansive circular driveway and spilling onto the lawn, as well as a number of less impressive vehicles that looked suspiciously like parents' cars. Most of the attendees had brought their cars to Shane's house, which was serving as the prom staging area. Our plan was to meet up with Shane and Jane at the dinner party and then take a limo that Shane's parents had hired down to the dance, which was being held at the Willard Hotel. Parking the Neon near the expansive four-car garage, I checked my bow tie in the mirror. Virginia prepared in her own way by swilling down some more Jack. Nice.

"So," I said, trying to be pleasant, "if you can put your bottle away, we should probably head in."

"I'm so hungry," she said, stuffing it in her purse and stealing the mirror from me to fix her lipstick. "They better have some major catered food inside."

Arriving at the front door, I pressed a small white button and the Bells of St. Mary's started to ring as some guy with a striking resemblance to Batman's butler opened the door with a mildly sinister "Welcome." On the other side of the grand marble foyer stood Mr. and Mrs. Wilson, decked out in formal wear themselves, as they greeted the other entering couples. Shane's parents were ancient compared to mine, both nearing the mandatory retirement age. The reason for this is that Shane was the last in a long line of Wilson children, five to be exact, whose ages ranged from thirty-five all the way down to eighteen.

As Virginia and I approached the party elders, we put on our best gracious act.

"Hello, Mr. and Mrs. Wilson," I said cordially, though slightly more familiarly than most in the receiving line. "Thanks for having us tonight."

They visibly perked up on seeing me.

"Hello, Cameron," said Mrs. Wilson, bussing my cheek. "How wonderful to see you. And look at you, all spiffed up."

On cue, Virginia let out a slight hiccup. I tried to cover with an introduction.

"This is Virginia McKinley," I said as Virginia offered her hand to Mr. Wilson, who was more polite than my dad, giving her hand a gentlemanly shake and wholly ignoring her cleavage.

"Pleasure to meet you, Virginia."

"Thanks," said Virginia, wasting no time on formality. "So where's the food at?"

Fortunately they laughed at her sassy remark, not fully getting her inebriated need for sustenance as they directed us downstairs to the Wilsons' finished basement. After a delicate and slow journey down the stairs, Virginia and I entered the main room to find an enormous buffet laid out on what was usually the ping-pong table, adorned for the occasion with a caterer's fancy, linen cloth, and countless green candles. Politely but firmly, Virginia released my hold on her arm and headed toward the spread.

"See ya—"

As she left me in her wake, I felt this amazing release as the burden of my fake date was lifted, my shoulders relaxing, my lungs expanding, as I let out a well-earned sigh. I could rest assured that the food would take care of Virginia, at least for a while. Or vice versa.

"Boy howdy!"

Shouting out his standard greeting, I turned to my left and saw Shane. I saw him in a tux. Maybe it's my infatuation with F. Scott Fitzgerald and old black-and-white movies on TCM but there is something about a man in a tux that is just . . . whoa. And then you put someone like Shane in a tux? Forget about it. Shane was an incredibly handsome guy wearing a dirty T and ripped up Levi's. But give the guy some formal wear and he's what *Teen People* likes to call a screamboat; six foot two, stocky build, square head, superhero's chin, darkly deep-set eyes with short-cropped chestnut hair. You get the picture, right? Basically, Shane looked like he could have jumped off the pages of A&F or be headlining his own show on the WB.

Not that he is not without his flaws. I mean, he was on the football team, after all . . . for three whole years. But that was more of his dad's thing, and although he was great at it, he went along for the ride mainly to please the old man. But that had all changed our junior year when he'd suffered a freakishly rough tackle at the homecoming game and lost most of the hearing in his right ear. That was the end of his sports career and, believe it or not, Shane was somewhat relieved for that, though the circumstances were pretty much a drag.

Since then he'd gotten used to dealing with his audio handicap. I'd only known Shane postaccident so I always took it for granted that I had to talk into his left ear, sit on his left side at lunch, and not talk too much when he's driving. Honestly, I'd always found something sad and sorta noble about it, like it was his secret weakness that no one can see. Like Clark and Kryptonite, you know? Though everyone at Prep knew about his injury, if he met someone new Shane usually didn't offer up the information that he was nearly 50 percent deaf which is totally understandable. Shane didn't want to be known as that hot semideaf guy, and similarly, I didn't want to be known as that skinny totally gay guy. I always thought that these mutual secrets gave us something in common, but who knows: Maybe I'm stretching things a bit.

"What took you guys so long?" he said, grabbing my shoulder in a manner like my dad grabbed it, but a thousand percent less annoying.

"Ohmigod . . . long story."

"Gimme the Cliffs."

I slumped my shoulders.

"I don't really wanna get into it here."

"Wow," he said, hearing my despondent tone of voice. "Sounds serious."

I glanced up at him and he smiled, Shane Smile No. 12, the intent of which is to lift one out of an intractable funk. Shockingly, it was not working. Smile No. 12 disappeared, replaced by Serious Stare No. 4.

"So," he said changing the subject, "where's your date?"

"Chowing down."

He looked over to catch a glimpse of Virginia piling her plate with enough ribs to feed to the offensive line of the Washington Redskins.

"Girl's got an appetite," he said wryly.

"Actually," I said, "girl's got a fifth of Jack in her purse. And a bottle of tequila in her system."

Shane Smile No. 8 popped into view, secretly bemused. I knew this one very well, as secret bemusement was probably the core of our unusual friendship. But I was not happy to see its appearance at this exact moment in time.

"Shane—it's not really funny."

"It isn't," he said, not really asking me a question.

"This is my date we're talking about."

He regarded my dour expression.

"Hmmmm," he said, thinking. Scheming. Uh-oh. "Okay—follow me."

"What . . . where . . . why?"

But Shane didn't answer. He just pointed me away from the ping-pong table and back toward the stairs. However, we weren't heading back upstairs. Instead we went behind the stairs to a short corridor that led to the laundry room. But we weren't going to wash our clothes or anything. With Shane a few paces ahead of me, he looked left and right as if he were in his own James Bond movie, then pulled open a door that led . . . I had no idea where.

"What the—"

"Please," he said in an oddly formal voice. "Step inside."

With that, he gave me a gentle push into blackness and closed the door behind us. We were now in a dark closet with a slanted ceiling, directly under the stairs, as I could hear the plodding of guests' feet descending above us. Then a light, a dim night-light Shane had plugged into a socket, flicked on.

"Ta-da!"

Shane pointed to a half-keg of beer in a small tub of ice that had been expertly stashed from parental view.

"How the hell did you—"

"Roger bought it for me," he said referring to his oldest brother. "He said it's my graduation present."

"But how did you get it here without your parents—"

"He came by the house this afternoon, created a diversion with my nephew, who kept my mom busy. Then he hustled the whole thing out of his SUV, slipped the cook a twenty, and smuggled it in the back door."

"Well, that's . . . wow," I said in a tone that was surprised but not as amazed as Shane wanted me to be. "Cool."

"Cool? Smuggling a half-keg of Bass Ale into my parents' house for my prom dinner party is cool? C'mon, Cam . . . my mom uses the word *cool* now. I need a little more than that."

"I'm sorry," I said, unable to be roused from my growing depression about the course of the evening. "This whole prom thing is just . . . it's not been so fun, really."

"Whattya mean?" he said, turning on Shane Smile No. 5, the supercharmer. "You're here at my party, Jane's here too, and we're all gonna have some chow, drink some beer, hop in the limo, head to the dance, and have a blast!"

"It's not what I was expecting. . . . That's all."

Finally Shane got it, and instantly his trademark smiles disappeared. He looked me right in the eye, deep in the eye, and he knew exactly what I meant. I didn't have to say anything more, and he didn't have to say another word either. And in fact, he didn't. He just leaned toward me, over the top of the keg, and kissed me. For about a minute. Okay—have you ever been kissed by the A&F catalog? Well, I would highly recommend it, because after that, I have to admit, I felt a million times better.

"Was that closer to what you were expecting this evening?"

"Uh," I said shyly, "more or less."

"More or less, huh?" he said playfully. "How about some 'more,' then?"

I didn't have to say yes. My eyes said it for me, and we went at it again.

So I guess at this point I should probably tell you that Shane is my secret boyfriend. Well, was my boyfriend? I don't mean to ruin this fairy tale moment for you, but what can I say? Things went downhill from this romantic high point. But again I'm getting ahead of myself. We still had quite a long night ahead of us.

# CHAPTER 5

As Shane released me from his second lip lock, I didn't want to go anywhere else. The dinner party, the prom, the after-parties . . . they could all take a rain check to the good time I was having in a dark closet in Shane's basement. And we had our own stash of Bass, too! We were totally set and could've spent the next few hours in there happily alone, drinking beer and getting busy. I tried to make this point to Shane but he was insistent that we rejoin the real festivities.

"C'mon, Cam, the sentiment is cute and all but this is *my* party."

Then I had a brainstorm. "I know . . . maybe I can feign illness, you know, like take some food into the bathroom and dump it into the toilet to make people think I'm totally puking, and then you could tell your folks that you'd have to stay and take care of me. And once everyone's gone we could call Virginia a cab and you could, like, pay her off for her troubles."

"Pay her off?"

"Believe me, she'll probably demand it," I said, referring to her negotiating skills. "But once we've gotten rid of her, you, me, and Jane can watch that *Punk'd* marathon on MTV and finish up the remains of the buffet and the keg and have a great night here at your place . . . a sleepover even!"

"Cameron," he said in that stern parental way of pronouncing every single syllable and consonant of my full name. I loved and hated this. "We are going to the prom. That was the plan. You and me and our dates are all going together. And we will have a great time. I promise."

"There's one minor little problem," I said, easing my way into the bad news. "Virginia kinda knows I'm gay."

"She . . . she what?!"

"I didn't *tell* her," I said, trying to defend myself.

"Then exactly how did she find out?"

With a sigh, I looked down at the floor.

"I, uh . . . I got her a matching corsage."

"Holy shit," he said, alarmed. "Why the *hell* did you do that?"

Needless to say, there was no mention of the secretive purchase of *Seventeen*.

"It was more than that, though," I said, changing the subject somewhat. "Virginia's brother's gay and she seems to have dated other gay guys too, so with all that experience, I guess she just kinda figured it out. And now she's totally pissed because she thought she was gonna get laid, and when she realized *that* wasn't gonna quite pan out for her, she decided to get drunk instead."

There was silence as Shane took all this in, as well as three deep, meditative breaths.

"Well . . . so what," Shane said, trying to put the best face on this major gossip leak. "She's a fun drunk. Like at that party on Q Street—remember, the night you two met?"

"Yeah—that's when she thought I was cute and available."

Shane's brow crinkled, still somewhat troubled by this breach in security. Now, if you think I've been secretive about being gay, with Shane we are talking For Your Eyes Only. Honest. The Pentagon doesn't have their secrets wrapped so tight. I mean, with me, anyone with three-quarters of an adult brain could probably figure out I might be into guys. At 130 pounds wet, I've never met a sport that liked me, I'm the editor of the yearbook, I'm also kind of a genius if I don't say so myself (ranked eleventh in our class), and here's the clincher: I've never really dated a single girl my entire young life.

With Shane, however, you'd really have to be a Drudge-type blood-hound to unmask the truth about his covert sexual preference. As I mentioned, he used to be Mr. Football at Prep; he worked on the yearbook but as the sports editor, so it doesn't really count against his heterosexuality; and he attracted teenage girls like a clearance sale at the Limited. You see, Shane had this whole jock-deflection shield that had kept him immune from Faggot Rays, or at least that's what the majority of people on the planet believed. However, Faggot Rays are strikingly similar to Kryptonite in that even the strongest can succumb. In Shane's case, believe it or not, I turned out to be his weakness.

I've never thought of myself as having supernatural powers, but apparently Shane thinks I'm cute. Like Kryptonite, I'm sorta smash-all-his-defenses cute. Me. I know—it's crazy, right? Well, I always joked with him that our whole attraction was like a Jessica Rabbit thing. You know, that I made him laugh, and that in reality he didn't think I was really that drop-dead cute. But he insisted that I was (no joke) "supercute" in a way that has always baffled the mind. Once a resemblance to Tobey McGuire was mentioned, but I think he might've been stoned that night. On more sober evenings, though, he has doted on the greenish tint of my eyes (especially on overcast days), the softness of my neck (I don't shave too much), and my supersize forehead (drive-in movies would be at home there). But when your boyfriend is a screamboat, after a while you tend not to dwell on the reasons why he thinks you and your geeky self are sexy. You just go along for the ride, even if it has some harsh bumps along the way. And believe me, it had been quite a ride.

Like most people in our high school universe, I had known of Shane before I actually met him. He was very Prep popular due to his football prowess as our number one pass receiver and winner of games that heretofore had been unwinnable by our sorry-ass squad. It was not until senior year, though, that I had a conversation with him when he started working on the yearbook last November as the sports editor. Though there was some weird energy between us from the start, it took a month of staff meetings and chats in the hall before we had an opportunity to spend some quality time together. This came about due to a regular feature in the Prep yearbook in which five people in the class are selected for full-page profiles based on their unique achievements at Prep. Shane was easily one of them, given the way he'd turned around the football team, and being the editor, I passed this plum assignment to me. I thought it would be interesting to conduct our interview the day of the homecoming game, the first one he'd actually watched from the stands. So in a weird way, I asked Shane to homecoming and ended up sitting with him through the whole game. And you know what? It was the first time I ever had fun at a football game. Hell—it was the first time I ever understood what was going on at a football game!

Later that night Shane invited me to a party that his best friend from the team, Ian Harrison, was having out in Reston. It was your typical posthomecoming blowout bash. Not that I knew what that meant, really, having never socialized that much with the Prep football team. This take on the party was courtesy of Shane. One thing, though, that seemed atypical about this party was the fact that I seemed to be attending it as Shane's unofficial date. Then after midnight passed and many beers had been imbibed, after Shane had ignored come-ons from about two hundred Potomac girls, after his ex-girlfriend Jane had gotten a ride home with some friends, leaving us alone in the midst of an increasingly hook-up friendly party, I found myself wandering around the upstairs hallway with Shane when he abruptly shoved me into the linen closet. I thought we were hiding from someone or that this was some big prank. But the joke was on me as Shane started to kiss me. Honest. And that was when this whole crazy thing began.

Now, more than six months later, Shane and me and our entire relationship were still in the closet, literally and figuratively. And Shane was determined to keep it that way until graduation. He felt there was no need to freak out his coaches, his jock friends, his sporty parents, or his heterosexual siblings with this shocking information. I went along with this plan too, believe it or not. Besides, I was in no rush to break this news to my parents either.

So Shane and I focused on making plans for the future, both of us deciding to attend UVA so that once we got to a new school, everything would be different. We would be honest and come out and everything would be beautiful, like in some tacky Hollywood love story where lovers run through swirling fall leaves and make out on picturesque campus greens. Except there was one problem: I don't remember seeing this movie with two college guys in love. (Oh yeah—because, *hello*, it hasn't been made yet!) But I was under Shane's spell and believed just about everything he told me. The whole idea of us staying totally in the closet at Prep seemed to make perfect sense to me, especially the way Shane explained it. I mean really, who couldn't agree with the guy when he flashed you Shane Smile No. 1, the total full-on I LUV U high beams. Please—you would be *sooo* weak!

Which brings me back to the closet in the basement of Shane's house, in the heart of the prom-dinner-party beast, which had been wholly created by Shane as part of what was beginning to look like a night of willfully orchestrated deceit.

"Do you think Virginia's told anyone else?" asked Shane, clearly worried about this loose alcoholic cannon in our midst.

"She was on the verge of outing me to my parents—"

"Holy shit!"

"That's when I bribed her with the bottle of Jack."

"Quick thinking," he said, satisfied by my save. "We should have no problem, then—my dad's got a huge liquor stash that I could dip into. And there's the keg for her too."

"Shane—we don't have to kill the poor girl!"

"Okay—relax," he said gently, trying to sound reassuring. "I'll have Jane talk to her too."

Shane and Jane had been an item decades ago, the fall of sophomore year to be specific, and best of friends since then. In fact, Jane was the only one in the known universe who was trusted with the knowledge of Shane's secret life and my role in it.

"It'll be fine, Cam. Trust me. And then we'll all have a blast tonight, right?"

"I guess."

"Please," he said, pulling me closer, his arms curled around my waist. Ohmigod—his arms! Don't get me started. "For me?"

What can I say? When the A&F catalog has you by the waist, there's not much you can do but agree.

"All right. I'll try to have a fake good time."

"Fake? C'mon, Cam," he said, nudging at my nose. "I want you to have a real good time. After all, you're my special guy."

"Oh yeah?" I said, milking this for all I could get. It worked, as he leaned in for another kiss. It was not as in-depth this time, but actually sweeter for its brevity and the true sentiment behind it.

"Yeah," he said, whispering between kisses. "And you know why?"

"Why?"

And then he planted another kiss not on my lips but on my cheek. Then some more on my ear, and then my neck. Oh, the neck. The neck always killed me, you know, totally destroyed any bad feelings I may have had or doubts that may have clouded my mind about why I was dating a guy like Shane. Not to mention the simple biochemical reaction it caused which drove me crazy with passion.

"Oh, Shane," I said softly. I loved saying this, his name. Softly. Shane . . .

And then he kissed me even more, going for the earlobe. Whoa. After half a year of this, he knew my weaknesses *way* too well.

"Shane," I said in a whisper. "Why do I love you?"

But he didn't hear me. Right ear. That is, the wrong ear.

"What?" he said.

Then in his hearing ear I repeated my confused sentiment. Sorta.

"I love you, Shane."

You see, I have this little problem with the truth. Did you get that already?

# CHAPTER 6

Emerging from the closet, Shane went upstairs to
check in with his folks, as I returned to the party downstairs. I took
a quick scan around the basement, and Virginia was nowhere to be
found. I imagined that she was again familiarizing herself with yet
another strange family bathroom. Or if I was really lucky, perhaps
she had passed out somewhere. Either way I decided I wouldn't
worry about it too much and, in Virginia-speak, I decided to get
some grub.

After filling a big plate with all kinds of fancy foodstuffs, I made
my way out to the back porch, where most of the guests had gone
to eat while enjoying the lush view of the backyard. Make that back
forest. The blond pine deck overlooked a dense green ravine
directly behind the house as well as an immense tract of lawn to the
right, bordered by tennis courts and a volleyball pit. I have to say,
the view off the porch was much more enticing than the people on
the porch itself. Honest. The social scene was like a woodsy version
of the high school cafeteria, with all the same cliques from school
transposed into this new, higher-scale environment. I navigated
my way through the clumps of jocks and their attendant babes, all
of whom I knew by name but only because I worked on the yearbook. Conversely, most of them knew me but only because I was
friends with Shane. However, without Shane's presence, they
merely nodded pleasantly at me as I passed, since on my own there

was no need for them to make a real social effort.

Near the side railing, I found an empty bench and took it. I was concentrating on eating when I heard a familiar voice.

"Hey, Hayes—what's shaking?"

It was Ian Harrison, Shane's best bud, whose homecoming party had set the course of our risky relationship. Ian was a linebacker type, a hulking guy with no neck to speak of and a chubby, baby face with cheeks for days. As for that rule about guys in tuxes being irresistible, I have to say that Ian was definitely the exception. His tux looked like it was about to burst from the tight constraints placed on it by his double-barrel chest and Herculean shoulders. Frankly, in his ill-fitting outfit, Ian looked like a mobster.

Asking if he could join me, he sat down on the opposite end of the bench, the force of his weight lifting my end seesaw style. Not wanting to catapult me into the ravine, Ian adjusted his seating physics and fortunately stationed his massive ass a little closer to the center of the bench.

"Pretty nice party, huh?"

"Yeah . . . nice," I said lamely, not knowing what to say about all these people I didn't really know and who didn't want to know me. I decided to focus on the food. "Good spread inside, huh?"

"Oh yeah," he said, digging into his plate. "Major ribs."

He chomped on some for a few moments, then looked at me quizzically.

"Hey, where's your date?"

"In the bathroom, I think."

"Girls. Always freshening up, right?"

Yeah . . . or puking their guts out.

"Where's yours?"

"Caroline's over there," he said, grunting in the direction of a picnic table with three blond bourgeois girls wearing three nearly identical black strapless dresses with three similarly bejeweled necks, chattering away as if they were auditioning for the junior version of *Sex and the City*. "The one in the middle."

"Cute," I said, more in reference to her dress than to Caroline. But Ian didn't need to know that.

"Eh," he said with less enthusiasm about his own date than even a gay man might muster. "She's all right."

So there was some trouble in preppy paradise. Not that Ian was going to discuss it with me. He had other things on his mind.

"Hey," he continued. "Tommy Devnan told me your date's hot. What's her name again?"

"Virginia."

"Yeah, yeah, yeah . . . Virginia. That tall redhead chick. You guys met at that party on Q Street, right?"

"Oh yeah," I said, recalling my make-out session with Virginia. Then I heard a little voice in my head that went something like this: *I will never do shots of Jagermeister. . . . I will never do shots of Jagermeister. . . . I will never—*

"I remember her. Man, she's built, too. How did you get with her?"

Ian gave me a playful manly punch. But from a guy like Ian, playful packs a wallop. My whole body swayed in response.

"Uh, dumb luck, I guess."

"C'mon, man. What's your secret?"

"I dunno," I said, fishing for something to say that would sound right to a big, burly dude like Ian. Then he peeked at me sideways, checking me out or something, except that Ian was definitely not gay. No gay guy would let himself get this fat this young.

"I always suspected you could be quite the player, Hayes," he said, grinning at me like the cat who ate the canary. Correction— make that the entire chicken. "It's the quiet guys you gotta look out for. So c'mon . . . give it up. What's your secret, huh?"

"Oh, man," I said, trying to suppress some rising sarcasm. It was useless. "Well, I'm a really good kisser."

This was not exactly the answer Ian was expecting. I don't know what he was expecting but it definitely wasn't this. So I had to convince him a little.

"Really . . . ask Shane."

Whoops. That slipped out. Honest. Well, maybe semisubconsciously it slipped out. Either way I couldn't let it sit there. Nor could Ian.

"Shane?"

"Yeah," I said, thinking very quickly. "He gets the reports back from Jane and all. She's very connected to the girls' gossip hub at Potomac."

Actually, Jane *was* the gossip hub at Potomac. That's why Shane's secret never got out. He had friends in very high places, and one in particular, who happened to be Jane. If Jane knew his secret and didn't tell, then no one was ever going to know because Jane was the number one source for all information in the Potomac-Prep nexus. This always made me wonder if that was the real reason Shane had dated her in the first place, you know, as a sort of preemptive gossip strike? He was crafty, that Shane. . . .

Anyway, after convincing Ian of my kissing skills, we talked for quite a while out on the porch, mainly about Virginia. Talking with Ian about anything for more than a few minutes was a significant accomplishment, as linebackers are generally not the most engaging conversationalists. But it was an amicable chat, mainly because it seemed I had risen in Ian's estimation due to the fact that I was taking a hot chick (his words, not mine) to the biggest dance of the year. It's like he suddenly saw me as a man whereas before, well, I don't think he ever really saw me at all.

Of course, the grand irony in all of this was that the only reason I was going to the prom with Virginia was because my boyfriend, Ian's best friend, had set the whole thing up in the first place so that we could be semitogether at the prom. Considering this fact, it made me a little sad to realize that Ian, Shane's oldest friend, really, didn't have a clue about the whole fake double-date scenario, you know? I mean, how can you be best friends with someone and not have them know secret stuff like that, right?

Shane's dishonesty with Ian made me feel a tinge of regret because, honestly, I'd been guilty of the exact same thing. I'd had a best friend who didn't know what was going on in my life. The only difference was I had let the friendship die.

Franklin Taylor and I had met in Honors English freshman year. Franklin was one of those smart, sensitive straight guys who, like me, didn't date girls either. However, his lack of action with the opposite sex was not because he was into guys; it was mainly because he was scared of girls. I mean, seriously, Franklin was even more frightened of them than I was. And it was this mutual lack of women in our lives that had kept our friendship tight over the course of our time together at Prep.

However, as senior year progressed and I spent more time with Shane, Franklin became increasingly puzzled as to why I was hanging out with a guy who to him seemed to be a big, jocky jerk. I explained my unusually late-in-high-school friendship with the excuse that Shane and I were working together on the yearbook. This was honest on the surface but not down deep where it counted, you know? Since I wasn't really letting Franklin in on what was going down with me and Shane, Franklin faded out of my life as Shane faded in. I mean, it's hard to manage a best friend that you can't be straight with, especially when you're gay.

I know it's hypocritical and all, but talking with Ian, it really bothered me that Shane was hiding his real life from Ian. However, I have to say that regarding Franklin, my case was even worse, as I'd let him fall off the face of my earth, so to speak, to such an extent that I had no idea where Franklin was on prom night or if he was even going to the dance in the first place. At least Shane's best friend was at his dinner party, chattering away with his boyfriend, even though he wasn't quite aware that's who he was talking to.

During the course of our heart-to-heart on the porch, Ian was kind enough to replenish my beer a couple times so that as the dinner party began to wind down, I started to wind up. I was feeling a bit buzzed, you know what I mean? Let me just say that due to my slight weight and general lack of a social life it doesn't take much for me to get plowed. A couple beers and I'm, like, a different person;

chatty and bubbly and downright personable. And this is how I was feeling when Shane came outside to retrieve us. In this newly frisky mood, it was all I could do not to jump Shane's bones when he planted that firm old hand of his on my shoulder.

"So we better get our posse together and hit the road. Where's Virginia?"

"I dunno," I said, grinning slyly at Shane. "Have you checked under the ping-pong table?"

I laughed hysterically at my own joke as Shane discerned my beer-inspired goofiness.

"Uh-oh," he said, looking over at Ian. "Has someone been refilling your cup with a certain fermented beverage?"

"No," I said with a straight face. "But Ian snagged me some beers."

Shane put his finger to his lips and shushed me.

"Zip it," he said ominously. "My parents have spies everywhere."

Shane's parents, as part of the whole dinner-party-at-home deal, had agreed to stay upstairs for the duration of the evening. Thus they were apparently none the wiser about the beer and the now-buzzing guests.

As we went back into the basement, the secret keg had been tapped and the noise level duly raised by half. The volume was deafening as all the drunk girls chattered on about how much their dresses cost and which swank stores in Tysons II they'd bought their accessories from. The guys' tipsiness was less obvious, though quickly evident to the male eye; they were looking at their dates with a newly charged lust, already planning ahead to the after-parties or hotel suites at which they might get some play. I know this because I was beginning to feel the exact same way about Shane. Walking at his side as we made a social loop around the basement, I fantasized about kissing my boyfriend somehow, somewhere, in the dark hours of the coming morning after all this formal fuss and bother was over.

"And where have *you* been hiding all night?"

Breaking me out of my Shane-induced fantasy, Jane materialized in front of me.

"Hey, Jane—I was hanging on the deck with Ian."

"Rrrrreallly," she said, employing her zippy delivery. "That must have been *fascinating*."

I laughed, and Jane's eyes twinkled at me. Let me say right off the bat that Jane is pretty damn adorable for a girl. Part of that might be due to the fact that she looks like she could pass for Shane's sister, as they have similarly dark coloring and square features. But in reality, they couldn't be more opposite. Jane is everything that Shane is not; outspoken, sassy, and totally petite. But despite their differences, Shane and Jane made a damn cute couple back when Shane was super-het and Jane was very much a sophomore, which translated from the Greek means "wise fool." (I'm sorry; I can't help being the smart one.) Even though their relationship ended as all sophomore affairs do, Shane and Jane became best friends.

Anyway, because of their tight friendship, Jane and I had become friendly too. I really dug her because she seemed to dig me and the fact that I totally dug Shane. Dig? And in a more general sense, Jane is really the coolest person I know in that she sees beyond all the BS of high school. She knows this is just the beginning of our lives, not the pinnacle, as Caroline and her bourgie trio seem to believe. Jane was always reminding Shane and me that real life was just around the corner. If we could all simply bide our time through high school with a decent amount of humor and a modicum of self-respect, then all of us could break on through to a much better side.

First, though, we would all have to deal with a problem called Virginia.

"So . . . we have a problem," I said to Jane.

"Oh, you mean Ms. McKinley?" she said, in her typically step-ahead-of-the-game way. "There's a rumor she's in the TV room, feeding smoked salmon to the fish."

As the guests began streaming up the stairs and out to their limos, Shane and Jane and I made our way to the other side of the basement in search of my date. At the far end of the Wilson rec room was the TV room, which I thought was closed off to partygoers. But once inside we discovered that the rumor was true, as we found Virginia leaning over the edge of the glass-enclosed tank, feeding the fish one of their own.

"Virginia!" said Shane, annoyed to see the mess of smoked salmon floating atop the water.

"They won't eat it!" she exclaimed. "I'm giving them dinner and they won't even bite!"

"They're not cannibals," said Jane, with brilliant reasoning.

"C'mon, li'l fishes . . . this is some good whores-doo-ooo-vers," she said in what had become a very slippery slur.

Shane approached Virginia delicately from behind, attempting to ease her away from her newfound friends. In the process he tripped over a couple cups of beer, spilling their contents across the floor.

"Jesus—are these yours?"

"Mostly," said Virginia, adding about ten additional s's to the word.

"You know what Virginia?" said Jane dropping another sarcasm bomb. "You give whole new meaning to the phrase *drinks like a fish.*"

That got me laughing uncontrollably. (I told you I was a light-weight.) Hearing my cackle, Virginia looked over toward me and didn't seem to recognize who I was at first. For some reason this made me laugh even more.

"Where does that phrase come from anyway," she said, suddenly curious. "Are fish big drinkers? Do they like beer or cocktails? What do you like, li'l fishies—martinis?"

She started tapping on the glass as Shane, gently reaching for her shoulder, tried to peel her away from her fishy friends. But she was not budging.

"C'mon, Virginia . . . we've gotta get to the prom."

"You go ahead without me," she said, her voice going soft. "I'm gonna stay here with my real friends. Hey, I hope these aren't fruit fish. Or fag fish . . . is there such a thing as gay fish? Maybe they're the ones with the flashy colors . . . I wonder if fish can give each other blow jobs?"

Reacting to this drunken monologue, Jane took a few steps toward the tank to try to ease Virginia away herself.

"Virginia, we've gotta get to the dance now, okay?" she said, as if coaxing a child to the dentist's office. "We don't wanna be late. It's gonna start in half an hour."

"Look, I'm *not* going to prom with a fag."

"Virginia—"

"Forget it, Jane," she barked. "You set me up with a total fag! And I'm not going to the prom with a fag date."

I felt like disappearing right there. Where's David Blaine when you need him?

"Cameron is not a fag," said Jane calmly. "He's just . . . bi."

That creative bit of invention didn't seem to help anyone, as Virginia ignored the comment and Shane rolled his eyes at the fabrication. Giving up on verbal inducement, Jane tried to gently tug Virginia away from the fish tank. Virginia teetered as she pivoted on her still-unstable heels and ultimately pitched backward toward the floor, falling with a bit of a thud. Jane stood there, hands on her hips, looking at Virginia like she'd look at a baby who still hadn't learned to walk after eighteen years. And Virginia suddenly looked bad . . . really bad. The color was draining from her face and she looked like she was really going to puke.

"Ohhhhh," she moaned. "I don't feel so well."

Jane went into panic mode, motioning for Shane and me to join her. As Virginia's face went a parchment pale and then faded into a sickly yellow, we yanked her to her feet and tried to turn her around to get her out of the TV room and onto the back porch. But as a deadly shade of green washed over her face, Jane was struck by a more efficient idea.

"Get her to the tank!"

And we did, just in time for her to emit a steaming stream of vomit right into the glassed-in tropical paradise. As Virginia continued puking, chunky globules of the Wilsons' fancy buffet sank toward the bottom of the tank, trailing packs of peckish fish along the way. Suddenly these colorful creatures were hungry for ribs and rice and Jack and Bass and whatever else had been churning around in Virginia's stomach. When the last of her foodstuffs were deposited with a deep *kerplunk,* the formerly clear and bubbly water had grown brown and cloudy, the fish disappearing into the murk of Virginia's bodily fluids.

"Well," said Jane, turning to her ex with an attempt to fill the postpuke silence. "At least you won't have to feed the fish for a while."

Shane was not amused.

"Clean her up and get her to our limo," he said with a severe face. "We're heading out in five."

Jane craned her neck around to get a better look at the makeover at hand.

"Uh . . . I'm going to need fifteen minutes, minimum."

Shane, still not amused, started heading back toward the rec room. Instinctually I followed. You see, when Shane moves I follow. That's how things worked.

"And lock this door when you leave!" he said emphatically. Then talking to himself, he muttered under his breath, "My mother is going to kill me when she sees this."

# CHAPTER 7

Without mention of the nautical disaster in the basement, Shane gave a brief and guilty good-bye to his parents up in the main foyer. Then we both exited the house and booked it to our limo, a basic black number that seated four; nothing crazy-fancy. No stretch SUV for the Wilsons. That would be too "new money," you know?

I thought about saying this to Shane as we sat there in silence waiting for our dates, but he did not look like he was in a mood to be joked with. He was in Serious Shane mode, Expression No. 4 in play, thinking deep Neo thoughts about life and fate and what it all meant anyway. Or at least that's what I imagined.

"I'm sorry about Virginia," I said, trying to ease us into a conversation.

"It's not your fault," he said, studying the gray carpet on the limo floor.

"Actually it's because I'm gay that she got all drunk and crazy in the first place."

"Yeah, but you didn't exactly hand her the liquor."

"Well, I sorta did, remember?"

And this got me a smile. Not a full-on Shane No. 1, but it was a start.

"Oh, man—this is such a mess," he said, sounding tickled and despondent all at once.

"So what are we gonna do?" I wondered.

"As long as she keeps her mouth shut at the dance, we'll be fine."

"You mean in terms of puking or gossiping."

"Both, I guess," he said, finally looking up at me again. "I'm sorry I made you take her."

"Really?"

"Dude—the girl heaved into my parents' fish tank!"

"Right," I said, hoping he had come to more of his senses than that. His apology should have been about more than my date's regurgitation. I was hoping for a full-scale realization of mistakes made due to the general conspiracy to cover up the true nature of our relationship, and maybe, just maybe, an actual expression of the desire that we could just go to prom together, me and him. But that would have been asking for the moon. Speaking of which . . .

"Full moon tonight," I said, staring up at the immense white orb visible through the open sunroof. "Total bad luck."

Shane gazed at the moon but seemed to see something different, his eyes narrowing and his lips parting to say the most extraordinary thing.

"I don't know . . . when I see a full moon I always get kinda romantic."

"You . . . really?" I said, floored.

"Yeah. It reminds me of that movie *Moonstruck* with Cher and the dude without the arm."

"Nicolas Cage."

"Right. That is such a great movie," he said, his eyes catching a glint of moonlight. Gorgeous. "Totally romantic."

"Except . . . doesn't the full moon drive them all crazy?"

"Sure," he said, turning to look at me. Right at me. "But in a romantic sorta way, you know?"

Oh, I knew all right, as he gazed at me with those WB eyes. I knew all over, you know? Maybe, I thought, this whole night is going to turn out fine after all. Maybe this prom thing won't be the mess I'd imagined. Maybe I *am* being a spaz.

"You know what I was thinking?" he said, his eyes in a dangerous holding pattern.

"You think?" I said.

This was part of this silly jock/brain routine we had. But he ignored my joke and got to what was a much more intriguing point.

"I think that after this is all over, after the dance and depositing Virginia on her front step and driving Jane home and coming back here to get your car, I think that you should probably just leave your car here and spend the night."

Now *this* had never been offered before. This was breaking new ground. Not that we hadn't fooled around before. We'd done that a number of times, at his house and mine when the 'rents were otherwise occupied or out on the town. But spending the night? That was boldly going where no gay boys like us had gone before. And suddenly, being the geek that I am, the *Star Trek* theme started soaring through my inflated-with-love head . . . *Oooohhhh-waaaaaaahh! La, la, la, la, laaaahhhhhh . . .*

"Are you humming?"

"Wha . . . huh . . . uh . . . I—"

"Okay, special guy," he said, using his unique term of endearment for me. It was as close as Shane got to actually calling me his boyfriend, which was okay but also sort of bugged me too, though I never really came out and said it. "Do you wanna spend the night or what?"

Of course I did. But there was a big "but" in the way. And I ain't talking 'bout his.

"But what about our parents?"

"What about them?" he said, acting all cool. "I'll just say you had to crash for safety's sake, you know. So you're not driving home tired in the middle of the night and all. You can give your folks the same story too."

"And you think they'll buy that?" I wondered. "I mean, you're not worried about what they'll think?"

"Nope," he said breezily.

My heart leaped up. Shane was changing. Things were changing. *Maybe,* I thought, *we wouldn't have to spend the summer making out in hall closets or dark bedrooms or the cramped backseats of cars. Maybe we could start making out like normal people, you know, doing it in the world. In broad daylight even.* The fact that he said this to me gave me such hope. Until he said—

"Besides, after my parents discover that fish tank, they'll be so pissed off about that, you know, that you spending the night won't even register."

Clever guy, this Shane. Some might say too clever by half.

After Jane's fifteen-minute makeover stretched into twenty, she and Virginia finally made their way out to the limo, Virginia more or less walking on her own power with minimal balance assist from Jane's shoulder. Jane had done wonders with the contents of what we began to refer to as her magic purse. In fact, Virginia looked better than when I'd picked her up earlier that afternoon. I realized the reason for this was because she didn't really have any makeup on then. Apparently her pre-prom prep session had been hijacked by her binge drinking. Now, though, with a nice Cover Girl sheen on, Virginia looked almost respectable, considering that only a half hour earlier, she'd been hunched over a fish tank, puking out her guts.

"You look great, Virginia," I offered, trying to mend our rift.

"Thanks," she said in a civil tone. Finally. "And you look like a fag."

So much for civility.

As the limo pulled away from the Wilson compound, Virginia reached into her velvet purse and pulled out some Camel Lights. Though Shane and Jane were vehement antismokers, always quoting some sort of disgusting statistic to anyone who lit up within fifty feet of them, they were surprisingly silent.

"I hope y'all don't mind the smoke," she said, noticing Shane and Jane give each other conspiratorial looks as they tensed up. "I'm generally not a big smoker, but they do help sober me up."

"That's an old wives' tale," said Shane.

"That's right, Shane," she said, blowing a plume of smoke in his direction. "I heard it from my mother."

Shane seethed and looked like he might try to strangle her. In an attempt at bonding with my date and making her hate me a little less, I tried to make Virginia feel like less of a pariah by offering to join her in a smoke. I'm not really a smoker, but sometimes I have been known to light up to make others feel less persecuted by their habit. I'm a sympathetic guy that way. And despite her behavior, I thought Virginia could use a little sympathy. It might help calm her savage beastliness.

"Can I have one?" I asked her, as Shane shot me an evil look.

"You need to sober up too?" Jane wondered.

"One beer too many," I said, which was true. After all, I didn't want to stumble into the prom past teachers and chaperones who expected better of me. Given my class rank, it was generally assumed that I would be responsible and sober at school functions.

Slipping me one of her smokes, Virginia lit me up off her cigarette. Leaning back into the comfort of the leathery limo seat, I let out a way-too-satisfied exhale. Shane was shooting me daggers with his eyes, none too happy about my smoking. Yet Virginia, on the whole, was feeling fabulous.

"You know what, you guys?" she said, suddenly confessional and buddy-buddy with us all. "I feel soooo much better having gotten rid of all that liquor!"

"Charming," said Shane.

Fortunately Virginia blithely ignored Shane's comment.

"It's like now I'm *totally* ready to party all night. Caroline was telling me about this after-party that sounds completely rad. . . . A bunch of people are going down to the Lincoln Memorial to go skinny-dipping."

"Yee-hah," said Shane, feigning fake excitement and again being something of a bitch. Though it was dangerous for him to treat Virginia like this given what she knew, it was equally awesome that

Shane was finally getting in touch with his inner gay bitch. Snaps to him.

"So you excited for the dance?" Jane asked Virginia, changing the topic with sincerely fake enthusiasm. When it came to stuff like this Jane was better than Shane and I combined. Still, Virginia was not buying it.

"I'd be more excited if I had a *real* date."

And that was it. Shane had had it, and he snapped at her.

"Virginia, stop harping on this whole thing!"

"Thing?" said Virginia, her ire rising again. "It's not some 'thing.' My date is a fag."

Jane sighed. I sighed. We all sighed in unison.

"Here we go again," I said wearily.

"Look, Virginia," Shane continued, "we all want to have a good time tonight. So when we get to the prom, we're all gonna dance and hang out with our friends and have a blast. I know you like to dance, right?"

"I don't wanna look like some fruit fly, hovering around *him* on the dance floor."

Shane tried to tamp down his temper.

"But if you were going with a straight guy, I mean, they don't even dance. Can't you at least be happy about *that*?"

"Aha," she said, sitting up and stabbing the air with smoke. "Even *you* admit he's gay!"

"Jesus Christ," said Shane, snapping again, if that were possible. "So what if he is? At least he's a good dancer, and he's with you. Hell, it's not like he's gonna be slow dancing with me."

Shane was trying to make a point, but he made it too well. He slipped. And he might have gotten away with the slip if I hadn't starting choking on my cigarette.

"Oh, no," exclaimed Jane. "Are you okay?"

No, I wasn't. I was really and truly choking on my cigarette. On hearing Shane's remark about us dancing together, I had bitten off the filter tip of the Camel which was now lodged in the back of my throat, perilously close to blocking off my airway. Shane, being the quick thinker that he is, moved Jane out of the way and, sliding across the backseat of the limo, wrapped his arms around my waist, not for a hug that would accent his accidental point that yes, in fact, we were a couple, but more to give me a sideways version of the Heimlich maneuver. Fortunately it worked. With one severe thrust, the filter popped out of my throat and, making a perfect arc across the interior of the limo, landed on Virginia's chest and rolled down into the gap between her cleavage. If there were judges in the car, it would have been perfect 10s across the board. Virginia didn't quite see it this way.

"Grrrooooosss!" she screamed, trying to pluck the slimy stub out of her décolletage. Shoving her breasts aside, Virginia dug right down in there, removing the butt from its booby perch and flicking it with her fingers back across the limo at us. It rebounded off Jane's purse and hit the side window, where it landed with a light *smack* and stuck in place. This set Jane off into gales of laughter. And really, who could blame her. Well, Virginia could.

"You think this is funny, Jane?" said Virginia, more incensed than before. "You set us up with a homo couple. Are you totally psycho?"

Stuck with a severe case of the giggles, Jane was unable to answer, so Shane tried to fill in for her.

"It was my idea, Virginia, all right?"

Virginia turned back toward Jane.

"Is this true, Jane?"

Jane was still not available for comment. Once you got her laughing like this, it was hard to get her to stop. But she did manage an affirmative nod between guffaws.

"So who else knows about you guys?" demanded Virginia. "The whole frigging school district? Am I supposed to be the laughing-stock of the goddamn—"

"No one knows," said Shane, dead serious. "*No* one. And it's gonna stay that way."

"What—are you, like, threatening me?"

"No," said Shane, relaxing his tone a bit. "I'm just telling you."

"Well," said Virginia with all the drama she could muster, suddenly aware that she was sitting on a veritable powder keg of gossip and holding a lit cigarette to boot. She exhaled like a Bond girl gone bad. "It might cost you, then."

"Virginia," said Shane, leaning forward in his seat to make his point, "the only thing this is gonna cost is possibly *your* life."

He Bonded her right back. Damn, this was getting good.

"Shane Wilson, I believe you are threatening me."

Shane fixed her with Serious Stare No. 4 and let her have it.

"You bet your ass I am."

# CHAPTER 8

The Willard Hotel, located two blocks from the White House, is incredibly famous and rich in history and all that: Lincoln slept there, Kennedy slept there, Walt Whitman slept there. You get the drill. But did you know that Walt Whitman was sorta gay? I mean, as gay as someone could be in the 1860s. It's not like there were rainbow flag stickers everywhere or TV shows like *Queer as Folk*. But from what I've read, Walt was digging on nineteenth-century dudes. Honest. In his book *Leaves of Grass*, which I had to read for AP English, there are all these emotional poems to his "comrades," which was basically ancient-school code for "gay lover" or "boyfriend" (or "special guy," if you're Shane).

Anyway, as we arrived at the stately entrance of the Willard, at least I didn't feel like the only gay guy to have ever been in such a straight historical joint. Walt and his Civil War boys had broken it in for me more than a hundred years previous. As Shane and I stepped out of the limo, I wondered if Walt's gay old ghost could see us. Did he sense that we were secret "comrades"? Would he have approved of our act of prom subversion? Would he have found it, I don't know, maybe even a little poetic? This I seriously doubted. As the evening progressed (or maybe *regressed* is a better term?), the misguided idea of Shane and me going to the prom together but separate was feeling more and more like a stupid idea. If anything, it was turning out to be more of a Shakespearean farce than a classic love poem that salty old Walt might pen.

To underline this point, even though Shane and I exited the limo first, we did not walk down the red carpet side by side. Instead we helped our dates out like the gentlemen we were pretending to be, and hooking them on our arms, headed through the spinning brass doors into the hotel's grand lobby. Entering the Willard was like taking a stroll back in time, the main room having been restored to its appearance around the turn of the previous century. The entire space was framed by four 30-foot marble pillars, and at the center of this formation sat a circular settee with an old, train station–style clock around which prom couples milled about in their rented finery.

The lobby was thronged with seniors, the girls all looking like Golden Globe nominees in their designer rip-offs, the guys looking like guys who had never worn tuxedos before. Virginia, however, looked fantastic as we strolled through the stuffy room, evidenced by the way she was turning male heads practically to the breaking point. Part of this was her aforementioned bust, but a bigger part was that I was shepherding her bust around for the evening. Consequently people were in shock. They couldn't believe that I, Cameron Hayes, had this totally hot girl for a date. Suddenly guys I vaguely knew from school and who had never said boo to me were now giving me the high sign and even offering an occasional thumbs-up. It was incredible! I went from zero to hero in the minute flat that it took us to cross to the circular staircase that led to the ballroom.

Downstairs the hotel's decor was a bit more sunny, with bright yellow Chippendale wallpaper and a royal blue oriental carpet covering the floor. As we passed through a pair of elegant French doors, we arrived at the entrance to the Willard's Crystal Ballroom. The only thing between us and the prom was the volunteer ticket taker and Mr. Moldonati, a.k.a. Mr. Mold. The nickname referred to his age, which, like most rotting organic spores, was pushing prehistoric. Mr. Mold was our beloved Vice Principal for Academic Affairs, a fancy way of saying he was The Law. As head disciplinarian at Prep, Mold would also be playing that same role at the prom, looking out for bad behavior and punishing it as he saw fit. Fortunately he was friendly toward me, as I'd never caused much trouble in my life. That was soon about to change.

"Mr. Hayes," he said, thrusting out his hand enthusiastically. "Wonderful to see you."

"Hi, Mr. Moldonati," I said, nervously averting his gaze and looking at Virginia. I was still feeling mildly buzzed from the beer and didn't want to give away my state of intoxication. Noticing my skittishness around him, he misread it as teenage hetero lust for Virginia.

"And who is this lovely lady you can't keep your eyes off of?"

I introduced him to Virginia and she said a few innocuous things about how nice the Willard Hotel was, how beautiful the ballroom was, how glamorous everyone looked, blah, blah, blah. Next up was Shane, whom Mr. Mold greeted warmly in honor of his status as former jock superstar. After some small talk about how he was attending UVA in the fall and how great that was going to be, Mold let us in. We had run the gauntlet! (Checkpoint Moldy?) Somehow I was certain Mr. Mold was going to bust us. Even though we weren't that drunk or messy, I thought, or maybe even hoped, that he would have looked into my panicked eyes and ascertained that this whole situation of pretending to have fake girlfriends was freaking me out. Secretly it was like I wanted to be stopped at the border and saved from any further charades because, by this point, all that lying was starting to make me tired, you know?

As we left Mold behind, Virginia leaned toward me discreetly.

"I'm exhausted," Virginia said, verbalizing my exact feeling, which was weird.

"Me too," I said, having what was probably our first true moment of date bonding that evening. "This whole thing's really been . . . draining."

"Ugh . . . you're telling me."

With that we shared a discreet, weary smile and entered the prom.

The Willard's Crystal Ballroom was well named, with ten chandeliers that hung from a basketball court–size ceiling. At the center of the room was an unscathed parquet dance floor, above which hung an implied second floor, with fake country-white railings framing painted pastoral scenes of incongruously mixed hillsides of ancient Greece and colonial Virginia, respectively. The desired effect of the trompe l'oilel was to create the illusion that the fancy-ass Willard ballroom was not, in fact, in the basement. But these tacky design tricks only seemed to make me more aware of our subterranean dance. They also inspired a bit of claustrophobia to boot. But that might have had more to do with my unique, paranoia-inducing circumstances rather than the ballroom itself.

Walking through a sea of seniors sitting at packed round tables, we sought our assigned table (number 13, of course), and after finding it in the far corner of the room, sat down. In addition to the four of us, there were already six other folks sitting there; Ian and Caroline and two other friends of Ian's from the sports world whom I recognized but didn't know. Still, they were all glad to make my acquaintance, mainly so that they could ogle my hot date as she sat down with a plop and then a reactive jiggle. If their less-endowed dates noticed their leering they didn't let on, or were so used to this primal male reaction to a large-bosomed woman that it didn't register. Conversely, I started to think that if I'd looked at every guy's crotch this way with Shane by my side, I would surely have heard about it. In fact, with Shane I would probably have felt his reaction. You see, when Shane gets angry, things tend to get beaten and/or broken. It doesn't happen often but when it does (e.g., threatening Virginia in the limo) he does not kid around. Honest. I'd been fortunate enough by that point in our relationship to have never been on the receiving end of his anger. I'd only witnessed it when friends disappointed him, siblings annoyed him, or parents contradicted him.

The DJ started spinning Fountains of Wayne and that cleared out our table, sending everyone racing to the dance floor. Except, that is, for our fake foursome. I wanted to take Virginia up for a dance because I love FOW (that lead singer is so cute for someone in his thirties) but turning to ask her, I discovered that she was out cold. Virginia was taking a nap, sitting straight up in her chair, eyes completely shut, mouth slightly ajar.

"Jesus," said Shane, looking at this sight and turning to his date. "Can't you do something about her, Jane?"

"Girl's tired," said Jane with a shrug. "Not much to do except let her sleep."

"Cam, do you have your sunglasses with you?"

Fortunately I did. I had them from driving that afternoon to pick up Virginia. So trying not to rouse her, I placed my Oakley's on her nose, covering her eyes so that she just looked freaky as opposed to sleepy. Not that a girl sitting in a basement ballroom wearing sunglasses and a slack-jawed expression didn't look suspicious. But at least she didn't look like she had passed out.

Seeing that this crisis had been contained, Shane got up from the table.

"I'm gonna do the rounds, say hi to some of the guys from the team," said Shane with a grunt, trying to act all butch. Ha. "You okay here?"

"Sure," I said, resigned to the fact that he had social obligations other than me.

"If we get bored," added Jane, "we can always dance."

"Yeah," said Shane, as if he were the host of the prom. "Have fun!"

Thus Shane left us with a sleeping Virginia.

"Cheer up, Cam," said Jane, sensing my funk at his departure. "He'll be back soon."

"Sure, but . . . I don't know," I said, suddenly feeling existential about the whole dance deal but not wanting to discuss it with Jane. You see, Jane and I were friends through Shane but had never really developed our own friendship independent of him, mainly because we had never really spent time alone. My outings with Jane always involved Shane. He was our degree of separation and one that actually served to keep us fairly separated from each other.

"What is it?"

"I don't know," I said trying to figure out my bummed-out thoughts.

"It's okay . . . you can talk to me about Shane if you want. I won't tell you all his secrets . . . just the good ones."

Jane smiled reassuringly and I suddenly felt one hundred times more comfortable with her. So, alone together with her for the first time ever, I took the opportunity to try to get some perspective on the man that I was going off to college with in the fall.

"Do you think Shane will ever be honest about us?" I asked, breaching the big question at an event that generally consists of small talk about where you got your nails done. But Jane didn't seemed shocked at all. She seemed interested and encouraged me to open up.

"About being a couple and all?"

"Yeah," I said, relieved that she got it. "I mean, Shane says that it's conditional, you know. That he's being so secretive because of Prep and all his jock buddies and not wanting to rock the boat before graduation. But now . . . I don't know . . . I'm beginning to wonder if graduation will actually change things that much."

Jane sat up in her chair and leaned in for confidentiality's sake.

"Don't worry. Graduation changes everything," said Jane, like she had already graduated three times before.

"What makes you so sure?"

"Once you leave high school, it's a whole different world out there. A huge world."

I looked at her skeptically. But she was undeterred in making her point.

"Look around at everyone here. Pretty big crowd, right?"

I nodded vaguely.

"Okay—this is about one two-hundredth of one-sixteenth of one percent of the people our age in the D.C. metro area right now. There is a gigantic world out there, Cam, and the majority of the people in that world don't really care whether you and Shane are a couple. If anything, they'd be totally jealous of the whole thing since you both are, like, catches."

Jane knew this because she'd been out in the real world for years. Unlike Shane, she didn't come from a fabulously wealthy family. Her parents worked for the government in jobs that provided safety and security but not a monster mansion like the Wilsons'. Because of this Jane had been working summer jobs since she was fourteen. But she was too smart for stuff like flipping burgers at McD's or slopping coffee at Starbucks. Instead her jobs were always esoteric, like selling tickets at the Smithsonian's American History museum or building stage sets for a community theater in Bethesda or teaching art to eight-year-olds at Glen Echo summer camp or, most recently, answering phones at National Public Radio. We all knew that someday, some way, Jane was going to take over this wide, wide world of which she spoke. Or at the least, she was going to majorly rock it.

"So," I continued, "you truly think Shane's being honest when he says that once we get to Charlottesville it's gonna be a different situation?"

"Totally," she said with utter assurance. "The big diff is that he won't have any of the sports pressures he had at Prep from his family. I don't think you know how much that shaped him. It's not really who he is, you know. It's who his dad is, and Shane had to play along with it to keep him happy. Otherwise, if his dad had not been happy he would never have let Shane go more than ten miles away to college. Remember, he's the last of the Wilsons, and they don't want to give him up so easily."

"Exactly what I'm worried about," I said, dejected again. "I think he is so concerned about disappointing them that he won't ever, you know, be honest with them or anyone."

Jane's sympathetic expression, though, began to grow less so.

"May I remind you that you're not Mr. Rainbows and Triangles with your folks."

"But that's different," I said, without thinking.

"Uh . . . why?"

"Because I'm the only child. They expect me to have kids and grandkids and all that."

Jane looked somewhat perplexed.

"They say this a lot or something?"

"Not explicitly," I said, caught. "But they *are* parents. It's what all parents want."

"Think about it, Cameron. Your parents are super young. If they loved kids so much wouldn't they be having *more* of them? Maybe they only wanted one because kids are kind of a pain in the ass. And your folks are youthful and fun loving and like to do stuff other than changing diapers."

"JazzFest at Wolf Trap is not my idea of fun loving."

"You know what I mean," she said, eyeing me sideways. "All I'm suggesting is that maybe your folks aren't exactly waiting around for you to ask them to baby-sit *your* future kids for the weekend. That might not be their idea of fun in their golden years."

Wow—I had never thought of it like this. But that's Jane for you. She gets you to think things you never would on your own. To put it in Chemistry 101 terms, she's like sort of a catalyst, you know what I mean? Shane, however, thinks that Jane's chemical abilities are also the one quality about her that can be a pain in the butt. But that's only because he generally doesn't like new ways of thinking. As I used to say to him, it's Shane's world and we're all just living in it, trying to get by.

Anyway, as Jane and I were hanging out and completely bonding over all this Shane talk and philosophy about the world, relationships, and parenting, we heard a dull thud. We turned to see Virginia, now slumped over our table looking more than suspicious—she looked passed out, my sunglasses smushed sideways against her face.

"Shit," I said looking around for Mr. Mold. "This does not look good."

"Okay. Don't panic," said Jane, her eyes a little panicky. "We're in a good position at least, far away from the door. Let's see. How 'bout we move your chair slightly to the left so that at least seventy percent of the room can't see her?"

I repositioned my chair to block the view as Jane checked Virginia's vitals.

"Is she asleep?" I asked.

"And alive, too," she said with her usual zippy-ness.

"That's grrrreat," I said, mimicking Jane in a way that I didn't intend to be mean, just frustrated. But it made Jane feel bad about the whole setup.

"I'm sorry, Cam," she said, putting her hand on mine. "I didn't realize Virginia was such a lush."

"It's okay," I said, trying to be understanding. "I don't think she realized it either."

"I mean, I've had a few drinks with her before . . . but she's never been like this."

"Well, in her defense, I think I'd have had the same reaction if I found out Shane was a lesbian or something."

Jane started cackling hysterically.

"That is rrrrrrich," she said, instantly happy again. "Can you imagine Shane as some big old dyke? Wearing lots of plaid—"

"Going to Melissa Etheridge concerts."

"Getting his hair cut in a wedge."

"Driving a pickup truck."

"Chunky glasses."

"No makeup."

We were both in hysterics, creating this alt-universe Shane as a sapphic teen goddess. It was in the midst of this hilarity that I smelled smoke. I thought that someone at a nearby table was snagging a cig and being daring, tempting fate and Mr. Mold himself. But this was not a cigarette smell. Clove maybe, but much worse than that. As the tears ran down our faces from laughing, I caught my breath and nearly gagged.

"What is that?" I said, wrinkling my nose.

Jane sniffed the air and looked over at the table next to us, an assortment of various fringe elements of Prep who were generally found hanging under the football stands.

"Maybe the punks at table twelve are sparking up?"

Then I noticed an actual trail of smoke rising from our table. I twisted around in my chair and following the trail downward, realized it was emanating from Virginia's voluminous hair, glowing a new kind of orange as a small brush fire burned through a clump of it that was surrounding the flame of a candle at the center of our table.

"Uh, Virginia's on fire."

"Hardly," said Jane, still in wisecracker mode. "She's totally out of it."

"No, Jane—her *hair*!"

Jane looked and her face went slack with shock. But being Jane, she did not let her alarm keep her from figuring out a way to deal with the situation. In a calm, measured voice, she instructed me to remove my jacket and, without causing too much of a commotion, place it over Virginia's head to cut off the supply of oxygen to the flame. (Jane excelled in all the sciences, thank God.) Once I did as instructed, I could feel the heat of the flame through the poly fabric of my jacket, sure that it was going to burn a hole right through it and thus start an even more obvious conflagration. Fortunately the heat subsided quickly as trails of smoke leaked out through my sleeves. The mission was quietly accomplished until Virginia, who, like the fire, had also been deprived of oxygen, woke up with a start, squirming and cursing under my jacket.

"Whoops," I said, still holding my jacket down as best I could. "She's awake."

As Virginia cursed a blue streak, she pushed herself up from the table, the force of which pushed me backward, knocking me and my chair onto the floor.

"What the hell are you doing!" said Virginia, frazzled to say the least.

Jane reached down and pulled me up off the floor.

"He was trying to save your life, Virginia, that's all."

"You passed out and your hair was—"

But before I could finish the sentence, Virginia got a whiff of her situation.

"My hair!"

She ran her fingers through the clump of melted and burned red hair. She looked like she was about to cry. Jane went into damage-control mode.

"Okay. Okay. Okay—don't panic, Virginia. Keep calm. It's only hair."

"But it's my hair. . . . And it's *ruined*!"

"All right," Jane said, leaning toward me urgently. "I'm getting her to the ladies'."

As tears began to stream down Virginia's cheeks, Jane whisked her up from the table and turning her charred side away from the bulk of revelers, extricated Virginia from the ballroom with hurried but not harried steps. Once they left I picked up my jacket off the floor and noticed the white satiny lining on the inside was gray with smoke, slightly singed where the candle had touched it. This would be hard to explain at the rental agency in my attempts to reclaim my $100 deposit. *Oh, uh yeah, and my date's hair caught fire when she passed out at our table after drinking too much because she didn't know that I was not really—*

Oh, never mind!

# CHAPTER 9

Okay—so what is it about high school dances and torture? I mean, why is it that these two things that should be polar opposites (no one intends them to be this painful, right?) are in fact synonymous, at least when it comes to my life? Of course, if I'd had the answer to all these theoretical questions then I certainly wouldn't have been sitting alone at the biggest dance of my life as my decoy date was in the bathroom getting a burn makeover, and my real date was somewhere in this swarm of two hundred-odd people, having a great time without me. But that's, sadly, what I was doing, sitting there all by myself and gamely smiling at classmates who passed my empty table, looking at me like I was a social leper.

You know what? It almost made me long for the simpler days of the freshman mixer in the gym, where even if you didn't have a date or a friend or a bodyguard you could at least salvage some dignity by slouching against the bleachers, unnoticed in the shadows. But here at the prom, under the glaring light of the Willard's orbiting galaxy of chandeliers, there was no escape from the prying eyes of The Crowd. And it was due to this fact that Franklin Taylor spied me from the other side of the room and actually came over to say "Hey, loser . . . why are you sitting by yourself at the senior prom?"

All right, Franklin didn't really say this. But it *was* sorta implied.

"Hey, Cam," he said. "Mind if we join you?"

See what I mean? C'mon, that's a pretty damn cheeky question.

Given the fact that I was alone, my response should have been something along the lines of "Well, of course I don't mind since I'm sitting by my-goddamn-self!" But I didn't say that. I never say any of the sharp, bitchy lines that come to me, for fear of seeming like some psycho-freak. So what was my response? Typical me:

"Sure."

What could I do, really? I mean, considering that Franklin and I hadn't said more than hi to each other in the last couple months, I decided to try to be sort of nice. I figured his simple act of at least making an effort had to be accepted and almost appreciated.

Okay—so the "we" Franklin was referring to was his date. Yeah, Franklin had a date for the prom. A real one, given the way she clung to him. She was an adorable Asian girl with a tight pink dress on who was actually taller than Franklin by about four inches (something I found unintentionally hilarious). Despite the height difference and the fact that she was a real, live girl, Franklin seemed unusually cool and not his generally anxious self.

"Have a seat," I said, trying to get them down to my level.

As Franklin pulled out a chair for his date, I noticed he was wearing a shiny, fancy-ass tux with a slick straight tie instead of the traditional bow. I guess he'd acquired some semblance of style since I'd stopped hanging out with him. Physically, though, Franklin looked about the same: shorter than average height with a pudgier than average face, and the kinkiest black hair that a white kid ever had. I used to call it his Jew-Fro, which when we were friends, he generally thought was hysterical. Franklin and I shared a lot of jokes and definitely had the same warped sense of wordplay humor. To be honest, I have to admit that I was maybe 20 percent attracted to Franklin when we were hanging out, but not so much in a physical way. I just loved the ease with which we made each other laugh.

"This is Franchesca," he said, introducing his date to me. After a few basic pleasantries regarding when we had all arrived and where my posse was, Franchesca joined the conversation.

"So how do you two know each other?"

"We used to be best friends," Franklin offered, saying it like he'd been waiting to for quite some time. Nice.

"Oh," said Franchesca, a little thrown off by her date's blunt but totally true response. "That's too bad."

"We're still friends though," I said congenially, trying to save some face. But looking at Franklin I could tell that even that was probably not the case anymore. Fortunately Franklin was kind and didn't call me on this lie. I think he probably sensed that I was already having a bad enough evening as it was. He knew all too well my dislike for dances.

"We just don't see each other that much anymore," said Franklin, which was correct in the barest way imaginable. It's true that we didn't see each other. However, the reason for this is that I'd kinda dumped him as a friend.

"So where's your date?" wondered Franchesca, wholly innocent of what a loaded question this was.

"In the bathroom," I said, rolling my eyes. "Uh, freshening up."

And if that wasn't the understatement of the year . . .

"Who is it?"

"Virginia McKinley . . . from Potomac. A friend of Shane's."

"Ah," said Franklin, nodding and taking note that since Shane had set me up on a date, he must be my new best friend. But what can I say? Shane was more of a *boy*friend, really. Not to say that Shane wasn't a close friend since, realistically, it doesn't get much closer than that. But we were not friends in the same way I had been with Franklin. Mainly we had a different level of interest in things artistic. I mean, unlike Franklin, Shane would never go to foreign films at the Hirschorn with me, or check out some random new punk band at Black Cat. He didn't have the sense of cultural mischief that I shared with Franklin. And seeing him again at my table, I was struck by how sorely I missed him.

"I heard you're both going to UVA in the fall."

"Yeah," I said. "Crazy coincidence."

Now, I don't know why I said this, because it was so far from a coincidence. Shane and I had jointly decided to pick UVA so that we could stay together. Still, Franklin could tell I was lying on this point, but not exactly why. He probably thought I was saying this coincidence thing so as not to make him feel bad about being dropped as my best friend. But I'd never done that intentionally. Honest. I lost touch with him because I couldn't lie to him anymore. And being truthful with Franklin, and everyone else, about who I was and what Shane and I were really up to totally freaked me out. And in the end our friendship took the fall for my fears.

Our already strained conversation hit a dry patch after this exchange about college. Realizing there wasn't too much more to say, Franklin and Franchesca rose from the table, making the excuse that they wanted to dance. Even though chatting with Franklin had been awkward, it had been nice not to be a loser hanging alone at my own table. But honestly, it had been even nicer talking to Franklin, if only for a few moments.

Stretching the limits of my ability to be truthful, I tried to at least be honest about this.

"It was great to see you, Franklin," I said in all sincerity.

"Yeah," he said, less so. "Good luck at UVA."

"Hey—where are you going in the fall?"

"Maryland. College Park."

"Cool," I said. "Let me know what your new e-mail is, okay?"

Surprised by this request, Franklin mulled it over, studying it almost to see if it was some kind of insincere party talk. But I really did want to stay in touch, at least at some point in the near future when my life had maybe reached a semblance of normalcy. *Maybe after high school,* I thought, *everything will be easier, just as Jane promised. Maybe . . .*

"Sure," said Franklin with an easy smile. "I'll let you know. Later!"

And again I was alone at the prom, though this time I felt slightly better about it.

After a few more minutes, Jane finally returned to our table from the ladies' room. Virginia, however, was still in there, as the extreme makeover progressed slowly. They had commandeered a resource-ful ex-Girl Scout with a sewing repair kit in her purse, using the scissors to excise Virginia's burned hair. Caroline had gotten in on the act too, slipping a twenty to one of the bellhops to heist some hair care items from a maid's cart. And this being a fancy hotel, they had scored some major Aveda product (that apparently soothed Virginia somewhat). So as the girls worked on gelling and styling her smoky mane into a new post-disaster do, I wondered if Jane had seen my real date, who was by that point officially MIA.

"Caroline got a text from Ian," she said. "The boys are seeking libation in the hotel bar with Shane's brother's ID."

"That's nice," I said, perturbed we weren't invited along on this adventure.

"Don't sweat it, Cam. I'm sure they'll be back soon enough."

"So what are we supposed to do in the meantime?"

"The word in the ladies' is that there's some weed to be had," she said with a devious glint in her eye. I was totally shocked. It was so not Jane to be into Mary Jane, which was exactly what I said to her.

"That's cute, Cam," she said with her dainty smile. "But I *have* partaken on a few special occasions. And it doesn't get any specialer than the prom, right?"

"Still, aren't you worried about getting caught?"

"Not particularly," she said, a bit too relaxed. "Because *you* have to get it."

"What?"

"There's a waiter here who's dealing. And he only deals in the boys' room."

"Well," I said, trying to worm my way out of participating in my first drug transaction. "I'm not *really* one of the boys, right?"

"Nice try, Cam."

She slipped her arm around my waist and spun me around to face the rear of the ballroom.

"That's our man, or your man."

With a slight nod of the head, she aimed my gaze toward the

refreshment table. Pouring some ginger ale punch into champagne glasses was a short and swarthy-looking guy wearing a maroon hotel jacket and matching bow tie.

"His name is Dmitri," she said, slipping her Nokia out of her purse. "I just have to text him your name and he'll meet you in the men's room. Third stall in. Then you go in and say you want some pie."

"Pie?"

"Code for high," she said, like everyone knew this.

"I dunno," I said, eyeing this Dmitri and trying to judge whether or not he was a narc in some *Cops*-like scheme to bust teenage stoners. "This all seems a little . . . shady."

"Uh, yeah—it's a *drug* deal. It's *supposed* to be shady."

"Thanks, Jane," I said, smirking at her.

"C'mon Cam, look around," she said, indicating the crowd of our classmates in the room, all of them laughing and conversing and cuddling and generally enjoying themselves. I mean, what the hell was their problem, having a good time at a school-sponsored dance? "Everyone's having a good time. Don't you wanna join them?"

"It's no use," I said sullenly. "I never have fun at dances. Ever."

"That's because you've never been stoned at one."

Well, she did have a point there. The only other attempt at getting any kind of high at one of these dances was the time sophomore year that Franklin and I took a ton of Sudafed thinking it would give us a big, speedy buzz. Instead it relieved us of sinus congestion for a month.

"Still, what if something happens?" I said, anxious about the possibility for disaster. "What if this all goes terribly wrong like just, uh, you know, just about everything *else* has gone terribly wrong tonight."

I will admit it. I'm sort of a pessimist when it comes to things in general, you know, working out. Especially things that just don't sound right in the first place. And I think I already had some rock-solid evidence to back me up on that one. (I direct your attention to Exhibit A: going on a fake double date to the prom without letting the date know about it.) Therefore, a hotel employee/pot dealer just seemed like yet another bad idea in an evening already brimming with them. Yet Jane was not having my doubts.

"What's the worst thing that can happen?"

"Uh, let's see, other than getting *arrested*?" I said with a mild case of hysteria. "Besides, how are we gonna smoke it without someone getting wise?"

"Smoke it in the bathroom," she said, as if this was the most obvious thing in the world. "Jeez—haven't you ever seen any teen movies?"

Believe me. I had seen my share of teen movies. And I enjoyed them, especially the ones with Freddie Prinze Jr. (Hot!) But please . . . nothing in those movies was ever remotely like real life. I mean, there was no one as attractive as Freddie Prinze Jr. in my lame Prep graduating class. Not that Shane wasn't cute but, well, let's face it— he's no movie star. (WB maybe, but movie star?) Which is to say that all teen movies are a total fantasy world created by a bunch of forty-somethings in Hollywood who, like our own parents, are always trying to sell us on the fact that being in high school can be fun. Hello—talk about people who must have been high back in the day! I mean, there must be some significant memory loss going on with this parental demographic.

Anyway, Jane's response to all my whining was simple and fairly predictable.

"Cam, I've never said this to anyone, but you *really* need to get stoned. Now."

So despite my vocal protests and better judgment, I reluctantly agreed to Jane's pot scheme. In seconds she sent her fateful text message, though I did make her provide a fake name for me so that I could at least pretend that I, Cameron Hayes, was not really doing something so damn illegal. It would all fall to my lawbreaking, pot-purchasing alter ego. That would be Freddie, of course, in homage to Mr. Prinze Jr.

Ten minutes later, there I was. I mean, there was "Freddie," standing in the men's room. Like everything else at the Willard, even the bathroom was super-swank, with its beige marble sinks, beveled mirrors, and brown wainscoting on the stall doors. I noticed that the third stall had the door closed. Crouching down for a better look, I didn't see any feet in the stall, which made me wonder if maybe the deal was off. Concerned that Dmitri was late, I checked my watch and saw that I was the one who was late, as it had been more than fifteen minutes since Jane's text. I secretly hoped that Dmitri had been waylaid by the police on his way to meet me.

Taking some tentative steps toward the third stall, I decided on a closer inspection. I put my hand on the door and, surprisingly, it swung open. Sitting with his feet up on the rim of the toilet and hunched over on his haunches was Dmitri. He had pale, ghostly skin and hair that was chocolate in color without any trace of gray even though he seemed pretty old. Definitely over twenty-five. He had a mournful face with deep-set eyes that were hazel, covered by big sleepy eyelids, darker than his skin and slightly oily too. His head was shaped like an apple, heavy on top but drawing to a double point at his cleft chin, a feature that made him resemble the Russian mobster that he likely was.

"Freddie?"

Dmitri's question threw me, having momentarily forgotten my alias.

"You Freddie?" he repeated in a thick Slavic accent.

"Oh—yeah," I said, remembering who I was supposed to be. "Yeah. Me Freddie."

As I responded with English that was even worse than his, Dmitri tilted his head to the side, regarding me like the retard I was.

"I'm Dmitri," he said, motioning me into the spacious stall. "Come."

"Thanks. So, uh, I wanted to get some pie?" I said with a certain lack of conviction.

"Apple or cherry?"

"Uh . . . well, jeez," I said, completely thrown off by this additional code. What could it mean? Was apple the regular stuff, and cherry laced with Ecstasy? Not a random mistake I particularly wanted to make, you know? "Well, uh, I don't know exactly which."

"Good," he said, taking my confusion as proof that I wasn't trying to bust him. Tricky these drug dealers, huh? "Lock the door."

I turned around and pulled the latch on the stall as he remained crouched on the john. He looked ridiculous hunched up there in his hotel uniform. He reminded me of a primate I'd seen at the zoo taking a crap. I stifled a laugh.

"Something funny?"

"Uh, no," I said, trying to cover my giddiness. "It's just, uh . . . are you comfortable like that?"

"I try to be discreet."

My laughter subsided as I stood there with a silly grin, the same one that numerous teachers had asked me to wipe off my face during my K-12 journey. Dmitri, though, unlike my teachers, didn't seem to mind it. In fact, he seemed to fancy it, if you want to know the truth.

"You got cute smile."

"Uh . . . well . . . I . . . uh," I stuttered, reinforcing my retardation.

"You never buy drugs before," he stated rather than asked, reaching into his jacket pocket. Though it was a true statement, I felt the need to defend myself anyway.

"It was my friend Jane's idea."

"Jane," he said nodding to himself. "This the girlfriend?"

And my grin returned.

"Uh . . . no."

Dmitri looked up at me with these luminous hazel eyes. Looked right through me in a way that basically got in a minute what my parents had not been able to figure out in eighteen years. Dmitri knew the score instantly: Boys 1, Girls 0.

"I see," he said, seeing all of me with his piercing eyes. Maybe it was my goofy smile that gave my gayness away. But part of it was that, well, how can I say this? I definitely was thinking that for a drug dealer, Dmitri was kinda cute.

"Thirty bucks," he said, taking his hand out of his uniform pocket and holding up two small joints, rolled tight in white paper that made them look like pregnant cigarettes.

"Whoops," I said, realizing that I'd forgotten to get cash from Jane. As for my own emergency fund, my dad's Benjamin was in my singed jacket, which I'd left to air out on the back of my chair in the ballroom. Not that I would've used that money for drugs. Honest. Anyway—

"You don't have?" he said, perturbed by my lack of green.

"Uh . . . well . . . I . . ."

Retard. Retard. Retard.

"Hmmm," said Dmitri, not as upset as I'd imagine a drug dealer might get in this situation. I'd seen plenty of movies on the narcotics trade, and this was usually the point where someone either pulled out a very large weapon or started beating the living daylights out of the moron without the cash. But Dmitri was just sitting there, still on his haunches. Staring at me. Right into me. Uh-oh.

"This is problem," he said flatly. *Not a very convincing line reading for a drug dealer,* I thought. Still, I tried to explain calmly. Ha.

"It's not like I don't have money," I said, my voice rising about three octaves. "I mean, I've got it . . . that is, Jane has it. Honest. We don't want to stiff you or anything like that, it's just—"

He interrupted my ranting.

"Take as the gift."

I stopped in midrant, my eyebrows arching skyward. A gift? Like for free? Hmmmm . . . I'd never seen *this* drug movie.

"Uh . . . well . . . I—"

"From me. Gift."

Then Dmitri took my right hand and turned it palm up. He placed the two "cigarettes" into my palm and, with his other hand, pushed my fingers around them, making my hand into a fist that concealed the contraband. And then he held my fist in his hand. His warm hand. For a while. Uh . . . you see where this is going?

"Really, I can pay you later," I said, seeing exactly where this was going.

"Yes. I know," he said, turning on the charm. "But a kiss will do."

Okay—clearly they have *very* different drug dealer movies in Russia.

"I . . . I can't," I croaked. Barely.

"Why . . . you no gay?" he asked, seeming confused.

"That's not the—"

"Is okay if you like both," he said, his other hand now coming into the action to make his case, gently caressing my wrist. Actually, it was more like working my wrist, kneading it deeply with his thumb. Damn, that felt good! "I am the bisexual myself."

And somehow, this made perfect sense for a drug dealer. Probably doubled his clientele.

"Besides . . . is just a kiss," he said, moving in closer. "Would be nice, no?"

Well, sure. Kissing a hot Slavic semi-straight dude could, objectively, be nice. But there was one little problem.

"I, uh, I have a boyfriend."

The sound of this phrase was as magical and as foreign to me as English probably was to Dmitri. The reason was that I had never, ever said something like this. I mean, ever. I had never had the need to, really. No one had ever hit on me other than Shane. But after having said it out loud in the bathroom . . . I don't know. It was so weird, you know? Okay—let me try a language lab analogy: It was like I had spoken French for the first time and was amazed that someone could understand what I had said, because I'd been such a poor student and used to fast-forward through all the tapes in class. Is that too crazy?

"Hmmmph. But this . . . boy-friend," said Dmitri, struggling with language himself. "He is not dancing?"

"Uh . . . what?"

"He is not here. Dancing. With you."

"Actually, he is here," I said. Where exactly I wasn't sure, but that was another matter. "We came together."

"You and boyfriend," said Dmitri, trying to add this all up. "You come to dance. Together."

I nodded.

"America," he said in a wondrous tone usually heard coming from immigrants getting their first look at the Statue of Liberty.

Though I neglected to mention that Shane and I weren't exactly walking through the receiving line of the prom together, Dmitri seemed to get the point that I had a boyfriend in the immediate vicinity and he released his grasp on my hand.

"I'll pay you later, back in the ballroom," I said sincerely. "Honest."

"No," he said nobly, shaking his head for emphasis. "Is my gift. To both."

Dmitri winked at me as I backed my way out of the stall, nearly tripping over myself.

"Wow," I said, charmed and surprised by this unlikely kindness. "Thanks."

I mean, really . . . who knew drug dealers could be so damn nice?

# CHAPTER 10

Once I got back to table 13, Shane had finally returned to the roost too, but not for long. He was there for barely two minutes when some other friend of Ian's dragged him away to say hi to more football folks, who were late arrivals. I didn't even have time to tell Shane about Virginia's hair disaster or get into the whole bizarre Dmitri situation, but frankly, I don't know if I would have, even if he'd sat down again. I doubted Shane would take too kindly to the fact that a) I was trying to buy drugs and b) I was actually getting them for free from a flirty Russian mobster.

At this point in the night, I have to say I was getting pretty damn annoyed by Shane's lack of attention to me. After all, the whole prom thing had been Shane's idea in the first place. Initially I thought his interest in having us go together was borne out of a sincere desire to actually go to the prom *with* me. However, having spent barely ten minutes of face time with Shane at the actual dance, I was beginning to see why he wanted to go to this thing. It was starting to look like his interest in attending the prom was so that he could hang with his football friends and relive his glory days as a popular jock dude. It made me almost wish that I had kissed Dmitri when I had the chance. Almost.

"I can't believe the drug dealer wanted to jump your ass!" said Jane, a little too excitedly, once Shane was out of earshot.

"Okay—*exaggerate* much?" I said, trying to bring some semblance of reality into play. "He asked for a kiss, Jane. That's all."

"C'mon, Cam . . . a kiss is *not* just a kiss. Especially with guys. And *majorly* with drug dealers. I'm sure he totally wanted to get it on with you in the men's room!"

"That is so revolting!" I said, trying to sound horrified. However, Jane wasn't buying it.

"Oh, please," she said not believing my shock one bit. "What's that line from Shakespeare? 'The lady doth protest too much.'"

"I protested a lot, thank you."

"That's what I'm saying," she said, making her point. "Admit it—you thought he was totally hot."

Though this was partially true, there was no way I would admit it to Shane's best girlfriend, even if she had proven trustworthy with the big secret of Shane's life.

"Jane—don't you ever, ever, *ever* mention the kiss thing to Shane, okay?"

"C'mon, Cam, I wouldn't do that to you," she said, shocked that I'd suggested it. "You and I are friends."

This was the first time Jane had come out and stated our friendship on its own terms. I thought that was one nice development in an evening that didn't have too much going for it. I mean, as a gay man you can never have enough straight female friends. At least that's what I've gleaned from *Will & Grace*.

So with our friendship newly cemented by the unlikely glue of a flirty drug dealer, we proceeded to "have some pie," as Jane put it. I slipped my dinner jacket back on in an effort to look more formal and less suspicious, and we both went off to our separate bathrooms with our conveniently separate joints. Then after doing the weed we reconvened in the basement parlor outside the ballroom, blissfully baked.

Honestly, I'd only been stoned once before in my life, so I was flying. My system was not acclimated to pot, and after taking about four deep choking inhales, I was in another world. And that was a good thing. It was truly something of a relief and at that point practically a necessity for my sanity, given everything I'd had to deal with. The world of the prom, with my real date off playing with "da boyz" and my fake date despising me because I was one of "da boyz," was not quite the ebullient end-of-high-school extravaganza I'd been brainwashed to expect from those stupid Freddie Prinze Jr. movies. It was more akin to a bad soap opera . . . you know, like *Passions*. No real stars, bizarre plot twists, and loads of bad acting.

As Jane and I headed back into the Crystal Ballroom, I scanned the crowd for my erstwhile boyfriend but still couldn't spot him. Then again, my vision was less than perfect due to the THC flooding my system. We were about to head back to empty old table 13 when the strains of Mary J. Blige's "No More Drama" started pumping through the room, the soulful lyrics speaking directly to me in the way music can when you're totally baked. Taking Jane's hand, we both raced onto the dance floor to groove out to Mary J. and sing along as best we could, given our condition. And you know what? We had a blast! As Jane did a superb Mary J. impersonation, I gave her some diva props with high fives and a few *You go, girls*.

When that song ended, the DJ segued into some Christina, the club remix of "Beautiful." Feeling sort of levitated by Dmitri's gift, I suddenly didn't give a damn what anyone thought, and that's when I really started dancing like a big, gay maniac. It was such an amazing relief to be out there on the dance floor going wild like that, letting loose in a way I never had at any previous dance or social event. It was then that I realized, with delayed clarity, the genius of Jane's earlier pronouncement that evening, that the high school world was so small and already beginning to recede into the distance, thank God. Suddenly I didn't care what anyone at Prep thought about who I was or wasn't. I found myself inspired by Christina's song, working my skinny body and ridiculously slender hips like nobody's business, as Jane and I screamed out the lyrics.

With all this inspired yelling and mad dancing, Jane and I were causing quite a scene. Correction—make that *I* was causing quite a scene. Jane spun toward me, shocked that I was starting to make such a spectacle of myself on a dance floor that was not exactly teeming. (50 Cent and Jay-Z were the songs that had created dancing traffic jams.) After twirling around like a top for an entire verse of "Beautiful," I grabbed Jane and yelled a question.

"Hey—am I dancing like a gay boy?"

"Honestly?" she said, her eyes happily bleary. "Yeah, a little bit."

"Good," I said, almost as surprised at saying this as when I'd stated my boyfriend status to Dmitri.

All our crazy dancing fun ended somewhat abruptly when the DJ put on a lame Mandy Moore song, clearly a sentimental request by someone's hypersappy steady. (And no, that would definitely not have been Shane.) However, unlike at most high school dances, the floor didn't clear out. It actually filled up as everyone took the opportunity of Mandy's song to get nice and close and sexy with their date. My intent was to exit the dance floor as quickly as possible, not being a fan of Ms. Moore or slow dancing with girls in general. Yet all escape routes were blocked off by the horny mob flooding the parquet. Thus in our chronic-induced stupor, Jane and I got stuck right in the middle of a swaying, slow dance mash-a-thon.

"If you can't beat 'em," said Jane, holding her arm out for me to take her for a spin, ballroom style. With nowhere for us to go, I took her up on the offer, clasping her hand as she grabbed my waist and rocking back and forth to the sugary Mandy melody.

"As my mother likes to say, aren't we a sight?" said Jane in an uncharacteristically dorky, un-Jane voice. But there was something melancholy about her delivery too, the usual Jane zippiness strangely absent.

"Whattya mean?"

"Well, in summary, your fake date's in the bathroom with a hangover and a crispy hairdo, while my fake date is out wandering the Willard, searching for his heterosexuality or something."

Nodding silently, I knew exactly what she meant regarding Shane. In the last couple of months, Shane and I had been spending a lot more time together, not only working late after school on the yearbook nearly every day of the week but also spending at least one, sometimes two, of our weekend nights together as well. This schedule had not given him much time to hang with his former football posse, which I took to be a good thing. Evolution, if you will. Shane was growing up, and even more so, we were growing together into a real couple. But thrown into the same social event with his old gang on the last week of school, Shane was suddenly feeling nostalgic for his lapsed jock identity. And missing him, I was feeling nostalgic for Shane.

"I mean, I really shouldn't complain since he's not *really* my date after all," continued Jane. "But, you—*you* must be mildly perturbed about the whole thing."

"Yeah," I sighed, resigned to my second-string status for the night. "I guess I should be, how you say, perturbed?"

Jane flashed me a stoner's grin.

"Shane's just nervous because of Virginia knowing," I reasoned. "He probably doesn't wanna risk blowing our cover now that we're just about done with school and all. Besides, after graduation next week, he's mine . . . all mine!"

I made a goofy Dr. Frankensteinesque gesture. Jane regarded me a little strangely.

"What about Beach Week?" she wondered, referring to the ritual migration to Ocean City, Maryland, for a week of postgrad decampment and debauchery.

"We're staying at his folks' place in Rehobeth, somewhat removed from the madness. Thank God."

"Actually, Caroline told me that Ian's rented some group house in OC for the team."

Really? This was news to me.

"There is no way he'd bring me to stay with Ian and Company," I said emphatically. "No friggin' football way."

"Uh," said Jane, trying to be polite. "I don't think he was planning on bringing you."

With this new nugget of information, a black hole opened up in my stomach. If Jane, the nexus of all Prep-Potomac information, was saying this, then it was most likely 99 percent true. I couldn't believe Shane would do this though. We had talked about the beach only a week before, and at that time I agreed that I'd go to the prom as long as he agreed that we'd go to Rehoboth and not OC. Now I really started to wonder if he could have totally lied to me as a means of placating me into going along with the prom scheme. Could I have been so gullible to believe he was telling the truth when he'd promised me that we would have Beach Week to ourselves?

Okay, not to make a huge moral point about this or anything, but this is one of those minor little problems you encounter when you live a life of lies; if you're fudging the facts on just about everything you say or do, you really can't expect the truth from someone else.

"Oh, Cam," Jane said in the most pitiful of all tones. "I'm sorry. I thought you knew or that Shane had told you or . . . are you all right?"

"I'm fine," I said, averting my eyes down toward my shuffling feet. You see, my eyes were getting a bit moist. "It's just . . . the pot . . . they're are a little red and all."

But who was I kidding? I was on the verge of tears as I spaced out about this whole new level of deception in our relationship. But there was no way I was going to lose it there on the dance floor. And not during a Mandy Moore song! Please—I had some dignity left.

"I thought for sure Shane had talked to you about it," she said, feeling as bad as I did. "That's totally shitty that he didn't. What is his problem?"

"If it were only one problem," I said mournfully.

Then Jane took my chin in her hand and gently lifted my face up to hers.

"It's okay if you wanna cry," she said.

"No, it's not," I said. "I'm not gonna get all weepy about this on the dance floor of the prom. I'll wait until I can find a nice empty limo or something."

Jane sorta smiled at my sorta-joke.

"It just makes me feel that, you know, Shane doesn't take this whole thing between us seriously. It's like we're a couple now, but maybe it's all some temporary thing. A marriage of convenience since I'm the only other gay guy in our class."

"Please, there are other ones," said Jane, matter-of-factly.

"Really," I said, intrigued. "And who would they be?"

"Using the ten percent rule, there's gotta be at least twelve others," said Jane with the authority of a statistician. "They just haven't figured it out yet. They aren't as evolved as you and Shane are."

"Ha," I said on hearing the words *Shane* and *evolved* in the same sentence. "They're probably somewhat better off delaying the disappointment."

Jane shook me gently to get me to look at her.

"Hey, bottom line," she said, very intently. "I know Shane cares about you. A lot."

"Sure . . . but," I stopped myself again. "Maybe he doesn't love me so much."

Now Jane looked like she might cry. The weed was getting us crazy emotional.

"C'mon, Jane, maybe it's true," I said, convincing myself of this awful notion. "You wanna talk bottom line—okay, *here's* the bottom line. It's the prom and I'm slow dancing with my boyfriend's best friend. . . . But where is he? Huh? Where the hell is he? *That's* your bloody bottom line. And it blows."

"So what?" she said defiantly. "You saying I'm not a great dancer or something?"

"You know that's not what I mean. You're a fabulous dancer, Jane. It's not that. It's . . ."

Taking a quick scan of the couples surrounding us, I calculated that four out of five of them were totally making out. I mean, seriously, there was some deep dental exploration going on, not to mention grope-age too. Hell, the dance floor was a veritable heavy-petting zoo, which made Shane's absence even more depressing. I wanted someone to pet too, you know?

Jane followed my longing gaze, and then with her dainty little hand again gently tugged at my chin, training my eyes back at her.

"You know what, Cam?" she said. "You're very handsome when you're all despondent."

I didn't know quite what she meant by that line. But it worried me.

Then her gaze shifted, staring at me in the same way Dmitri did in the bathroom, like she wanted to do more than compliment me on my depressed good looks. She wanted to kiss me. First Dmitri and now *Jane?* Apparently there was something about Shane's absence that made me way kissable. Come to think of it, that's how Virginia and I got macking the night we met at the house party in Georgetown. So maybe Jane had a real point, that there was something to be said for the attractiveness of my more despairing moments. But kissing Jane? Even stoned, it seemed fairly questionable. *Kissing Jane* . . . the more I thought about it, the more it kinda sounded like the title of some tacky teen movie. And being baked and all, I felt like I was sitting in the Wheaton Plaza Loews, watching the movie version of my life unfold under the glamorous and glittering chandeliers of the Willard's Crystal Ballroom. To be honest, the scene did look mildly romantic. Soft, sparkly lighting. Cute girls in glam formal wear. Slow, moody Emo music (they'd finally segued out of Moore-land). So as I watched this flick of my prom unspool in my mind's multiplex, I found myself intrigued by these two decent-looking, if a little square, dateless kids, staring at each other for what seemed like an eternity. In fact, I started getting a bit frustrated watching their emotional stalemate, and suddenly I got that ghetto urge to start yelling out at the screen. ("Christ, just kiss the damn girl already!") And listening to my own rowdy interior audience, I did it. I kissed her. *Kissing Jane.* Rated PG-13.

Maybe it was the pot or my down mood or the fact that I thought that Shane didn't love me, but, man, did I kiss her. Actually, now that I think about it, it was probably a dangerous confluence of all these factors (not to mention Jane's not having had much action lately either, if I can be frank) that conspired to create, if I can borrow another movie analogy, a perfect storm of kissing. It was like our two whacked-out emotional weather systems collided there on the dance floor and set into motion all kinds of waves and swells and wetness, if you know what I mean. Basically Jane and I went at it like we had been stuck at sea for months and—all right, already . . . *enough* of the nautical analogy! All this is to say that once it started, I got carried away. But the truth is, so did Jane. I mean, who would've ever expected sly old Jane to be such a voracious kisser? At one point I thought she was going to accidentally amputate my tongue. The girl even grabbed my ass, and you know what? It was kinda hot!

Okay, now I know you're thinking this doesn't make sense because I'm this totally gay guy who hates girls and all that standard straight-guy, fear-of-a-gay-planet bullcrap. But honestly, I've never really had anything against girls. This make-out was not psychologically fraught with meaning or working out of emotional issues or anything. It was all about technique and having a good time. Seriously. Jane was a damn good kisser, and to quote her, when you get to the bottom line of it all, lips are lips. Oh, and she did have that resemblance to Shane, which kinda helped too.

So our big make-out was going on and on for, I don't know, maybe five minutes or ten minutes. Or maybe it was a minute. (Time gets so elastic when you're high, you know?) Anyway, it was all fine and sexy and surprisingly good until I felt someone's hand on my shoulder. Initially I thought it was Mr. Mold, playing the role that nuns used to play at those cotillion dances in eighth grade, where if you got a little too close to your dance partner, decrepit Sister So-and-So would come up and ask you to "make room for the Holy Spirit." But upon opening my eyes and dislodging my tongue from Jane's mouth, I noticed that the dance floor was not so full anymore. A decent pocket of awe, I'll call it, had formed around Jane and me as we apparently had been making something of a public spectacle of our passionate selves. And that's what this mysterious hand on my shoulder was reacting to.

Finally when I turned all the way around to see whose hand it was, it was even more clear why we'd become the de facto floor show. The hand belonged to Shane.

"Oh," I said, sounding totally surprised to see him. "Hi, Shane."

Shane looked at me dead in the eye, but he was not flirting this time. He was very, very angry.

"What the *hell* are you doing, Cameron?"

Behind him, I noticed Ian and a couple of the other guys from our erstwhile table. They regarded me with even angrier looks than Shane. It was as if I'd really done something terrible, like taken the name of our school in vain or, God forbid, had made out with a guy. But I hadn't done anything of the sort. I didn't get what all the fuss was, and this unfortunately came across in the sarcastic tone to which I responded to Shane's query.

"Uh . . . I guess I was makin' out with Jane."

I looked at Jane. She was frozen like a statue. A stone statue. Ha. Stone/stoned. Get it? Well, I did at the time. I started to laugh all by myself, which was the wrong reaction.

"You think this is funny?" asked Shane, his voice rising with a weird fury.

"Well, not *this* per se," I said, eager to explain. "You see, I was looking at Jane and thought that she was a statue and—"

But Shane was not interested in my baked musings.

"Jane is my *date*, Cameron."

Oh. My. God. Was he joking? He didn't look like he was joking. Was he, like, actually jealous that I made out with a girl? With his fake date?

"Oh, right," I said, with a straight face. "I forgot. Sorry. My bad."

Then I couldn't help it. I started laughing again. I mean, really . . . what other normal response could I have had to Shane telling me "Jane is my date"? C'mon, the whole thing was absurdly hysterical. My boyfriend was mad because I made out with his beard?

"Cam!"

That was Jane's warning yell, which unfortunately came about a half-second too late for me to dodge Shane's balled-up fist, which landed squarely on my cummerbund. Yep, Shane had slugged me. Not too pleased by my laughing reaction to what he took to be a grave situation, my boyfriend had given me a swift right hook to the gut. Well, if there was any clearer sign that maybe Shane didn't love me, I couldn't think of one at that moment.

# CHAPTER 11

"Shane!" screamed Jane as I doubled over from his punch, my knees collapsing to the parquet. "What are you doing!"

As I felt the unique burn of this blow, I realized that I had never been hit in the stomach before. Actually I'd never really been in a conventional fist fight since . . . well, never. I was not that kind of a kid growing up. If people didn't like me, I basically ran. I always thought this was a pretty reasonable approach. It had kept me out of trouble. Until prom night.

"He was making out with you, Jane!"

"No," said Jane, insistent. Defiant. Making trouble. "I was making out with him!"

In response, a general "ooh" rose up from the impromptu assembly of promgoers watching this tacky scene unfold. Jane's reversal, though highly clever, was a questionable tactic. But she had been in fights before and knew the right thing to say to really escalate matters. See Jane make things worse! See Shane's face turn beet red! Go Jane, go!

"Keep out of this, Jane! This is between me and Cam."

Well, at least he got *that* right.

Finally I was able to get up on one knee and get a better look at the whole situation. I noticed Ian and Co. standing behind Shane, looking like his very dangerous and bulky backup dancers in a bad production of *West Side Story.* Ian grabbed Shane's shoulder as if to say, *Good job, killer.* And then, at this moment, I glanced up at Shane. I must have looked pathetic—hair out of place, face pale, eyes blazing red from the weed. And it was then that Shane gave me The Look. You know, like in one of those heist movies . . . the look that says *Play along,* that the whole thing is a highly orchestrated ruse, that this so-called fight is actually all for show. A diversion. But what was he diverting people from? Then it hit me—*why* he'd hit me. The whole fight was a big lie. (Shocker, right?) Shane was trying to save face in front of his football friends so that they didn't think he was a wuss for letting some skinny retard take advantage of his date.

Struck by this revelation, I met Shane's conspiratorial look with a different look. My eyes narrowed, my heartbeat raced, my blood might as well have turned Incredible Hulk green as I totally lost it. You remember how I said before that I usually ran away from fights? Well, that finally changed.

"You fucking prick!"

And with that shocking exclamation I lunged at Shane, grabbed his right ankle, and yanked it skyward. This had the desired effect of sending him earthward with a resounding thump. Jane yelled my name in vain, trying to stop the insanity, but I was unstoppable. Shane had gone one lie too far, and it was my turn to escalate things. As I scurried across the slick floor to where he was lying, prone and stunned and rubbing the back of his head, which had met the parquet before his body did, I wound up my right arm as best as a nonfighter could for what would be my first retaliatory strike. I was about to let loose on Shane's adorable face when my arm stopped in midpunch. Someone had me, and I knew from the strong grip on my bicep it wasn't Jane. It was a man's grip. An older man. A wiser man.

"That's enough, gentlemen," said Mr. Mold as he grabbed my left arm with his other hand and pulled me up on my feet. "I think we need to have a little talk."

So as not to disturb the romance of the evening for the rest of the real couples, Mr. Mold removed Shane and I from the Willard's ballroom and led us to the men's room for our "little talk." After clearing out a couple guys taking a piss, he led Shane and me inside. Standing at separate sinks, Shane held an ice pack to the back of his head while I massaged my aching belly. Then, clearing his throat, Mr. Mold planted himself in front of us and asked us what the hell was going on.

"We got in a fight," said Shane, barely looking up from the smooth marbled floor.

"I can see that, Mr. Wilson. Not only am I a college graduate, but I also have a master's in education, which has enhanced my powers of elucidation so that I can discern when a physical altercation between two parties has taken place."

Just so you know, Mr. Mold always talked like this, sounding like he was giving a seminar on something other than the topic at hand. I guess that's what happens when you spend too much time in school, then end up back in another one, even if you are sorta in charge.

"My question to both of you," he continued, like a trial lawyer, "the said parties in this dispute, is simple and was previously stated—what the *hell* was going on in there?"

The real answer was that my boyfriend had been ignoring me all night in lieu of his jock posse so that he could reinforce his faux heterosexuality by doing shots with them at the hotel's bar utilizing his brother's ID, thus leaving me with his best girlfriend (that's *girl*friend, in the drag-queen sense of the word), whereupon out of sheer boredom we procured some marijuana, which made us incredibly stoned to the point where I was struck by the epiphany that Shane probably didn't love me because he'd lied about Beach Week, at which point my depression on this topic led to a desperate game of tongue hockey, partially out of said boredom but, I have to admit, partially out of a desire to, well, have some desire on my big lame night at the prom.

"I don't know," I said.

brian sloan

You see, this happens a lot. I'll say, like, a frigging novel in my head, but then when it comes time to speak, nothing really comes out. I have been told repeatedly that I need to work on my verbal skills. This has been a habitual problem throughout my education, as it was in the bathroom that night, trying to explain everything to Mr. Mold and then saying nothing.

"Well, Mr. Hayes," Mold continued haughtily. "I can see that your verbal skills are still somewhat underdeveloped."

See—I *told* you this had been a bit of a problem.

"He started it, so maybe you should ask *him*," I said, stupidly acceding to my boyfriend to fill in the blanks. A very bad idea.

"I can explain, Mr. Moldonati," said Shane a little too eagerly. Uh-oh. I knew this was going to happen, or at least suspected it: that Shane was going to give a fake cover-story version of what happened. And that's exactly what he did. Not that he was going to out-and-out lie. But still, there are definitely different levels of truth in life, as I was discovering this momentous evening. There were the actual events at hand, which Shane laid out somewhat honestly and objectively, but there were also the motives and rationales behind those events. When considering *that* bottom line, as Jane liked to say, the real reason Shane punched me was not to save Jane's honor or express some genteel notion of decorum in which one is supposed to be physically enraged when another man pecks at your date. No, no, no. You see, the reason my boyfriend had punched me was to make his friends think he was straight. The whole fight had been a ruse to reinforce Shane's faux heterosexuality in front of his jock-ass friends. But as he told his version of the event that had brought us to the bathroom, Shane had no intention of getting into this subterranean level of the truth. He was not going to dig that deep. No way.

As I stood there listening to Shane's retelling of events, which basically blamed the whole altercation on me, the above thoughts began to coalesce in my brain and a strange thing happened. I started to feel angry. Really angry. I mean, Shane-style angry. It was like this big lie of his about our big fake fight was the lie that finally broke my back, or at least broke my heart. As Shane continued talking, making up this whole madness to Mr. Mold of how he and Jane were soul mates or something and I had always been jealous of their relationship, blah, blah, blah, suddenly I couldn't take it anymore. In fact, I could barely stand looking at Shane as he lied and lied about the whole thing. So I turned away from him and found myself looking at myself in the bathroom mirror.

I didn't look so hot. I looked terrible; my face was flushed from the fight and my eyes were mottled pink from the pot, their cute green qualities totally obscured. Staring at my awful face in the mirror, it was like I experienced this disconnect, standing there looking at myself and not really recognizing myself. Okay—have you ever had one of those moments when you're at a party, feeling a little too drunk or stoned and you look in the bathroom mirror and are kinda like, *Hmmm, who the hell is that?* Well, that's what this was like, because staring into the mirror, I didn't see myself. What I saw was this dumb kid who was dating a cute, fast-talking, easy-lying, loser and even worse, not saying a goddamn thing about it. I was like, *Who was this lame-ass moron?*

When I realized with a certain amount of horror that it was me, Cameron Hayes, soon to be a high school graduate, I was shocked into action, because for the first time in my life, after years of looking into various mirrors and not really seeing anything of interest, I suddenly saw who I truly was and the tragic reality of my so-called life: that I was stuck in a bathroom on prom night, listening to my boyfriend of six months continue to lie about our relationship. And you know what? I wasn't going to stand for this sorta behavior anymore. *Cameron* wasn't going to stand for it. No one should friggin' stand for it!

"No one!"

"Pardon?" said Mr. Mold, regarding my newly energized face in the mirror. "Did you have something to add, Mr. Hayes?"

"Yes, Mr. Mold—" I said, catching myself quickly, "—donati. I'd like to tell you the truth. The *real* truth about what happened tonight."

Hearing this, Shane tensed up immediately, putting his angry face back on. The dreaded Pissed-Off Shane No. 7. *Oh shit*, I thought. Seeing his expression turn, I didn't know if I could really do this. If Shane had slugged me for a stupid indiscretion on the dance floor, then it was likely that he'd probably beat the living crap out of me if I completely spilled the beans about our covert love life. But you know what? *Screw it*, I thought. I was so damn tired of keeping the novel of our relationship in my head, having all these thoughts and feelings and no outlet for them, that I just couldn't keep it inside anymore.

"I did make out with Jane. But the real reason Shane punched me has nothing to do with jealousy."

Shane was now glaring at me, his dark brown eyes having gone black. Yeah—he was getting *that* worked up.

"Then why did you punch him, Mr. Wilson?" asked Mold, turning around to face Shane as he did his best *Law & Order* impersonation.

"Because . . . I was jealous," said Shane.

Ohmigod! *He is unbelievable,* I thought. *Unstoppable. Like the Terminator or something.*

"Mr. Moldonati—that's so *not* the truth."

Exasperated, Mr. Mold turned back to me and crossed his arms.

"Then what exactly are you getting at here, Mr. Hayes?"

"Shane is . . . Shane is lying."

Shane's back stiffened, his whole body tightening as his eyes spoke their own silent novel to me. And believe me, it wasn't a Harlequin romance.

"All right then, Mr. Hayes—what *is* the truth then?"

"Shane is . . . he's my boyfriend."

Well, I might as well have told Mr. Mold that I just burned the school down. He was *that* skeptical about the believability of my claim. In fact, his eyebrows just about met his receding hairline in their incredulity at my statement. Simply put, he was not buying it. At all. So I tried to explain a bit, to make this all seem less impossible.

"Okay, you see, Shane is only good friends with Jane and the real reason he punched me was because no one knows we're a couple and Shane was trying to keep it that way by pretending to be jealous of me, making out with Jane, thus punching me to make this point to his straight friends that he was straight too, you know?"

Again there was an awful silence. It looked like Shane would have strangled me if Mr. Mold hadn't been there. As for Mr. Mold, well, he looked like he wanted to be anywhere but stuck with us in the men's bathroom of the Willard hotel.

"Mr. Hayes," he said, sounding offended. "Do you honestly expect me to believe that what you're saying about you and Mr. Wilson is the truth?"

"Uh, yeah," I said, my voice wavering because suddenly my version of events was somehow suspect. "It is . . . the true truth. I swear."

It certainly didn't sound like it to Mr. Mold.

"I have to say I'm gravely disappointed in you, Mr. Hayes," he said, shaking his head mournfully. "To not take responsibility for your actions tonight but instead create some incredible fiction in a last-ditch attempt to avoid punishment. And then to go even further with a claim of homosexuality in a desperate move to gain sympathy for yourself in all this? It is *truly* beyond the pale."

I couldn't believe what I was hearing. Shane couldn't either, but Mr. Mold's nonbelieving take on all this was certainly making him breathe easier. I, however, was practically hyperventilating.

"But Mr. Moldonati, that *is* the truth. I swear to you that—"

"I don't have time for any more of your stories," he said, summarily cutting me off. "Now, though neither of you have acted as model Prep students tonight, it's clear to me this whole situation was precipitated by Mr. Hayes's actions in the first place."

"*My* actions?"

Ignoring me, Mr. Mold pointed a judgmental finger at me, and I knew I was doomed.

"Thus I will be phoning your parents to come and retrieve you from the Willard within the hour."

As if bad could not get worse.

"Isn't that a little . . . severe?" I asked.

"Not any more 'severe' than stealing a classmate's date at the senior prom."

"But that's not what happened, I—"

"Mr. Hayes, I told you that I'm not interested in any more of—"

At that moment, Mr. Mold was interrupted by the ringing of his cell. Removing the phone from his jacket pocket, he answered with great annoyance.

"Yes—"

As Mr. Mold listened to his phone, Shane flashed me a satisfied grin. The bastard.

"What?" said The Mold. "A dealer . . . selling pot . . . on the wait-staff? I'll be out in one minute."

Mr. Mold clicked off his phone and shook his head gravely.

"I have an emergency situation out in the ballroom," he said, heading towards the door. "You will both remain here while I deal with this other matter."

Then as he turned to leave, he made a final statement to no one in particular.

"Drug deals and fisticuffs—I utterly *long* for the days of kids spiking the punch."

# CHAPTER 12

Silence. After Mr. Mold exited the bathroom, that was all that was left between Shane and me, and it was the most terrible silence of my entire life; an insane and echo-like sound of dead air. I remember thinking that this is what it must sound like in outer space, terrifyingly empty and without hope, without life even. So what does one say when confronted by such a silence? I didn't know where to begin so I started small. Sarcastically small.

"Thanks."

Shane looked at me, his eyebrows jumping to attention as if to say, *It's not my fault.*

"What did you want me to do, Cam?"

"You could have told him I *wasn't* lying," I said, my long-suppressed anger rising within me. "You could have told him that we *were* boyfriends."

"Yeah," said Shane casually. Too casually. "Right."

"Yeah, right?" I said, amazed at his tone. I mean, it was one thing to deny that he was my boyfriend by omission. But then to respond to my statement about our relationship with that sort of dismissive line? C'mon—that was a huge, up-front betrayal. It was like Judas squared, you know?

"Mold wouldn't have believed me the same way he didn't believe you," Shane said, by way of justification.

"You don't know that."

"C'mon, Cam, it's Mr. Mold. Old Mr. Mold. He probably has trouble believing guys get past first base on prom night . . . with *girls!*"

"Still, you could've said something," I said pressing my case. "Stood up for me at least and not make me sound like I was a crazy person."

"Why should I stand up for you, huh?" he said, challenging me. "You've ruined this whole night—"

"Me?"

"Cam, you were macking on Jane like a maniac!"

"Only because I couldn't mack on you!"

"Oh, now there's nice reasoning," said Shane, throwing up his hands. "You *knew* that was not gonna be an option at the prom. That was a given, Cam!"

Then it came out. My sense of betrayal morphed into a more visceral response, and I let him have it.

"Fuck you, Shane."

Shane froze. It was as if I had finally connected with my *punchus interruptus* from the dance floor. And I wasn't even finished.

"Fuck you and fuck your lies and fuck everything. I mean . . . *fuck!*"

For the record, let me state here that I usually don't curse at all. Honest. So this run-on of expletives not deleted was a major shocker, not only to me but to Shane as well. Then add to that the fact that I was sorta telling him off for the first time ever; I mean, that was major. That had never happened before. Ever. Seeming winded, Shane reacted to all of this like I'd delivered a series of Tyson-strength body blows.

"What is wrong with—"

But I wouldn't let him finish. I was on a fucking roll, you know?

"There is nothing 'wrong' with me. The only thing 'wrong' with me is the fact that I've been in love with you for, like, the last six months."

Another blow. He was reeling. He tried to steady himself on the sink.

"Cam—I know you're upset about our fight and—"

"This is not about the punch or your lame attempt to make everyone think you're straight. This is about us and the fact that you don't love me. Period."

Okay, you know how Shane's deaf in his right ear? Well, for a while I thought this was cute and gave him character and almost made me feel bad for him, even though he had everything else in life going for him. But now that I think about it, there was also this symbolic thing that bothered me about his lack of hearing: Sometimes Shane just didn't seem to *hear* me. Seriously. He often ignored things I said, brushed my repeated concerns about our relationship aside, and was constantly telling me to stop worrying. But standing there in the bathroom, I realized that the real problem with our relationship was not that Shane couldn't hear me, it was more that I couldn't hear the nuance of what Shane was saying. Or in his case, not saying. He never, ever, not even once, said that he loved me.

Whenever we'd had previous tiffs on this issue of him not being demonstrative enough, Shane's response had always been that he was there for me and that that should be enough. But you know what? I finally realized that night that it was not enough, because saying it, saying that you care about someone, matters. It fucking matters! (Sorry, there I go again with the cursing.) The shocking reality of our relationship was that *I* was the truly deaf one all along, not even realizing what I wasn't hearing. It was like I was tone deaf to the fact that Shane didn't love me. Sure, he certainly liked me a ton, wanted me to be his pal/compatriot/co-conspirator and all that, but he didn't truly love me, wanting me to be his boyfriend/lover/soul mate for life.

"C'mon, Cam—don't say that."

"Why . . . because it's *true?*" I said, suddenly feeling my bitter oats. "You don't love me, Shane. Just admit it!"

"You know that's not—"

"Oh, no," I said, winding up for the knockout. "Well, I know it's true for the simple reason that you never say it. Never once have you said you love me. I mean, you can't even say that we're boyfriends. Not even to *me!* You just call me your 'special guy' which makes me sound like I'm a friggin' retard—"

"I thought you liked that."

Ugh—where he got *this* idea . . .

"I can't stand it! I make a face whenever you say it. But you don't notice. I don't think you notice anything sometimes. It's like you just want me around, trailing you like some faithful dog, and every now and then you'll throw me a biscuit with a pat on the head or a kiss or sex if I'm really lucky, and no one else is within a ten-mile radius. I'm sorry, that's not enough anymore . . . hell, it never was enough but I was too blinded by my own stupid feelings for you to realize it!"

Shane exhaled, trying not to get angry. It was a struggle.

"Okay, I know you're . . . upset about tonight, but high school is almost over. I've told you that once we get through all this it'll be a piece of—"

"Ohmigod . . . this is *not* about tonight, Shane," I said, utterly exhausted by him. "It's about *everything*. And it's *not* going to change when we get out of school. I know that because I heard about Beach Week from Jane. You told me we were staying at your parents', by ourselves!"

He looked caught on this matter and tried to downplay it.

"I'm only gonna be in OC a few nights."

"Oh, right—just like tonight and how you went to hang out with the whole football posse for a 'few minutes.'"

Shane ran his fingers through his hair, messing it up, frustrated by all these accusations that happened to be true.

"Cam, you act like this whole thing tonight is somehow *my* fault."

"*Is* your fault."

But I didn't say this. Nor did Shane. We both looked at each other, mystified by who the hell had just said this.

"Is *his* fault, not you," said Dmitri, peeking out at us over the top of the third stall. He'd been there the whole time.

"Who the hell are you?" asked Shane.

"Oh," I said, wondering if I should introduce him as my drug dealer. All right, maybe not *my* drug dealer. "Uh, this is the drug dealer. Dmitri."

"The drug dealer," said Shane flatly. Dmitri gave him a strange little salute. Then Shane looked back at me, back at Dmitri, and then to me again, as if he was watching a tennis match but couldn't quite figure out who had the ball.

"Uh . . . Jane and I bought some pot from him."

"Was a gift," added Dmitri.

"What!" said Shane, even more confused as we all entered the Surreal World.

"I forgot the money and he . . . uh, gifted us. But I owe him."

"S'okay," Dmitri said, smiling at me. Flirting with me? "Was gift."

"Wait a minute," said Shane, piecing it together. "You mean to tell me you've been *stoned* all this time?"

Shane's revelatory tone seemed to suggest that my drug use was the ultimate explanation for all that was going down; that my truthfulness with Mr. Mold, my indignation at Shane's betrayals, and my own revelation about the sorry state of our affair were all a direct result of getting high. Okay, now I'll admit that maybe being stoned helped me connect the dots on all this emotional stuff and probably reduced my inhibitions about doing so in such an un-me, confrontational manner. But I was not going to let Shane blame our disintegrating relationship on my being a bit baked.

"That's *not* what this is about, Shane," I said. "Besides, you're not exactly Joe Sober here tonight, having downed God knows how many shots at the hotel bar."

As Shane was about to reply to this accusation, Dmitri chimed in.

"So you are the boyfriend?"

"*You* know?" asked Shane, astounded, as he whipped his attention back to me. "He *knows* about us?"

"Well, uh . . . yeah."

"Jesus, Cam—you wanna tell the hotel manager too?" said Shane, his tone rising to new heights. "How 'bout the friggin' DJ so he can make an announcement to the whole class!"

"You are not such a nice boyfriend," said Dmitri, shaking his head, *tsk-tsk* style.

"Excuse me?"

"Freddie spoke very highly of you," continued Dmitri. "And you are like shit to him."

"Wait a minute—who the hell is Freddie?" said Shane, his face getting red again as he looked at me, newly furious. "Someone *else* you told about us?"

"I'm Freddie," I said, trying to explain.

Shane was dumfounded.

"How are you Freddie?"

"It's . . . uhm, it's my drug handle."

Before Shane could react to this tidbit of info, Dmitri interrupted things again.

"This relationship is not good," said Dmitri, pointing at Shane offhandedly, then addressing me. "He is not so nice."

"No one asked you, buddy," said Shane, practically yelling.

"I have idea," said Dmitri, jumping down from his perch on the toilet. "I must go and leave hotel because of your Mold. Too much trouble here. So I say, you come with me."

He meant me. Leaving with him. *Not a bad idea*, I thought. Shane, however, disagreed.

"What?" said Shane, his voice going through the roof. But Dmitri ignored him as he continued to lay out his plan to me.

"I'll save you from the troubles . . . get you out before your parents come."

Dmitri, the bisexual drug dealer. My savior. Who'd a thunk it, right?

"Oh, Jesus," said Shane, getting freaked out. "This is ridiculous!"

"Actually," I said, not nearly as freaked, "I kind of like it."

"But we need to go now," said Dmitri, coming out of the stall. "The Mold will be back . . . very soon."

"I can't believe you're actually considering this," said Shane to me, astounded.

"I know," said Dmitri, turning to me with an idea. A bunch of them. "We wear disguise to leave. I give you my uniform. You slip out and Mold won't know you. I wear your tux and my bosses won't know me. And then I meet you out front in my car. We go."

Okay—I know this all sounds crazy, but think about it from my perspective for just a second. At this point in the evening there were basically two scenarios on my horizon: I would either have to propagate the Shane lie about me stealing his date and be punished for that or I would have to be honest with my parents about my relationship with Shane and be punished for that. Frankly, both of these scenarios were equally unappealing to me at that point. It was total lose-lose, you know what I mean? On top of those specifics, things at the prom had gotten into such a state of insanity with Virginia and Jane and Shane that I just wanted out. So the only thing that seemed like a decent option was leaving via Dmitri and thus avoiding all repercussions and punishments, at least for a while. On balance, escaping from the prom sounded simple and easy and an ideal way to avoid my parents.

I whipped off my tux jacket and started unbuttoning my shirt.

"You're not really leaving?" said Shane, looking at me as if I were newly insane.

"Why not?"

"Good," said Dmitri, seeing my preparations for escape. He took off his belt and slipped out of his uniform trousers, tossing them to me. "Now, the pants may be tight. . . ."

"Wait a minute—you can't be honestly thinking about doing this, Cam."

"You have any better ideas?" I said, undoing my belt buckle.

"Mold is still gonna call your parents."

"Sure. But at least I won't have to see them when they get here."

"The jacket should fit," said Dmitri, slipping off the maroon coat.

"You're stoned," said Shane, trying to reason with me. "You don't know what you're doing!"

"C'mon, Shane, you sound like one of those antidrug commercials."

"I keep my shoes," said Dmitri, looking at my floppy feet. "Won't fit you."

"There might be serious consequences if you do this, Cam. Mold could get you suspended."

"Uh . . . school's over next week."

"You have cute legs," said Dmitri as I removed my tux pants.

"Really?" I said, charmed and surprised. I mean, I'd never gotten a compliment like this before. It was sorta sweet, you know?

Shane didn't think so.

"Hold on—you're *really* gonna leave here with some drug dealer pervert?"

"I am not pervert!" said Dmitri with much offense, ignoring being tagged with the drug dealer label.

As I slipped on Dmitri's jacket, Shane looked at me, resigned to my madness and future status as a fugitive from the prom.

"You're making a huge mistake, Cam. Massive."

"I have my car in garage," said Dmitri, planning.

"Not any more massive than going to the prom in the first place."

"That was cold," said Shane, wounded. Good.

"Oh—your phone," said Dmitri, fishing my cell out of my tux pants and tossing it to me. I slipped it into my new hotel pantspocket and was ready to go. Patting down my hair with some water, I checked my new look in the mirror. I was a hotel employee, all right. A very young one.

"This is crazy," said Shane to himself, giving up. "Truly and totally crazy!"

Sure. But not escaping really would have been way worse. Look at it from my perspective. You see, the source of all my insanity that evening was Shane, and I was finally leaving him behind. For a while, at least.

# CHAPTER 13

As I slipped out of the bathroom into the basement
hallway, the theme music to *MI:2* pounded in my head. *DUNT-dunt
. . . dada-DUNT-dun . . . dada. Diddlydooooo . . .* I looked left and
looked right and imagined myself a junior Tom Cruise as I snuck out
of the hotel in my clever disguise. (Ha.) Before taking off, though, I
spied Mr. Mold about forty feet away, heavily immersed in a conversation with the hotel manager over the whereabouts of Dmitri.
Scoping out the other end of the hall, I saw that the coast was clear
that way. *DUNT-dun . . . dada-DUNT-dun . . . dada.* My heart raced
to the beat of the song. *DUNT-dun . . . dada-DUNT-dun . . . dada.*
And taking a deep breath, I made my move.

Dmitri's uniform fit snugly, especially around the waist, making
me walk like a penguin. Still I was able to move fast, taking brisk
baby steps so as not to rip the tight poly-spun fabric and blow my
cover. I have to say, the one unexpected advantage of this hotel get-
up was that, as I passed by a full wall mirror, I noticed that the pants
made my ass look hot, which, when I wore real trousers that fit, was
generally not the case. The fact that I even noticed this under such
duress clearly meant one thing: As Shane had suspected, I was still
way high on pie.

Hugging the wall, I made my way up the stairs to the main lobby
of the Willard. Just before crossing the wide-open room, I spied a
few classmates milling about by the Chanel store. I ducked my head

so as not to be recognized and made my way toward the Pennsylvania Avenue entrance, keeping my head down and following the maroon lines woven into the fancy oriental carpet that lead to the front entrance. This method of navigation worked until I ran smack into some girl's backside. Raising my head, I was about to say "sorry" when my lips suffered total paralysis. It was Virginia.

She looked at me, bewildered, her face equally paralyzed too. After the night she'd had, her reflexes were—how can I put this?—somewhat dulled. However, I detected some murky thought of recognition forming in her brain, but I wasn't going to stick around for it to come to fruition. Before Virginia said anything, I made a ninety-degree turn and headed away from her, doubling the pace of my tiny steps. Just before spinning through the revolving door, I gave a quick glance over my shoulder and saw her standing under the antique clock at the center of the lobby, her new lopsided hairdo making her head list toward the east, as she wondered how on earth she knew a waiter at the Willard.

When I finally got outside, I inhaled deeply, taking in the fragrant, flowery June air. The night suddenly seemed fresh and new and filled with exciting possibilities. Standing there on the red carpet, I turned my back on the Willard, trying to forget "the troubles" (as Dmitri called them so succinctly) that I was leaving behind. With a simple and ludicrous act of deception, I had escaped my boyfriend, the prom, and high school in general. Amazing, right?

"Three bags in the trunk," said a deep, drawling voice. "Thank you."

To my side stood a couple of elderly tourists from the Deep South, as indicated by the ten syllables they'd managed to shoehorn into *thank you.*

"Oh, I'm not a—"

I tried to explain that my hotel uniform was a ruse, but before I could finish, the Stetson-wearing husband slapped a twenty in my palm and disappeared through the revolving door with his big-haired wife. Feeling a tinge of responsibility (easily traced to my fine moral education at Prep), I was about to seek out the source of their luggage when a squeal of tires diverted my attention. A silvery RX-7 was hooking a 180 out of the parking garage entrance and heading my way. This sleek blur-mobile came to a screeching stop at the curb, with Dmitri at the wheel fully sporting my James Bond tux, which looked perfect on him.

"Okay, Freddie—hop in!"

Forgetting my drug alias again, I suffered a split-second delay on hearing his command. This time, however, my delay was nearly fatal, as the Stetson cowboy ambled over, seeking his bags.

"Where's my goddamn luggage?"

Not wanting to be discovered as a fraud or an escapee, I took this as my cue to stuff his twenty into my pocket and jump into the passenger's seat of Dmitri's car, the RX screeching away from the scene of all my crimes.

"Hit it!" I said to Dmitri, feeling like some outlaw. Which I guess I was now, both in the eyes of Mr. Mold and Mr. Luggage.

"Hey," the tourist screamed. "Come back here!"

"Who was that?" asked Dmitri.

"Oh . . . some guy thought I was a bellhop."

"Happens to me all times," he said, glancing over with a warm smile.

Turning his attention to the road, Dmitri gunned the engine and shifted into fourth as we shot down Pennsylvania Avenue toward the glowing dome of the U.S. Capitol, heading God knows where. Wherever we were going, though, we were due to get there in record time. Dmitri drove like an astronaut—all thrust and no brakes, just highly tactical steering. The gray government buildings of the Federal Triangle swished by in a dizzying blur as we weaved in and out of traffic down America's Main Street. As the wind whipped my hair around, instantly I felt like I was free; free from my drunk date and the boring prom and lying old Shane and everything that everyone at Prep ever expected me to be. It was like I was living a manifestation of what Jane had been preaching earlier that night, about high school being this small, insignificant place when compared to the whole wide world that was out there. Suddenly, as I left my small existence behind, I not only had the whole night ahead of me, I possibly had my whole life too. And I had a cool hundred (and twenty!) bucks to get started with, which seemed like a fortune. I mean, there was a lot you could do with that if you were crafty. I thought I could maybe rent a cheap motel room in the Virginia suburbs, lying low for a while, or I could even skip town entirely, taking the cheap Chinatown bus to New York, leaving me with money to spare for a youth hostel up in Harlem. Or even more drastically, perhaps I could purchase a one-way train ticket out of Union Station and head West, all the way to California. Hell, I felt like I could do anything, you know? With the roar of the RX engine filling my head and the whoosh of the wind blowing past my ears, it was as if the whole damn world had exploded, shooting me out of it like a freakin' cannonball into the circus of life!

Did I mention I was still stoned?

"You look good in uniform," said Dmitri, bringing me back to reality a bit.

"Yeah? It feels a bit tight."

"Yes," he said, his glance shifting into leer category. "Uniform is sexy."

Whoa. So apparently Dmitri really did think I was hot. I have to admit, he looked hot too, even though he was bi. In fact, we both were kinda checking each other out when our cruisy bliss was interrupted by the dissonant honking of many horns. Angry honking. Turning to catch a glimpse of the intersection we'd just barreled through, I noticed we'd ignored a shining red light. Delicately I tapped Mr. Bond's shoulder.

"Hey, that was a red light."

"Oh yes."

Okay—not quite the response I was looking for.

"Aren't you worried about the police?" I said, trying to be heard over all the noise. "You know, breaking the *law*."

Okay, so I was too stoned to realize what a stupid question this was to ask a drug dealer. Anyway, Dmitri shrugged and drove even faster as I wondered aloud where we were headed.

"Back to my office," he said.

"I thought you worked at the hotel."

"My other office," he said with an air of mystery.

As the James Bond scenario seemed to get more real with this remark, I wondered if our next stop might be, oh, I don't know, maybe the counterintelligence division of the CIA in Langley. He was Russian after all. This type of destination seemed even more likely when, without warning, Dmitri threw us into a near tailspin of a right turn, rocketing us down into the tunnel that went under the Capitol and led to I-395, the main artery to Virginia.

"Are you really Russian?" I asked just as we entered the brightly lit, white tiled tunnel.

"Too many questions," he said, flicking on his Bose stereo. Turning up the volume to 11, he blasted some techno music as we burrowed under the Mall at a speed that I was too scared to take note of. Plastered to the back of my bucket seat with fear and something approaching 5 g's, we tore through the tunnel, my hair whipped up into a punk rocker's do. Noticing my terror, Dmitri stared at me again, looking at me slightly too long for someone who was supposedly driving. And then he let out a wild man's scream, something akin to what a cowboy might yell before battling an entire army of Indians in an old Western. I have to say it was almost hard to believe that this drug dealing, fast-'n'-furious driving, war-whooping dude was into guys at all. At least not what I understood that to mean in a high school gay-boy context. Let me put it this way: Dmitri probably didn't know what a drama department was. His life *was* drama. He didn't need to make the shit up, you know what I mean?

Which made me begin to wonder; was my life actually in danger from all this real drama? I began to fret that perhaps my escape, which had been his idea after all, was a setup of some sort. Maybe in actuality Dmitri was really an evil straight guy who was in charge of kidnapping me into some Eastern Bloc teen porn ring or something. Not that that would have been so bad . . . I mean, who hasn't wanted to be a porn star at some point in his young life? But Eastern Europe? That's kind of a long way from home. And the weather there is *really* supposed to suck. So I began to worry that being kidnapped, if that's what was happening, could be, you know, something of a drag.

Anyway, all these thoughts were swimming around in my buzzing head when outta nowhere, Dmitri leaned over and kissed me. On the lips. Taking his hands off the wheel too! I guess Russian driver's ed didn't cover the 10 and 2 wheel positions.

"Dmitri!" I said, nearly flipping out as he took hold of the wheel again, righting the car before its imminent collision with the tunnel wall.

"You no like kiss?"

Tough question. I tried to be honest for a change.

"Not while you're *driving!*"

Okay—so I let a drug dealer kiss me and partially enjoyed it. Though the kiss was abrupt and wholly unexpected, I have to admit I liked it—even though at that point, technically, I still had a boyfriend. I think the reason behind this (if there was reason behind any of this) is that the kiss reassured me that Dmitri was not a spy or porn pimp or an Eastern Bloc kidnapper. He was just a horny guy. A sexy, horny try-anything guy who seemed to fancy me and what the hell is wrong with that?

With a wicked grin, Dmitri turned the car's stereo up even louder and whooped again, the sound of his yell echoing off the tunnel. So what could I do except whoop along, which I did, even louder and longer than he had. This pleased him greatly, and you know what? I thought it was kind of a kick myself.

When we emerged from our subterranean joyride on the other side of Capitol Hill, Dmitri pulled another offensive-driving maneuver, this time abruptly altering our course off the freeway and onto

South Capitol Street. At least it was clear now that we would be staying in Washington and not crossing state lines to Virginia. Still, I was baffled by our ultimate destination. The area south of the Hill, known as Southeast, was something of the bastard stepchild of all D.C.'s neighborhoods; a hodge-podge of failed urban housing developments, old crumbling warehouses and burned-out residential blocks left over from the 1960s riots. I had never really been down to Southeast, my knowledge of the area limited to stories I'd read in the *Post* about failed plans to build a sports stadium there and an equally unsuccessful attempt to revive the Anacostia waterfront. Both of these projects went nowhere, because persistent homicides and drug busts plagued the area. Which made me wonder, with a shudder of concern, maybe *this* is what Dmitri meant by his "office"; that Southeast was his territory, as it were, his home base for sales.

Ignoring two more red lights, Dmitri made an alarming, S-like turn that took us off South Capitol, swooped us left onto M Street, then swerved us right onto the curiously named Half Street. I had never heard of this street before. All the grid streets downtown were either letters or numbers, not fractions. Finally Dmitri slowed to below 50 mph, due to the fact that Half Street received about half the maintenance of most normal streets, given the number of potholes disrupting the pavement. Looking for clues to our actual destination, I noticed an enormous Metrobus parking lot on our left and a Metrobus repair shop on our right. Yet as I discreetly checked out Dmitri's smooth hands on the steering wheel, it seemed unlikely he was a mechanic. His fingers were too thin, his hands too unmarred for that sort of "office" work.

As we continued down Half, the car slowing as it bounced from crater to crater, the street growing dimmer and dimmer, the light posts scarcer and scarcer so that after a couple blocks the only light was from the full moon, now perched high in a midnight blue sky. I glanced over at Dmitri, his skin nearly translucent in the moonlight. A chill ran up my spine as he downshifted, pulling the Mazda parallel to a rusting barbed wire fence and cutting the engine.

I looked around, curious as to where the hell we might be going. I could see zero options ahead of us, as Half Street dead-ended into a cement factory.

"Let's go, Freddie," said Dmitri.

Finally I tried to make it clear exactly who I was.

"It's Cameron, actually," I said, apologizing for my own name. "Freddie was my drug handle."

"No, Freddie is good name," said Dmitri. "Cameron is car."

"That's a Camaro," I said, trying to correct him.

"No, is good. You look like Freddie."

And I gave up.

"So where are we going exactly?"

"Secret."

"Uh, it's a secret?"

"No," he said shaking his head. "Secret."

"Wait a minute—are you saying you can't *tell* me?"

"No Freddie, lis-ten," he said, acting as if I was the one with ESL skills. "We go Secret."

I gave up on any further clarification, deciding to instead just follow him as he wandered off towards the gloomy cement factory. As we neared the end of Half, I saw that this pockmarked street wasn't exactly a dead end. Ahead on the right, blocked by a concrete mixing truck, was a bent traffic sign for O Street. Walking at a leisurely pace, we turned onto O, which was a little less desolate than Half. There were a number of parked cars on both sides of the street, an unnatural purple light cast over the middle of the block. The source of this odd glow was a lavender neon sign hanging over the entrance to a squat warehouse. Getting closer, the scripty neon spelled out what Dmitri had been telling me: SECRETS.

"Come," said Dmitri, beckoning me to catch up with him.

"What is this place?"

"Is Secret," he said obliquely. "You like."

"Yeah—I can *see* that," I said, feeling somewhat testy. "Is this . . . is it a gay bar?"

Okay, full disclosure time. I had never really been to a gay bar. Not that I hadn't wanted to go to one or anything. I mean, they seemed like they might be fun in theory—drunk gay guys dancing with each other and making out in public and all that. (Almost sounds like the average Prep party, minus the girls.) But in practice, me in a bar would have been so illegal.

"I'm only eighteen, Dmitri. I can't go into *any* bar."

"Is okay," he said, walking toward me and taking my hand. "You are with me."

Tugging gently on my arm, Dmitri succeeded in rooting me from my fixed position in the middle of O Street. So with hesitant steps I approached the black metal door of Secrets. It swung open, revealing the bouncer, a beast of a man with nearly inhuman proportions, both tall and wide. I mean, seriously, he probably weighed three me's. I tried to slip my arm from Dmitri's grasp but he held me tight, waving at the bouncer.

"Hello there, B," said Dmitri, in a cheery and overly friendly version of his Russian accent. I wondered, *Is the B for Bouncer?* "How are you?"

"Hey D—who's da kid?"

"A good friend," said Dmitri nonchalantly, as I tried to hide my shock at this description. Without even a cursory look, the bouncer let me pass, and I racked up yet another illegality for the evening. It's no wonder that the police caught up with me eventually. Yet I digress. First let me introduce you to the Wonderful World of Secrets.

So Secrets is basically a gay bar in that there is a bar with gay guys both behind and in front of it. But Secrets is so much more than this, which (surprise, surprise) Dmitri neglected to tell me. And wisely so, because if I had known I was entering the world of a gay strip club I probably would have demanded he return me to the prom. Not that I have anything against 90 percent naked guys in jocks or G-strings. But you know what? The sight of eight of them, shaking their wares up and down a running-light-rimmed "runway" is enough to give any gay teen newbie like myself a full-on heart attack. I mean, c'mon, doesn't the whole thing sound kind of overwhelming? If you're straight and need an analogy, take a moment to think about, I don't know, maybe a night at Hooters, except for the small fact that the girls aren't wearing any uniforms.

"Here," said Dmitri, handing me a dollar bill. "Which one you like?"

With a poke at my back, Dmitri pointed me in the direction of the T-shaped runway, with the intent that I stuff one of his bucks in one of these young bucks' white athletic socks. (As if!) Still, he insisted on pushing me forward toward the stage. Then as one of the dancers lingered in front of me, jiggling his package in a generally counter-clockwise direction, I felt something amazing. My pants started to vibrate. Honest. It was my cell phone.

"Where the hell are you?" asked Jane.

Having gone on a journey to the other side of Washington (in all senses of that phrase), I had practically forgotten about the prom and all I'd left behind; the fighting with Shane, the kissing with Jane, the burning of Virginia. Even though I'd only been away from the Willard for less than half an hour, the events of the prom seemed days in the past. A lot of that was the effect pot had on me, turning minutes into hours and stretching one evening into a timelessly fluid infinity. The pot also had a tendency to make distances seem all screwed up too. Thus standing at the lip of Secrets' racy runway, the prom seemed, oh, maybe about a zillion miles away.

"I'm at Secrets!" I said, trying to yell over the deafening thump of a disco song.

"What do you mean it's a secret?" said Jane, insulted. "I'm not going to tell Shane. We're not exactly talking to each other right now."

"No—no, I'm *at* Secrets . . . this bar down in Southeast."

There was a pause in the conversation as Jane lowered her voice.

"Cam—are you at a *gay* bar?"

"Well," I said, regaining some of my sense of humor. "With a name like Secrets, it ain't a sports bar."

# CHAPTER 14

According to Jane's recap, it appeared my escape from the prom had caused surprisingly little stir. This shouldn't have shocked me too much considering I made a stealthy exit in disguise (if not a terribly clever one), and also since the only one who really might have truly cared about my absence (other than the Mold) was not so fond of me anymore. I did expect, though, that Mr. Mold would have been more upset about my disappearance on the verge of his disciplinary action, but according to Jane, his attention had been sidetracked by the search for the drug dealer who was rumored to be sparking up seniors all over the joint.

Still, given what Mold had said before my exit, I wondered where I stood on the crime-and-punishment front.

"Do you know if he called my parents?"

"Cam, I'm not exactly friends with the Moldmeister."

Though I had my dad's emergency money to keep me far and away from the homestead for a while, the more I thought about my runaway scenario, the less likely it seemed I was actually going to be hitting the road and heading out West or anything rash like that. Ultimately my final destination was going to be Silver Spring. The question was, Would it be sooner or later?

"I'm just wondering if it's safe for me to go home."

"That's a relative statement," said Jane, extra dry. "Pun intended."

"Not funny," I said, sounding a bit down.

"C'mon, Cam, your folks are going to find out about what happened at the prom eventually. You might was well go home and break it to them in person, because no one wants to hear their son is gay from the Vice Principal of Academic Affairs."

"But Mold didn't believe me!"

"Cam," she said in a tone that sounded like my mom on a rare bad day. "You know what I mean."

By this point the prom was starting to wind down, and Jane told me their next destination was going to be the after-party down by the Lincoln Memorial, the one Virginia had been talking about earlier. Shane had already called the limo and told the girls to meet him in front of the Willard at a quarter to one.

"So you *are* talking to him!" I accused.

"We are conveying travel plans," said Jane, denying the accusation. "I would not say that we are talking in the conventional sense of the word."

I asked her this because I was beginning to wonder if Shane and I had officially broken up. I mean, we'd definitely had a major fight that actually led to blows, or at least one real and one intended. But we'd had fights before, a bunch of times. The difference was that I had never really walked out on him in the middle of one. Usually our fights ended with Shane saying he was sorry and me accepting his apology, thus restoring our status quo as the happy, top secret gay couple. But the prom fight had been different. I mean, seriously, *no* one apologized. That was way different. I asked Jane what she thought.

"Sounds to me like a major separation that could lead to divorce," she said in her future litigator voice. "If it does, you should *definitely* get the house."

Again very not-funny.

"Jane, this is severe."

"I know," she said, sympathetic again. "If you want my real opinion, I think it'll all work out in the end—or at least by tomorrow. You know how Shane gets angry and then it always passes. Like one of those late-afternoon summer thunderstorms."

"But I don't know if this storm is gonna pass for *me*," I said, surprised by the resonance of my newfound anger at Shane, namely over his betrayal in the bathroom.

"Wow," said Jane, a bit taken aback by my tone. "That *does* sound severe."

After promising to check in with her in an hour, I looked around to discover that Dmitri was gone. Totally disappeared. So there I was, all by my lonesome, sitting on a rickety bar stool with two strippers approaching from opposite ends of the bar. I caught the eye of the bartender, a husky bear type with a silver beard, and gave him my best low-key look of panic. He lumbered over to me and leaned on the counter.

"You lookin' for D?" he asked in a raspy smoker's voice tinged with a streetwise accent. Apparently, it was required that everyone working at a gay strip club had to be related to the Sopranos.

I nodded.

"He went back to his office to get some work done."

"Really?" I said, shocked that he actually *had* an office.

"You think I'm lyin' to you," said the bartender in a way that was half menacing and half playful. I didn't bother to figure out which half was which.

"No. Uh, no sir."

"Good," he said sauntering over toward me. "He did tell me to get you a drink. What'll it be?"

I ordered a Coke, not wishing to break any more laws for the evening. Sitting there by myself, I decided that I would keep to myself. Let me tell you, this was not easy. When you're a teenager sitting by yourself and wearing a way-too-tight waiter's uniform at a gay strip bar, you tend to draw attention. So in less than a minute, one of the strippers was hovering above me. Again I looked to Tony Soprano's uncle for help.

"If you give 'em a tip, they'll leave you alone, kid," offered the bartender.

Realizing I still had Dmitri's dollar bill in my left hand, I slipped it into the beefy dancer's sock without even looking up at him. Sure enough, his tan, muscled legs sauntered down the bar, seeking more attentive customers. A few minutes later, however, there was another pair of socks straddling my soda. Unfortunately I was plum out of petty cash, my dad's Benjamin tucked into my tux, which Dmitri was still wearing in his "office" somewhere. Then I remembered the tip I'd accidentally received back at the Willard. I have to say, there was a twisted yet divine irony that this elderly Texan's twenty was going to end up as part of some male stripper's booty. Deliciously pleased by this fact, I stuffed the crumpled bill into the dude's right sock in hopes he would move along. Yet this time my tip had the opposite effect, as the dancer crouched down right in front of me.

With his privates bunched into a glittery gold spandex pouch at eye level, this go-go gay just sat there, bouncing on his thighs and smiling at me. Unlike most of the dancers at Secrets, who were muscle freaks with enormous shaved heads and bulbous arms the size of my waist, this guy who'd stopped in front of me was refreshingly funky-looking. He was über-skinny, with a build only slightly taller than mine but not any more filled out. He had a rosy, open face with pinkish skin, his face topped off by a shock of blond hair, most of it sticking skyward. With earrings in both ears, pirate style, and a sparkling stud glamming up the left side of his nose, he had some bad-boy bling-bling going on too. If it wasn't for his lack of clothes, you might mistake him for the bassist in a glam-rock band with a name that would make your parents freak. Maybe something like, I don't know, Glitter Ass?

Anyway, as he bumped and ground away to a Cher song, I decided that a simple hello might be in order. He didn't say anything back, however. He just nodded, his smile growing bigger and more intent. It was a blinding, Cheshire cat grin, with two matching movie-star creases that framed it beautifully. Wow. I tried again to say hi, this time speaking louder to be heard over the din of the Cher.

Still nothing. Then I tried a more conversational "What's up?" which also fell flat. Finally, instead of getting a response from the dancer, the bartender replied for him.

"Hey, kid—he can't hear you."

"I know," I said. "Can you turn Cher down?"

The bartender looked at me like I had asked him to concoct a Sex on the Beach or something. Then I realized why. As the dancer recognized someone entering the bar, he started signing to the new patron.

"Buck is deaf, kid. He can't hear the music or a goddamn word you're saying."

*Okay—wait a minute*, I thought. *A deaf go-go boy? Who's giving me the full-on flirt? Named Buck? Someone is definitely not in Kansas anymore.*

Buck turned to the bartender with a flurry of signing.

"He wants to know your name," said the bartender. "Says you're cute."

Feeling an overwhelming surge of honesty and, I admit it, curious attraction to this deaf stripper, I offered my real name. The bartender passed on a signed translation of Cameron, which seemed to please Buck and, I have to say, looked kinda pretty from a nonsigners perspective, like he was mimicking a bouquet of flowers. Then I asked the bartender if the me-being-cute thing was why this dancer was still parked in front of me. He signed and Buck signed back as the music blasted away, and I was struck by this thought: Being deaf is a major advantage in a nightclub, because you never have a problem hearing what your friends are saying.

"Sure," said the bartender in response to my question. "That and the fact that you tipped him a twenty."

"He could see that?" I said, amazed that Buck discerned the bill's denomination from his height.

"He's deaf, kid, not blind," said the bartender with no humor at all. "Any pro knows the denomination going down into his sock."

With this Buck turned his full, smiley attention back toward me, and my stomach did a dance of its own on the bar. Whoa. This Buck was kind of a babe, you know? But what is it with me and gay guys with hearing problems, right? Are you sensing a theme? Well, to be honest, I can see that in hindsight. But at the time, sitting at the bar, the real theme going on was the mutual attraction we both seemed to be feeling toward each other. I mean, c'mon . . . when that sorta lightning strikes, what can you do except get fried, right?

Standing up again, Buck placed his right hand on the top of my head and mussed up my already disheveled hair. Then he started talking again in midair, the bartender kindly translating.

"He wants to know if you're an amateur."

"A . . . a what?" I said, confused.

Then the bartender pointed to a sign by the door advertising an Amateur Strip Contest later that night. Buck continued signing, the bartender interpreting.

"He says you'd be a cinch to win," said the bartender. I glanced at Buck and he threw me the high beams. Damn! "Personally I don't agree with Buck, but that's what he said."

"Tell him I'm not here for the contest," I said. Not by a long shot. My God—could you imagine? Please. If I was a contestant in something like that, it would be more like people tipping me to put my clothes back on! "But thanks for the compliment anyway."

I glanced up at Buck, and looking right back at me, he made some more noise with his hands.

"He says he'll come back on his break."

"Uh—cool," I said, beaming back. "Can you tell him that's cool?"

The bartender shook his head ruefully, my goofy expression needing no translation at all.

So I sat there, sipping my Coke and discreetly following Buck with my eyes as he did his rounds. After hopping off the far end of the bar, he crossed the room with a stylish skip and jumped onto the tacky runway that ran down the center of Secrets. Whereas most of the go-go guys had walked up and down this blinking platform, breaking stride only when greenbacks presented themselves along the way, they were all generally oblivious to the incessant disco thump. Buck, however, actually danced. And I mean Danced. He had this whole choreographed routine, a *Flashdance*-meets-*Fame* thing, where he grooved to the beat and catapulted himself back and forth down the runway, commanding it like it was his own personal stage and he was its singular star.

My favorite part of Buck's set came at the end. There were a bunch of full-length mirrors lining the wall at the back of the runway where the dancers would strike these lame poses, as if they were modeling underwear for Hecht's. It was totally unexciting because you could tell they were just into themselves, you know, checking out how hot they thought they looked in the multiple mirrors. However, when Buck got back there, it was crazy! He threw his whole body onto the mirrors, splaying out his limbs like he was being arrested by an invisible cop. Then he rolled himself back and forth across his reflection (front side, back side, repeat) about three or four times in each direction. Finally, with his barely covered ass facing the bar, he put his hands on the mirror and started doing these standing push-ups, swaying his butt to the beat at the same time. I looked down the bar to see how this was going over and all I could see was a line of male jaws scraping the floor, eyes wide with wonder, as they followed Buck's gyrations, back and forth, like the eyes on a tacky kitty-cat clock that you'd see in the dentist's office. Well, at least *my* dentist's office.

When the song ended there was some wild applause for Buck, most of it from me I admit. Jumping off the stage, Buck trotted over to me and proceeded to sit right on my lap, as he threw some signs the bartender's way.

"Coming up," he said, responding to Buck's silent drink order. I had to wonder, though . . . was the bartender also alluding to the future condition of my lap with Buck in it? Yikes.

"You're amazing," I said to Buck, meaning in general but with the intention of complimenting his moves. "Your dancing was just . . . I mean, wow."

"Thank you," said Buck, speaking. Speaking? My look of shock was so damn retarded that the bartender swooped in to save me from my totally mortified self.

"Relax, kid," he said, placing a glass of OJ on the bar for Buck. "He can read lips a little when he's not working, and can speak some too. Like that chick who won the Oscar."

"Marlee Matlin," offered Buck. "Gorgeous."

I didn't know if he meant me or this Marlee chick. I figured the latter, as I'm probably cute on a good day, not gorgeous.

"But you are very cute," he said, confirming my suspicions as he played with my hair again. All right, I have a weakness that I can admit; it's whenever someone starts messing with my mad mass of generally unruly hair. I know it sounds silly, but secretly I love it. In fact, Shane used to do this all the time, saying how he was amazed at how thick it was, even after a haircut.

"Thanks," I said, turning to my translator. "How do I sign *beautiful*?"

The bartender gave me a sour look.

"Jesus Christ, kid," he said leaning toward me. "Why don't you just kiss him instead?"

Well, the thought had crossed my mind. It's like, hell, here was this sexy go-go guy who'd literally fallen into my lap. I mean, c'mon, it seemed like the logical thing to do, right? But at the same time, I started thinking about Shane. The big question was, Should I truly feel guilty for being attracted to Buck? According to Jane, Shane and I were at least separated, so given that I figured I was technically clear on the cheating factor.

"Yeah," said Buck, concurring with the barkeep in his uncertain, lip-reading voice. "Just kiss me."

And when he put it like this, what could I say? Honestly, it was all somewhat hard to resist. So repositioning him in my lap, I was about to make contact with Buck's luscious cherry lips when there was an abrupt change in the music. The pounding disco-dance beat segued harshly into the Whitney Houston version of the "Star Spangled

Banner." You know, that cheesy histrionic one from the first Iraq war? It seemed a curious choice in a place like Secrets. I wondered if it was being used as the intro to some naked-dancer sporting event, like mud wrestling or maybe even boxing. Buck's response to the music indicated that was not the case.

"Shit," said Buck, jumping off my lap as if it was on fire. For the record, it was. But that was not the reason for his jump.

"What's going on?" I asked.

"Police raid," said the bartender as a couple of the younger-looking dancers hopped off the stage and shuffled out a swinging door in the back. "How old are you, kid?"

Giving him my age, the bartender freaked, hustling both Buck and I toward the swinging metal door in the back.

"Get your butts to Dmitri's office and get the hell outta here!"

# CHAPTER 15

So this is where my prom night transitioned from being a racy John Hughes movie to something more like a dangerous Quentin Tarantino movie. I mean, for a while it was all cute PG-13 fun, but the minute the D.C. police were on my tail, I was in R territory. Jail was only a few steps behind and closing fast. Hell, I was probably just hours from NC-17-land with some hideously unthinkable prison scene in my narratively doomed future. At the time, I tried to keep those Oz-like thoughts out of my mind and focus on the positive, namely the fact that we were running from the police and hadn't been caught. Yet.

"Where are we going?" I yelled to Buck, who had taken me by the hand and was leading me through a labyrinth of locker rooms, dank hallways, half-stairways, and empty storerooms. After asking him about our destination a couple times, I finally realized that Buck couldn't hear me and/or read my lips, as I was behind him, huffing and puffing and trying to keep up with his panicked pace.

Finally we came to a scarred door, dim gray light leaking through the crack at the bottom. The home office, I presumed. Shoving the door open with his shoulder, Buck busted us into the room and, sure enough, there was Dmitri, sitting at a computer and smoking a cigar. He was now wearing some jeans and a wife beater, my tux mysteriously absent.

"Hi Buck," said Dmitri with a nod. "What's—"

136

Before he could finish, Buck started signing, positioning his right hand over his left armpit and forming his fingers into something resembling a talking sock puppet.

"The cops?"

Apparently an imaginary sock puppet is sign language for the police. Which made me wonder . . . did the police know about this?

"So this is your office?" I said, wanting to change the topic and pretend for a minute that the police weren't on our tail. (Have you got that I'm into denial a lot?) Actually, despite all the hustling and running the threat of the police didn't seem that imminent. It felt more like a rumor of a hurricane before all the wind shows up.

"I make the IDs," said Dmitri, distracted by thoughts of escape. "Was making you one."

"Cool," I said, distracted by thoughts of how industrious this Dmitri was; hotel waiter, drug dealer, ID forger. This all helped explain two things: the fancy car he drove, which was far above a waitperson's salary, and the fact that he'd left me alone at the bar. Dmitri was actually looking out for my underage welfare. "Can I see it?"

But I didn't get an answer as Buck did some more sock-puppet signing, this time impatiently.

"We must go now," he said, flicking off the computer monitor.

"Can't we stay here and just wait?" I suggested, totally out of breath. "Lock the door and hit the light and hide out or something."

"No—we wait, we fuck."

That sounded pretty good to me! (Okay, kidding!) But that was not exactly what he meant. I tried to clarify.

"Dmitri, do you mean, we're *fucked*?"

But there was no time for proper English or correct verb tenses. Dmitri killed the light and we slipped back out into the foreboding hallway, heading down another long, dim corridor. After a short sprint, we arrived at a scary-looking wooden freight elevator. Dmitri grabbed two frayed leather straps, pulled apart the elevator doors and pushed Buck on board. I, however, remained in the hallway, holding my ground.

"Wait a minute. Exactly *where* are we going?"

"You want arrest?" he said, annoyed with my questions. Grabbing me brusquely by the arm, he yanked me into the elevator.

"But what about my tux?" I wondered as he pulled the freight doors closed and shifted the elevator into gear manually. With a mechanical thud we lurched downward.

"In locker room," he said. "We get later."

As the freight elevator descended, accompanied by eerie sounds of cables stretched too thin and rusty gears clanking too loudly, I turned to Buck with some trepidation. At this point my demeanor was morphing from that of mellow stoner-dude to something more like freaked-out horror-movie victim, you know? My expression was like something you'd sport midloop on an inversion coaster at King's Dominion, except, of course, this elevator was no ride. It was not even a highly realistic Xbox game rated "M for Mature." This was real and live and merely the first leg in one criminal's hastily arranged escape, in which I was, of course, a full accomplice.

Sensing my newfound mortal fear, Buck reached out and took my hand. His grasp was strong and warm and kept my heart rate under 150. Then as Buck flashed me his blinding grin on top of that, my pulse dropped some more. (Ah, the calming effects of a gay stripper . . . there should be a study or something.) It was at that moment that I thought, *Hey, maybe this is love. Or is it fear? Or maybe they are one and the same?* All right, hear me out for a sec. I thought this crazy thought because, honestly, it was sometimes how I felt around Shane, this intense mixture of love and fear. Hell, that was the basic yin and yang of our secretive affair; love of him and fear that we'd be found out. But as much as I cared about Shane, some of that fear was actually *of* him as well: his judgment on whether or not I was acting "too gay," his quicksilver temperament that could turn on a penny, his unpredictable outbursts over stupid things like us leaving the yearbook office at the same time. As if there were paparazzi outside or something!

Basically that had been life with Shane and thinking about it all in that groaning elevator, something hit me: Love and fear are really *not* a cute combination. You know what I mean? They are *not* one and the same, an intertwined emotion, or at least they shouldn't be. They are separate and should be kept that way. That was my break-through, accomplished by the hold of a stripper. It's like, at least with Buck, the love and the fear I felt were happening at the same moment, but definitely they were coming from wholly separate sources; my nascent love of Buck and my fear of dying in an indus-trial accident while escaping the cops. I mean, realizing that love and fear didn't have to be intertwined . . . for me that was huge!

With a resonant thud as the elevator hit bottom, my love for Buck transitioned back to fear. Dmitri threw open the doors and we found ourselves outside somehow, on a street that was wholly unfamiliar to me. Not that I really knew my way around Southeast, but still I had expected us to emerge onto Half or O Street. But this street was neither.

"Where the hell—"

But Dmitri had no patience with me or my questions. With an index finger to his lips, he silently motioned for Buck and me to follow him. I remember thinking that were a stranger to come upon us, we would have been quite a sight: the stripper in his glitter thong, the prom drop-out in a hotel waiter's uniform, and a shady Russian all trying to evade the D.C. police.

So with soft steps and hushed voices, we crept down this mystery street, burned-out row houses on one side of us, monolithic ware-houses on the other. Ahead of us I saw a fence with barbed wire that looked familiar. It was Half Street. It was such a relief to know where we were that it almost felt like home. Almost. Peering down Half, we could see a flurry of red, white, and blue police lights spinning and flashing and reflecting off the side of Dmitri's RX-7, parked about fifty feet away from us.

Dmitri assessed our situation.

"We fuck."

Well, you didn't have to be a criminal genius to figure that out. Still Dmitri's phrasing could have used some work.

"You mean fucked, Dmitri. We're *fucked*," I said, trying to be helpful with his grammar. Dmitri just glared at me. "Maybe we should go back to your office?"

"No, they search building."

As the three of us huddled behind the corner of a rusty warehouse, Buck signed something to Dmitri, who responded with some more broken English.

"Maybe—I know before—but with you—"

The suspense was killing me.

"Uh . . . what are you talking about?"

"Buck says . . . and I agree," said Dmitri, giving me a quick glance. "I think we go."

"Go where?"

"Car."

Given the car's proximity to the constellation of police lights shining down on Half, this seemed like a bad idea. I'll even go out on a limb here and say that this was probably the worst idea ever! And I was about to say as much when Dmitri exploded into a sprint, making a diagonal dash across Half toward his vehicle. Remarkably he made it to the car in five seconds flat, and whipping out his key ring flicked on the remote lock and lights, causing the the car's alarm to bleep. Of course, that was enough to get the cops' attention, and instantaneously the scream of sirens shattered the night.

"Now, we are *really* fucked," I said to Buck's back. He couldn't hear me but it didn't matter. I mean, we were sitting ducks, standing ones actually, hanging out on a corner where no eighteen-year-olds doing anything legal would ever be found at nearly 1:00 A.M. on a Friday night. And then add to that the fact that Buck was wearing his glitter panties. With my money in his sock. It was fairly obvious what both of us had been up to, and it wasn't studying for finals. I mean, given the circumstances, the arc of my prom night was headed toward the toilet with touchdown likely in the jailhouse crapper. As images of my bleary-eyed mug shot flashed in my brain, I realized that it was "Game Over" time.

Dmitri, however, taking no heed of the sirens or showing any fear of the law for that matter, revved up the RX and threw the car into reverse. Shooting backward across Half Street and coming to a smoking stop, the car arrived in front of Buck and me.

"We go," said Dmitri, flinging the car door open. "Now!"

Without warning, Buck dove into the front seat, and with my hand still surgically attached to his, I followed quickly behind, landing in *his* lap for a little role reversal. Though the door was still wide open, it didn't stop Dmitri from pumping the accelerator and getting us the hell outta Dodge. Spewing a spray of gravel and dirt in the direction of two fuzz-mobiles coming up on our rear, he peeled out again, heading down Half in the opposite direction.

Now, to be honest and all, this is the part where I sorta screamed. "Ahhhhhhhhh!"

I know, what a big girl, right? Well, in my defense, let me see you try to keep your shit in line when you're speeding away from the cops at twenty, thirty, forty-plus miles an hour, your hands barely gripping the roof of a tricked-out sports car as you try to keep your ass from falling onto the pavement that's rushing by inches away through the open passenger's side door. C'mon, I know I'm gay and a sissy and all that, but cut me some slack here, okay?

My scream was relatively short-lived, however, as Buck's lap started vibrating. It was my phone again. As we raced away from Secrets, the whine of Dmitri's engine rising and falling with each new gear shift, Buck slipped my cell out of my back pocket and handed it to me. Looking at the caller ID window, I caught my breath as the screen read simply, MOM & DAD.

So did I ever tell you how I have seriously bad phone karma? I've had this for many years, missing calls at home by seconds and calling back only to miss the caller by seconds. Anyway, this sort of bad telecommunications timing only logically increased when I got my cell junior year. (See "the time my parents rang while I was in midst of dark passions in Shane's bedroom.") But with this call in Dmitri's car I had reached the pinnacle of bad karma timing, as my parents decided to buzz me during the opening minute of my first ever high-speed police chase.

Given Mr. Mold's disciplinary promise earlier that night, I knew my folks weren't calling just to say hi. So needless to say, I didn't answer the phone. However, sensing that this would be the first of many calls from them, each one growing increasingly frantic and angry as the evening wore on, I realized I had to do something about my cell. Something that was seemingly illogical, but really the only reasonable solution given the fact that I had no intention of answering their calls. I mean, what was I gonna say? "Hi, Mom. I'm in the middle of a hot pursuit with a stripper and his dealer, so I'm probably gonna be a little late"? You get the point. So with the pavement still rushing by through the open door, I released my tentative grasp on my vibrating Nokia. After bouncing off the car door, it hit the black street and skittered into oblivion.

"Can you do something about the door?" I yelled over the rush of the wind, the door handle out of my reach.

Nodding and checking the rearview, Dmitri made a hard left onto M Street and the door did its action-reaction thing, swinging to a slamming close and missing my fingers by about a millisecond. After nearly losing all my digits, that was the moment when my high from Dmitri's pot officially ended. I mean, it was gone so instantly. It was as if someone had flicked a switch, turning a nice warm light off. Or more accurately, someone (namely, the District Police) had whacked that light with a hammer, shattering it into a billion pieces. Yeah, I'd have to say that being chased by the law really is *that* much of a downer.

C'mon, you've seen *Cops* . . . you know the deal when they're after some bad boys. Well, as a regular viewer of the show, here are your basic options when the real cops come for you: a) you're going to run like hell, and then b) you will inevitably get your ass caught. On *Cops*, though, the pursuit is always seen from Officer Friendly's perspective, which means that you're rooting for them to get the bad guys. But believe me, it's a wildly different perspective when you are trying to get away from the police, knowing damn well from count-less *Cops* re-runs that they are gonna get you. It's just a matter of time and maybe a commercial break. That's when you come to the horrific realization that you have somehow ended up on the wrong side. That *you* are the bad guy. That's when you start to ask yourself, Hmph . . . now, how the hell did *that* happen?

Thinking about all this, I was instantly sober and way too alert to all the flashing cars fast encroaching on our tail. Dmitri, however, seemed undeterred by our desperate situation and gunned the engine even more, the speedometer pushing sixty. Approaching South Capitol, we plunged down into an underpass, leaving my heart somewhere above sea level. Emerging from the underpass, I checked out the chase action in the side-view mirror. There were two D.C. police cars in full, blazing pursuit, and as the Mazda's mirror advertised, these objects were already way closer than they appeared.

"Hang on," said Dmitri as we banged a right through a McDonald's parking lot, nearly taking out a light pole. Soon enough, Johnny Law duplicated our turn with disarming ease, leading me to the conclusion that if this was an escape, it really wasn't going so well. That was when Dmitri took severe action. As we continued tearing through the Southeast warehouse district, the streets getting less paved and much less lit, Dmitri hit the lights. That is, he turned ours off.

"What are you *doing?*" I screamed.

"I see this on TV," he said, to my astonishment.

Well, yeah, dude, I used to watch *Dukes of Hazzard* reruns too, but that was, you know, fake. Like TV has a tendency to be! However, this nuance of American television was completely lost on Dmitri.

"Hang on," he said, this time really meaning it as Dmitri exe-cuted a series of rapid ninety-degree turns on and off various side streets, zigzagging his car through the deserted neighborhood. On the first of these maneuvers, my lips kissed the passenger's-side window, and then on the second, I was nearly tossed off Buck's lap and into Dmitri's. After the fifth of these harsh turns, Dmitri's strategy was clear: He was literally trying to shake the cops.

"This is a bad idea," I said, my voice tremulous with reason. "Not good, Dmitri! Bad!"

"I know streets," he said with assurance as we made another screeching hairpin turn. "Is good."

My stomach was feeling quite the opposite of good as we careened through another intersection, despite the protests of a red light. But amazingly enough, all these wild turns were somewhat effective. After a few minutes of extreme maneuvers I could still hear the sirens in the distance but we had lost a visual on the cops. After another couple minutes even the sirens were beginning to fade out in the distance. Stunned that this insanity had actually worked, I looked over at Dmitri, and he returned my disbelief with a wry, Bond-like grin.

"Is good, huh?" he said, his stolid face breaking a smile. "No jail tonight!"

He said this as if it was the exception to the rule of his average night out. But I couldn't complain. All I can say is that I'm glad I caught him on a good night.

Exhausted by the tension of our chase, all my muscles finally able to relax, I collapsed back into Buck, my human bucket seat. Without a word or a sign or anything, Buck wrapped his arms around my waist and sensing my fatigue, held me tight. It was a simple gesture really, nothing terribly sexy or insanely romantic. But it was done without prompting and without prescience. And that was . . . something unique. Feeling Buck's casual hold as we raced through the city, going God knows where at God knows what illegal speed, it struck me that this was something that Shane had never done. He'd never touched me at all out in the world, the only shared intimacies occurring in dark bedrooms or locked closets. So to feel the touch of another guy, even someone I barely knew, holding me in the midst of the real world of cars changing lanes (if a little too fast) and buildings buzzing past (if a little too blurry) was like . . .

wow. It was, I dunno, so real and simple and, well, simply heaven not having to hide from someone's affection, you know?

"We go celebrate," offered Dmitri. "Back to my place."

"Uh, I think we need to get my tux first," I reminded him.

"Oh, no—cannot return to crime," he said with authority on the matter. "Always not good."

"Really, Dmitri. I need to go get it," I said, meaning not only the tux but also my dad's cash, which was still tucked away in the front pocket. "Where will I stay tonight without my money?"

Buck held me tighter. Was this a silent answer to my question? Unlikely, but a guy can dream . . . .

"You stay with me," offered Dmitri.

Though spending the night with a fugitive seemed like an outrageously bad idea, I realized that I didn't really have any other options. My parents' car was still parked at Shane's house with the keys in it. Still, I couldn't exactly take their car anywhere, as I'd surely be tracked down via an APB and other police actions. Also I couldn't get a motel room without my dad's one hundred bucks. And of course, I couldn't really call my parents (phone or not) because they were going to ground me for the rest of my life or, at the least, the entire summer before I headed off to school.

"Where do you live anyway?" I said, resigned.

"Dale City."

"Virginia?"

"Is not so far."

And with this Dmitri executed a series of sharp turns and he had us racing up a steep highway ramp, rocketing us into orbit on the Southeast Freeway. Instantly I tensed up again as Dmitri drove with renewed purpose. Though we weren't running from anyone, it didn't keep him from driving like Anakin Skywalker in the race for his life.

After a couple exits we veered off the highway, sped past the Jefferson Memorial, and whipped around the serene waters of the Tidal Basin at not-so-serene speeds that were double the posted limit. This did not seem wise given the fact that we probably wouldn't want to attract any more attention from the law. But I kept my mouth shut, knowing that my safe-driving tips would likely be ignored. Zipping past the Lincoln Memorial and dipping under the grand arches of Memorial Bridge, we were on our way toward I-66, the freeway that would lead us out to the wilds of Virginia, when Dmitri's halogens revealed something alarming in the road. It was a blur of red and it wasn't a car. It was a person. Someone whose back was toward us as we raced toward them at, oh, seventy miles an hour. Now it was Dmitri's turn to scream.

"Arrrrrrrrgggggghhhhhhh!"

Jamming the wheel hard to the right in a last-ditch attempt to avoid a vehicular homicide, the RX spun off the road. Buck's grip on my waist tightened like a safety seat belt as the Mazda tore into the slick grass, the rear tires catching up with the front, and so on, and so on, sending us into two full revolutions before our circular spin-out came to a sudden halt. Fortunately we had not hit anything, which made it something of a mystery why we'd come to such a quick dead stop. Maybe, I thought, we were actually dead. But then I felt Buck squirm underneath me, and Dmitri, letting out a sigh, once again assessed the situation in his typically perceptive way.

"Fuck," he said, his tense correctly deployed. "Everyone okay?"

"Yeah, I think so," I said, making sure that my limbs were all present and accounted for. Then I looked out the front windshield and saw what appeared to be a gigantic spider's web.

"What the *hell* is that?"

To answer this question, Dmitri unclicked his seat belt and got out of the car. I followed his lead, and jumping out of Buck's lap, my foot hit the not-so-solid ground on which we were stopped, sinking a few inches into a dense white sand. Backing up a bit, I saw that Dmitri's car had spun off the road and into one of the volleyball pits just north of the Lincoln. The spinning tracks of the RX's tires were dark reliefs in the dewy grass, a peculiar pattern that looked like infinity on acid that led toward the sandy pit, which had stopped the car cold. Talk about good luck, right? Well, yes and no.

"We are fucked," said Dmitri, getting the tense right for the second time in a row. "Look at wheels."

Sure enough, all four tires were embedded deep into the sand, the left front wheel bent at a discordant angle that would not facilitate any future forward motion. Which is to say, his car truly was fucked.

"Are you trying to kill me?"

But this was not Dmitri speaking. A woman's voice—an oddly familiar woman's voice—had interrupted our damage assessment.

"My father could sue you, asshole! What's your name?"

An electric shock buzzed down my spine as I realized I knew this voice very well.

"Virginia?"

"Cameron?" she said, looking me up and down and trying to get a fix on where she'd seen me before in my hotel outfit. Standing there, hands on her hips, she was still wearing her red velvet prom dress, which had survived most of the night's trauma. In general she was more alive and perky and not so stinking drunk anymore. Virginia's new hair even looked better. One thing that hadn't changed, however, was Virginia's distaste for me.

"Look, Hayes," she said in her inimitable tone. "I know you don't *like* me and all, but isn't trying to run me over a little . . . uh, psychotic?"

"You know her?" said Dmitri, utterly mystified.

"Yeah—this is my date," I said.

"I thought Shane is date."

"So this guy knows *too!*" said Virginia, getting worked up again. "Who the hell are you?"

"Hello, I am Dmitri," he said, as if greeting aliens from another planet.

The offering of his name wasn't enough for a confused Virginia, so I filled in the blanks.

"He's the pot guy . . . from the prom," I said, as Virginia tried to take this in. Then I tried something of an apology. "So I'm, uh, sorry I left the dance and all."

"Don't be sorry," she said curtly. "It was the best thing that's happened to me tonight."

"Okay," I said, trying not to get mad at her since I really had no right to. I deserved her hatred. I had, in fact, earned it. So as a counterpoint, I tried to lighten the mood. "Well, nice running into you again. Literally."

Ignoring my lame attempt at levity, Virginia took note of Buck, who had emerged from the car and was signing in our general direction. Ignoring the fact that he was deaf, Virginia instead focused on Buck's glittery package. Then her head cocked to the side, her face beautifully blank, she regarded me with a pure, baffled silence.

"Uh . . . that's Buck," I said to explain. "He's a go-go guy."

Virginia blinked once. Twice. And gave up on us.

"Ohhhh-kaaay," she said dropping her hands to her side. "Nice meeting y'all, but I'm gonna head back to the party."

"Party?" said Dmitri, intrigued.

"Yeah. There's a prom after-party over in Constitution Gardens. I was using the ladies' at the Lincoln."

"The restroom is open this late?" I wondered.

"I had to use the bushes."

"You peed in the bushes of the Lincoln Memorial?" I said, offended for Abe and the sanctity of all national monuments in general. Not happy to be judged in this manner, Virginia glared at me, her eyes narrowing into a squint.

"This from a fag who tried to mow me down in a Russian pimp-mobile."

Dmitri laughed. "I am no pimp," he said casually, turning to address me. "She is funny."

"Not really," I said, annoyed by my date's continuing insistence on using the f-word.

"So where is party?" said Dmitri, taking a few steps toward Virginia.

"Wait a minute—this ain't some fag party," she said harshly.

"Virginia," I said, bristling.

"Party is a party," said Dmitri in his best philosopher-king tone. "Maybe your friends like to smoke the pot?"

You see, Dmitri wasn't interested in the party at all. He simply saw it as a business opportunity. I, however, saw only a chance for further humiliation by returning to the now-mobile prom a) without my tux and wearing a hotel uniform, b) with both my dates severely angry at me, and c) with a deaf stripper in tow. Buck signed to Dmitri and Dmitri signed back, seeming to indicate that they'd made up their minds to check out the party anyway. I interjected vocally. "Uh, what about the car? And going out to Virginia?"

"What?" said Virginia, hearing her name as she studied Dmitri.

"Not you—"

"Look, don't be talking about me behind my back, Hayes."

*Oh, good God,* I thought. *When will my torture end?*

"I was just saying—"

Then Dmitri interrupted me with the verdict. "This car is not good," said Dmitri. "It is stuck and so are we."

As for me, what can I say? I was stuck and, as Dmitri might say, totally fuck. "So," said Dmitri in a grand, theatrical voice. "Let's go party!"

# CHAPTER 16

North of the Reflecting Pool, tucked away amid
an oval of landscaped hills and knolls that hide it from Constitution
Avenue, is this really cute pond. Constitution Pond? I don't know if
that's exactly what it's called, but this kidney-shaped, man-made
body of water is located at the center of an area called Constitution
Gardens, so it's a reasonable guess, right? Anyway, the whole joint is
a surprisingly intimate little park in the middle of the monumental
Washington Mall. Most people don't even notice it, as they tend to
focus on the big tourist magnets that surround it on all sides: the
Vietnam Memorial to the west, the Washington Monument to the
east, the White House to the north. Also most folks who live in D.C.
and never do anything touristy have probably never even heard of it.
In fact, it was this quality that probably led to it being chosen as the
location for the wholly unauthorized Prep postprom party.

Our motley crew arrived at this outlaw party around 1:30. There
were about ten guys splashing around in the pond under an
immense ceiling of sky, the stark white shaft of the Washington
Monument the only thing visible on the downtown horizon. As we
got closer to the edge of the pond, I noticed a bunch of tiny black
and white piles of tuxes, which indicated that the guys were skinny-
dipping. Their female dates, however, were not joining them in this
racy endeavor. They were Potomac girls after all. By way of explanation, these are the kind of girls who go to the beach and don't even

go in the ocean, preferring instead to laze about on the sand, reading *Marie Claire* and painting their nails. So the skinny-dippers' dates were sitting on a gently sloping grassy hillside in their now incongruous gowns, smoking Parliaments and gossiping like mad. And that's exactly where I found Jane.

"Ohmigod," she said, jumping up to greet me. "*What* are you wearing?"

Jane took hold of my hotel uniform sleeve with its martial buttons and gold-braided cuffs.

"My escape outfit."

A couple of Jane's pals popped up from their perches, having heard rumors of my escape and wanting to get the full dish. Apparently my fight with Shane and ensuing flight from the prom had become something of a legend in the couple hours since it had happened. So with Jane's prompting, I regaled the girls with my tale of high-speed adventure and derring-do through the mean streets of Southeast. As I did, Dmitri worked the other half of the party, trying to sell his weedy wares to everyone who wasn't listening to me. Unfortunately he only had a couple takers, as most of the girls were not big stoners. Again these were Potomac girls, and the term *smokin'* usually referred to some sort of ultralight cigarette. They all had scruples and good breeding. Except, that is, for Jane.

"So, is *that* one of the Secrets strippers?" she asked breathlessly, pointing to Buck who was following Dmitri around like a loyal Labrador.

"Oh yeah," I said. And in a stroke of good timing, Buck glanced in my direction and gave me some sign that looked like it meant "rock on" but actually meant "I love you." He'd taught me this one at Secrets moments before the police arrived.

"Ohmigod, Cam—he is totally hot!" said Jane, not so discreetly checking him out. All of him. "What a bod!"

"Yeah. And he's also pretty much deaf."

"Perfect," said Jane with aplomb. "He never speaks—the ideal man!"

"Jane," I said, correcting her misassumptions about the hearing-challenged in the same tone the bartender had corrected mine. "He's not dumb, just deaf. He can speak and read lips and all that stuff. Like that chick who won the Oscar."

"Charlize Theron is deaf?"

Now, in her defense, I think Jane was still baked from our Dmitri weed at the dance. So I ignored her absurd question and focused on more relevant celebrities.

"So . . . is Shane here too?"

In a case of bad timing, it was at this moment that Shane emerged over the top of the opposite knoll, zipping up his fly after having relieved himself.

"Ask and ye shall receive," said Jane in a weird, mystical tone.

Yeah, she was definitely still stoned.

"Great," I said, stopped in my tracks. As was Shane. We regarded each other warily across what might as well have been an impassable ocean of grass. After a minute of this stalemate, Shane raised his right hand and motioned like a traffic cop for me to come over to where he stood, somewhat removed from the gaggle of girls on the hillside. Though I should have known better, you know, like giving him the finger and walking away or something rash like that, I didn't do anything of the sort. I just started heading toward him. It was force of relationship habit, I guess. When Shane beckoned, I came running. Or at least walking briskly.

As I neared him, Shane's dark eyes zeroed in on my own. Ducking my head toward the ground, I stopped a few feet short of what might be normal conversational distance. Then after a pleasant moment's silence, he spoke quietly but firmly.

"Have you lost your mind?"

"Uh, I don't think so," I said with a sarcasm that surprised even me. Having outfoxed the District Police, I was feeling bold. "Why?"

"Oh, I don't know," said Shane, matching my sarcasm to a T. "Maybe leaving the prom with a drug dealer—"

"Mold kicked me out, so I left."

"And then going to some seedy gay strip club."

"It wasn't *that* seedy," I said, trying to lessen my adventures. No dice.

"But it was a bar. You're not even twenty-one . . . barely eighteen!"

"I know how old I am, thanks."

"Cameron, you could get arrested for that."

"Oh yeah," I said pointing toward the pond and his frolicking friends. "Like skinny dipping in Constitution Gardens is *so* legal!"

Shane tried to get his rising anger in check so as not to make a scene. "This party was Ian's idea," he said coolly. "And I am *not* in the water, if you didn't notice."

Oh, I noticed all right. Metaphorically, Shane was never in the water, if you know what I mean. And I told him as much.

"Don't get all metaphoric on me, Cam," he said, wholly annoyed by this literary tact. "This is some serious shit. The things you've done tonight and the things you said to me earlier. That was so totally out of line."

"Why?" I said, challenging him in a way I never had before. "Because I actually *said* something and told you what I really felt?"

"Because what you were saying to me, about me . . . what you were going on about in the bathroom . . . it's not true."

To translate, this was Shane referring in his atypically indirect way to my statement that he didn't love me. But I was not going to let him allude to something this important. I needed to know, out loud, exactly what he meant. "What, Shane? *What's* not true?"

"You know what I mean," he said, searching the expansive sky for words that worked, things he could manage to say about this guy in front of him who, granted, did love him in some strangely dysfunctional way but simply wanted to hear that, somehow, despite everything, it had not all been in vain. But Shane didn't find anything to say, really. He just turned his attention to his friends horsing around in the pond, nervously checking to see if they were watching us.

"You know what," I said, newly annoyed by his paranoia. "I better go before your friends think we're having some sort of lover's spat."

Then Shane fixed on me again, his eyes somewhat hurt. In a voice that was strangely vulnerable, he spoke. "What happened to you, Cameron?"

"I don't know," I said with an exasperated sigh, unable to sum up in one hundred words or less all the things I was feeling and suddenly understanding that night. "But if the same thing doesn't happen to you sometime soon, I don't see how we can keep this going."

Shane looked stunned, wondering if I meant what I seemed to be saying.

"Do you mean—"

"Are we breaking up?" I offered. "I don't know, Shane. It's a tough question, really. I mean, according to what you said to Mr. Mold, we were never a couple in the first place."

That stung. For me, that is. Maybe it stung for Shane too. But I honestly don't think he ever really saw us as a couple, whereas I actually did. Suddenly by saying this, I'd blown apart my own illusion of our great love. Unintentionally I'd totally harshed on myself. Damn . . . talk about irony. As my eyes started to feel teary, Shane tried one last defense.

"Just because I didn't say something about us to Mold—"

"Not just him," I said, trying to keep it together. "You never said anything to *me* about us. Not once."

He started explaining something, but I had no more time. Literally. I was about to burst forth with a major, full-scale emotional breakdown.

"Cam— I— Wait!"

Turning on my heel, not intending to be dramatic but more to keep Shane from seeing the water welling in the corners of my eyes, I started speed walking away from him, not exactly sure where I was going. As I passed by the edge of the pond, a spray of water crossed my path as some of Ian's pals tried to douse me. I ignored it, though, and kept on walking. Then I heard Jane's voice yelling out my name from the girl's hillside, and still I didn't turn around. Giving her a backhanded wave, I merely yelled back one simple word.

"Peeing!"

At this point I picked up my pace, as tears started spilling down my face and streaking across my cheeks, my breath getting short and quick. My face was becoming a wet mess, crisscrossed with the tracks of tears and snot and saliva. (I mean, if I'd had makeup on it would have been totally destroyed!) So given my disastrous condition, I kept on walking as fast as I could, out of the Garden and over a low rise of hills. As I started choking on my own breath, my shoulders shaking with sorrow, I thought that maybe I would just keep on going, booking it out of the city, across Memorial Bridge, through Virginia, into Kentucky, Missouri, etc., until I got all the way to California. Apparently that's where all the gays go when they come out, the twin Meccas of San Francisco and Los Angeles, and at that moment, getting that far away from my problems sounded like a great idea. Even the sound of those Left Coast cities held promise, a sort of cool, vowel-filled hope that the hard consonants of official-sounding Washington didn't seem to offer.

As I continued stumbling under the dark boughs of the oaks, I saw a glint of white ahead of me. The shadows of the trees subsided as I reached the edge of the Reflecting Pool, its smooth, mirrorlike surface reflecting the rays of an achingly full moon. It was like one of those perfect scenes from a tourist postcard, the Lincoln Memorial at the far end of the pool casting its Taj-like reflection onto the water. All this perfect scenery only served to make me cry even more, because it was so damn beautiful that I thought I should have been standing there and sharing it with my boyfriend, holding hands like a couple of romantic goofballs or playing footsie in the water with our pants legs rolled up or simply making out like a couple of horny teenagers on a moonlit June night. But I was doing none of this. I was just standing there all by myself, taking in the whole tragically picturesque scene and losing it like a champ.

As I continued to sob, the whole of my life began to seem

incredibly hopeless. That's when I thought of, you know, ending it all. The Big S. Never having learned how to swim, I imagined I would toss myself very dramatically into the waters of the Reflecting Pool and that would be that. A monumental suicide. I'd probably make the front page of the *Post*! Okay, I know this all sounds a little crazy and everything. But, c'mon, I think I'd earned the right to some insanity given what was going on that night. I mean, my boyfriend wouldn't even admit that we were a couple or in love or anything. If that's not enough to make a person consider the worthlessness of it all, then I don't know what is.

So as all this was spinning around in my head, I thought about how I might pull off the Big S. Then moving closer to the granite edge of the pool, trying to judge the murky depths of the water before taking the final plunge, something quite unexpected happened. Wearing a pair of very slick rental dress shoes with no-traction soles, I slipped on the edge of the smooth stone and, losing my balance, fell into the water butt first. *Kerrrplassssshh!* Feeling the creepy chill of black water on all sides of me, I did what any normal nonswimmer might do: I panicked. I was thrashing my arms around, kicking my feet like a maniac, trying to figure a way out of my lame suicide attempt when suddenly there was an enormous explosion of water right next to me. *KERRRRPLASSSSHH!* A second later I felt something lock around my chest in a manner that made it impossible to breathe. I wondered if this was some lost Loch Ness Monster, or an even more misplaced intergalactic beast from *Star Wars,* like that slimy thing from the trash compactor in Episode 4. Yet instead of this thing pulling me under, as evil, inhuman beasts tend to do, it tugged me back toward shore, extricated me from the water, and tossed me like a caught fish onto solid ground.

Lying on my back I opened my eyes and could make out the form, sure enough, of a beast of some sort hovering over me. But with the moon looming behind its enormously round head, thus creating a blindingly appropriate halo effect, I couldn't quite tell what or maybe who this thing was. I wondered, *Could it be Shane?*

156

Had he saved me from self-inflicted death? Would this serve as the glue that could repair our busted relationship?

Well, not exactly.

"You okay, Hayes?"

The beast was Ian, Shane's best friend. His massive body was dripping wet as he wore nothing but a pair of drooping boxers that were in danger of revealing a true watery monster. Yikes!

"I . . . I can't," I sputtered, coughing up water.

"Can you breathe?" he asked with real concern as he crouched down next to me. Then placing his meaty hand under my neck, he propped me up slightly, preparing to give me mouth to mouth. Granted, my breathing was not great and my lungs could've definitely used a jump-start, but holding up my right hand, I declined Ian's mouth. You see, I'd already made out with one of Shane's friends, so smacking lips with his best friend, even if the reasons were semi-medical, seemed ill-advised.

"No," I said barely. "I'm good. Thanks."

"Damn, Hayes, you scared me there," he said exhaling deeply, as if his breathing had been affected by all the drama as well.

"Wow," I said, amazed to realize that Ian had saved my life. "I could've drowned."

Ian laughed as I said this. Not the response I'd expected, you know?

"Unlikely, Chief," he said. "The Reflecting Pool is only a couple feet deep."

"It . . . it is?" I said, feeling like I'd been fighting the Atlantic in my struggle to save myself.

"I'm guessing you're not a big swimmer."

"Um," I said, averting my gaze. "Not so much."

"I lifeguard summers in the city," added Ian. "I get at least two of your type a month, losing their shit in the shallow end."

Ian stood and offering me his hand, reeled me up too swiftly, not realizing how little I weighed. Dizzy from the rush, I tilted into his chest and grabbed his arm to keep from falling back in the water again.

"Whoa," he said, misreading my lack of balance. "You're trashed, Hayes."

"I wish," I said plainly. "So what were you doing over here anyway?"

"Got bored of swimming naked with a bunch of guys."

One man's hell is another man's heaven, right?

"But, uh, what about your girlfriend?"

"Who—Caroline?" he said, sorta surprised. "It's not a big thing with her. At all. We're just friends and shit."

Friends and shit? Yep, that definitely did not have the ring of high romance.

"Anyway, she was fine . . . getting baked and hanging out with that Russian drug dude."

"Uh-oh," I said.

"What . . . is that bad?"

"Uh . . . it could be," I said, not wanting to get into the bisexual details of it all.

"Well, maybe we should head back to the party then," suggested Ian. "Also, Shane was wondering where you went off to."

And with the simple mention of his name, it all came back. Instantly. The tears, the snot, the shaking. It took one word and the dam was broken for the second time that evening. Except this time, I was doing it while holding on to Ian.

"Shit, dude," said Ian, freaking. "What is *up?*"

"Nothing. Everything. Never mind." More crying. More shaking. More Ian getting freaked.

"Can't be *that* bad?" he said, as I continued to bawl. "Uh, can it?"

And then I made my seventy-third mistake of the evening. For those of you keeping count. "It's Shane," I said.

"Oh—you mean that fight?" he said, referring to our Jane-joust on the dance floor. "Don't sweat it. It was a heat-of-the-moment thing and all. Besides, we were all sorta smashed by that point— Shane did something like four shots of Jagermeister in the cigar bar."

Seventy-four. Calling mistake number seventy-four . . .

"No, you don't understand," I said, sniffling. "He doesn't love me." More sobbing and shivering. At this point, Ian was starting to pull away some.

"What . . . uh . . . whattya mean?"

And finally number 75.

"I think we're breaking up. Shane and I."

Ian looked at me not unlike Mr. Mold had in the bathroom. You know, serious skepticism. But seeing my condition, my total and unabashed unraveling, Ian was somewhat more inclined to believe me. I mean, what moron would lose it willingly in front of another guy . . . *over* another guy? Basically, I was so publicly pathetic that it *had* to be true, right?

"Whoa," he said, troubled. "You guys are *gay*? Like Will and Grace?"

"More like Will and Will."

Even when losing it, I can manage to get off a good one, huh?

"Whoa," he said. "That is, uh . . . man, that's some serious shit."

Despite Ian's harsh language, it was hard to get a handle on how he was taking all this. He was shocked, certainly, but appalled? Yes, but not exactly in the way I'd expected.

"Man, I can't believe Shane never told me about this."

"He didn't tell anyone," I said, between sniffles. "He was scared. I was scared too."

"Still, I thought Shane and I were tight," said Ian, sounding slightly wounded. "I thought we told each other everything."

Suddenly I realized I was treading on the solemn ground of their friendship. Even though it was sorta too late, as I had already trespassed, as it were, I tried to backtrack. "I shouldn't be talking about this," I said, realizing that I was now blowing Ian's world apart as well as my own. If I continued blabbing at this rate, Ian would soon be feeling the need for the Big S, too, though he'd definitely have to seek out the deeper waters of the Potomac.

"I'm not supposed to say anything about it," I continued. "It's a secret . . . was a secret. Shit. Can you forget I said anything . . . okay?"

"Uh—that's gonna be, like, impossible, dude," said Ian before going back into an uncharacteristic contemplative mode. "I can't believe Shane didn't say anything to me. Shit."

"He was probably scared what you'd think," I said, now trying to console Ian. Crazy, right?

"Oh yeah," he said. "Well, you know what I think?"

I was a bit nervous to hear the answer to this question.

"Uh . . . what?"

"I think Shane's a dick for not even telling me in the first place." Shaking his head back and forth as if to forget a bad dream, Ian sat down to take this all in. I joined him.

"No wonder he's been acting so weird tonight," said Ian.

"Yeah," I said ruefully. "That's the understatement of the new millennium."

So then Ian and I sat down on the edge of the Reflecting Pool, bonding over what an asshole Shane was for being such a liar to both of us. Strange, huh? I mean, he'd known Shane since freshman year, so the gay revelation was really hitting him hard. Not that Shane had really been hiding it that long from Ian, but still; hiding it at all was what seemed to get him. Which only made me wonder how incredibly disappointed my parents would be when they found out the true reasons behind my eviction from the prom. I'd known them for a little longer than four years.

After processing the Shane info, Ian turned to me to figure out the rest.

"So then . . . you and Virginia—"

"Sorta hate each other."

"Really?" he said, apparently finding it impossible to hate someone as bodacious as Virginia.

"Well, it didn't start out that way," I said, explaining Shane's whole double-date scenario. And you know what? Saying this scheme out loud to another person made me realize how truly misguided that plan was.

"Ohhhh," said Ian, getting it. "So you and Virginia really aren't a couple or anything?"

Ian seemed strangely more interested in this question than he should have been.

"No. Definitely not."

"Wow, man," he said, visions of her breasts dancing in his head. "She's hot."

"She looks good, I guess," I said, unable to deny Virginia's outward attraction.

"So . . . you like guys," he said, still ruminating on the issue. "And Virginia's available."

But before I could play matchmaker, our chat was interrupted by the not-so-distant whoop of a police siren. Then another.

"Not again," I said, my stomach tightening.

Standing up, we both could see intermittent flashes of blue and red in the vicinity of Constitution Gardens.

"Looks like the party's over," said Ian. "I hope Caroline isn't too zonked to run from the cops."

In the distance I could hear the panicked pitter-patter of seniors running for their lives. I took this as a strong hint for us to leave as well.

"I suggest we get out of here. Fast."

"But my tux," said Ian, looking down at his drenched boxers. "It's over by the pond."

"Forget it," I said, putting a hand on his shoulder. "I've managed without mine for a couple hours."

Then with the resigned air of a professional con on the lam, I took charge of our escape.

"All right, dude. Where's your limo?"

# CHAPTER 17

It was a suspiciously long line of limos parked on Constitution Avenue that tipped off the police to the outlaw party going on in the park. Fortunately Ian had been savvy enough to have his driver park on Independence Avenue, way on the opposite side of the Lincoln Memorial. So heading away from the police action, Ian and I took off, heading up the side of the Reflecting Pool as fast as we could. He was in a running crouch as I tried to keep up with a spastic skipping gait, given the snug nature of my pants. Again the *MI:2* theme music started pounding in my head. *DUNT-dun* . . . *dada-DUNT-dun* . . . *dada. Diddlydooooo.* Except this time it wasn't only in my head.

"Are . . . are you . . . humming?" said Ian, curiously out of breath for a jock.

"Sorry."

"*MI:2?*"

I nodded sheepishly, and Ian cracked up.

Approaching the front of the Lincoln, I glanced up at old Abe, who sat on his marble throne, looking down on us with indignation. I mean, Abe had seen a lot in his time, but had he ever seen a skinny gay guy in a wet hotel uniform and a massive football player in plaid boxers streaking across his front yard? Unlikely.

As we passed the Memorial, I noticed that our sprint was having one fortunate effect; my outfit was drying. But in the unfortunate category, it was also beginning to shrink, the already tight fit on my legs and butt getting even snugger. So much so that I was in danger of pulling a Hulk-like move that, if successful, would leave me in an outfit not unlike Ian's.

Just as I was starting to feel out of breath myself, I caught sight of Ian's limo idling on the opposite side of Independence. After crossing the empty avenue Ian slammed on the driver's-side window of the stretch, waking the chauffeur from a nice nap. The auto locks clicked up and we both hopped inside, nearly falling on top of each other as we scrambled into the backseat. Then Ian slapped his meaty paw on a green button next to the window, barking into the intercom.

"Get us the fuck outta here!"

There was a pause. The car didn't move an inch. A calm, drowsy voice crackled back.

"Where the 'fuck' are we going?" posited the sleepy driver.

Seeing Ian without his tux, I was reminded of my own.

"I know," I said, leaning over Ian toward the speaker. "Take us to Half and O Streets, Southeast. . . . and *step on it!*"

What can I say? I'd always wanted to say that and I just couldn't resist! Surprisingly, the driver responded to the urgency of my order as the limo lurched from the curb, made a squealing 180, and sped off into West Potomac Park. Driving away from the lights and sirens converged on Constitution Gardens, we were finally safe. Looking out the window, I stared at the placid waters of the Potomac, trying to lull my heart back into a state of non-cardiac arrest. Meanwhile, Ian reached for his own type of calm, opening the minibar and popping a Bud. After a gulping silence and a refreshing burp, Ian wondered aloud what was to be found at the corner of Half and O.

"Secrets."

"It's a secret?" he said, fairly irritated by my answer. "Christ, Hayes, I think I've had enough secrets for one night."

"No, it's the name of this bar where the drug dealer who was wearing my tux took me, and then he changed into another outfit and we had to leave it there when the police came and—"

"Wait a sec," he interrupted, not so interested in my complicated adventures. "Is this place a *gay* bar?"

I thought about using the sports bar line that I'd played with Jane, but thought it might not be so funny to someone who actually liked sports.

"Uh, yeah," I said.

Ian's eyes sorta bugged out at this point.

"You're taking us to a fag bar?"

"Okay—wait a damn minute," I said, fiercely annoyed by the umpteenth use of this derogation that night. "Can you *please* not use that word?"

"What—*fag?*"

"Yes, fag!" I screamed in response, my voice heading for the heavens as I geared up for a rant. "Your best friend is one, I'm one, and using that term to describe us is . . . it's *incredibly* offensive!"

Ian was a little taken aback.

"All right. Chill, dude."

"*NO,* I'm not gonna *chill,*" I said, getting even more worked up. "It's like, do you want people sitting around calling you a fat ass to your face! Or a friggin' two-ton tub o'lard? Or maybe a goddamn walking bucket of blubber!"

The instant I said this was the instant I regretted it. I mean, the fag thing is beyond wrong and all that but what was I thinking? Ian wasn't merely big, he was severely muscular too. Was I trying to get into yet another fistfight, except this time with Hercules? Did I have some sort of prom night death wish?

"Shit, Hayes," said Ian, a grin slowly inching across his lips. "I didn't realize you were such a Barney badass."

"It just . . . it's . . . I've heard it one too many times tonight."

"Okay, man," he said, chastised. "You won't hear it anymore from me. That's for sure."

And then he hit me playfully on the shoulder, a male-bonding tap. Still, a playful hit from Ian was enough to send me laterally onto the other side of the backseat, my face smacking the shiny leather seats.

"Whoops . . . sorry," he said, as he started laughing at me. And then I started laughing at me. Then he started laughing at me laughing at me. I can only imagine that at this point, the limo driver probably started laughing at us in general. I mean, it was all so damn absurd that what could we do but laugh our asses off? Ian's, of course, being immensely larger than my own.

When our fits of hilarity subsided, Ian gave me a sideways glance. "You're all right, Hayes," he said, pleased with himself. "For a—"

I tensed, waiting for it . . . .

"A gay guy."

Turning toward him, I smiled for the first time in a long time. "Gee, Harrison," I said, using his surname in a familiar way. "Thanks."

Ten minutes later, Ian was halfway through his second beer as the limo began inching its way through the obstacle course of potholes on Half Street. I was on the intercom again, instructing the driver to slow to a stop at the intersection of Half and O so I could take a look up the block and make sure the cops weren't still staked out at Secrets. Once I saw that O was clear of all law enforcement, the driver turned onto the street and pulled up to the club.

"So . . . you gonna stay here?" I asked.

Ian looked at himself, splayed out across the backseat in his boxers and sipping a Bud. "Uh, yeah."

"You sure?" I said jokingly.

"Just get in there, get your monkey suit, and let's get the hell outta here, okay?"

Taking a deep breath, I pushed open the limo door and crouched forward to get out. At that instant, a large tear ripped through the seat of my pants. Ian let out a snort.

"Damn, dude," he said, laughing and slapping his knee for effect. "Your ass is all hanging out and shit!"

Nice. Just the kinda support I needed when entering Secrets. But I pressed on, getting out of the car and taking tiny baby steps to where the bouncer was planted at the front door, just under the purple neon sign. Seeing my return, he glared down at me menacingly. Uh-oh. Then I had a rare flash of brilliance as I remembered his name. Sort of.

"Hey, B!" I said, with as much style as I could muster. "'Sup?"

No response. Only a look. A very unfriendly look.

"I was here earlier . . . with Dmitri . . . he was wearing a tux . . . and—"

"Son, you think I'm gonna let your ass in here again after the cops busted us for letting your ass in in the first place?"

Actually I was sorta hoping he wasn't going to bring this up.

"Well," I said, trying to be helpful. "I don't want to hang out, really. I just want to get my tux from Dmitri—"

"Dmitri ain't here, son."

Actually I figured as much. By my estimate, he was either in police custody or cruising down I-66 in some Potomac girl's stretch, firing up some chronic on the way to Dale City for the post-post-prom party. All of which is to say that, without Dmitri, I was fuck. His presence was the only reason I got into Secrets, as he seemed to know this B guy on a first-initial basis. Without Dmitri, I was stuck and I needed that tux. Not only would the one hundred dollar deposit be a loss, but also I really needed that other hundred in cash for sustenance and lodging since it seemed highly unlikely that I was going home anytime in the near future. With all these worries jostling around in my big head, I started panicking and my scary, high-pitched freak-out voice kicked-in.

"Okay, if you could just let me in for, like, two seconds it would mean a lot to me, because that tux is a rental and it's got my dad's money in it and I'm gonna be in major trouble if they find out I lost not only the tux but also the money, and besides I'm pretty sure I know where Dmitri left it downstairs in the dancers' locker room, so if you could please please *super-please* just let me have a quick look—"

For the first time ever, my crazy voice served me well. It actually drove the bouncer crazy!

"Hold up, son," he said placing his hands in front of him like I was spewing pepper spray. "Damn, that's annoying."

"Sorry—I just need to—"

He put his hands up again, cutting me off. "All right, you've got five minutes."

Back inside Secrets, I expected the place to be empty after the raid but it was even more full than before, surprisingly packed for 2:00 in the A.M. Apparently, since the cops hadn't found me or Buck or any other underage kids, they had no choice but to retreat in defeat and leave the joint open for business.

I walked with my hands over my butt, resembling a butler inspecting the house staff as I tried to cover up my revealed rear. Elbowing my way toward the bar, I made three attempts to hail the husky bartender. Finally I caught his eye, and he looked just about as pleased as the bouncer had been to see me.

"*You* again!"

I tried to ignore his animosity and keep to my task, which was to get my tux back.

"Hi there, I wanted to get my tux—"

But he cut me off.

"They took it."

"They—they *what?*"

"The cops took it with them. It's gone."

"But . . . why?"

"Said it was evidence or something."

"Evidence?" I said, totally confused. "Of what?"

"Do I look like a cop?" he said, raising his voice and leaning in toward me for emphasis, his tart breath providing harsh punctuation. "Look, kid, you want another Coke or something? If not, I got customers."

Before I could say a word, he ambled away to his next customer, leaving me to contemplate this new and unexpected disaster. With the tux gone, I was now out not only the one hundred-dollar deposit but also the one hundred-dollar bill that was in the front pocket. I certainly wasn't going to be able to go the police to reclaim it either, as a visit to the station house would likely turn into a permanent stay once my infractions were tabulated. So the question of the hour became this: Where on earth could I get two hundred bucks, and fast?

I was sulking my way back to the exit, my eyes cast toward the floor, when I accidentally bumped into someone entering the club. Looking up to apologize, I instead saw the answer to my problems. I got a sign. Literally.

AMATEUR NIGHT @ 2 A.M.!
CASH PRIZES! $200 FOR 1ST!!!

It was the sign Buck had pointed to earlier that night. It was the sign that explained why Secrets was hopping when I returned. And though it was not exactly a sign from God, it *was* something of a miracle nonetheless. How perfect, right? The two hundred dollars would be exactly enough to cover the tux deposit and my dad's money. I would simply enter the contest, do my thing, and claim first prize! It all seemed like the most amazing solution to my compounding problems, except for one small thing—there was no *way* I was going to get on a stage half naked and dance at a gay bar! I had some scruples left. Please.

Besides, even if I could in some alternate universe actually win, the whole idea of me in that kind of contest just didn't compute in my head. Now, I know that Shane thought there was something interesting about my looks, but honestly, the bartender had been fairly accurate in his earlier assessment of my chances. In Janespeak, the bottom line was, I was not really hot enough to win some strip contest. Now, not to be too self-hating and all; maybe I could have secured third place, but what would that have gotten me? According to the fine print on the sign, a mere $25 worth of humiliation, leaving me $175 short of my goal. Frankly, I'd had all the free humiliation I needed that night, thank you very much. On top of all those good reasons not to give Amateur Night a go, I was totally stone-cold sober. However, I did know of a certain linebacker waiting for me outside, downing his fourth beer and wearing only a pair of comely boxers.

"Where's your tux?" wondered Ian, as I poked my head in the limo two seconds later.

"There's a little problem, and I need a little help."

"Dude," he said, his tone dropping. "The way you say that makes it sound like exactly the opposite."

All right, so maybe not all jocks are brain-dead. Jocks 1, Gay Guys 0. Confronted with Ian's smarts, I fessed up the truth in record time and waited for Ian's reaction.

"So let me get this straight," he said with surprising calm. "You want me to dance at Secrets so I can win some cash for you?"

"Uh . . . pretty much, yeah."

Ian sat there, shaking his head in a manner that had become familiar to me that evening.

"Are you outta your friggin' *mind?*"

In response to his question, I assured him that I wasn't nuts (yet) and that I would have done the deed myself (maybe) except for the small fact that I wasn't as hot as he was (true). Even though he was a straight guy, I figured flattery should still work pretty well, right?

"Dude, you called me a fat ass about, oh, five minutes ago."

"I know," I said, trying to finesse my insult. "But . . . uh, gay guys like big butts."

He didn't even respond to that one.

"All right," I said emphatically. "So you're a little husky. But it's all in a very jocky way. Besides, all gay guys love teenagers."

"Dude," he said with some horror in his eyes. "You are *really* creeping me out now."

Frankly I think I was creeping myself out with that point. So I took another tack. Glancing over Ian's shoulder, I noticed his mini-bar was kicked, the last beer in his meaty hand. And thus, I was inspired.

"Oh," I said, struck by brilliance. "And the winner of the contest also gets free beer!"

"Free beer, huh?" said Ian, perking up a bit at this. *Free beer* were magic words to a guy like Ian, especially given his present condition without any. All right—I know what you're thinking: Who said free beer was part of the contest? Okay, I admit that even though this reward wasn't technically true, I surmised that once Ian won the contest, the patrons of Secrets would be more than willing to buy a few beers for a high school linebacker wearing his underwear and a sporty grin. Base, yes, but admit it . . . so beyond true.

"That could be cool," he said. Mulling . . . mulling. "But I think I'm gonna need something more than that. Something bigger."

Suddenly Ian had a crafty glint to his eye, like a Bond villain. Or Dr. Evil.

"Uh, like what?"

"Virginia."

I gasped.

"The whole *state!*"

"No, dumb ass," he said, punching my arm. "Your date."

Oh yeah. Her. I think I was trying to block her out of my mind. Well, this seemed somewhat reasonable. I mean, hell, I didn't want her, and she sure as hell didn't want me. But how could I truly deliver her to Ian? I mean, would a phone number suffice?

"I can get her number out of the Potomac directory," he said testily. "You gotta put in a word for me, talk me up, set me up. Get me the hookup."

Talk him up? This might be a bit of a problem.

"I don't know if Virginia wants to really talk to me so much."

"That's the deal, Hayes. Take it or leave it—the beer and the babe," he said, making it all sound so simple and so scary. "Whattya say?"

I didn't say anything. What could I say? I just shook his hand and sealed our deal.

# CHAPTER 18

Dragging Ian and his massive ass out of the limo, I pushed him toward the door of Secrets. Fortunately the bouncer was not so much of a problem this time, as he gave Ian the once-over. You know, checking him out and all. Big was apparently his type.

"Hey, B," I said to the bouncer, sounding crazily familiar. "This is my friend E."

You know, like street for Ian? They shook hands.

"Word," said Ian, as I rolled my eyes. Unnecessary coolness; five-yard penalty. But the bouncer didn't seem to care about this breach of street etiquette. He was too busy sizing up Ian's colossal figure.

"He's in the contest tonight," I explained.

"Oh yeah?" said B, stripping Ian with his eyes and imagining what he could do with him. "You got it in the bag, son."

"You think so?" said Ian, with an almost girlish surprise. "You really think I can win?"

"Oh yeah," said B with a sexy grin. "But you better get in. They already started."

And with that the bouncer let us in uncarded, thus gaining my third illegal entrance of the night. I was getting good at this, huh?

Back inside Secrets, a raucous crowd of fifty or so guys formed a rowdy horseshoe around the front of the runway. From the back of the room, the DJ served as master of ceremonies while providing the

---

appropriate theme music for the amateurs. Yes, that's right, more crappy disco.

"All righty, now—let's hear it for contestant number three . . . Wayne!"

This Wayne was a mess; a highly inebriated, bushy-haired redneck who was fairly out of shape too. This fact was revealed all too fully as he whipped off his green softball T to display a farmer's tan. Very *Green Acres*. Next, he unbuttoned his 501 jeans, and while trying to extricate his left leg from them, tripped on the cuff and fell onto his side. Ouch. Sporting a pair of blue boxers with Ford trucks imprinted on them, he struggled to right himself on the stage as the audience started losing it. If this was our competition, I thought, the contest was going to be a cakewalk.

Leaving Ian by the front door, I pushed my way through the crowd to the DJ on the other side of the room. Telling him my friend was a late entry to the contest, I gave him Ian's dancer handle, the Big E. (Pretty sweet for an impromptu idea, right?) Then returning to the back corner of the bar, I stood next to Ian as he nervously chugged down his last Bud.

"Okay," said the DJ, as Wayne tripped offstage. "Get that man another drink . . . and then a taxi home."

Crickets. No one ever said DJs were known for their sense of humor.

"All righty, now—let's hear it for our next victim, folks. It's . . . Coleman!"

Next up was a black dude who was decent-looking, if a little short for my tastes. Having planned ahead for his performance, he was modeling some fancy stripper-style underwear (Day-Glo lime spandex briefs), probably hoping to detract attention from his burgeoning belly. Even though Coleman showed a knack for shaking his hips to the beat, his gyrations just weren't doing it for the audience. It was maybe too hard of a sell. That wasn't going to be Ian's problem. He would be the king of amateur realness, you know what I mean?

"You're gonna kill," I said, throwing my arm over his shoulder and patting him on the back.

He responded with a noisome burp. Nice.

"Okay, folks," said the DJ. "Let's get it up for Billy Boy!"

The next amateur was not half bad; a lanky cowboy wearing a Stetson and slick brown leather boots. He had a pleasant face, round and corn-fed, as well as a nicely defined square chest and even decently bulging arms, which were revealed in their full glory when he took off his denim shirt. But Billy Boy was not exactly a boy any-more. He was definitely over thirty, an instant disadvantage for a crowd of spectators who were, on average, pushing forty. Thus Billy received polite but unenthusiastic applause.

"And now let's give a big Secrets hand to our final amateur tonight. The aptly named . . . *Big E!*"

Scrunching up his beer can and tossing it behind the bar, Ian parted the crowd and made his way to the runway. The same lame disco music continued to play as Ian hopped up onto the stage to a general holler of approval from the crowd and stood up in his Joe Boxers under the soft red spotlights. The racy lighting gave his gen-erally pale skin a dark, nearly russet tone. With the faux tan, the boxers, and his linebacker lineage, I thought we had the whole thing in the bag. I mean, damn . . . Ian looked good!

However, once Big E started swaying awkwardly to the disco beat, the hollering of the audience conversely started to die down. Having already stripped down to his shorts way back in Constitution Gardens, Ian really didn't have much to do up there in his boxers other than dance. And to make matters worse, he was not much of a dancer, especially when it came to music he'd never heard before in his life. So Ian just stood there, smiling dumbly and squinting into the spotlights, his feet planted like cement in the center of the runway with no intention of moving them from that spot until the announcer said, "Thank you very much," and handed him the loot.

As the crowd grew increasingly restless and disinterested, it seemed that first prize was slipping away by the second. I had to do something fast or that two hundred dollars would be riding off into the sunset with the cowboy. Pushing and shoving my way past the stage, I returned to the DJ.

"Hey, do you have any good music?"

He regarded me in the unfriendly manner I'd become accustomed to at Secrets.

"Ex-*cuse* me."

"Big E doesn't know this seventies stuff. You have anything . . . current?"

"Yeah, yeah," he said, begrudgingly. "I got the new Britney."

"No way," I said, shaking my head.

"What's wrong with Britney?"

"What's right with her?" I said, trying to gain the pop music high ground. "How 'bout something else . . . like . . . you got any Good Charlotte?"

Annoyed, he flipped through some CD's and found one of those *Now . . . That's What I Call Music!* compilations.

"I got something by them called 'Boys and Girls.'"

"Perfect," I said.

As the DJ cross-faded discs, Ian suddenly came to life as the band's familiar punk 'n' thrash beat roared through the bar. Pushing my way back through the throng, I maneuvered up to the front of the stage to yell some encouragement to Ian.

"Go on, Big E, " I said as loud as I could. "Show them what you got!"

But the song was so bloody loud he couldn't hear me.

"What?"

I moved closer. The music pounded in my ears as Ian bent down to me.

"Just dance a little, okay?"

"Dude, I don't know how to dance."

All right, I guess I should've asked Ian this before submitting him to an amateur dance contest. My bad. My disaster. My two hundred dollars going, going . . .

"Just dance," I said, illogically hopeful despite what Ian had just said. "Like in the video, you know?"

Still, all I got from him was a blank look. Maybe he was one of those underprivileged kids who didn't get cable. Or maybe he just didn't like TV. Regardless, I had to do something. So standing there at the lip of the stage, I did my best Good Charlotte imitation, jumping around like a moron. After what my parents claimed were wasted hours of watching MTV2, I found a real-life application for what I'd gleaned from all those music videos. And you know what? I wasn't half bad. Then, as imitation is the sincerest form of flattery, a couple spectators in the crowd started getting into it and copying me. Maybe it was my moves. Or maybe it was the ever expanding, risqué rip up the backside of my pants, revealing the seat of my Fruit of the Looms. Either way I didn't care. All I cared was that Ian started dancing as well as I was.

I bellowed out his name and he bent down again, speaking right into my ear.

"Dude, that's awesome!" he said, referring to my dancing.

"Thanks," I said, pleased with my new role as his stripper Svengali. "So now you know what to do? You got it, right?"

"No . . . but I got *you*."

Ian clamped on to my forearm and with a Herculean heave-ho that only a 250-pound linebacker could have managed, single-handedly lifted me onto the stage. I landed front and center under the rosy lights of the runway and was immediately petrified. I mean, c'mon . . . have *you* ever stood in front of fifty guys salivating for a strip show? Yeah, I thought not. Turning around and seeing Ian's big mug behind me, I felt a little less alone. But still my feet were glued to the floor. Ian tried some sports-based motivation.

"Just do it, man," he yelled, chanting like a most unlikely cheer-leader. "Go . . . GO . . . *GO!*"

Of course, the crowd joined in this chant, and after a few repetitions of it rang in my ears, what else could I do except dance? What could anyone do really? When you are standing in front of an unruly mob, you generally end up doing whatever the unruly mob wants, if you value your life. So as the boys of Good Charlotte thumped toward the first chorus, I closed my eyes tight and just pretended I was in the video as I screamed along to the lyrics, pogoing my ass off.

Instantly the crowd went wild. My eyes snapped open on hearing this, and then, sensing a large presence next to me, I saw that Ian had started jumping up and down too, doing what was a reasonable facsimile of my slam dancing. This encouraged me some more and I started going even crazier, bouncing around the stage like a dirty dancin' Tigger, my formal shoes seemingly made of rubber. This springy move sent the gathered audience into a sustained roar of pleasure, which seemed a bit disproportionate response-wise. I mean, Ian and I were just rocking it out to the song. It was no big deal really, just a little moshing, you know? The only thing I could think to explain the mob's explosive reaction was that two teenagers bouncing up and down can really get a bunch of middle-age men very, very excited.

As I continued dancing like a punkster, leaping around and tossing my head about like it was a salad, I started getting hot. Temperature hot. Sweating under the lights, I started to feel somewhat constricted in my newly shrunk-to-fit uniform. So after a few minutes I had no choice but to take off my waiter's jacket. This produced yet another eruption of excitement from the mob below. Whoa . . . this was crazy! After that, what can I say? I totally went with it, giving them what they wanted, I guess, as I whipped the jacket over my head and tossed it out into the crowd. Another roar went up, and you know what? This was getting fun! Next I removed the white hotel uniform shirt, busting a few buttons in the process, and they got even wilder. Finally, feeling possessed by the spirit of Sid Vicious or something, I raced up to the lip of the runway and screamed, from the bottom of my lungs, for everyone to—

"DANCE!!!"

Despite the advanced age and infirmity of the Secrets demographic, they actually responded to my call by dancing like maniacs, reliving their lost rebel youth as they coalesced into an aging mosh pit. I turned to Ian and he was grinning like an idiot now, amazed at the frenzy we'd spawned. Taking it to the next level, I intentionally crashed into Ian's backside, safely knowing that not much would happen when a skinny guy in motion meets a huge dude at rest. This move was meant to set the proper slam-dancing example for the crowd in their newly formed pit. And, sure enough, in an instant they were willfully colliding into one another too. I glanced back at Ian and he was completely cracking up, beyond amused at the chaos we had wrought.

*What to do next,* I thought? Even though my pants were already completely split up the back, I was definitely *not* going to take those off. Please . . . I still had some scruples left. Ian, however, didn't. To my shock, as the song reached its crescendo, he slipped out of his boxers! To everyone's surprise, he was wearing a pair of XXX-tra large, Under Armour briefs to keep things relatively decent. As Ian twirled his boxers triumphantly over his head, I looked at him with an expression that can only be described as, I don't know . . . stunned wonderment?

"What?" he said, in reaction to my reaction. "You thought I was free-balling it all this time?"

Then with a forceful point of his finger in the direction of the flash-mosh pit, Ian seemed to have an idea.

"Jump!"

Lumbering to the front of stage, he raised his arms in the air like we'd scored a field goal, shouting and bounding up and down.

"Jump! JUMP! *JUMP!*"

In seconds, the crowd joined him in this chant, as if they were playing a twisted version of Simon Says. It was at that moment that I understood the giddy rush of being a rock star, as my "fans" called for more. Seriously—that shit was intoxicating, like no alcoholic beverage or pot, for that matter, that I'd ever had. Honest! I totally loved it and wanted to make this merry mob even happier.

And of course, I wanted to win. Correction, I *had* to win.

So backing myself up to the mirrored wall where the runway began, I prepared for my daring leap. Then out of the corner of my eye, I caught a glimpse of the door opening in the back of the bar as a couple people entered Secrets. I assumed they were latecomers for the show, except that I noticed they were oddly in formal wear. My first, hopeful thought was that Dmitri had returned with my tux. But as I recalled that my tux was in lockup, one of the disco lights flashed into the back corner, revealing the handsome gentleman in the tux to be none other than Shane.

"I fuck," I said, catching my breath.

Shane's jaw truly reached for the floor as he was confronted with the sight of me, topless on the stage of Secrets, bouncing on the balls of my feet to Good Charlotte. But he was not alone in his amazement, as following close behind him were Virginia, Jane, and good ol' Buck. Jane's eyes looked like they just might implode from the sight of it all, while Virginia looked awfully confused by the whole sordid scene. Buck was the only one of them who seemed to be enjoying the spectacle of my starring role in Amateur Night. *Perhaps,* I thought, *he'd been there before . . .*

"JUMP!"

It was Ian yelling again, his back to the crowd as he exhorted me to make my move, totally unaware our classmates had entered the room. Now, don't think for a minute that just because my three prom dates had walked in the door it meant I was going to stop what I was doing. Oh, no . . . quite the opposite. In a weird way their presence only encouraged me. So averting my gaze from my friends and enemies, I took off down the runway, sprinting toward the blinking end of the stage and springing up, up, and away into the sea of upraised hands with a heartfelt rebel yell.

"Whooooeeeeeyyyyyyaaaaahhhhh!"

Landing with an unexpectedly elastic bounce on the cushion of the crowd's hands, I started laughing uncontrollably. It wasn't that my leap had been particularly funny. It was more that the ticklish feel of all those hands on my bare back was giving me a gigantic case of the giggles. The crowd seemed to sense this as they rolled my slight, wiry frame back and forth, body surfing me across the room with ease. At this point, with all the jostling and rolling, I couldn't see Shane. In fact, I couldn't see anyone really, my field of vision consisting mainly of the dingy black ceiling tiles of Secrets. And that was fine. I needed a moment to myself before the storm that was surely going to follow this outrageous escapade.

I was zoning out on some curious stains on the ceiling when a new call of "jump-JUMP-*JUMP*" rose up around me. This time, however, it was not coming from Ian. This time it emanated from the pit as they chanted for Ian's tighty-whitey-clad figure to be tossed into their midst before the song reached its conclusion. Heeding this call, I was let down at the far side of the room as the crowd's attention shifted to commanding Ian to make the leap. This was ill-advised, Ian being more than twice, maybe even thrice, my size. But these folks were hardly clear thinkers. To be frank, they were a bunch of boy-hounds who were wasted and horny and, by this point, under the spell of a rowdy mob mentality.

"Jump—JUMP—*JUMP!*"

With four beers in him, Ian's judgment was not what it should have been, to say the least. In addition to that, as a member of the varsity football team, it was impossible for him to ignore the alluring siren song of any crowd yelling for more—MORE—*MORE!* He knew this call all to well, and conditioned by years in the athletic arena, he was compelled to answer it.

"Yyyyyyyeeeeeeeaaaaaaaaahhhhhhhhaaaaaaaaaa!"

And so Ian leaped into the Secrets abyss, the image of his hulking frame in midair having the same implausible look of a 747 at the moment of takeoff, in the way it seemed scientifically impossible and dangerously doomed. I then turned my attention to Shane, watching him react with an inaudible but heartfelt *holy shit* while Jane's jaw joined Shane's on the floor. As for Virginia, she watched Ian's incredible flight with, how to describe it . . . a perverse awe?

After an all too short journey, Ian crashed into the tiny hands topping off the pit. I flinched, turning away from the disaster as his body took the express elevator down to the first floor, landing with a soft crunch on top of at least three forty-something moshers. The moment of Ian impact was severe enough to get the CD player to skip, voiding the room of music for a few dead seconds. Then after a tense moment, Ian thrust his right hand into the air, still holding on to his boxers, with a defiant V for victory. With help from a couple of the huskier patrons, he righted himself and stood up, revealing that the poor souls beneath him had not been smothered, just smushed a bit. Nothing fatal. In response to this the crowd roared its approval of Ian's colossally stupendous, not to mention stupid, stunt.

"All righty—I think we have ourselves a winner, " exclaimed the DJ. "Let's hear it for Big E and . . . Little E."

We heard it. Loud and clear. We had won! Amazing, huh? Though I could have done without the Little E part.

"Thanks for quite a show, guys," said the DJ. "Claim your prize from the bartender and keep on rockin'!"

Then the DJ threw on the new Britney. Whatever. At least we were going to get our prize money. I mean, my prize money.

"You rocked, dude!" said Ian, slapping me on my back as I tried to find Dmitri's white shirt on the dirty, beer-stained floor. "Let's go get our free beers!"

Slipping his boxers back on, Ian headed directly for the bar, leaving me to contemplate how I was going to manage my false beverage promise. I was about to try to cut him off at the pass, before he got to the bartender, when suddenly I couldn't move. I felt a strong presence behind me, like a disturbance in the Force. Damn, did I know how Luke Skywalker felt or what?

"You *have* lost your mind."

I turned around to face down Darth. I mean Shane.

"Actually I lost my tux."

Okay, I wasn't trying to be sassy. Honest. I was just trying to explain. All right, maybe it was a little sassy, but I was somewhat emboldened after winning my first nonacademic contest ever (I mean, EVER!), so maybe I got carried away. Not that it mattered to Shane. He looked at me, stone-faced, as I tried to explain.

"No, really—that's why Ian and I were in the contest," I said, trying to convince him there was a reason behind all this insanity. "You see, the cops took my tux after Dmitri was wearing it but then left it in the dancers'—"

"Whoa," he said, putting up his hands like what I was saying sorta stank. "You think there's a real, actual *excuse* for you to be dancing in some seedy bar for *money?*"

"Well . . . actually, when you put it that way, there *is.*"

Again not trying to be sassy. I was merely trying to give him the truth, which just happened to sound sassy.

"I can't talk to you right now. Just get some clothes on and come back out to the limo in ten," said Shane, averting his eyes from me as if I was deformed. I mean, c'mon, I wasn't wearing a shirt, but it's not like he hadn't seen *that* before. "We're going home."

And Shane was outta there.

Once he'd left me safe to approach, Jane and Virginia came over, both of them looking at me like they'd never really seen me before. Jane tried a compliment.

"That was . . . I mean . . . it was . . ."

But Jane was speechless. Virginia, however, never was.

"Totally raw."

"Gee, Virginia," I said, not knowing if this was a compliment or an insult or both. "Thanks?"

"That was sheer unadulterated genius, Cam," continued Jane, bubbling over with enthusiasm. "Good Charlotte in a gay strip bar? And you . . . you were hot up there!"

"Ah, you're just saying that," I said, fake playing.

"Who was that other guy with you?" wondered Virginia.

Ah . . . the strange awe was making some sense.

"It was Ian, Shane's best friend," I said.

"Is he gay too?"

Jane, exasperated, swatted at Virginia's arm with her purse.

"It's not like *everyone* is gay, Virginia. Give it a rest!"

"No, he's severely het," I said, realizing I had an opportunity to fulfill the other half of my dancing deal. "Actually, Ian was asking about you. Thought you were kinda hot."

"Really?" said Virginia, slyly checking him out as one of the patrons he'd landed on bought him a beer. (That was a relief!) "I dunno . . . he's kinda fat."

Christ.

"He's a nice guy, Virginia," I said, trying not to get agitated by her dismissiveness. "Maybe you could at least talk to him."

"I dunno—he seems like one of those jock-ass bores."

Christ on a cracker.

"Okay, look," I said, trying to reason with the woman. "At least talking to him might be better than talking to me, and maybe not as much a waste of your time?"

With an arched brow, Virginia got the hint and strutted her way toward the bar. Returning my attention to Jane, I saw her mouth was wide open in shock. Super shock.

"Cameron Hayes," she said in her best Southern belle voice. "My, my, my . . . how *bold* you've become this evening."

"'Tis a mighty bold evening, Miss Scarlett," I said, continuing the accented riff. "Narrowly escaping the cops . . . twice. Speakin' of which, I'm amazed *you're* not in the slammer and all."

"It was a close call, that's for sure," she said with great relief. "We booked it the second we saw the police lights. The cops did nab a couple guys in the water who were still trying to get their clothes."

"And Dmitri?"

"He was last seen racing off toward the Washington Monument with Caroline in tow."

*Now, there's a charming couple,* I thought; the bi-Russian mobster and the preppy Potomac princess. So utterly mismatched, it could be the perfect relationship . . . at least for a night.

"So how did you find us here?" I wondered.

"Your young Buck."

"The deaf leading the deaf, as it were?"

Jane snorted a laugh.

"Yeah . . . they had some serious hearing-impaired bonding in the car."

"Great," I said, bummed that my soon-to-be ex was already on the make.

"Cam, it's not like they were making out. Give Shane *some* credit."

"Do I have to?"

"At least til you get home . . . he is our ride after all."

Then it hit me. Home. I recalled what Shane had said moments before his speedy exit from Secrets. He'd said, "We're going home." Not "I'm leaving" or "You better leave" or "You should get your ass home" or any other singular variation on the night-is-way-over theme. He'd used *we*. The relationship *we*.

I tried to think. . . . Had he ever labeled us a "we" before? I couldn't recall, but then again my memory banks were a little screwy, so overloaded with the strange names and new faces and, uh, unusual experiences of that night that it was problematic to do an instant database search for the pronoun *we*. But even if it had been used before, Shane's use that night, given everything that had been going on, definitely had meaning. Or at least the potential for some real meaning that could turn the whole disastrous *Titanic* of a night around.

*We're going home. Hmmmmm.*

I played the audio like a sample, back and forth, slow and fast, studying the phrase in my head like a scientist might, or maybe a really intense English professor. You know, trying to dissect it and all. I wondered if by *home* Shane meant that he was taking me back to his folks' place? I wondered if the *we* meant that we were back together? I wondered if maybe, miraculously, Shane had seen the relationship light, realizing that maybe he truly did love me somewhere deep down in his hidden heart?

The answer would be mere minutes away.

# CHAPTER 19

As the Amateur Night crowd dispersed, I eventually found my hotel uniform stuck to the floor of Secrets. Trampled by the mob and stained with beer, it was not exactly ready to wear. I was in desperate need of some post-show clothing. Fortunately Buck reappeared from the back of Secrets, and sensing my fashion dilemma, led me to the dancers' locker room, where he had some extra clothes. No, not a G-string or anything racy. (Though the thought of hopping in Shane's limo wearing that might have been a kick. However, on balance, I thought that I'd had enough kicks for one night already.)

Scavenging through his locker, Buck offered me a pair of Diesel jeans and a Gallaudet University T-shirt. I then thanked him for his help, speaking with exaggerated lip movements since my translator/bartender was out front serving drinks. In response Buck said he'd had a great time meeting me and hanging with my friends. He thought they were all a lot of fun and that we should all reconvene again in the summer. Amiably I agreed to this plan, secretly doubting if there was ever going to be a night on which this same contentious crew would willfully hang out with each other. But I didn't say that to Buck. I just smiled pleasantly and on my way out offered my hand as a good-bye gesture. Buck took my hand but didn't let it go.

"Your boyfriend's very nice," he said.

"He can be."

"He really likes you, very much."

"Maybe . . . " I said, rolling my eyes.

"No," said Buck emphatically, placing my hand on his heart to make his point less verbally. "He loves you."

This was a stunner given the events of the last couple hours.

"He said this to you?" I wondered skeptically.

"You don't need to hear love to know it's there."

Even though it sounded silly, Buck said this in a manner that was wholly sincere and hard to dismiss. Why *did* I have to hear Shane say he loved me to know it was true? Maybe my doubts about our so-called relationship said more about whether or not *I* loved Shane. Still, I knew I *did* love him, even though maybe I had never quite said it myself until that night. But I didn't have to really. Shane knew I adored him, that my world revolved around him, evidenced in the way that I always deferred to his every whim and command (e.g., going to the prom in the first place, hello!). Still, Buck's bit of wisdom got me thinking too much as I often tend to do when it comes to this sorta emotional stuff. The only way to figure it all out would be heading out to the limo to see exactly whose home we were going to.

Leaving the dancers' locker room, I found Ian and Virginia happily ensconced at the bar, doing shots of Jagermeister under the bemused eye of the bartender. Apparently this guy had no problem serving Ian drinks, in the same manner that the bouncer had had no problem letting him in without proper I.D.

"C'mon, Virginia," I said wearily. "We're gonna hit the road."

"We?" she said, adversely reacting to my use of the relationship *we*. "What's this *we* stuff?"

"Shane wants to get going. He's waiting outside in the limo."

"Oh, shit—I've gotta get my clothes," said Ian, gulping down a shot. "Jane picked them up for me before the cops arrived in Constitution Gardens."

Ian hopped off his bar stool and waddled outside, the bartender longingly watching his ass shake its way out the door.

"That guy is something else," said the bartender.

"Well put," I said, agreeing. "C'mon, Virginia."

"Ease up, Hayes. One more round and then we'll head out."

Not wanting to fight anymore with anyone, I acceded to Virginia's unbelievable wish to consume yet even more alcohol, as if the first round of boozing that night hadn't been enough to wean her off the stuff for the rest of her life. But then I remembered her mother and how her insatiable appetite for liquor was probably in the genes. I also remembered what her mother had said as we left the house.

"Hey, aren't you gonna be late for your curfew?" I said, pointing at the clock on the wall that indicated it was 2:30.

"Oh," she said turning around to face me down. "*Now* you're worried about my well-being?"

"Sorry I brought it up," I said, wishing I was dead or something.

"Look, my mother is *not* the boss of me."

Leaving me to wonder: Could anyone, anywhere, *ever* be the boss of Virginia? Maybe Ian could. At least he was bigger than her.

"So it seemed like you and Ian were having a good time."

"He's all right," she said offhandedly. "He can drink like a pro, I'll give him that."

That seemed promising. Matching Virginia drink for drink is not in your average guy's playbook. Seeing this opening, I decided to breach it a bit. After all, now that Ian had secured my fiscal solvency for the night, I really did owe him more than free beer. I owed him free Virginia.

"He *really* digs you," I said a little too enthusiastically.

"Oh yeah?" said Virginia, her eyes fixing narrowly on my own. "What exactly are you up to, Hayes?"

"Just relaying a friendly message."

"Thanks for the bulletin, Scoop, but he's dating Caroline."

"Oh—not really," I said like I was now her confidant. "They're just friends. And she ran off with Dmitri anyway, according to Jane."

"The pimp?"

"Drug dealer."

"Hmmmm, interesting," she said, standing up and suddenly ready to leave. She seemed somewhat pleased that I had provided something useful to her, even if it was coming toward the end of an otherwise disastrous night.

Outside, the early morning air was brisk. The full moon was still there though slightly farther away now, not as exaggerated and pie-in-the-sky-looking as it had been when the madness of the night began.

I was walking toward our limo when Virginia started to veer off.

"Where you going?"

"I'll catch a ride home with Ian," she said in a new and improved polite voice. "If you don't mind."

"Uh . . . no," I said, trying to hide a burgeoning smile. "That's cool."

"Okay, then," she said, not able to hide hers anymore. Finally, Virginia was gonna get laid that night, and it seemed to make all the difference in regard to her temperament. "I'll catch you later, Hayes."

She would? Highly unlikely, really, but at that point I decided to play along with this fake-friendly vibe.

"Yeah . . . later Virginia."

I ducked into our limo to find Jane and no Shane.

"Hey—where's the man?"

"In the other limo," she said nonchalantly. "Ian said he had to talk to Shane about something and they both went off."

Suddenly the moonlit serenity of the night dissipated. No, more like it disintegrated. Wait—hold on a sec—can I make that *exploded*? I realized that Shane and Ian were probably discussing my little breakdown back at the Reflecting Pool where I happened to mention that Shane and I were boyfriends.

"You know, maybe I'll grab a taxi home instead," I said motioning for the door, desperately trying to get out the limo before it was too late.

"What are you talking about?" said Jane.

"I've got enough money now . . . with the contest cash and all," I continued, scrambling over her toward the door. "I'll be fine, really. I'll leave you two to have a nice ride home together."

Then, as I dove for the handle, the door opened at the same time in another case of unfortunate timing, pulling my body halfway out of the car and leaving my legs halfway in. Twisting my neck around to look up, I saw Shane looming over me. A very angry, upside-down Shane.

"Hi," I said in a perky, friendly voice.

Smile and the world smiles with you, right? In this case, wrong.

"Get in the car," replied Shane in a not-so-perky and entirely unfriendly voice.

Grabbing me by the back of my Gallaudet T, he lifted me up off the ground and shoved me back into the limo. With the force of this unnecessary push, I fell across the floor of the limo, knocking my head on the other side of the car.

"Ow," I said, as Shane got in and slammed the door shut. Then as the engine kicked into gear, we pulled away from Secrets.

"Shane," said Jane, coming to my aid and helping me up onto the backseat of the car. "That's not very nice."

"Not very nice, huh?" he said, his voice winding up in a way that, by this point in the night, I knew all too well. "Not very *NICE?*"

"No," said Jane. "To push someone like—"

I interrupted. "Jane—it's a rhetorical thing."

It was at that moment that Shane's rhetoric exploded into invective.

"You know what's not nice? I don't think it's very *nice* to talk about your friends to another friend. I don't think that's very nice at all, is it, Cameron?"

"I dunno," I said, trying to play dumb. But you know what? This playing dumb bit never quite works for me.

"What do you mean you don't know? You know *exactly* what I'm talking about."

"Well," said Jane, chiming in. "I certainly don't."

"Cameron told Ian everything. EVERYTHING!"

Jesus—Shane made it sound like I had blown some major criminal scheme we'd been planning for years that was going to make us billionaires. His tone was that ridiculous! So hearing this, I was not going to take that kind of fall for confiding in someone during the middle of a near-suicidal nervous breakdown. I was not the loose-lipped, stool pigeon Shane was implying, at least not intentionally.

"I told Ian the truth," I said plainly. "What's so wrong with that?"

"What's wrong with *THAT*?"

Shane's face grew red again, the veins on his forehead popping into throbbing definition. If he didn't calm down, his head was going to explode.

"You *outed* me to my best friend, Cameron. It is so not your right to have that conversation with anyone, more or less my best *FRIEND!*"

Jane gasped. In fact, she even covered her mouth like in the movies when someone dies or some terrible revelation is made about who the real killer is. But to be honest here, Jane's reaction was not an exaggeration on her part. Jane knew the gravity of this situation immediately. I, on the other hand, had nearly forgotten the gravity of my revelation to Ian, it having been lost somewhere in the rush of so many other extraordinary events, namely my near suicide/drowning in the Reflecting Pool. On balance, it didn't seem so bad or evil or awful that it had slipped out about Shane and I being a couple. But seeing Jane react like I had done something unspeakable, I knew that by sharing this with Ian, I had probably made a huge, end-of-the-world mistake.

"I didn't mean to," I said in my feeble defense.

Okay, some legal advice here. If you're ever going to defend yourself, you'd better make it a strong defense. Feeble defenses have a tendency to make those who have suffered a perceived injustice due to your actions very, very angry. Like, *insanely* angry.

"Didn't *mean* to?" he said, loudly returning to his rhetorical theme. "Is that supposed to make me feel BETTER?"

"Well, yeah," I said, gaining something of my voice back and trying for a somewhat stronger defense this time. "It's not like I said it on purpose or to make you mad or to get back at you. It just sorta came out."

"How does something like THAT just come out, Cameron, HUH?"

Shane was on the verge of tremors, he was so pissed off. Reminding myself to breathe a couple times, I took a pause and then tried to explain the whole thing in a calm, rational voice.

"After our fight in the park, I was upset and crying and panicking and drowning, so when Ian saved me and was talking me down, it just slipped out and I said that you didn't love me."

Jane gasped again. She even put her other hand up by her mouth. I had never seen this scary position before, even in really bad horror movies. I knew I was in a whole new territory of shocking.

"I can't believe—"

But Shane stopped himself, choking on whatever the next word was going to be. He couldn't speak he was so damn mad. Shaking something loose in his head, he tried again.

"Why do you keep saying that, Cameron? WHY?"

"Because it's true. Or at least I thought it was after you didn't say anything to Mold about us being a couple and then us fighting again about it in the park and . . . well, is it true?"

Now Jane closed her eyes, not wanting to be in our limo and hoping, like Sabrina, she could magically blink her way somewhere else. Shane's reaction to this question, however, was strangely Zen, as looking away from me, he regarded the sharp creases in his pants, smoothing them with his palms.

"I don't wanna talk about this anymore," he said, flattening out the straight line across his thigh.

"Uh, why not?"

"Because you've ruined my friendship with Ian."

"Ohmigod," I said, losing my Zen. "That is so ridiculous that—"

"I'm serious, Cam," said Shane, looking at me again.

"But you don't even get it. Ian doesn't really care that we're a couple," I said, trying to get him to understand. "He's mad you never *told* him about it. That's all."

There was a glint of recognition in Shane's dark eyes for a moment but it passed, clouded over by the usual mixture of fear and loathing that had a tendency to kick in regarding his interest in the same sex. It dawned on me there in the back of the limo that the really tragic thing about all of this was simply that Shane couldn't see past his own fears to know that his best friend actually had no fears about him dating another guy. But getting Shane to see that in his current state was psychologically going to be a bridge too far.

"I said I don't wanna talk about this. Okay?"

"But that's what Ian—"

Again he cut me off.

"And I'm sure Jane doesn't wanna sit here and listen to us fight."

Jane opened her eyes on hearing her name. She glanced at Shane and then at me, offering a slight nod for me to knock it off. At least for the time being. And I did.

It was now 3:00 A.M. and all was not well. As we drove in silence through the sleeping city, past the Jefferson, past the Lincoln, past the Kennedy Center, I stared out the tinted windows, looking for answers to some pretty important questions. Unfortunately they were not to be found anywhere on the blank white surfaces of the city's colossal monuments. There were so many questions swimming around in my head that all I wanted to do was ask them and find out, one way or another, where I stood. Where *we* stood. Did Shane, in fact, love me like Buck had suggested? Or did he truly hate me because I'd told Ian we were a couple? Was he ever going to get over all the secrets and lies inherent in his take on homosexuality? And more importantly, what did he mean in that moment back at Secrets when he said we were going home?

As we sped through a shuttered Georgetown, continuing to parallel the river on McArthur Boulevard, it seemed clear we were not going to his place off Foxhall but heading farther out. I surmised that we were making our way to Jane's house first. Jane's folks lived in the Palisades, a classy but not aggressively swank area of the District just south of where Maryland began. As we curved our way around the placid waters of the Dalecarlia Reservoir, Jane broke the calm as she spoke the obvious.

"So . . . we going to my place first?"

"Yep," said Shane with no discernible inflection or meaning.

"Then you're going home?" she continued, speaking on my behalf.

"Yep."

Though Shane's tone was flat, at least it wasn't sharp. Thus I speculated that maybe there was some hope left. Maybe Shane had just needed some quiet time to chill out and all. Maybe in the end he wouldn't be so mad at me after all. I thought that once we dropped Jane at home we would go back to his parents', and then, alone for the first time since the beginning of the evening, we would make up and I would spend the night as he'd offered in the first place.

All right, you can stop looking at me like I'm on crack. Sure, maybe this was all a little optimistic. But I at least had some modicum of hope. I had to. It was the only option left really. I mean, my parents probably didn't want to talk to me for the rest of my life given all the illegality I'd been up to that night. So that meant that Shane was about all I had left family-wise, and the thought of losing him too would have been—I just couldn't even go there. At least not yet.

# CHAPTER 20

As our limo wound its way through the dense, leafy streets of the Palisades, we made our final approach to Jane's house. All was quiet, both in her slumbering neighborhood and our sleepy backseat. Unfortunately this calm turned out to be one of those before-the-storm deals.

Shane clicked open his door as we sat in silence parked in Jane's driveway. Quietly gathering up her dress, Jane got up from where she sat between us and got out of the limo. Turning around, she was about to give us her good-byes when Shane, staring straight ahead at the glass panel that separated us from the driver, strangely raised his right hand and pointed it like a traffic cop in the direction of Jane's front lawn.

"Okay," he said in a robotic voice. "Get out."

"Shane," said Jane, ruffled by his rudeness. "Uh . . . I am out."

"I'm talking to Cameron."

"What?" I said, blindsided not only by the order but also by his monotone, something I'd never heard from him before. "You want *me* to get out? Here?"

"That's what I said. Last stop. Get out."

"Uh, this is *my* house," said Jane, now standing defiantly on her lawn, arms crossed over her satiny dress. "You can't just drop Cam here at three in the—"

"I can't?" said Shane, getting all rhetorical on us again. "I think it makes perfect sense now that you and Cam are such close pals. I thought that you'd wanna, you know, spend some more time together."

Jane just sighed and said something that sounded like "Oh, brother."

"Maybe you can even make out a bit on the living room couch," Shane continued. "It's a nice couch and Jane is a good kisser, right Cam?"

"Shane—that is so raw," said Jane, intensely pissed off.

"Raw?" said Shane, turning sarcastic on us. "Hey, I'm just speakin' the truth. And since Cameron is such the crusader for truth and justice and the American way tonight, I thought I'd take his lead. Follow his good example."

You know what? It's really not cute when someone throws your own dumb quotes back at you in this sorta snarky manner. Especially when it's three in the morning.

"But you can't just leave him here like this," said Jane, her voice becoming strident. "At this time of night? With no way to get home?"

"Yeah," I said, belatedly joining my own battle, the initial shell shock of being ditched by my real prom date having passed. "My car's at your place."

Shane sat up from his reclining position on the backseat, and adjusting his finger, pointed it at me.

"You know what, Cam? I don't care where your car is. I don't care how you get home. All I care about is that you get out of the limo . . . *now.*"

"Is this about the whole Ian thing?" I said, a little too dismissively.

"The Ian *thing?* You say that like it's nothing. Like it doesn't *mean* anything. It means a lot, Cameron. I've known Ian four times as long as I've known you. It means a helluva lot."

"Yeah, but Ian's not your boyfriend," said Jane. "Cameron is."

Wow—I wish I had said this. Anyway, props to Jane for making this point.

"I'm not so sure anymore."

Wow—I wish Shane hadn't said this. It was chills-down-the-spine time.

"But, Shane—" I said and couldn't say anything more, gasping for air and my own words, neither of which were in plentiful supply. Not that he cared. Not at all. Not one bit. He turned toward me and let me have it.

"Cameron, get out of the limo or I will make you get out."

As Shane said this his warm eyes went absolutely cold on me, like he was some android or something. This wasn't the guy I dated. In fact, even his voice wasn't his, sounding mechanical and harsh. It was like Shane had become a Terminator-like imposter who was intent on destroying my world. Deciding not to test the strength of this new hideous machine, I opened the door on my side of the car and got out, trying to avoid crossing in front of Shane for fear of being tripped or something else vindictively petty along those lines.

The second my shoes touched the grass, Shane pulled the door closed behind me with a harsh slam. Turning around, I stood there in shock as the limo slowly backed out of the driveway, angled sideways into the street, and drove away down the shadowy lane.

"What an asshole," said Jane, standing on the other side of the void in the driveway where the limo with my former boyfriend had been idling only a minute before. Now all that remained were a couple shiny oil stains, catching the waning gray rays of the moon. Fixated on the driveway splotches, I shuddered.

"Seriously," I said, not knowing what else to say.

"I'm sorry, Cam," said Jane, crossing the driveway to put a hand on my shoulder.

"Thanks," I said mournfully. "But it's not your fault."

"I kinda think it *is*. Things were fine until I started making out with you."

"We made out with each other, Jane. Besides, things were not fine with Shane and me. . . . This whole thing tonight had been building up, I guess, over the last few weeks. Fighting about Beach Week and the prom and everything."

"But I had no idea you guys were on the verge of breaking up."

"Funny . . . neither did I," I said, dropping my head and checking out Jane's incredibly lush lawn. It looked so cushy and comfortable at that moment, a rich bed of fragrant green, that I imagined myself lying down on it and taking a long summer's nap. Forever.

"I mean, shit," I said to the lawn. "What am I gonna do now?"

Not only did I mean that with regard to my relationship with Shane, but in a more specific sense too. I was physically stuck in the Palisades. Jane didn't have much assistance to offer either, the Pierce household being completely carless that weekend. (Her dad had taken their Explorer to North Carolina for a golfing expedition, and her mom's Camry was in the shop for repairs.) It was like, all around I just couldn't catch a break, you know?

Saving me from my middle-of-the-night melancholy, Jane invited me into her house and said I could spend the night. Okay—it's not what you think. We weren't going to do anything dirty. Jane just thought that given the hour, it would be better for me to crash at her place for the night and get some rest so I could face all my troubles, not to mention my own parents, bright eyed and bushy tailed, in the morning.

As we entered Jane's kitchen, the first thing I noticed was the time flashing blue on the microwave. 3:07 A.M. Then as Jane flicked the lights on, the second thing I noticed was Jane's mom.

"Hey, kids—what's shaking?"

Jane's mom was as cute and petite as Jane, her brunette hair, peppered with gray and cut into a professional bob that framed a face that was as naturally pretty as Jane's. Wearing some casual sleepwear that consisted of a pair of Georgetown sweats and a pair of big owl-eye glasses, she seemed guileless that we'd we caught her in her adult jammies.

"Mom?" said Jane, equally as startled as I was to get this parental hi-ho at such a late hour. "What are you doing up so late?"

"*Trading Spaces* marathon on TLC," she said blithely, heading toward the fridge. "I'm feeling snacky. . . . You kids want some ice cream?"

"No, thanks," said Jane.

I was especially shocked to meet Jane's mom at this hour because my parents never stay up late, usually hitting the sack by eleven. You see, they are total morning people, bustling around the house at 6:00 A.M. and always trying to rouse me with the promise that it was a beautiful day. Okay, but if it's a decent looking day at 6:00 A.M., it's only going to look better to someone like me after 9:00, you know what I mean?

As Mrs. Pierce scoped out the contents of her freezer, Jane and I regarded each other warily, unsure of what exactly to tell her mom about the awkward situation that had stranded me at her house. Having retrieved a pint of Ben & Jerry's, the lady of the house became aware of our strange silence and curiously regarded us. Namely me.

"Who's your new friend?"

"Oh, sorry," said Jane. "This is Cameron."

"Nice to meet ya, Cameron," she said, waving from across the island in the center of the kitchen, searching for a spoon. "What are you kids doing up so late anyway?"

"We, uh, we were at the prom," I said, neglecting to mention the rest of the evening's itinerary. Talk about a half-truth . . . more like a one-eighth truth.

"Holy cow," she said, looking up from her late night snack. "I'm sorry, Janey. I totally spaced that was tonight. I've been going nuts with these congressional oversight hearings all week: In the office at eight, on the Hill all day, then back in the office till nine and barely getting any sleep, obviously."

"No biggie," said Jane, meaning it. The prom had certainly not been some Cinderella-like fantasy for her, that's for sure. If it had been that would have made me her prince. Ha.

"You work on Capitol Hill?" I wondered aloud.

Jane eagerly provided the bio. "She's the Assistant Secretary for Research at the FDA."

"She's always bragging like that," Jane's mom said dismissively, spooning some Chunky Monkey into her mouth. "But I wanna hear about your night. So how was the big ol' prom? Anyone spike the punch?"

If it had only been that simple.

"Hmmm—a little problematic," said Jane in a less-than-enthusiastic tone. Unlike me, Jane was not one to lie to her parents.

"I see," said her mom, thoughtfully enjoying her snack. "Proms never are easy affairs. Then factor in the drinking, the drugs, and God knows what else is available these days, and I'm sure you kids could get into some real trouble."

Silence. Jane and I shared complicit looks. Neither of us was going to take *that* bait.

"But now it's, what, three in the A.M. and you two look like you survived. You're standing up straight and not puking in my sink and don't seem to be reeking of anything."

"Actually I did get a little stoned," offered Jane, to my outright astonishment.

Her mom stopping chewing for a moment.

"But you weren't driving and no bong hits, right?"

And the lack of bonging made it better?

"Uh, nope."

"Good," she said, strangely satisfied by Jane's frankness as much as I was shocked by it. So this was what it was like living in a house with full disclosure? I felt like I'd entered a weird parallel universe, like you'd see on an episode of *Voyager*. You know, the show with that superhunky captain. . . . The one who is always without a shirt on, baring his hairy chest. Can it get any sexier than that? But I digress . . .

"So then," Jane's mom wondered. "What exactly was the problematic part?"

"Basically Shane and Cam got in this huge fight and Shane wouldn't take Cam back to where his car is parked in Foxhall so he's stuck here."

I sighed with relief that Jane didn't give her the full-on story.

"Bummer," she said, shaking her head at this abridged version.

"So is it okay if Cam spends the night?"

"Sure. The couch is free now that my marathon's over," she said, smiling. "But I have one question. . . . What happened to your tux?"

"Uh," I said, jumping in and stopping Jane from saying a truthful word on this subject. I still had my dignity. Or at least I had the illusion that I had my dignity. "It's a majorly long story."

"Hmmmm," she said, savoring her ice cream as she contemplated the real meaning behind my opaque answer. "Sounds like it'll be something for your memoirs someday, right?"

"I don't know if I wanna remember anything about tonight. Well, except Jane maybe."

The Mrs. smiled at me warmly and quickly nodded at Jane.

"I like this one," she said to Jane.

"Uh, he's not available, Mom," offered Jane.

"Girlfriend?"

"Gay."

If I'd had some ice cream, this would have been the moment I would have choked on it. Or done a creamy spit take. You see, in true what-goes-around-comes-around fashion, it was apparently Jane's turn to out me in front of her mom. But given Mrs. Pierce's lack of reaction, Jane might as well have told her that I was left-handed.

"Oh, well," she said flippantly. "Sounds like good company, though."

"The best," said Jane as we exchanged smiles. "And a great dancer."

That at least was totally true, both in terms of the prom and my winning performance at Secrets. Jane was such a sly one sometimes, huh?

"Well, I've got a ten o'clock tennis match tomorrow with Madame Secretary so I better get my six hours in. Nice meeting you—"

"Cameron," I said, reminding her and adding my surname, as I have a tendency to do so when in the vicinity of adults. "Cameron Hayes."

"Hayes—really?"

"Uh . . . yeah," I said, wondering if I had said it right.

"I work with a Barbara Hayes out at NIH—I'm heading up the grant panel on their molecular research. Any relation?"

And that would be my mother.

"Unfortunately yes," I said, starting to feel slightly faint.

"Unfortunately?" said Jane's mom, turning to address Jane. "His mother's a wonderful scientist. Absolutely brilliant. I think I met your father, too, out in the parking lot one day. Isn't that something. . . . here I am with the son of the brilliant Hayeses in my kitchen at three in the morning. Ain't that a kick?"

More like a kick in the pants. That would be the front of my pants. Got it?

"Well, definitely tell your folks I said hi," she offered, heading to bed. "Good night, kids."

Jane and I stood there in silence for a few moments, listening to her mom's receding footsteps go upstairs. Freed from the post-parental gag rule, I spoke as if I'd been underwater for the duration of her mom's time in the kitchen.

"Ohmigod," I said, breathless. "I can't believe you told your mom I was gay!"

"I can't believe she knows your *parents,*" said Jane with wide eyes.

So yeah, I was fairly mortified to have been outed in this manner. But it was a total karmic boomerang that I should have seen heading my way after doing the same thing to Shane earlier that night. The bigger shock was that I'd never imagined that karma moved *that* quickly. I'd always understood it as an epic, life-spanning process when, in fact, payback was swift and painful.

"This is awful," I said, feeling woozy. "Just terrible. Horrific even."

"What—are you worried she's gonna tell your mom?"

"Yes . . . no . . . I don't know," I said, trying to sort through the thicket of feelings around this issue. One thing was clear though: One way or another, my parents were going to find out about me, if not through Mr. Mold then through Jane's mom or maybe some item in the Metro section about a certain underage Secrets patron who walked away with first prize at Amateur Night. So given that inevitability, running away from my folks didn't seem to make that much sense anymore. Despite my earlier more adventurous plans concocted during the whirlwind of excitement surrounding my escape from the prom, it seemed somewhat doubtful there were going to be any Motel 6s or late-night train rides in my immediate future. The endless possibilities of my night on the lam from the prom and high school and reality in general didn't seem so endless after all. In fact, the course of the rest of my evening, which had been a little fuzzy in the limo drive out to Palisades, was now coming into clear focus.

Though staying at Jane's had initially sounded appealing, I realized it was only delaying the inevitable confrontation with my parents by about six to eight hours. The haze of the night having lifted, I could see what I had to do: grab a cab to Foxhall, pick up my car at Ravenswood, and drive to Silver Spring to face the Jazz music, as it were. Even though returning home was not something I was looking forward to, knowing full well that it meant coming clean to Mom and Dad about everything, it did seem to be the most rational option. (Me thinking rationally . . . crazy, right?) But when the bad starts outweighing the good, there is something to be said for a plan of action set by reason and not emotion.

Still Jane tried to convince me to stay at her place, saying that the jig wasn't really up since her mom could keep her mouth shut. "Carol can keep the gay thing on the DL if you want," she said, surprisingly casual with her mom's real name.

Jane was trying to be helpful. But it struck me that more deceptions and secondhand cover-ups were not what I needed in my life. I'd been preaching the gospel of The Truth to Shane all night when the real truth was I needed a dose of it in my own life, maybe even more than he did.

"Thanks, but at this point it doesn't really matter," I said, my shoulders falling on the released weight of this burden. "I'm just gonna have to tell my folks all about tonight and Shane and everything. It feels inevitable at this point."

"Yeah, I guess you're right," said Jane, the heaviness of it all hitting her too. "I hope they're cool about it."

"Well, they are brilliant scientists, according to your mom. So in theory, they should be clinically objective about it, right?"

"Right," said Jane, encouraged. "But if they're not so scientific about the whole deal, give me a call and Carol will talk them through it. She went to school at Berkley in the seventies. . . . She knows her stuff when it comes to the gays."

I released a reluctant smile.

"Like mother like daughter."

Jane found the number for National Taxi and placed
my cab order. Since there were a bunch of proms happening that
night, they told her the wait would be about thirty to forty-five minutes. Checking the clock again, it was nearly 3:30 and Jane was
seriously dragging. I told her she could hit the sack and didn't have
to stay up with me, that I could wait outside. Jane didn't think it was
such a great idea to have me sitting out on her street alone. However,
after pointing out to her that Palisades was a safe neighborhood,
even at that hour, she conceded. With a kiss on the cheek this time
and zero tongue action (honest!), we said our good-byes.

Leisurely making my way down the Pierces' curved front walk
toward the curb, I glanced over at the driveway and saw the shiny oil
spots. Jesus. I mean, who'd have ever thought that friggin' motor oil
could get a person all choked up? I felt another episode of losing it
coming on as my eyes welled up again and I thought about how, in
only a few hours, everything about my relationship with Shane had
seemingly fallen apart. Yet I also recalled how, back in the beginning
of this whole boyfriend misadventure, everything about our relationship seemed totally improbable in the first place.

The first time I met Shane, I mean, actually talked to him one-
on-one, had been back in November. My original sports editor had
quit to focus on getting into an Ivy League school so the yearbook
advisor, on a recommendation from Shane's former football coach,

had named Shane the sports editor. When I heard this, even though I thought Shane was cute and all that, I was still fairly annoyed since as editor-in-chief I was under the nutty perception that *I* was in charge of the yearbook. So when Shane came to meet with me to discuss his duties, I was determined to be a bit of a hard-ass.

After making him wait in the hallway about ten minutes, I finally called him in and sat him way on the other side of my desk in a stiff old chair, giving the impression that he was being called in to be punished for something. And in a weird way, that was true. I was punishing Shane for being so damn attractive and popular and well liked. You know . . . for being everything that I wanted to be in high school but never quite had the looks or social ability to attain. Thus I'd decided I was going to make his life on the yearbook staff not so much fun. So I started talking a blue streak about how being sports editor sounds easy, like all you have to do is throw a bunch of pictures and scores into PageMaker and you're done, but in reality it's probably the hardest job because there are so many pictures and scores that you have to pick and choose the right ones and use them to tell the story of sports at Prep for that year blah blah blah. Basically I was being a total bore and barely letting Shane get more than a few *yeah*s or *cool*s in between my incredibly long-winded dissertation on sports editing.

After about ten minutes of this I hit a lull in my lecture and something utterly embarrassing happened. I completely lost my train of thought while looking at Shane, something that tends to happen to the majority of people who stare directly at him for more than a few minutes. So as I sat there dumbly, mutely even, Shane looked at me and smiled, thus forcing me to rustle around some papers on my desk, pretending to look for something very important. The weird thing is that, glancing up at Shane, he seemed equally as dumbstruck and awkward as I was, which I thought was pretty damn odd. Maybe he'd actually been impressed by what I had to say. Wondering what was up, I squinted at him, the late afternoon sunlight from the window making it difficult to see his face at that point. Then Shane said the most remarkable thing.

"You know, your eyes are incredibly green."

Honest. That's exactly what he said. Word for word. I know this because I scribbled it down a minute or so later under the pretense of taking notes. I mean, talk about one of the most improbable things to come out of the mouth of this guy, this god, this gorgeously sporty dude sitting in my office! So that was the moment I knew something was afoot. What exactly was going on would not be completely apparent until the end of that month at homecoming, but oh, the promise of his words. I can't even begin to tell you the dizzying heights that simple sentence raised my hopes to. And then when those hopes were actually made real with his kiss in the dark, the whole thing was so damn . . . overwhelming. It was frankly too good to be true. Yet unbelievably, it *wasn't!* Making out with Shane *was* true. It had happened!

Homecoming night was followed by a number of subsequently random acts of making out in December, until we finally fooled around on New Year's Eve at his house, his parents safely attending a charity ball. That's when things took a more intense turn, and soon enough actually being boyfriends with Shane *was* true. But you know what? After all the revelations and disasters of prom night, it turned out that my instincts from the moment Shane laid eyes on my eyes were right. It *was* too good to be true, because as it turned out I was merely his "special guy" and not really his boyfriend. Our "relationship" was, in many ways, one big lie.

Anyway, thinking about all this only bummed me out even further, and my eyes started tearing up again. Another breakdown was minutes away. Looking down Jane's drowsy lane, I was relieved to see that this time, there was no one around to witness me losing it—not a person in sight, not a single window lit up, not a car in motion. The neighborhood was void of all life. That vast emptiness, however, only served to amplify my own exponentially growing feelings of loneliness and, as one tear slipped through my weakened defenses, it felt like the whole dam of sorrow was going to burst again.

In the instant before this happened though, a bright light flashed on my backside, casting my long skinny shadow across the pavement against streaks of luminescent white. For a split second I thought maybe it was God or something, appearing to me in my darkest hour like he's supposed to. You know, like in all those Bible stories? Or *Touched by an Angel*? Maybe it was some crazy angel, sent down from up on high to save me from yet another suicidal spiral. But then I remembered that God and angels are more of a fictional concept than an actual bright light, and besides, that shit never happens in real life anyway. Only in lame Jimmy Stewart movies they show in an endless loop around Christmas.

So I bet you'll never guess who it was, shining this revelatory beam on me? Not that it was anyone I knew or anything. It was merely the District police again. And you know what? After their haphazard pursuit of me twice before, it looked like the third time was going to be their charm.

"Okay," I said holding my hands aloft. "I give up."

A squad car was slowly inching toward me down the block, the silver sidelight casting its stark beams on me. Then as it came to a stop about ten feet away from me, I noticed something odd. The roof lights were not flashing red and there was no siren wailing. Also there was only one squad car, as opposed to a fleet of vehicles in hot pursuit, indicating that this wasn't the posse that had been after me before.

The front door of the cop-mobile creaked opened and out stepped a very tall police officer whose features were somewhat obscured by the light still shining directly into my eyes.

"You can put your hands down," the policeman said in an easy, almost friendly tone. "You're not under arrest."

"I . . . I'm not?"

"Not yet at least," he said, ambling over to where I stood, his heels clicking menacingly on the street. As he approached I could see this cop more clearly. He had a lean figure and a long, narrow face with protruding, Alfred E. Neumanesque ears. Did I mention he was tall? Like, basketball tall. Stopping directly in front of me, he was at least 6'5".

"You mind telling me what you're doing sitting out here at three thirty in the morning?"

"It's, uh, it's kind of a long story," I said, repeating my escape clause that had worked with Mrs. Pierce. Now, in case you find yourself in a similar predicament, let me be the first to tell you that this vague approach doesn't work so well with the police.

"It always is," said the cop, like he had heard this excuse about a million times. Then as he looked me over for weapons or wounds or stolen property, all he found was the lonely track of a tear cutting across my left cheek. And you know what? He had the friggin' nerve to ask me about it.

"You feeling okay?" he wondered, an actual note of concern in his voice.

"Uh, well . . . honestly?"

He swallowed a laugh.

"Well, I wouldn't advise lying to me."

"Okay, then," I said, relieved to be forced into the truth. "It's been, I don't know . . . kind of a hard night."

"Uh huh," he said, like he had also heard this line way too many times before. "Why don't we get back to why you're sitting out here, okay?"

Taking a huge breath, I explained the basics of leaving my car at Shane's for the prom and then coming back here in the limo, as well as the more recent cab-to-the-car scenario. The cop nodded suspiciously.

"Are you drunk?"

"God . . . I wish," I said, forgetting for a moment that I was talking to an officer of the law.

"You do, huh?" he said, sounding like he was going to write me up for being a smart-ass. Taking a more formal tack, I tried some old-fashioned decorum.

"I'm sorry, Officer. I didn't mean it that way. You see . . . I'm not totally . . . myself tonight. It's been a really, uh, emotional evening and—"

I stopped. Not on purpose but because I was choking again, on the verge of having yet another breakdown. In fact, that last sentence had been enough to send another fugitive tear heading for the border, making its way to freedom across my right cheek. I slapped it away like a gnat but it was too late. Johnny Law had discovered, much to his dismay, that the criminal element (uh, that would be me) had emotions. Very intense ones, too.

"All right, how 'bout you get in the patrol car with me."

And then I snapped.

"Oh, please, Officer," I said, relapsing into my crazy, high-pitched pleading voice as a couple more tears slipped out. "If you have any mercy or heart or soul I beg you to please not do this. I fully regret everything that I—"

Putting a calming hand on my shoulder, he tried to get me to relax. "Hold on there," he said in a tone generally used for talking down a horse. "I was just going to offer you a ride to your car."

"You—-you were?"

"There are seven proms going on in the city tonight," he said. "You'll be waiting for that cab until the sun comes up."

Once it was clear to me that this cop had no idea about my near-miss record for eluding his coworkers twice that night, I realized that he was actually trying to help me out. Imagine that, huh? The police coming to my rescue? Given the endless improbabilities the evening had already spawned, this one seemed, on balance, not so improbable.

"But, uh, don't you have to work?" I wondered.

"This *is* my work."

So taking the kindly cop up on his offer, I walked with him to his car. Reaching for the door to the backseat, he stopped me.

"You don't have to ride in the back," he said, somewhat bemused.

"I . . . I don't?"

"Not unless you *want* to feel like a criminal."

Since I already knew that feeling well enough, thank you very much, I quickly went around and opened up the front door. Settling into my seat, I realized that I had never been in a police car before and shared this remarkable trivia with my cop. His response was as follows: "Don't touch anything and you'll do just fine."

As he shifted into gear we pulled away from Jane's house, leaving her sad, oily driveway behind as we headed toward what would hopefully be the end of my endless night. I say *hopefully* because by this point I knew that nothing on this night went as planned.

"So is this your regular beat?" I asked.

"Usually I patrol the Spring Valley area," he said. "But I was responding to a call we got about half an hour ago, about a domestic."

"What's a domestic?"

"A domestic argument," he said. "Apparently someone on that block heard a couple arguing. Something about a car, from what I got. Except the caller also said they sounded like kids."

As it turns out, he was responding to a complaint regarding the argument Shane and I had in the Pierces' driveway. Not that I was going to mention this. I mean, c'mon, this was a cop I was talking to. What was he going to understand about two guys having a "domestic"?

Driving through the thickly forested neighborhoods of the Palisades, the trees casting eerie shadows as we buzzed past them, it took us about ten minutes to get to Foxhall from Jane's. In that time my Friendly Neighborhood Policeman gave me the rundown on his life. I know it sounds strange, right? But his audio autobiography came about solely because I was somewhat reluctant to discuss the specifics of my own sordid existence, namely the shocking itinerary that had led me to Jane's curb in the middle of the night. So I let him do all the talking, and thankfully he obliged quite willingly.

My cop's name was Sean, and at twenty-two, he was certainly a bit younger than your average policeman. The story about how this had happened was actually kind of interesting. You see, Sean's conservative parents had raised him to be a Washington lawyer, just like his dad. But after two fairly unsuccessful years at Georgetown University on the pre-law track, Sean opted out of school for the more exciting end of justice, passing D.C.'s law enforcement exam with ease and breezing through six months of training before being deposited on the mean streets of upper Northwest. Patrolling the sedate glens and coves of the Second Police District he'd seen all sorts of lame action, such as breaking up illegal teen parties in Wesley Heights and searching for runaway dogs in Spring Valley. He even admitted that his discovery of me was probably the most unusual thing that had happened to him on patrol in the last month. However, because of this lack of action in his district, Sean had been itching for an assignment in the rougher parts of town.

"You mean like in Southeast?" I said, like the expert in lawlessness that I was becoming.

"Yeah," he said. "The First District is very high incident. Always something going on down there. In fact, earlier tonight they had a hot pursuit through the warehouse district."

"Wow," I said, feigning ignorant excitement on the matter. And the Oscar for Best Supporting Surprise in a real-life role goes to . . .

"Did they catch him?"

"Nope," said Sean, disappointed and surely thinking that had it been on his watch, Dmitri would be behind bars. (Along with me, of course.) "The guy had some tricked-out sports car."

"An RX-7," I offered.

Whoops.

"Hey—how did you know?"

"Uh," I said, desperately looking for cover. "I think I heard something about it on the news."

"I don't think it was on the news yet," he said, eyeing me with a hint of suspicion. "It happened well after eleven."

"The radio, I mean, on WTOP. They said they found the car at the Lincoln Memorial."

"Yeah . . . it was totaled, too, stuck in a volleyball pit. But they didn't find him," he said, believing me, fortunately. "Just some morons skinny-dipping in Constitution Gardens."

"Uh, those would be my friends."

"Really?" he said, bemused. "Were you down there too?"

"Uh . . . maybe," I stalled, unsure of where my guilt began or ended at this point. "Are you gonna arrest me if I was?"

"Not now," said Sean, laughing to himself. "It's a little late for that."

Seeming more relaxed, Sean took off his police hat and put it on the seat between us. In the reflected reddish glare of a stoplight, his face seemed more open, less authoritarian without the brim of the hat hiding it. His hair was auburn and wavy and somewhat beyond standard cop length, most of it having been shoved up into his hat.

"All right, now that you know everything about me, I think it's time I get the full story about how you ended up in the Palisades at three thirty in the A.M.?"

"I don't know," I said cautiously. "What's the rule on things I say being used against me in a court of law."

"Were you doing something illegal tonight?"

Deciding to focus on the positive, I thought I'd start with the things I *hadn't* done.

"I didn't go skinny-dipping in that pond."

"Okay—but was there something else that you *did* do?'

Here's where I had a moment of memory recall from my American Government class.

"I'm gonna take the Fifth on that."

Hey, not to be all public-service announcement or anything, but let me tell you for the record: Sometimes it really *does* pay off to pay attention in class. Especially when you find yourself riding in a police car in the middle of the night after having broken and bent the law in various and sundry ways.

"Look, here's the deal," said Sean, taking on the authoritative voice of a law professor. "If you're not in police custody, which technically you're not even though you're in my car, nothing you say can be held against you."

"That's a relief," I said with a huge exhale.

Sean raised his finger to make a big point. "That is, unless you murdered someone. Then I'd probably have to turn you in."

Swinging his goofy head around, Sean flashed me a lopsided grin.

So since I was pretty sure that no one had died yet in the course of my misadventures, I decided to give him the basics of my really nice prom mess, as I've taken to calling it. Or at the least, I made a valiant effort to do so.

"Okay, but it's hugely complicated. There are so many things that happened tonight."

Frustrated, Sean gave an annoyed sigh. "How 'bout this," he offered, trying to be helpful. "What is the main thing that happened tonight? The thing that had you so upset when I first saw you."

"Oh, that," I said, my face going crimson. "I don't know if I can talk about that."

There was a dramatic pause.

"*Did* you murder someone?"

"No!"

When he made murder the worst-case scenario, telling the truth was more of a breeze.

"I think my boyfriend dumped me."

There was a studied silence. Sean nodded his head a bit, fake concentrating on driving when he probably didn't have to since we were only going about twenty miles per hour through the empty side streets of Spring Valley. After a minute of mulling over my unexpected confession, Sean offered a response that was not quite what I expected.

"What do you mean by 'you think'?"

Sean, as it turned out, was actually curious about the whole thing. He didn't express horror that I was gay or even disgust that I actually had a boyfriend. He seemed to just want the dirt, as it were, about what happened between Shane and me in our biggest fight ever. So I presented the details from my own crazy perspective, which is that I had done absolutely nothing wrong and that Shane was a total dick. I know—not exactly the most objective rendering of the night, but on some level it was basically true, right?

After a couple minutes retelling my troubles, I wrapped things up.

"And then Shane kicked me out of the limo and drove away."

"Hmmmm," said Sean thoughtfully, contemplating the details like the detective that I guess he sorta was. "Did Shane say anything like 'I don't want to ever see you again'?"

"Uh . . . nope."

Pleased by my answer, Sherlock then presented his findings in the case.

"Sounds like you just had a fight, then," he said with relaxed reason. "A big fight, but it doesn't sound like the end of a relationship."

Coming from a guy in uniform with a deep voice, this theory sounded logical. Maybe Sean *was* right. Maybe it wasn't The End—drop curtain, roll credits—of the Shane epic.

"So you really think there's hope for us?"

Even though I was being very serious with this question, Sean chuckled a bit.

"Yeah," he said with a pleasant smile. "You're both, what, eighteen? There's *plenty* of hope."

And didn't that make me smile for the first time in hours.

# CHAPTER 22

It was almost four in the morning when we arrived at Ravenswood. I told Sean that it was okay for him to turn into the Wilsons' driveway, saying how they were too old money for an electronic gate, but he said that he probably shouldn't. In his time on the force, he'd learned that people tend to stress out when a police car pulls into their driveway at that hour. He did say, however, that he would wait on the street until I got my parents' car started to ensure that I didn't get stranded for the second time in the evening. I tried to tell him that he didn't have to do that, but he insisted. I thought that was sweet, you know, for a cop.

Given the late hour and the odd circumstances of my visit, I tip-toed my way up the driveway to where my car was parked, not wanting to wake any of the Wilsons. I remember thinking that Shane was probably not asleep since he had a tendency to be a bit restive when worked up over something. (And there had been a few things to be worked up over—that I couldn't deny.) Still, I decided that I wouldn't bother him and that I would let insomniac dogs lie, you know? The best course of action would be to give him a full day to calm down. Then I could ring him on Sunday to sort everything out if, as Sean claimed, there was stuff left to sort out. But I was very optimistic about our prospects after Sean's encouraging interpretation of our crisis as being just that: a crisis and not a conclusion.

I found my parents' car easily, as it was the only one left in the driveway that didn't belong to the Wilsons. Quietly I opened the front door, delicately buckled my seat belt, and went to start the engine when I realized there was a minor problem—there were no keys in the ignition. Instinctually I checked my pants pockets but realized I was not wearing my pants; I had Buck's jeans on. Then somewhat frantically I pawed the passenger's seat, rifled through the glove compartment, and scanned the floor, looking for the keys. But they were nowhere to be found.

As my mind raced, I thought back to the beginning of the evening. I was pretty sure that I had left the keys in the ignition, thinking a) they were making an unsightly bulge in my tux pants and b) leaving them in the car parked in the Wilsons' driveway would be safe. Then a grim thought clouded up my sunny mood. Maybe Shane, in one of his uncontrollable fits of anger, had taken the keys to get back at me for the whole Ian/outing thing. However, something like that would have been too petty and mean even for Shane. I wondered, though, if maybe he had taken the keys but not in anger. Maybe it was yet another obscure and typically indirect Shane message, indicating to me that when I came to retrieve the car, he wanted me to come see him, too.

I walked back to Sean's patrol car.

"No keys," I said, whispering to him through the window.

"Do you know where they are?"

"I think Shane has them."

"Hmmmm," said Sean, looking concerned. "I wouldn't advise ringing the doorbell."

"No, no, no," I said, like, duh. "I'm going to head around back to where his bedroom window is and get his attention."

"I don't know," said Sean, eyeing the imposing mansion behind me. "You think that's a great idea at this hour?"

I explained to Sean how before the big fight Shane had actually wanted me to spend the night at Ravenswood. So maybe, I hoped, Shane was over our fight and had taken the keys as a sign that all was, in fact, well.

"I don't know," said Sean, eyeing me again with some concern.

"I'm sure it'll be fine," I said breezily.

"So you really going to spend the night, then?" asked Sean skeptically.

I shrugged. "Guess I'll find out, huh?"

Sean grinned nervously at this and told me to let him know either way what happened, that he would be waiting. I agreed, and stepping gingerly I went back up the driveway and made my way around toward the rear of the house.

Familiar with the layout of Ravenswood from countless visits over the past few months, I found Shane's ground-floor window easily, as it was the only one with a light on, confirming my insomnia suspicions. However, his shade was pulled down, making it impossible for him to see me in the backyard. And I wasn't going to bellow out his name for fear of waking his parents. So bending down, I rummaged in the plantings under his window for a small pebble or branch I could toss at the window to get his attention. Finding a quarter-size piece of bark, I lobbed it at the corner of the window. No response. However, after a minute I did see Shane move across the room toward his stereo. The sound of a loud but muffled CD could be heard playing, A Simple Plan's second album. All right, I did think that perhaps turning on the music was a blow-off move. But also maybe he just hadn't heard the noise the bark had made. Feeling optimistic, I went with the latter explanation and decided to try again.

Finding a candy-bar-shaped chunk of dead branch, I flicked it sideways so as to avoid potential window breakage. It skittered across the glass, making a decent racket but still garnering no response from Shane. *Maybe,* I began to fear, he was ignoring me, or maybe with the music going it was hard to hear the sound of twigs and bark. Scouting around for something with more heft, I found a moist clump of dirt that looked like it would be more effective in making a deep thump to counter the noise of A Simple Plan. I tossed it window-ward and it hit the upper reaches of the pane, breaking into a rain of dirt that cascaded down the face of the glass and hit the sill with the crackle of a brief but heavy rain shower.

Instantly the shade flew up and Shane appeared.

I smiled upon seeing him, relieved that he was not ignoring me. However, Shane was not smiling. Not at all.

"Cameron," he said, after cranking open the side pane. "What the hell are you doing here?"

"I, uh . . . I came to get my car."

Shane rolled his eyes, his level of annoyance with me having not abated at all. If anything it seemed to have increased.

"I am not your car, Cameron."

"But I—don't—uh," I said, stumbling all over my words. "You've got the keys."

"What makes you think I have your car keys?"

But before I could explain how I thought the missing keys were a sign that he still wanted me to spend the night, I was cut off.

"Maybe you didn't understand what I meant over at Jane's," he said harshly.

"You kicked me out of your limo, " I said. "I think I got that part."

But Shane shook his head. Clearly there was some other Shane message that I had not received or interpreted. And it went a little something like this. . . .

"I really don't want to see you anymore, Cameron. Ever," he said with steely conviction. "You ruined my prom night, you ruined my friendship with Ian, you've ruined my life. I thought all that was pretty clear. But if it wasn't, it should be now. Because of all this disaster that you've created I . . . don't . . . want . . . to see . . . you. Ever again."

I couldn't believe what I was hearing. It was as if Sean's mention of that penultimate sentence of doom on the drive to Ravenswood had actually willed the phrase into existence and thrust it into Shane's mouth.

"You don't?"

Shane looked suddenly uncomfortable.

"You really should get home. It's been a long night."

"But my keys—"

"Good-bye, Cam."

"Good-bye?" I said, hoping he had meant to say good night and it just came out wrong. But he didn't retract the phrasing. Shane had meant exactly what he said, and with a sad squeak he closed his window and drew his shade. Curtain down. The end. Roll credits.

I couldn't believe it. At 4:00 A.M. on prom night (friggin' prom night!) my boyfriend had just dumped me as I stood outside his bedroom window. I mean, c'mon . . . when a guy shows up at another guy's house in the middle of the night, especially if this jerk is that loser's boyfriend, shouldn't there be professions of poetic love rising to the balcony and sparks of passion raining down onto the lawn? Apparently not in my case.

Not only was I in shock at the act of the breakup, but also with the situation itself. Of all the odd ways and means to break up with someone, this one was truly bizarre. I mean, we weren't even face-to-face for it, the window screen coming between us. Seriously . . . it was like breaking up at the Taco Bell drive-through! You know, here's your change and have a nice life.

Contemplating the horror of it all, I sank into the Wilsons' perfect wet grass and realized that, in the realm of my life, there was actually a certain sick sense about the whole window-dumping thing. You know how I was talking about how I have bad phone karma and terrible timing in general? Well, on top of those handicaps, I also have this problem of things often turning out the exact opposite of how I expect them to. For instance, once I figured out back in the tenth grade I liked guys, I imagined that my first kiss would be on a brilliantly gorgeous beach, rolling around with some totally hot Jams-wearing surfer on a colorful beach blanket, making out and going at it as the July sun warmed our backs. Of course, the reality of my first gay kiss was the absolute opposite, crammed as it was into a pitch-black closet at someone's parents' house in the middle of a homecoming kegger. Not exactly the roar of the Atlantic in my ears, you know what I mean?

So continuing on this theme, I also had a stupid fantasy that prom night might actually be a romantic evening, ultimately ending in the coziness of Shane's bed. Except there I was, at the end of the night, sitting alone in Shane's chilly backyard after having my ass summarily dumped. It was at that moment that I felt like I was so tired of this type of incongruity in my life. So damn sick of it and sick of Shane's role in it too that I decided to take action.

Crawling on my knees, I searched the muddy garden for another piece of bark and flung it toward the window. *PLUNK!* Shane's reaction? He turned out his light. This only served to infuriate me. Scrambling for another branch, I threw it too. *CLUNK!* Shane turned the music up louder. Feeling an amazingly frustrated rage bubble up inside me as if I were a human volcano, I channeled that energy into explosive action. I discovered a small rock and without thinking whipped it at the center of the window. *CLANK!* But that was only the beginning of the sound that rock made. In one of life's awful slow-motion moments, the sharp end of the stone spawned a spiderweb of cracks, causing the whole window to shatter into a billion pieces, collapsing into heap of broken glass on the sill. In a word . . . *CRRRRAAAAAASSSSSHHH!*

Then, of course, the Wilsons' security system went off. I mean, went off!

"Burglary! Burglary! Burglary!" an inhuman voice barked out from some hidden speaker somewhere, echoing through the valley behind the house in a manner that seemed to triple the volume.

"You have violated a secure area!" screamed Big Brother. "Leave immediately!"

Then as an alarm started to wail all the floodlights in the backyard started to strobe like mad. Up on the second floor of the house, a couple lights flipped on in the Wilsons' master bedroom, while on the ground floor Shane's bedroom shade flew up and he came into view, freaky horror-movie shadows courtesy of the floods flashing across his face. Now that I had his full and undivided attention, Shane glared at me through the gaping hole where his window used to be. There was nothing between us but air. About twelve feet of it. Though this distance was not long enough for even his long-armed reach, I truly thought that at that moment he was going to reach out and strangle me.

Jolting my body into action, I jumped up from the wet grass and bid Shane adieu.

"Bye!"

He didn't say anything in response to this. Not that I expected him to. But as sick as this sounds, I have to say it was very satisfying to know that I got the last word in our relationship.

Running like a maniac as all hell broke loose around me, I sprinted around the side of the house and down the driveway, heading for the squad car. Looking as alarmed as Shane, Sean rolled down his window.

"What's going on?"

But I didn't have time to answer. I ran around to the passenger's side and hopped in, locking the door behind me. Sean, however, sat there like a statue, not nearly in as much of a hurry as I needed him to be.

I turned and practically screamed at him.

"Go!"

Then his radio crackled to life.

"Second District, any units in the vicinity of 1280 Fuller. We have an automatic 10-14."

"A prowler?" said Sean, truly perplexed as he regarded me with a certain shock. "I thought you were getting your—"

"I broke his window . . . with a rock . . . but it was an accident. Just go!"

"Oh, man—," moaned Sean, incredibly disappointed with me.

I looked back at the house. On the first floor, a couple more lights blinked on.

"Just go—I can't deal with this now. Pleeeease?"

"Cameron, I can't leave the scene of a crime," he said, trying to be all law and order with me. Can you believe it?

"But it's not a crime," I tried to explain while in full hysterics. "It was an *accident*."

Sean was not getting the distinction.

"Still, we have to straighten this out."

He was trying to be responsible and logical, as cops are expected to be. But you see, I was not living in a logical or even a lawful world that night. So the trick at that alarming moment was convincing the police officer next to me that it was imperative that he too must break the law to save my sorry ass. That somehow he actually owed it to me. And you know what? Having a total eureka moment, I realized that in a way, he did. He totally did!

"You were wrong, Sean . . . totally wrong," I said, getting frantic as I tried desperately to get him to put that police car in gear. "Shane hates me and was still mad at me and—"

The police radio came to life again, with the voice of another officer this time. "Unit 148. I'm at McArthur and Foxhall, responding to 10-14. ETA three minutes."

I turned to Sean again, my face in full-on panic mode. The dragnet was closing in on me.

"Ohmigod," I said, pleading with him. "Just go . . . *please?*"

"Look, Cameron. There are proper procedures and—"

But I couldn't hear about proper procedures. I had bigger problems, of which I began to inform him in my highly effective, high-pitched crazy person's voice.

"He dumped me! Shane broke up with me! Just now!" Cue tears. Not that they really needed any cuing . . . by this point they were a fairly natural occurrence. "And he said . . . he said he didn't want to see me! Ever! He said good-bye . . . *forever!*"

As I screamed this last sentence, my dam fully broke. (That's right, *again.*) But this time it was even worse than at the Reflecting Pool. Take two of my breakdown involved not only endless tears cascading down my face while my lips trembled as if they were having an 7.8 earthquake, but my breathing went totally AWOL. I think it was this last symptom, my inability to retain oxygen, that truly freaked Sean out. His instinct as a police officer, of course, was to stay and figure this all out with reason and the bright light of the law. But the reality was I was losing it in his car, gasping for air and starting to look like a fright. I mean, when a cop is more scared of your physical state than the circumstances of aiding and abetting a fugitive, you know you are looking seriously scary. It was a decisive factor in Sean's momentary leap to the Dark Side.

"Oh, man," he said, torn between duty and a real concern that I might expire in his front seat. He picked up his radio and clicked it on.

"This is Unit 130. In the general vicinity but going 10-10."

"Roger 130. 148 responding. Have a good night."

"Ohmigod," I said, thinking he was actually turning me in via code. "What the hell is 10-10?"

"It means off duty, okay?" he said, annoyed by this predicament I'd gotten him into.

Careful not to make a tire-squealing exit, Sean gently shifted his patrol car into gear and we left Ravenswood behind at a rational speed. Arriving at the intersection of Foxhall, we hung a smooth left without even stopping, and headed north in the opposite direction of the approaching Unit 148. At the end of Foxhall, Sean finally flipped on his roof lights, and with a severe right we flew down Nebraska Avenue and out of the neighborhood at top cop speed.

Though I greatly appreciated Sean's illegal efforts on my behalf, our escape from the law had not abated my tears. Despite his repeated verbal attempts to calm me, I kept on gasping and weeping and shaking like a madman. Slowing down a bit, Sean leaned over and popped open his glove compartment, wordlessly sliding a box of Kleenex into my lap. I turned to thank him but in my shaky condition couldn't even form that simple phrase.

After a few minutes, his radio crackled again.

"Unit 148. We're at 1280 Fuller. Residents claim to know the responsible party. No charges are being pressed."

With this Sean heaved a sigh of relief, turning his flashers off and slowing down to a more leisurely speed. "You are one lucky bastard," said Sean.

"I don't . . . really . . . feel . . . so lucky . . . right . . . now," I said between sniffles. "But thanks . . . for . . . getting . . . me . . . outta . . . there."

"Like I had a choice?" he said. "I can't stand it when a guy starts bawling. Drives me nuts!"

"Still, thanks," I said. "You took a . . . big risk . . . there."

"Not that big of a risk, really," he said, trying to downplay his daring. "I was guessing your boyfriend wasn't going to press charges. Even if he *does* hate you."

And this set me off on a mild wail of pain. Sean winced on hearing this. He really did have an adverse reaction to male tears.

"Sorry," he said, a little late. "I didn't mean it like that."

I tried to tell him it was okay, even though it wasn't. But I was having trouble formulating sentences again.

"Man—you're really a wreck," he said, looking at me sideways.

"Gee," I said, mopping up my face a bit. "Thanks."

Sean glanced at his dash, checking the time. "It's about four thirty now. We should probably get you home. Aren't your parents going to be worried about you?"

"No," I said, feeling a lump of something rise up my throat. "After everything I've done tonight, they probably hate me too."

"I'm sure they don't hate you," said Sean, trying to console me. Or maybe he was just trying to keep me from crying again.

"Oh, right. You were sure my *boyfriend* didn't hate me," I said, still perturbed by his bad advice.

"Now, wait a minute—don't get pissed at *me*," he said, his demeanor taking an unpleasant turn. "I had a basis for my advice. A sound basis actually."

"What, some book about gay guys they forced you to read in training?"

"No. Real-life experience."

This sounded odd. I turned to him with a dubious expression.

"Look," he said, sounding a little bummed out. "The truth is that Shane sounded exactly like my ex-boyfriend, that's all. I thought it was a similar situation. "

My tears seemed to freeze on my face as the cop outed himself to me. My renegade cop was a homo? Go figure.

"You mean you're—"

"Well, yeah," he said, surprised that I was figuring this out now. "How else could a guy give you boyfriend advice?"

# CHAPTER 23

Driving through the predawn quiet of Georgetown, we pulled over at an all-night falafel joint on Twenty-eighth Street, the King of Pita. Kindly reminding me that I looked like hell, Sean said I should go use their bathroom and get cleaned up before he took me home. I told him that he didn't have to drive me out to Silver Spring, that I could just call another cab, but since his shift was over he said it wasn't a problem.

King of Pita was ridiculously bright inside, lit with way too many fluorescents stuck at odd angles to the ceiling and blue neon Arabic letters hanging over the counter. The restaurant was fairly devoid of people at that hour, the only sound of human voices coming from an old color TV in the corner tuned to CNN. The only person in the joint was the cashier, a heavy-set, mustached man with a prodigious gut. Walking up to him and asking where the bathroom was, he insisted that I buy something; following some debate on this topic, I agreed to purchase a soda after using the bathroom. As the cashier got a closer glimpse of my distraught and messy face, he averted his gaze in the way that guys often do when they see another guy who has been crying. (Like Sean did, actually.) Fiddling with the register, the cashier produced a large key and without looking at me pointed it in the direction of the men's room.

After locking the bathroom door I did what I always saw people on TV do: I ran some cold water, which I then splashed on my face a few times. In the fictional world of television, this always seems to make criminals feel better and less guilty about their misdeeds. However, in the real world, splashing water on your face doesn't have this soul-cleansing effect. It simply makes your face even wetter and more unattractive than it was before. In my particular case it also turned the dirt on my cheeks (which had rubbed off from my hands during my time in the Wilsons' yard) into dark streaks of mud that literally looked like shit. I thought that maybe some soap was in order.

After scrubbing my face twice, I realized that my hair looked awful too. Ducking my head under the faucet, I flushed hot water through my mop. I noticed too late that there were only a couple paper towels left on the roll—enough for my hands but not for my hair. With no other options for drying, I shook my head like a dog, spraying water all over the bathroom. Staring at the mirror again, it was splattered with drops running south in jittery streaks toward the sink. I'd made the mirror look like it was crying. And you know what? That was fine by me, as by that point I was all cried out.

Stranded without any product or styling tools, I improvised a mini-makeover as I slicked my hair straight back, fashioning it flat and wet like I was a suave male supermodel. (Ha.) I checked out the new me in the mirror and growled. Until, that is, I started laughing, because basically I still looked like the old me. The only difference was that my dirty mop of hair was finally out of the way, providing an unobstructed view of the expanse of my forehead. Confronted by its panoramic size, I was bluntly reminded why I always combed my hair forward. But after all I'd been through, I didn't really care anymore what anyone thought of my hair, my forehead, or me for that matter.

So finished with grooming, I headed back into the world, my forehead leading the way. I was on my way to buy a Diet Coke from the cashier when I discovered Sean sitting at a round plastic table, a blue cafeteria tray crammed with hummus, pitas, falafels, and a couple of Diet Cokes in front of him.

"Hey," I said, puzzled by the spread. "What's up?"

"You were taking so damn long in there that I decided to get some food."

"Sorry," I said, wondering if he noticed why I'd taken so long. No luck. "Had to fix my hair."

"You hungry?"

"Definitely," I said, fishing in my pockets for my Amateur Night winnings. "How much do I owe you?"

"Don't worry about it," he said, as I sat down across from him. "It's on me."

"Wow," I said, slightly blindsided by the first true act of charity that evening. "Thanks."

"I was starving. I've been on duty since five o'clock yesterday."

"Me too," I said, which seemed to confuse him. I meant that I'd been on social duty, but I guess it's really not the same thing as being at work, though in my case it certainly had felt like it.

He grabbed one of the sodas, twisted off the top, and handed it to me.

"How did you know I wanted a Diet Coke?"

"I didn't," he said, picking his bottle up and raising it toward me. "Cheers."

Sean took a hearty chug and then dipped his pita triangle into the pool of yellowish oil that had formed in the center of the hummus. After dredging up a greasy mound of spread, he popped the whole thing in his mouth like it was a piece of popcorn. You see, Sean had this huge mouth.

"Mmmmm, they're warm," he said, talking with his mouth full in a way that was somehow not gross. Sean's mouth was so big that he could chew on one side and talk out of the other without revealing everything inside. "Have some . . . s'great!"

He pushed the tray in my direction. Thanking him, I nabbed a wedge of hot bread and after dipping it into the cool creamy sauce, the whole thing actually made for a pretty decent taste combo in my mouth, I have to say. I didn't realize it until taking that first bite but, man, I was starving too! Basically I had been running on fumes since midnight. The last time I'd eaten had been nearly twelve hours previous at Shane's buffet and those calories had evaporated, having been all used up by activities such as dancing, making out, getting in a fight, evading the cops, nearly drowning, evading the cops again, stripping for dollars, getting dumped, and accidentally breaking into my ex's house. Hey, maybe I could write a diet book based on this. Something like "Go to the prom and screw up your life, but *lose the weight!*"

"Easy there, chief," Sean said, as I devoured the whole bowl of hummus, shoveling mountainous heaps of it into my maw. I must have had the ravenous look of an exile recently arrived from some desert island, with bits of falafel clinging to my chin as a trail of hummus drooled out of the corner of my mouth.

"Sorry," I said, my mouth jammed with food. FYI, I have this way of talking with my mouth full that is far from graceful. Having a relatively smaller mouth than Sean, it was not nearly as cute and effortless as when he'd done the same thing. In fact, the sight of my full-frontal chew totally made him cringe.

It was at that point that I noticed something about Sean that I hadn't seen in the shadowy light of the patrol car; he had the most amazing and sparkly sky blue eyes. Maybe their hypercrazy color was due to the combo of the blazing fluorescents, the shining neon, and his matching blue uniform collar, but damn they were mesmerizing.

"What?" he said, catching me staring. But I'm sure he knew exactly what was up. He knew this look because I knew this look. You see, I could always tell when Shane was staring at my eyes and not at me, his focus shifted slightly lower for some reason even though technically he was gazing directly into my green orbs. Anyway, the bottom line here is that I was caught checking out Sean's eyes. In response I thought of co-opting Shane's line, the one that he'd used on me in the year book office a decade ago. But I didn't want it seem like I was trying to pick up a cop. Even if he was gay and single and handsome. Please! I had enough problems without dating the law.

"So do I look any better now, postcleanup?" I said, avoiding him and his eyes as a topic.

"Much more presentable," he said, glancing up at my hair. "Nice new do, too."

Really?

"Ohmigod, it's awful. My hair is a mess from the Reflecting Pool," I said without thinking. This was my new and unfortunate mode of speaking that night; talking without thinking.

"I *don't* wanna even know," Sean said, shaking his head and staring deeply into my . . . hair? "You know, you have a massive forehead."

"Uh . . . thanks," I said sarcastically, so as to make him feel bad.

"I didn't mean it as an insult," he said, lamely trying to convince me this was true. "I think big foreheads are cool."

"Okay—that's a very weird thing to say."

"Yeah," he said, laughing. "Still, I like them. I think they can be kinda sexy."

Big foreheads are *sexy?* Snatching a falafel, Sean popped it in his mouth in an attempt to distract me from this blatant and bizarre bit of flirtation. As he chewed on his falafel, I sat there wondering if Sean really thought I was going to be into the fact that he had some sort of pervy forehead fetish, even if the forehead in question was mine. Uh, nice try, but I don't think so.

"So you have a thing for . . . foreheads?"

"I don't know," he said, embarrassed and uncoplike. "Sort of. My ex had a huge forehead, like a Cro-Magnon man."

"Interesting," I said, not knowing exactly what to say when a guy compares you to his ex, whom he's also classified as subhuman. Should I agree with the assessment of the similarity? Should I jump on board the bash-the-ex bandwagon? Was there any kind of protocol for this? And if there was, how the hell would I know it anyway? I mean, Christ, I had just had my first breakup about a half hour previous, so all this was, you know, sorta new. So on the question of the ex, I decided to take the high road. The curious high road.

"So . . . exactly why did you guys break up?"

"Oh, man," he said, shaking his head ruefully. "Long story."

"Hey, I told you mine."

"Not all of it."

"Believe me," I said, dead serious. "It's all you need to know."

"All right," said Sean, trying to figure out where to begin his tale of romantic woe. "He was this guy who lived on my floor sophomore year. George. We used to have the same nine o'clock class and started having breakfast together all the time. And then studying and then . . . not studying."

Okay, a little too much information from a cop. I tried to ignore this and focus on the guy's name.

"George at Georgetown," I said, cheekily. "Cute."

"Oh, he was that, all right—actually he was really hot with—"

"I meant the name . . . George."

"Right," he said, catching himself before going TMI on me again. "Anyway, it was a very volatile up-and-down thing. We were both very serious about it and monogamous. But George was also intensely Catholic and had issues about the whole gay thing."

"Sounds like Shane," I said. "Except sports were more his religion."

"Same thing," said Sean, drawing a blank from me. He explained his point. "Look—they're both strong, ancient institutions that inspire irrational loyalty to questionable ends. You've seen how crazy Redskins fans are."

"Totally," I said, cracking up big at the expense of D.C.'s tragically inept football franchise. Sean smiled so much at me laughing at his lame joke that it seemed like he was maybe flirting with me. Again.

"George was a very sweet guy, but he got so caught up in what the Pope thought about our relationship that he couldn't see the forest for the trees."

"Whattya mean?"

"Belief in God and any religion is a belief in love, when it comes down to it. But George couldn't see that our love was a good thing simply because the Church said it was wrong."

Wow. That was some crazy shit, you know? I mean, I could

understand Shane's fear of what his friends and his parents might think about his being gay, as in many ways it was my own fear too. But being worried about what some ninety-something dude in Rome thought about your boyfriend seemed a little absurd. And I said as much.

"That's exactly right," said Sean, excited that I got his point. "It's absolutely ridiculous. People always point to the Bible as justification for this antigay stuff, but you know what Jesus said about homosexuality?"

I didn't have an answer to this, not having picked up a Bible in, oh, about eighteen years.

"Nothing," said Sean. "Not one holy word."

Even though I was no Biblical scholar or anything, this was a bit of a shocker. I wondered aloud why all the Catholics were freaked out about the gay thing.

"Recruiting," said Sean flatly. "Their numbers are diminishing, and gay Catholics won't exactly be cranking out new baby recruits for them. That's why the Church has problems with birth control and women being empowered. The only role for women as far as the Church is concerned is to make more Catholics."

"Wow," I said, truly shocked by this revelation. "It's just like *The Matrix*."

Sean looked up from scooping some hummus, somewhat baffled. "Wha?"

"You know, the Church is like the machines, harvesting babies and all."

"Hmmm," he said, considering this thoughtfully. "Interesting analogy, though a little exaggerated. I wonder, though . . . would that make Neo a gay crusader?"

"Shane always said he'd heard rumors about Keanu."

Sean nearly fell out of his chair when I said this. I mean, it wasn't *that* funny, right? But he thought it was the most hysterical thing he'd ever heard. Either that or this cute, blue-eyed cop kinda liked me.

After wiping that cafeteria tray clean of food, I was still hungry.

So on our way out, Sean bought me a baklava to take with me in the car. When I whipped out my winnings to try to pay for it, Sean busted in front of me and offered the cashier a fiver. I was going to pay for it myself, really, but he insisted. Isn't that sweet, you know, for a police officer and all?

As I munched on my dessert, Sean revved up the squad car and, shifting into gear, we left the King of Pita behind. But instead of heading out on Wisconsin Avenue toward Maryland, he turned onto P Street. When I questioned him about this he said that he shouldn't be driving around in his patrol car, being off duty and all. Since we were already in his neighborhood, Sean wanted to park the car at his mom's place (where he was living temporarily) and drive me out to the 'burbs in her car, an old Taurus. This was mildly disappointing, as I thought that showing up at my house in a cop car would have been pretty cool and might have momentarily distracted my parents from all my troubles. But Sean said that crossing the District line in his vehicle would have been pretty illegal. And at this point I wasn't going to argue for anything not legal.

Driving to his mom's, the stretch of P Street we traversed seemed somewhat familiar to me. I tried to remember if I'd been to one of those illegal no-parents parties on P, but none was coming to mind. The party at which I'd originally met Virginia was on Q Street. I definitely remembered that because I had shared a joke with Shane about it when I gave him the address, saying Q for *Queer*. Needless to say, it was a joke that landed on deaf ears. (That is, Shane's right ear. )

"Here we are," said Sean, noticing a place to park. "And there's actually a spot."

Angling the steering wheel toward the curb, the patrol car's headlights illuminated something, something red, in the gutter. As we pulled closer into the parking space, this object looked like a bunch of roses. Red roses and a rubbery wristband. In fact, it was a corsage that looked awfully familiar.

"What the hell is that?" exclaimed Sean. But he was not talking about the corsage.

Leaning forward in his seat, Sean was staring at the front of his mom's house. It was an eighteenth-century, two-story, brick Georgetown row house, generously set back from the curb to make room for a square, perfectly manicured lawn. However, it was not the house's appearance or immaculate lawn that had caught Sean's eye. What he was reacting to was a man, clad in black, who was clambering up the front of the house using the white vine-covered trellis as a makeshift ladder.

"He's breaking into our house!" said Sean, incredulous at the sight of a criminal act in progress at his very own place of residence.

Reaching behind the steering wheel, Sean flicked a couple of switches and suddenly P Street was lit up like the Fourth of July as his sirens bleeped out a couple warning cries. Hearing this, the crook in black craned his neck around in our direction and, like the corsage in the street, he looked awfully familiar as well.

"Ian?" I said, dumbfounded.

"You *know* him?"

Wearing his tux, Ian raised both of his hands up in a gesture of surrender. However, he forgot to factor gravity into his actions, as without anything to hold on to, he plummeted toward the ground. Fortunately, though, he didn't hit the ground itself as his fall was broken by the indestructible lady in red—yes, Santa, Virginia herself. Standing in the bushes and assisting her man in this curious crime, Virginia disappeared behind a row of boxwoods as Ian crashed into her, both of them hitting the ground with a comical thump.

"Virginia?" said Sean, equally dumbfounded.

A tingle ran up my back, like the kind you'd get in a horror movie, you know? Slowly I turned to Sean, terrified as to how he might answer my question.

"You know *her?*"

# CHAPTER 24

Jumping out of his patrol car and racing up the lawn, Sean headed toward the boxwoods, which seemed to be shaking with a struggle. Following Sean, I got out of the car too, and running toward the house spied the address marker: 2842 P Street. That sounded *very* familiar. Too familiar. Then it hit me: This was Virginia's address! As I studied the front door lit up by the police lights, I realized that this was the house where I'd picked her up for the prom. So then if this was Virginia's house, that meant that Sean was . . . ohmigod! Her brother?!

"Sean," shrieked Virginia. His sister. His bloody sister! "Get him *off* of me!"

Sean dove into the bushes, and after more screaming and struggle, emerged with Ian, holding him brusquely by the collar of his tux jacket. Wearing a fairly terrified expression on being manhandled by a cop, Ian got a glimpse of me and it was like I might as well have been Jesus Christ.

"Cam . . . Cameron?"

And that was about all he could manage.

Virginia, however, never one lacking for language, had a lot more to offer.

"Hayes! *Again?*" she shrieked. "What are you, like, *stalking* me?"

Since everyone involved in this farce seemed to know me intimately, Sean turned in my direction for an explanation of what the hell was going on. It was at this point that I noticed Sean's name tag, just below his badge—McKINLEY. I hadn't quite seen that before, having been a little distracted by my post-Shane breakdown and, frankly, the color of his eyes.

"How the hell do you know my sister?" asked Sean.

Needless to say, I was somewhat, uh, reluctant to explain the exact circumstances of my relationship to Virginia. The whole sordid story of the prom date who wasn't really my date didn't seem like something her brother, the straight-talking policeman, would appreciate. So I decided that I would be best served yet again by invoking my knowledge of American civics and taking the Fifth. Thus I stood there in a state of shrugging muteness, hoping I could pantomime my way out of this predicament. That approach worked until Virginia decided to jump right in and explain to her brother what happened anyway.

"Cameron was my gay prom date," she said, brushing some dirt off her red dress. "But I traded him in for a straighter model."

"He . . . he was?" said Sean, astounded.

"Yeah, I was," I said. "But it wasn't my idea. Honest."

But Sean had moved on to other more confusing matters.

"And you," he said, turning to address Ian. "What were you doing climbing up the front of our house?"

Ian wisely also decided to take the Fifth, though he probably didn't understand the exact legal ramifications of his silence. He was just keeping his trap shut. Virginia, however, had no qualms about telling her brother the full story on this front. Maybe as a family member she had immunity from embarrassing herself in front of her sibling. Or maybe, as I'd suspected from the start, Virginia was just slightly insane.

"Look, Ian and I were making out in the limo for a while, but it got cramped. I mean, we are both plus-size people, if you get my drift," she said with a hoary wink that made Sean seem physically ill. I thought the hummus might make a return appearance.

"So we decided to come back to my room to get it on. But then I couldn't find my keys and Mom didn't answer the door since she's probably passed out or something, so I thought Ian could just climb up to my room and get us in that way."

Realizing that he had not interrupted a break-in, Sean released his grip on Ian's collar. On her man's release, Virginia smiled her bitchy smile and then cuddled up to her new and improved date. I have to say, they were actually a cute supersize couple, and seeing them together made me relieved that I'd fulfilled my side of the Secrets bargain with Ian. Still, Sean did not seem so pleased by his sister's tramping around with a hulking member of the football team, and scolded her for it.

"You think Mom is gonna let some random guy who wasn't even your prom date spend the night in your bedroom?" said Sean, his voice going squeaky as he suddenly sounded a lot like someone's big brother in a standard-issue sibling fight. Then I realized something else: Sean was Virginia's gay older brother, the one she talked about at length in my car at the beginning of the night. The one she didn't get along with so well. And this was all very apparent in the tone she took toward Sean.

"She wasn't gonna know about it, asshole."

"Oh, she *wasn't*?" said a voice out of nowhere.

In all of the break-in confusion, none of us had noticed a weary Mrs. McKinley open the front door to see what all the excitement was. Draped in a black silky robe and wearing a turban instead of her fiery wig, Virginia's mom did not seem pleased to discover this gathering on her front lawn at five in the morning. Virginia, however, tried to act like there was absolutely nothing wrong with this picture.

"Oh, hi, Mother," said Virginia. "I'm home."

"Virginia McKinley," declared her mother, eyes wide with rage. "What the devil is going on here?"

"Mom, this is Ian," she said proudly. "My new date."

Ian displayed a wan grin as Virginia threw her big arms around his big waist. The astounding thing was, given Virginia's wingspan she could actually do this with ease, cinching him in her grasp as if he was her very own oversize teddy bear.

"Wait a minute," said Mrs. McKinley, recognizing me despite my lack of a tux and a forehead-positive do. "Isn't Cameron your date?"

"Yeah, that's him," she said with a bubbly and highly un-Virginia like enthusiasm. Then she tilted her head curiously at me. "Hey, did you get a makeover or something?"

"My hair."

"Oh. Looks good, actually."

A compliment? From Virginia? It's amazing what a little love can do, huh?

"Thanks," I said, turning to her mom with a sheepish wave. She looked utterly baffled. "Hi, Mrs. McKinley."

As the lights from Sean's police car flashed across her face, she seemed to get even angrier and directed her rage at her son.

"Will you turn those blasted lights off, Sean!"

On his mother's urging, Sean ran back to kill the lights. Then composing herself again and gathering up what was left of her wits, she crossed her arms, lowered her voice, and tried to figure out what was going on.

"Virginia, dear, I don't understand this at all."

"Okay, Mom," said Virginia, echoing her mom's calm tone. "If you can relax for, like, a minute, it's really not that hard. I just had to make some decisions for myself about my prom experience to make it more . . . fulfilling."

Virginia went on in this manner, addressing her mother as if she was Virginia's own child. That was pretty ballsy, I thought. Which got me thinking, you know, the reason I probably liked Virginia to start with was that she was a woman who had balls. Ha.

"And Cameron, you see . . . he turned out to be . . . well, let's just say not available."

Amazing. She didn't call me a fag. Progress!

"So I ditched him and he ditched me, and then I found someone much more to my, uh, liking."

Virginia purred into Ian's ear as he tried in vain to keep her friskiness at bay. Meanwhile, Mrs. McKinley was not so impressed with her daughter's reasoning for swapping dates.

"Well, that is just," she said, flustered and at a loss for proper words. "I think that is the very height of rudeness, Virginia. No one switches dates at the prom!"

"Oh, don't worry, Mother," she said dismissively. "I didn't do it *at* the prom. It all happened much later in the evening."

This line of reasoning, however, didn't make things any easier for her mom to swallow. As far as Mrs. McKinley was concerned, there was no excuse for such impropriety. She was clearly upset about the breach of all the good manners and etiquette she'd tried to instill while raising this wild girl. With this in mind, I tried to alleviate some of her mother's concerns on the matter of propriety.

"It's okay, Mrs. McKinley," I said, almost defending my nightmare. "Virginia and I being dates was kind of a mistake. And . . . uh, actually the whole thing was my fault."

Virginia looked at me, shocked that I'd taken the fall for the whole prom insanity when I could have easily let her mom continue to wail on her lapsed breeding. But with the police somewhere behind me, I figured this was no time for more deceit. Though the whole prom mess was Shane's initial idea, I was the one who agreed to go along with it. I could have said no and I didn't. I said yes, and in doing so hadn't really thought about the consequences of that for anyone but myself.

"Well, Hayes, at least you made up for the whole thing," said Virginia, with a warmth that was creepy coming from her. "You were nice enough to introduce me to this hunk of butter."

"Oh, Virginia!" exclaimed her mother, recoiling at her daughter's loose lingo.

"C'mon, Mother," replied Virginia, not getting the immodesty of it all. "You have to admit that Ian is superhot, right?"

Embarrassed, Ian dropped his head and concerned himself with picking some twigs off his trousers. Sean, having returned from his squad car, arrived just in time to save Virginia's mother from answering his sister's question regarding Ian's hot quotient.

"Well," said Sean, filling a pregnant silence. "Isn't it about time for everyone to be getting back to their proper homes?"

"I should say so," said Mrs. McKinley, gathering up the collar of her sleek black robe and shaking off a chill. "It's past five in the morning."

"Wow—it's that late?" said Virginia, truly surprised to hear this. She turned again to her mother. "Ian lives all the way out in Reston. You think he could spend the night?"

Mrs. McKinley gave Ian the once-over, providing the impression that if she'd been thirty years younger, she actually might have thought he *was* superhot. Or at least handsome, which is probably more in line with her vocabulary anyway.

"He can stay," she said, initially to everyone's shock. Until, that is, she qualified her answer. "He should be fine on the big couch down in the den."

"That is so *not* cute, Mother," said Virginia, her shoulders sinking. Yet Mrs. McKinley paid no attention to her daughter's complaint, instead shifting her focus to my plight.

"And what about Cameron?"

At that instant, another silent void engulfed the lawn as everyone turned toward Sean and I in unison, staring and wondering what the hell was going on with the gay boys.

"I'm giving him a ride home," said Sean, tilting his head in the general direction of Silver Spring. "I have to change out of my work clothes first, and then I'll take the Taurus."

"That's very kind of you, Sean," she said, pleased that at least one of her children had been raised properly. Virginia, however, sneered at Sean, indicating a long-running sibling rivalry of good versus evil, and I don't think I have to tell you which was which, right?

After everyone got their good nights and good-byes in, Mrs. McKinley headed back inside with Ian in tow. That left me on the lawn with the younger McKinleys, who immediately started bickering; Sean chastising his younger sister for her misbehavior while

Virginia protested Sean's habit of always claiming he knew what was best for her. As they yammered away at each other, volleying insults and accusations back and forth, I was shocked to notice their physical similarities and surprised I hadn't made the family connection before. They were both equally tall, Sean topping Virginia but only by a couple inches, and they had the same big-boned features and enormously versatile and wide mouths (his for eating falafels, hers for talking trash). It was suddenly obvious to me why I'd found Virginia to be so beautiful when I saw her in that calm, lovely moment at the top of the stairs, looking like a fiery princess. I guess you could say she was "my type," except for one small thing. . . . She wasn't a guy. Fortunately her handsome brother was.

"Virginia, stop arguing with your brother and go to bed!"

Their squabbling was interrupted by Mrs. McKinley, leaning out her window with an exasperated expression. Virginia, however, beamed back at her.

"Good night, 'Mother'!" she said, with sarcastic quotes on the formal version of her mom's title. In response Mrs. McKinley just shook her head and closed her window.

As the sky began to transform from night back into day, I observed that the big devil of a full moon was finally, thankfully, nowhere to be found.

"Later, Hayes," said Virginia, drawing my attention back to earth as she thrust her manly hand out for a friendly shake. I took it and squeezed as hard as I could, which was only half as hard as she could. Ouch. "Thanks for a memorable night."

"Ditto," I said. Then stretching for some final greeting, I offered this: "Good luck with graduation and life and all that."

Sean turned and looked at me with a screwy face.

"You sound like you're never going to see her again."

Well, I didn't see any reason why I *would* ever see Virginia again, except maybe while waiting in line for the keg at an illegal graduation party. Still that was not the point Sean seemed to be making.

"Look," she said to Sean in her plainspoken manner. "If you're gonna start dating this guy, I am sooooo telling mom."

"What?" we both said, incredulous at the assumption that Sean and I would be dating *and* that she would tell poor Mrs. McKinley. I mean, seriously, the woman had enough problems with a vixen for a daughter. She didn't need to know her law-abiding son was dating a newly minted criminal.

"Don't play all coy with me," she said, pointing toward me. "Just because you two are guys doesn't mean *you're* gonna get away with having him spend the night. Sex is sex, right?"

"Virginia!" said Sean, horrified, his face going as red as her hair.

"Oh, please," she said, backing her way into the house. "Don't act all shocked. You know you two are totally gonna get it on eventually. I'm just thinking of the future."

And with her last wicked grin of the night, she closed the front door of the McKinley residence with a dramatic thud. Of all the deadly silences that night, this was the deadliest. Virginia really had a way with an exit line, even if it was sorta honest. I mean, there definitely had been some flirtation going on between Sean and me. Actually I'd noticed it the instant he saw me sitting on the curb but had blocked it out of my mind, given that the breakdown of my relationship with Shane was consuming my thoughts at the time. (Go figure.) But honestly, even though Sean was a decent guy, it was hard to wrap my brain around even that simple fact, as I was still trying to figure out how my six-month relationship with Shane had self-destructed in one way-too-momentous night. I mean, c'mon, I had just gotten out of an awful relationship. Did I really want to jump right back into another one, even if it was with some cute, charming cop who was out to his family and actually seemed to have his life together?

All right, I'm taking the Fifth on that question, too.

# CHAPTER 25

Twelve hours had passed since I'd first driven out
Connecticut Avenue with a very drunk Virginia beside me, justly
accusing me of being a fag. Now I found myself making the journey
back home again, this time with her sober sibling at the wheel, a guy
who also happened to be a so-called fag. Needless to say, this
second ride was much more pleasant.

Gazing out the open window of the Taurus, I could see the sun
shooting its rays through the towering oaks that lined the avenue.
The air streaming in through the window was murky, thick with
pollen and the scent of lawn clippings. The night sky had been fully
replaced by day in a shade that was a near match to Sean's eyes. As
my parents liked to say, it was going to be a beautiful day.

*Oh, shit,* I thought, *my parents.*

"I fuck," I said to myself.

"What?" said Sean.

Suddenly the heady buzz of hanging with Sean and the boost his
flirtatious presence had provided in the face of my breakup doom
was gone. Even though I hadn't had a drink since Shane's party, I
instantly felt like I had a hangover. The party was over.

"I am gonna be in sooooo much trouble," I said, my mood going
south.

Stopped at a light, Sean checked out my drooping face. He didn't
like what he saw. "You look awful again," he said.

"Even my hair?"

His silence indicated an answer I didn't want to hear.

"You know," I said, annoyed. "You'd look terrible too if you'd been through half of what I've been through tonight."

"So . . . what exactly did you go through tonight?" he said quizzically.

Hanging my head gloomily, I glanced over at Sean. I could see his point about my appearance, since by comparison he looked perfectly respectable. He had changed into a pair of Old Navy carpenter pants and a clean white Izod shirt. I was still wearing Buck's baggy Gallaudet sweatshirt and a pair of Diesel jeans that weren't mine.

"I never did get the full story," continued Sean. "About the prom itself, namely the parts involving my sister."

"I don't know," I said, trying to judge how safe it was to tell him of my illegal adventures. "You sure that you won't take me to jail or anything?"

"I'm off duty, Cameron," he said, sounding very relieved that this was the case. "Nothing you say can be used against you in a court of law."

I eyed him suspiciously, wondering how trustworthy a cop could be. Sitting there without his uniform on and looking like a normal guy, Sean now seemed somewhat easier to confess to. Staring at me with anticipation, seeing if I had a story for him yet, those eyes of his began to have a crazy hypnotic effect on me. After a few seconds of his flashing those blue blinkers my way, I would have told him just about anything he wanted to know. Damn!

"All right, I'll tell you."

So taking a deep breath, I gave him the rundown on the night. I breezed over some of the more awful stuff regarding his sister, like puking in Shane's fish tank. But on the whole I was pretty honest about everything. Anyway, as I rambled on about my prom night, Sean listened attentively, nodding and not getting too hysterical about my misadventures, except for maybe the part when I attempted to buy pot from Dmitri. However, I told him that in retrospect it had been a huge mistake because getting stoned hadn't laid the best ground-work for my decision-making process during a time of intense emotional crisis. I mean, thinking back on it all I cannot *believe* some of the things I did that night, namely that I got in some drug dealer's car, even if it was for the A-plus reason of skipping out on the prom. Still, in hindsight that was really not the greatest judgment call. At all. And as I told Sean all this, I came to realize this educational fact about the evening and was struck by my careless, weed-induced stupidity.

Sean also got a bit freaked out about the whole Amateur Night at Secrets. But once I started telling the details of the story, about how I changed the music and got a bunch of homos slam dancing into each other, he actually laughed. When I capped the story off by telling him that Ian and I both won the contest and the cash, Sean nearly ran a red light, he was so hilariously stunned. Then with a sidelong glance he let loose this whopper.

"You must have a decent body then," he said, half joking. At least I *thought* he was half joking. If I had thought he was half serious, I would have had to immediately ditch out of the Taurus, knowing that a crazy person was at the wheel.

"Uh, no," I said, in my new zeal to be honest, even when it came to something like my lack of a body. "I'm ridiculously skinny and have never met a sport that liked me."

"Spoken like a true homosexual," said Sean, weirdly pleased by my line. "But still, you must be in good shape to win that sort of contest."

"All right," I said, trying to make my point as clearly as possible. "Here's the deal. You know how some jocks have zero body fat? I have, like, zero body."

Sean thought this was majorly funny too, slapping his knee and nearly losing control of his vehicle. I have to admit, making this guy laugh was fun and pretty damn easy and just about took my mind off all the problems that lay behind and ahead of me.

"I don't think I could ever do something like that," said Sean.

"Really—why not?"

I mean, please. Sean was a cop with a very big, law-enforcing body. Guys like big, I told him, recalling the wholly positive reaction Ian got at Secrets. And big guys in uniforms? Forget it. I mean, that's the stuff porn movies are made of, right?

"Hell," I said way too enthusiastically. "I think you could easily beat me."

"I doubt it," he said, regarding me warily. "Age before beauty."

"What?"

"In the gay world a teenager trumps a twenty-something any day of the year."

I didn't know what to make of this. Was it a compliment or an insult or what? Basically I thought it was sorta sweet and demented at the same time. Which is to say that, yeah, I liked Sean's sense of humor if it was this disturbing. I thought it was pretty cool for a semi-grown-up.

"Still, I think you could win," I said to him. "No problem."

Thinking about the notion of Sean in a strip contest, I have to admit, got me mildly excited. Sitting there in the front seat of his car, checking out his long, lean frame, I had this flash, a sexy premonition of sorts. Now, maybe this will sound dirty to you, but here it is anyway: It was like I knew exactly what Sean looked like without his clothes on. Honest! I know that I'd never seen him naked or even without a shirt on, but somehow I just knew.

All right, I imagined that he had this slightly concave chest with an inverse triangular patch of reddish hair on his breastbone, which wasn't that thick but was still pathetically cute for the simple fact that it was trying, you know? As for his arms . . . oh, man, let me just say for the record that he had arms! (Most of which I could actually see.) They were incredibly long limbs, coated with a thin, practically invisible layer of blondish hairs. But the most defining feature on them was a purplish raised vein that ran up each forearm, outlining each thoroughly muscular bicep in relief, before disappearing under his shirt and heading with a ninety-degree turn all the way into his very decent heart. As for his stomach, it was totally flat with one of those squished belly buttons, you know, that look like they got ironed or something, and a light brown trail of hairs that disappeared into his pants. All right, don't get too nervous, because that's where I'll stop before this gets too NC-17. But you get the picture, right? Well, that's the picture, literally, that I saw, sitting innocently in his car heading toward my parents' house and doom.

"You got awfully quiet," Sean said, referring to my silent stripping fantasy that had killed our conversation.

"Telling that story is exhausting," I said, bummed out about everything I'd been through. "It was not a good night."

"At least it had a happy ending," he said cheerily.

"Uh . . . it did?"

Which got me wondering: Which part of my own story did I miss here?

"You met me," he said, with this annoyingly sunny conviction.

This bugged me a bit because I guess he did have a point. Still, I wanted to be immersed in my own self-inflicted funk over the whole Shane disaster. But when you think about it, the fact that I actually did meet Sean that night is nearly miraculous, you know? Seriously. I mean, it was so random that this nice gay police officer would pick me up, since technically only about 10 percent of all guys are into guys (and that includes the ones who are just "fooling around"). Then you look at the police force, which is pretty het considering you have to shoot and tackle criminals for a living, and that knocks the percentage down to probably 5 percent if you're lucky. So you have to admit it was a mad coincidence that I met a gay cop the way I did, sitting out on Jane's curb in the middle of the night. Being newly into honesty and all, I shared these thoughts with Sean.

"Well," he said, mulling over all my musings on fate, chance, and the percentage of gay men in the general populace. "It is true that, on balance, there aren't that many gay guys out there. But in my experience it seems like you'll meet the ones that you need to meet."

Hmmmm. I thought that was interesting and philosophical and

all that. But it didn't quite jibe with my reality, namely having met and wasted so much time with a certain individual named Shane.

"What about the ones you *don't* need to meet?" I asked.

"Oh," he said, caught off guard a bit. "You mean like Shane?"

"Or your friend George."

At this point we both flashed the secret grin of two guys who share a healthy hatred of their ex-men.

"Well," he continued, "even those losers have their role to play in everything."

"Which is what?"

He eyed me, surprised to be challenged again on his impromptu theory of life. Then he turned away to concentrate on the road.

"I don't think you find *that* out until the end."

"The end of what?"

"Your life."

*Whoa,* I thought. Basically he was saying that I had to wait something like sixty years before everything makes some sort of sense? I mean, come on! I was under the impression that the whole point of having this conversation with him was for me to gain some clarity on my last twelve hours from someone with a more adult perspective. But Sean wasn't helping by saying I had to wait until I was collecting Social for the meaning of all this. I mean, *that* was his advice?

"You know what?" I said, pissed. "Comments like that aren't really helping me cope with my current situation."

"Sorry," he said, chastened but also defiant. "But I gotta tell you. . . . Sometimes there's no easy answer, especially immediately after you've been through this kind of emotional turmoil. I don't mean to bring you off your whole teenager high, but life can be a pain in the ass sometimes. And for no good reason."

Okay, teenager high? I don't know who he was referring to, as I was never high on being a teenager. Ever. And especially after that night. Please! In fact, the only thing that I'd been high on was Dmitri's pot, and that was only for a few hours.

"I know life is hard and all that adult BS," I said. "But there must be something that makes it all worthwhile, right?"

Sean seemed stumped. This was not good. I didn't want to stump him, really. I was truly hoping for another reassuring, mildly philosophical answer from him. However, in my bitchiness and annoying desire to be right, it seemed I'd eliminated any future answers that might be of assistance.

"Okay, relax," he said, hearing my tone go desperate. Then he tried to change his tune. "All right. You know what makes it worthwhile?"

"I'm on the edge of my seat," I said, slouching back for antidramatic effect. I didn't really think he would have something to say on this question that would interest me. Really.

"This."

"What?"

"Driving with no traffic on a perfect June morning with an impossibly smart but not-so-wise guy like yourself sitting next to me and talking my ear off about bullshit questions like the meaning of life."

Well, that was not what I expected to hear at all. That wasn't philosophical or meaningful or anything. That was just stating the obvious, that driving in Sean's car and bickering like this was almost kind of fun. It nearly made me forget our final destination: home.

Given the events of the night and my very late return, I was sure my parents would be awake and waiting up for me. What I did not expect was that the Montgomery County Police would be waiting for me as well. And turning onto Crestwood Drive, Sean and I were confronted by that surreal sight.

"Holy shit," said Sean, seeing a bunch of cop cars parked in front of my house. "All right, Cameron—is there something you didn't tell me?"

"No," I said, which was true. I had told him everything that happened to me that night. I was done with lies. Honest. All right, I might have skipped over the part where Dmitri kissed me somewhere under the Washington Mall, but that was it.

"Cameron," he said, his voice taking a turn for the worse. "I'm not kidding. What did you *do* tonight?"

But before I could say anything else, the all-too-familiar sound of police sirens broke the pristine silence of that clear blue morning. Hearing this, Sean slammed on the brakes, bringing us to an abrupt stop in the middle of the road, a couple houses down from mine. We were now sitting ducks for an ambush-in-waiting. Then an authoritative voice boomed out from one of the patrol car's PA system.

"Get out of your vehicle with your hands up."

Let me be the first to tell you that you have not lived, I mean seriously lived, until you've heard that cheery announcement greeting you on your return home at six in the morning. I mean, really. I could've died at that point and not missed a helluva lot, because truly there's not much else that's ever going to top that one. And speaking of my death, it looked like it was on the morning schedule, either via the police or my own failing circulatory system. You see, it was at this point that I believe my heart stopped functioning.

"Ohmigod," I said, clutching my chest in a lame attempt to give myself CPR. But there was no heart to start. It had escaped from my chest, bounced onto the floorboards of Sean's car, ricocheted off the fuzzy ceiling, and plopped into my lap, where via osmosis, it made its way into my stomach, where it remained for a few nauseating seconds before returning to its place of honor behind my rib cage. But it was not going to stay there for long. . . .

Looking toward my house, I noticed two officers shuffling my parents out the front door and leading them down the walk to a crouched position behind one of the leading police cars. Meanwhile the other policemen, who moments before were lounging around their cars, chatting and eating doughnuts, had suddenly assumed menacing, offensive positions with their shiny firearms aimed in our general direction.

"Holy shit," I said to Sean, my heart going for another out-of-body experience. "They have guns!"

"Cam, look at me," said Sean, grabbing me by the arm. "*What* in God's name did you do?"

"All right, all right," I said, exhaling heavily. "I . . . I kissed Dmitri."

"What?"

"You know, the drug dealer."

"What!"

"But he started it and I didn't really kiss back and—"

Another wail of sirens and the PA crackled on again.

"Let Mr. Hayes go and we can talk with you about everything else."

"Let me go?" I said baffled.

"Everything else?" wondered Sean, equally confused. "What are they talking about?"

"I . . . I have no idea."

Turning his X-ray eyes on me, Sean assessed the truth quotient of my answer. Believing what I said to be authentically earnest and on the whole correct, Sean formed a plan of action.

"Okay," he said with a passably fake calm. "Let's do what they said. We'll both get out of the car calmly and in unison. Very, very slowly."

"O-kay," I said, my hands shaking like a crack addict's. Sean grabbed them and held them together for a moment in hopes of my getting it together. His hands were very warm and strong, and that was reassuring for about a second.

"Now . . . no abrupt movements, Cameron. Smooth and cool and relaxed . . . okay?"

"Ohmigod—you honestly think I can *relax* with a firing squad aimed at me?"

But Sean ignored my hysteria and concentrated instead on attempting to normalize relations with our armed adversaries down the block. He put his hand on the door latch and indicated that I do the same.

"On three. Ready?"

"Uh . . . no."

But he ignored my reluctance.

"One . . . two . . . three!"

The sound of our doors clicking open was met with the danger-ously corollary sound of a hundred .45 Magnums being cocked. This did not bode well for the future of my life. My heart, sensing it was history anyway, took off in the other direction down Crestwood.

"Mr. Hayes," said the disembodied PA voice. "Step away from the vehicle and move toward the police cars."

I looked at Sean, wondering if this was the right thing to do, fig-uring he knew police shoot-out etiquette. He nodded solemnly but firmly, as if I was truly making my way down death row. Was this a look of good-bye? It was not an encouraging look, to say the least. I started thinking that all I needed now was a final cigarette or a final meal. Hey—did you know that the vast majority of death row guys choose a cheeseburger and fries for their last snack, with a shake on the side? I never understood this. That's like going to McDonald's or something. I'd at least order a filet mignon or some gourmet dish. Maybe my very own lobster, dripping with melted butter, with a fancy side dish, like braised polenta. Or a spinach soufflé perhaps . . .

(So in case you're wondering, this is what a burgeoning gay boy thinks about at the end of his life.)

"Mr. Hayes, step toward the police cars."

Finally putting one foot very slowly in front of the other, I started to make my way to the afterlife, when suddenly my mom's head popped up over the roofline of one of the cars.

"Cameron!" she squealed, leaping over the hood of the cop car in an uncontrollable fit of motherhood and dashing down the street toward me. In no time at all, she had a full body-lock hold on me, hugging me like I don't think I had been hugged since I departed for my first day at kindergarten.

"Oh, Cameron," she said, losing it like I had been losing it only an hour previously, but for much different reasons. No wonder I was such an emotional wreck that night. It was, like, a totally genetic thing. "You're alive!"

The second she got hold of me, a phalanx of county officers advanced down the street and surrounded Sean with their guns drawn. Sean reached for his wallet in an attempt to flash his own badge, but the cops thought he was reaching for something a little more menacing. They had him flat on the hood of his Taurus in the time it takes to blink.

"Hey, leave him alone!" I said, with way too much emotion because, like my mother, I am a Hayes and we are not only excitable but emotionally unstable as well. Not understanding what was happening to Sean, I tried to make my way back to the Taurus, but my mom yanked me in the other direction.

"That monster," she said in a manner that was usually heard in earnestly bad Lifetime movies.

"Mom," I said plainly. "What are you talking about?"

"You're safe now, Cameron," she said, sobbing. "It's all over. Don't even look at him."

She talked about Sean like she knew him intimately, like she and the police and everybody there knew him, which seemed curious and impossible. But before I could sort this all out, my dad joined our family-therapy moment, vigorously throwing himself at us, creating a big group hug with even more emotion than my mother. They were both crying all over me, getting Buck's T-shirt all wet and totally ruining my new hairdo. After some deft squirming, I managed to come up for air and tell the truth.

"Sean isn't a monster," I said breathlessly. "He's the guy who gave me a ride home. That's all."

My mom turned to my dad with a conspiratorial tone.

"He's in denial, honey," she said.

"It's okay, Cam," my dad said, in manner of speech usually reserved for in-patient screening at St. Elizabeth's. "You don't have to tell us anything right now. . . . It'll all come out in time."

"Actually," I said, not really that fazed by the reality of my prom night anymore, "I can tell you everything now if you want."

(Ummm—minus the part about kissing the drug dealer, of course.)

Once they stopped crying, that's exactly what I did. Standing there in the middle of my street, I explained to them that Sean was a D.C. police officer who had picked me up at Jane's and given me a ride home. It wasn't the whole story, but given the tales I had to tell about the rest of the night, I figured that I would start small, you know?

"He's *not* the man who abducted you from the prom?" asked one of the county cops.

Abducted me?

"The principal called us and said that you had been abducted by a drug dealer outside the Willard Hotel," said my dad, wiping away his tears.

A couple more cops, starting to pay attention to what I was saying, moved over to where we stood, and with their help I began to unravel what had become a gigantic misunderstanding. You see, everyone had apparently gotten the wrong idea when I sped away from the prom in Dmitri's RX-7. They all thought that I had pulled an Elizabeth Smart on them. Or that Dmitri had pulled an Elizabeth Smart on me. Whatever. So when Mr. Mold couldn't find me anywhere at the hotel, he asked Shane where I was and Shane pretended that he didn't know anything about my whereabouts, thinking, in true Shane fashion, it was better to say nothing than to come out with the truth. (Thanks, Shane!) Then when Mr. Mold went to talk to the hotel manager about my disappearance, the Texan tourist was found complaining to the manager about a mysterious teenager who disappeared with his twenty. Thus putting all of their misinformed heads together, Mr. Mold and the hotel manager added one and two and somehow came up with five, falsely believing that Dmitri had kidnapped me from the curb and abducted me into drug slavery or something.

With an ID on Dmitri's RX-7 provided by the Texan, a police officer in Southeast spotted Dmitri's car on Half, fostering the whole Secrets raid, which was not an attempt to flush out underage patrons but in actuality a search-and-rescue operation to find me. (Thus the tux's disappearance into evidence.) Then after the failed high-speed pursuit of me and my "kidnapper," detectives scouting the area for clues found my smashed and battered cell phone on the curb of South Capitol Street. That's when my parents got severely worried, spurring on a search through the entire Second District of Southeast. Meanwhile I was hanging out in Northwest at Jane's house, totally unaware of all the chaos and concern I'd left in my wake. Then having been picked up by Sean, a First District guy who was severely out of the Second District loop, they never made the connection between the missing senior (who was supposed to be wearing a hotel uniform) and me. So when Sean finally ended up driving me home, the county cops thought that my savior cop was actually my outlaw, drug dealer-kidnapper. Got that?

I was in the middle of explaining this to the police when my mom, seeming to suffer from a migraine, held one hand to her temple and waved the other hand in my direction. She had heard enough of this madness and wanted to focus on what counted. "All that matters is you're alive, Cameron."

And then she hugged me again, this time without tears and only mild hysteria. It was still somewhat tighter than the average hug, but after all I'd been through, that really wasn't such a bad thing.

Meanwhile over on the hood of the Taurus, the county cops had finally realized that Sean was one of them, apologizing and handing him his wallet with the badge facing out.

"You wanna meet Sean?" I said to my mom.

My parents looked at each other.

"He's in denial," said my mother . . . again. This was all going to take a while to sink in.

"No, no—Sean is *not* the drug dealer, you guys."

I tried to laugh that one off, but my parents were not amused.

"So there *was* a drug dealer?"

Okay, so they were having a little trouble dealing with the facts of my bizarro night. Given that, there was no way I was going to get into details like Dmitri. At least not yet.

"Sean's a cop. From D.C. He picked me up at—"

"You mean he's the one who *found* you?" asked my mom, her eyes getting wide with tears again.

"Well . . . I mean, I wasn't exactly lost," I said, trying to make things less scary to them. "At least not technically . . . maybe a little emotionally lost, but—"

As I rambled on to myself about my mental state, I discovered that my folks were not even listening. In fact, they had left me and were making a beeline for a wholly unprepared Sean. I tried to catch up with them, but I was too late. Walking right up to Sean without any sort of warning, my mom hugged him even tighter than she had hugged me. Remember my parents' infamous enthusiasm for life in general? Well, it was essentially doubled when it came to the matter of what they thought had been my near-death experience.

"Thank you for saving our son," she said to Sean, all soap-opera dramatic. "Thank you so much!"

With her back to me, she hugged Sean, his long face hooked awkwardly over her much-shorter shoulder. As she held him, Sean glanced up at me with a bit of shock at all this emotion and all I could do was smile, not too much, though.

"It was really nothing, Mrs. Hayes," he said, leaning back to see her tear-streaked face. "He was just sitting on a curb and—"

"We owe you so much," she said.

"Come inside," said my dad, pointing over at the house. "Have some breakfast with us."

Ohmigod—my parents were actually inviting Sean over for a meal? This was beyond mortifying. I mean, I thought that this really would kill me in a way the firing line hadn't managed to. So in a last-ditch attempt to avert this sort of humiliation, I started vigorously shaking my head at Sean, mouthing "no" behind my parents' back. Though Sean saw me doing this, he still said yes. (The bastard.) I think he thought the whole thing was funny or something. I, however, did not see the humor in inviting this handsome stranger whom I barely knew into my parents' house for an excitable thank-you breakfast. As if I really needed any more embarrassment for one evening? Or morning? Please.

## CHAPTER 26

Once the county police had dispersed, my mom headed immediately to the kitchen to prepare some pancakes while my dad headed toward the basement to locate his tripod so that he could document the morning of my near death and miraculous rescue. Surprise, surprise, right?

As my folks ran off in different directions, Sean and I were stranded in the living room. Left alone after all the excitement of my homecoming, I didn't know what to say to Sean. I actually got shy around him. After all the praise my parents had heaped on him as my hero, I was feeling a bit intimidated, you know? It even got me wondering if maybe Sean *was* my hero. I mean, he had been there, literally by my side, after the breakup with Shane. Thinking back on it, I couldn't imagine having gone to Shane's by myself, suffering such an utter rejection and then not having anyone help me through the implosion of my relationship, especially someone like Sean, who could completely relate. I mean, without his presence I might have done something irrational, you know, that I probably don't even want to think about.

Anyway, despite all the hero worship in the air, Sean seemed mainly unfazed by it. In fact, he was much more interested in checking out all the embarrassing pictures of me that lined the bookshelves of our living room.

"Nice smile," he said, referring to a picture of me in the seventh grade in which I was doing everything I could not to reveal the lattice-work of braces in my mouth.

"Thanks," I said, mortified and wishing I could crawl into my shell, if I had one.

But my mortification didn't keep him from looking at the rest of the photos. I mean, really, these pictures are not exactly the first impression you want someone to see. It had taken me a good three months before I'd invited Shane over to peruse the gallery of my retarded youth; a complete and unfortunately unabridged history of Dad-inflicted haircuts, Mom-inspired Garanimals combos, and my very own sour looks on being told to smile while holding my head at a thirty-six-degree angle, chin aimed toward the ceiling, torso turned in counterbalance to the left, rear shoulder forced down an inch by some sadistic school photographer who somehow believed that was what natural looked like.

"Awwww," said Sean, teasing me about a particularly bad early nineties cut. "Look at your hair . . . it's sorta mullety."

"What can I say?" I mused, wondering what defense I could muster for a seven-year-old's bad hair day. "I tried to stay behind the trends as a second grader."

Sean turned to me and pursed his lips into an uncharacteristic smirk. You know, like an expression his sister would make.

"Your parents really like to take pictures, huh?"

"Yeah," I said. "It's their avocation."

"What?"

"Sorry," I said, apologizing for being such a smart-ass. "Fancy SAT word for hobby."

Sean nodded thoughtfully as he turned his attention to a naked picture of me tearing across the backyard at age three. Wonderful. Suddenly I found myself longing for the Montgomery County Police Department's death squad.

"Cute butt," he said, trying to keep himself from laughing at my parents' kiddie porn. "Now I can see why you won that contest at Secrets."

"Okay, that's enough," I said, dragging him away from the wall by the back of his untucked Izod. "I'm going to get you a magazine or something not me to look at."

I forcibly pushed him down on the couch, tossing an issue of *Smithsonian* magazine in his lap. He looked up from the cover, which heralded the End of the Universe, and wholly uninterested, narrowed his gaze at me in that disarming, investigative way he had.

"So . . . when are you going to tell your folks the whole story about tonight, huh?"

"I did," I said, referring to my explanation in the street.

"I mean the real story . . . about Shane and everything."

"Oh, that," I said dismissively. "I don't know . . . maybe at breakfast?"

"Really," he said, surprised. "And you want me to be here for *that?*"

"Why not? You're a pretty big part of the story. You're supposedly my hero or something, having saved me and all that. Hey, I bet you'll probably get some big award or medal for it from your boss!"

As I was standing in front of the couch, trying to block his view of the Wall of Me, Sean continued giving me that intense look and I thought, you know what? Sean could have a really great career with the CIA, professionally making people nervous for a living or something.

"So . . . you're really going to tell them about Shane and everything? At breakfast?"

*Oh, man,* I thought. *Why on earth does he have to keep harping on this?*

"Yeah," I said, sighing and collapsing onto the couch. "I mean, they're gonna find out one way or another through Mr. Mold or Jane's mom or the Wilsons' insurance agent, so I might as well get it out there now."

After a moment of silence Sean stood up, and with his hands in his pockets, angled his shoulders toward the front door.

"Well, I should get going, then," he said. "This is probably something you should talk about minus a third party."

Then panic set in as I realized I couldn't do this all by myself. I wouldn't be able to speak without an accomplice, especially one like Sean, who had helped me make it through so much already that night.

I leaped up from the couch and grabbed Sean's shirt again, begging him to stay.

"C'mon, Sean," I said, pleading like a big baby. "I need you here. For support. Don't go yet . . . please!"

"I don't know, Cameron," he said, trying gently but firmly to evade my grasp. "This is really something you should discuss with them by yourself."

As he removed my grip from his shirt, I got hold of his belt loop. What can I say? I was a desperate man, looking for any way to get him to stay. Then I remembered something, courtesy of his sister.

"But Virginia told me that *she* was there when you had the big talk with your mom."

"Yeah, only cause she *outed* me!"

"Still, wasn't it easier having someone else there?" I said, fishing.

"Not someone like Virginia," he said with a sour face. "She wasn't exactly the most supportive person in the room."

Having succeeded in extracting my fingers from his belt loop during this conversation, Sean started to make his way across the room to the front door. I sprinted to his left, dodging around him and blocking his entrance into the foyer. Go defense!

"Cameron," he said, addressing me sternly as I stood in his way.

"What?"

"I've gotta go."

Sean was very firm about leaving, and that, it appeared, was going to be that. I dropped my head and studied the floor, pouting. Delicately he skirted my position, and turning the doorknob, headed outside. But before he was totally gone he stopped on our welcome mat for some final words.

"Look," he said, using his sister's trademark phrase but in a much sweeter manner. "You'll be fine, Cameron. Your parents are really young and seem totally cool. It'll all be fine."

"You really think so?"

Sean nodded in the affirmative and that made me feel, I don't know, maybe 10 percent better about the whole looming parental conversation. Actually I have to say that in the end, Sean was right by insisting I have my confessional with my folks solo. His presence would only have been awkward, not to mention improper. Yet still, there was something in me that just didn't want him to leave. I'd spent, I don't know, maybe three hours with him, but it felt like it had been more like three days; three of the most terrifying and unexpected and interesting and trying days of my life. And I guess, in a sick way, I didn't want them to end.

"You all right?" said Sean, in the same concerned voice he'd used when he found me at Jane's. Wow. That was a question. Was I all right? The answer, off the bat, was definitely no. I had had the worst prom night imaginable, and to top it off had just broken up with my first-ever boyfriend. But despite all these downers I didn't feel as awful as I should have. I was weirdly . . . optimistic? Having made it through that terrible night alive and intact and somewhat smarter for it all, I actually thought that things might get better for me (you know, start going the way I wanted them to for once!) and that my life might start turning out right for a change.

The really strange thing was I didn't know where the hell this unlikely optimism was coming from. It was not a general personality trait of mine. Honest. I always saw the worst in every situation and expected most things I got involved in to be doomed to failure. But having this tall, oddly compelling guy standing outside my front door changed everything. It was very clear where this sense of hope came from, clear like an early June summer sky. That breathtaking kind of crystalline-blue clear. Basically it was Sean who had given me this wacky hope and that was an amazing gift, you know? I mean, that's bigger than getting your own car even.

"Thanks," I said. "For helping me out tonight . . . with everything."

"Hey, just doing my job," he said, all dopey and Joe Policeman-like. I don't think he was getting the seriousness of my point. And believe me, this was serious.

"I mean it, Sean," I said, disheartened. "I really, truly, honestly mean it."

"Thanks, Cameron."

And then I had an idea about what I could give him to show my thanks for all my hopeful hero had done for me. Except I didn't really know if it was something he wanted. It might be presumptuous to just give it to him, you know, without asking. I wasn't sure. In fact, I'd never really offered this to anyone, at least this directly. Not even Shane. *But,* I thought, *what the hell.* I'd tried out all sorts of other nutty things that night, so why not give this a go? So with my heart somewhere up in my nose, I did it. That is, I offered him my thanks and something else, too—a kiss.

Now, let me be totally clear. This was not some super, major make-out thing. (Frankly, Jane and I had more going on tonsil-wise at the prom.) This was only a briefly sweet meeting of lips with some mild nose rubbing thrown in for extra credit. But the most extraordinary thing about this kiss was not its length or the warmth of Sean's lips or the slight scratch of his cheek. The best thing about this kiss was that it took place in the world, not in the dark of a closet or under cover of night, but on the front porch of my parents' house, the morning sun blazing down on us, the birds chirping away like mad, the air smelling like fragrant—

"I found my tripod!"

Yep—that would be my dad. Interrupting *my* kiss. Oh. *My.* God.

"Hey, Dad," I said, spinning around to face him and try to pretend I was not just macking on a guy in broad daylight. My dad, of course, was stunned by this discovery, his chunky camera in one hand, his long tripod in the other, his very blank face stuck in the middle. Since my kiss with Sean was definitely not the photo opportunity he was expecting, I tried to explain what was up.

"I was just, uh, saying good-bye to Sean," I explained, trying to play it off like I kissed all my friends good-bye on the lips. "He has to head home."

Still, this explanation was not helping, as the color continued to drain out of my poor father's face. Conversely, Sean's face was beet red, but in a good way, if you know what I mean. Which is to say that I think he enjoyed the kiss, if I don't say so myself.

"Uh, okay, then . . . well, good-bye, Sean," I said, like I was acting out a bad scene from *7th Heaven*. "Thanks for everything!"

Sean smiled at me and gave me a wink. In front of my dad even! Then my mom stumbled upon this awkward domestic scene, totally unaware of the crazy male love going down on the front porch.

"The pancakes will be ready in about ten minutes."

No response. From anyone. Bewildered, she assessed me and my dad and Sean, all of us standing completely still and looking like human-size lawn ornaments. "What is everyone standing around out here for?"

My dad jumped in. "I was gonna get some pictures before Sean left."

"Oh, he has to leave?"

Sean nodded.

My mom's face fell. "That's a shame."

"Major drag," I said with a sly glance in Sean's direction.

"Oh, well," she said enthusiastically disappointed. "Let's at least get some shots before you leave."

Busying himself with his equipment, my dad went to set up his tripod on the front lawn as my mom chatted away with Sean on the porch about life on the police force and how exciting it all must be. Slipping away from my mom's bonding moment with Sean, I casually walked over to where my dad was, hunched over his camera and adjusting a lens or something. Discreetly I leaned in so that only he could hear what I had to say.

"Dad," I said, wincing. "Uh, I think we need to talk about some stuff at breakfast."

"About . . . Sean?" he said, echoing my wincing.

"Yeah," I said, somewhat relieved that I didn't have to spell it out. But I guess being a scientist and all, his knack for deduction could be applied to less-than-empirical situations like my own. "And some other people too."

His face draining again, my dad looked mildly concerned that there were more men in my life other than Sean. But at the same time he seemed equally relieved to know that the full story was on its way. He put his hand around the back of my neck in a friendly, dadlike way.

"Cam—we're just glad you got home safe," he said, practically getting teary on me again.

"Me too," I said.

So I guess if you're gonna come out to your parents, the ideal setup is to make them think you're dead first so that, on balance, being merely gay ends up really being not such an issue. Okay, I was *kidding* there! Still, like they say on TV, do *not* try these sorts of emotional stunts at home, you know? Coming out to your folks is all well and good, but a small word of advice: Try to keep the police out of the picture.

With the camera finally set up on the lawn, my dad set the self-timer and we both ran over to where my mom and Sean stood on the porch steps. My dad cut left, going to my mom's side, and I split right, heading to where Sean was. As the camera's red light blinked down the seconds to the click, my mom cajoled us to get all happy.

"Okay, everyone—smile," she said, cuddling up to my dad. "Say . . . prom night!"

I totally burst out laughing at this, and of course that's the moment the camera snapped, capturing my openmouthed guffaw for posterity on the Wall of Me. Due to the hilarity of the moment, what I didn't notice (but my mom pointed out to me when we got the prints back) was somewhat more interesting. In the split second of the photo being taken, Sean had surreptitiously slipped his hand around my waist. The reason my mom pointed this out was because it was the exact same position as my dad's hand around her waist.

She seemed to sense something romantically portentous in the moment, and who the hell knows? Maybe she's right. . . .

Honestly, though, it's hard to say where the whole Sean thing may or may not go. Sure, we've talked on the phone a few times since we met, and that's been cool. But it's hard to predict how this might develop romantically since he lives in D.C. and I'm heading to Charlottesville in the fall. Oh yeah . . . I'm still going to UVA, as it's a little late to change my choice of college just because of some stupid guy. All right, I know Shane's not stupid. I mean, he did get into UVA, which is not easy, especially if you're out of state. But I'm still mad at him and vice versa, so there you have it—sometimes I call him names. I know, really adult and all, right? Well, guess what? I'm not an adult, as Sean likes to point out to me all the time. I'm only eighteen and trying to figure everything out still, so sue me for being a little retarded, okay?

However, in a groundbreaking effort to be less retarded, Shane and I have talked since the big night. I called him the Sunday after the prom to apologize for breaking his window. I even offered my two-hundred-dollar prize money from Secrets to replace it, and, begrudgingly he accepted the offer, though was quick to point out that he was not telling his parents where the money came from. And that was about all we discussed. I mean, we are still very broken up and I can't really see us getting back together. The main reason is that after everything that's gone down, it is beyond apparent that we have wildly divergent views about what being honest means. You see, Shane has not breached the truth over at Ravenswood about the events of June 6. (Shocker, huh?) He stuck with the original Moldy-prom story about me making out with his date as the explanation to his parents about why we suddenly weren't friends anymore. To explain my bizarre behavior he even came up with a charming cover story, telling his folks I was a first-time stoner. I mean, really. You want to talk about stupid? But there's not much I can do about it when it comes to Shane and his life. As I said before, it's Shane's world and we're all just trying to get by.

One thing I've realized about Shane, that Sean turned me on to actually, is that people are on their own timetable when it comes to coming out. When Shane is ready to deal with it, he will. But until then, frankly, I just can't deal with him. It sucks and all, but what can you do? Answer: Nothing. As for attending the same college come September, I'm not too worried about running into Shane down in Charlottesville since our class has something like three thousand students, a far cry from Prep's 140. But still, I hope he figures out all his issues soon, because it would be nice to at least be friends with him. I mean, damn—otherwise I'm not gonna know a soul down there!

As for my own parents, I did come totally clean at breakfast about Shane and all the terrible things that happened prom night. Believe me, they were *not* happy to hear all of that! In fact, they were pretty shocked and upset, but hell, so was I. I mean, I still can't believe all the stuff that went down that night. Anyway, due to all the bad things I did (namely leaving the prom in the first place), I got grounded until the Fourth of July, which I thought was harsh. But actually it's not that bad on balance as it still gives me at least half the summer to have something resembling fun.

Until then, though, I am stuck at home. Because of this and my new thing of being honest, I'm certainly talking to my parents more these days as they have a lot of questions about gay stuff, most of which I don't even know the answer to. (I made www.pflag.org the new default page on their Web browser.) In fact, I spend a lot of my time online now since I'm sorta trapped at home. Lately I've been getting lots of IMs from Buck, which has been cool. He even called me on the phone once, which was wild, mainly because I didn't know deaf people could do that. What happened was this operator came on and said I had a "relay call," and after explaining to me that it meant a deaf person was calling me using a TTY machine, she then translated my voice into typing as I filled Buck in on the boring details of my house arrest. Buck enjoyed my whole home-prison analogy thoroughly and kept LOLing, which I don't think the relay operator, who sounded somewhat ancient, understood.

Wondering what my favorite drug dealer was up to, I inquired about Dmitri's whereabouts and whether he'd avoided jail since our big night on the town. Buck relayed that Dmitri had continued to evade the not-so-long arm of the law. He even still had his "office" in the back of Secrets and was up to all sorts of no good, per usual. I was also curious about the fate of Dmitri's car, and Buck informed me that wasn't really Dmitri's car after all. (Surprise, surprise.) I was like, you mean it was *stolen?* Not exactly. You see, Buck told me that Dmitri borrows lots of cars from mysterious friends who don't seem to demand their return. (That fact alone is almost enough to make me want to be a bisexual drug dealer when I grow up—ha.) Anyway, the biggest joke of all during our relay "chat" was that he saw Caroline and her trio of blond fembots hanging out with my Russian stud at Secrets last weekend. And how did those underage girls get into a gay strip bar? Dmitri made them all IDs, of course.

As for my favorite Potomac girl, Jane has embarked on her latest summer job adventure: She is currently in training to be a tour guide on this red-white-blue bus that drives all around the monuments downtown. She calls me every day after work with every new and exciting fact she's learned; did you know the Washington Monument sways 1/8 inch in a thirty-mile-an-hour wind? Or that the Lincoln Memorial statue of old Abe has his hands forming sign language for his initials, A and L? Or how about the factoid that the Reflecting Pool is a mere twenty-one inches deep? Actually, I informed Jane, I knew *that* bit of trivia pretty well. Anyway, Jane is totally digging on her job and has insisted that next summer we do it together. She says that it's the perfect gig for a couple of teenage smart-asses like ourselves. And, she added, there's lots of cute tour guides who are in college, too.

"Sexy and mature," said Jane, with her usual zip. "Bingo!"

Jane hasn't seen much of her old pal Virginia, however. The reason is three letters: I-A-N. That's right, my prom sweetheart seems to have found a man who can not only tolerate her offensive

language, insane behavior, and off-the-scale drinking, but can actually top it. Why these two nuts never realized they were the perfect
couple before is beyond me. I mean, what was Ian doing with petite
and perfect little Caroline in the first place? Well, not too much as it
turned out. Now, though, he and Virginia are fairly inseparable, and
apparently, are quite the dynamic couple when spotted out at parties. To put it mildly, they tend to go a little, uh, overboard when it
comes to the PDA factor. Jane thinks it's fairly revolting when they
start going at it, but I think it sounds pretty damn cute. I mean,
really . . . the fact that Virginia is showing anyone any affection whatsoever is remarkable in and of itself and something, I think, to be
celebrated. Seriously. That girl had some major issues, and it's good
to see that she is working through them in a positive manner, even
if it happens to be in the pool at someone else's graduation party.

Oh yeah—I almost forgot about *that*. The Big G. So I did actually
graduate from Prep earlier this week, which was a bit of a relief. Mr.
Mold was angry about everything, sure, but when my parents
explained to him that what I was saying at the dance about being a
big homo was the actual truth, he was less inclined to punish me,
figuring correctly that I had already been punished quite enough by
the experience of the prom itself. It was that rare instance of an
adult actually understanding that being a senior is not all fun and
games and "best time of your life," you know? So I marched with my
class onto the football field and, like a normal, law-abiding senior,
got my piece of parchment, which serves as official proof that I survived high school. The ceremony was long and boring and with
more pictures taken by my parents than any previous Hayes event.
Ever. I kept joking that I could do a whole yearbook supplement
with their photos alone. They didn't find this funny, but instead were
intrigued by the notion of having their photos published. Really. You
know, sometimes I don't think they get my sense of humor.

Afterward, at the reception in the caf, I managed to avoid Shane
for the most part, other than a drive-by hi on the way to the cake
table. In fact, I spent most of the event hanging out with Franklin,

which was unexpectedly fun. I haven't had The Talk with Franklin yet, but maybe I'll do it this summer if we continue on the path to normalizing relations. However, I think that Franklin might suspect the gay thing already. When we were talking about making plans to do something once I'm granted my freedom, he mentioned checking out these Bollywood musicals at the AFI Movie Theater. Musicals! Okay—I clearly have to educate him about what a real gay guy is like, you know?

As for the rest of the excitement in my postgrad life, well, there is none. And guess what? It's my own damn fault being grounded and all. So mainly I'm just biding my punishment time this June, hanging around the house and trying not to obsess about all this future uncertainty regarding Shane and college and Sean, all of which are on my mind on a regularly rotating basis. But it's not, like, making me crazy or anything. Honest. And the reason for this new, less spastic attitude is a huge lesson thing I've realized postprom: Life is fairly unpredictable.

You see, you can think things are all set, like with me and Shane, only to have them unravel in the most ridiculous ways. But conversely, it was because of the meltdown of our relationship that I even met Sean in the first place. That was totally unexpected and majorly cool, too. Then as if meeting him wasn't enough, there was this bonus, too: Sean gave me hope on a night that didn't seem to have any. And as he gave me hope about myself, I have to admit that I secretly have great hopes for Sean. I mean, really . . . he's such a decent and upstanding guy that knowing him almost makes me want to be a better person, you know? Crazy, huh?

Still, I don't even know how this whole thing might work out with Sean and I being different ages, in different states, with very different hair. On top of all that, there's one major thing that could be semiproblematic: If Sean and I got together as life partners or something down the road, it would kinda make Virginia my sister-in-law. Ohmigod! I mean, how weird would *that* be, right?